"I re ... e de-
serv ... wists
in the werewolf's tail that are very cool."

—Laurell K. Hamilton

"This unusual, artfully constructed, and enticing blend of horror and romance will have wide appeal with its male point of view, intensely sexy love story, and caperlike action."

—*Booklist*

"This incredible novel is inventive, totally riveting, as well as surprisingly tender in spots. Adams and Clamp are a powerhouse team that has opened the door to an amazing new world."

—*Romantic Times BOOKreviews*
(4 1/2 stars, Top Pick)

"Filled with an abrasive charm, intriguing characters, and a dry wit, *Hunter's Moon* is a must-read for the fall season."

—*Romance Reviews Today*

Moon's Web

"Adams and Clamp are adept at writing intensely sensuous, hot lovemaking scenes, but where they really shine is in the creation of an unforgettable world where secret shapeshifters live, love, and scheme. Laurell K. Hamilton readers will enjoy this edgy world."

—*Booklist*

"It's only taken two books for the dynamic duo of Adams and Clamp to cement their position as premier authors of paranormal fiction. Gritty and unique, with amazingly Byzantine character development, this inside look at the unconventional world of shapeshifters is a page-turner in the truest sense."

—*Romantic Times BOOKreviews*
(4 ½ stars, Gold-Medal Top Pick)

"It's rare when a second book surpasses the first, but *Moon's Web* explodes onto the scene, earning a Perfect 10. If you're a fan of Laurell K. Hamilton or Kelley Armstrong, *Moon's Web* is definitely a book for you!"

—*Romance Reviews Today*

Captive Moon

"Firmly grounding these extraordinary characters in the modern world helps increase the emotional stakes in the gripping Sazi reality. Like few others, Adams and Clamp's writing style successfully blends romance, adventure, and the magical. As their latest confirms, this outstanding duo is unbeatable!"

—*Romantic Times BOOKreviews*

Howling Moon

"After being a dangerous footnote in previous books, the true evil of Sazi serial killer Jack Simpson is now revealed. Layer by layer Adams and Clamp build their compelling Sazi world with its strict laws that give this unique universe dramatic shape and form. Besides captivating plots, it is the rich, dark characterizations that make these books distinctive and mesmerizing. True genre luminaries!"

—*Romantic Times BOOKreviews*

"*Howling Moon* is a fantastic story! Authors C. T. Adams and Cathy Clamp just keep getting better and better. . . . [*Howling Moon*] is a true masterpiece and a joy to read."

—*ParaNormal Romance Reviews*

PRAISE FOR THE WORLD OF THE THRALL

Touch of Evil

"Unveiling a new paranormal series, the brilliant team of Adams and Clamp crafts an exceedingly intriguing heroine trying to survive a dangerous and complex world. Told in first person, the resilient Kate's struggles and choices are both vivid and terrifying. This is an unbeatably good paranormal!"

—*Romantic Times BOOKreviews*
(4 ¹/₂ stars, Top Pick)

"Adams and Clamp are adept at incorporating riveting plot twists into this fully imagined world, and they don't stint on the romance."

—*Booklist* (starred review)

"*Touch of Evil* receives *The Road to Romance* Reviewers' Choice Award for the great writing of the author duo C. T. Adams and Cathy Clamp. This book has it all and more. Readers don't want to miss this perfect example of fantastically vivid paranormal fiction."

—*The Road to Romance*

TOR PARANORMAL ROMANCE BOOKS
BY C. T. ADAMS AND CATHY CLAMP

THE SAZI
Hunter's Moon
Moon's Web
Captive Moon
Howling Moon
Moon's Fury
*Timeless Moon**

THE THRALL
Touch of Evil
Touch of Madness

*Forthcoming

Moon's Fury

C. T. ADAMS
and CATHY CLAMP

tor paranormal romance

A TOM DOHERTY ASSOCIATES BOOK
NEW YORK

This is a work of fiction. All of the characters, organizations, and events portrayed in this novel are either products of the authors' imagination or are used fictitiously.

MOON'S FURY

Copyright © 2007 by Cathy Clamp and C. T. Adams

A Tor Book
Published by Tom Doherty Associates, LLC
175 Fifth Avenue
New York, NY 10010

www.tor.com

Tor® is a registered trademark of Tom Doherty Associates, LLC.

ISBN-13: 978-0-7653-5664-2
ISBN-10: 0-7653-5664-3

First Edition: October 2007

Printed in the United States of America

0 9 8 7 6 5 4 3 2 1

Dedication and Acknowledgments

First, as with all of our books, we dedicate this novel to Don Clamp and James Adams, who have stuck with us through thick and thin! You guys are wonderful and we love you! Then (again, as always) to our wonderful agent, Merrilee Heifetz, and terrific editor, Anna Genoese—both of whom continue to help us grow and shine! Next, we'd like to thank some specific people for their help in pulling this book together: Lupe M. Gonzalez of San Antonio Romance Authors (SARA) for tirelessly helping us put together the terrific Salinas Tejano family of Santa Helena over the course of many months. Super big thanks also to those absolutely wonderful, helpful, inspiring, caring, friendly, and downright great officers of the www.realpolice.net forums. (They made us say that, but they're right!) Comprised entirely of working LEOs (law enforcement officers) they answered all of our "stupid author questions" without laughing—at least not in print to our virtual faces. Special thanks to PO1IC3M4N, whoever you are and whatever Texas badge might grace your shirt in real life. Also, big thanks to the biologists of the Red Wolf Recovery Program of the Wolf Education and Research Center for their help in writing the differences between timber and red wolves. Finally, a big thanks to the rangers at the South Llano State Park, who were incredibly friendly and knowledgeable about the area. Several threads of the book came out of chats with them.

Authors' Note

Moon's Fury is set down here where we live in the Texas Hill Country, and Texans are notorious for wanting the state's history told properly. So, we had to do a *lot* of research just to insert a few bits and pieces in the book.

For those present and former Texans keeping track, this book is set in the fictional town of Santa Helena, the county seat of the also fictional Tedford County. Santa Helena and Tedford County are located in the wide-open spaces between South Llano State Park and Devils Sinkhole S.N.A., pulling corners from Sutton, Edwards, Kimble, and a tiny bit of Real counties.

In keeping with state tradition, we named the county after John Tedford, the county sheriff of nearby Kerr County from 1870 to '76, who gained "hero" status in the state when he defended the small town of Camp Verde against a band of Comanches intent on burning it down for several hours before help arrived. He permanently lost the use of an arm from an arrow in the process, but still managed to continue to serve as sheriff for his full term!

Cara's wolf pack are Mexican red wolves, which used to inhabit the Texas Hill Country, but are presently presumed extinct. Red wolves are smaller and faster than timber wolves, and better adapted to the hot climate, all of which we used in the book. They are also a threatened species in most parts of the world, but on the road to recovery in several places. Researching red wolves took a really long time, and included conversations with wolf experts at several locations.

Moon's
Fury

Chapter 1

CARA PRESSED DOWN harder on the accelerator as she replayed the phone message in her mind. *I hope you can make it here before I'm gone.* The old man's voice had sounded shaky and out of breath, which worried her. He'd always been such a tough old bird. She flipped the switch to turn on her cherries, but not the siren, and watched the lone vehicle in front of her on the highway dutifully pull into the emergency lane and slow to let the sheriff's truck pass.

Sheriff. She still hadn't gotten used to the title—even if it was only temporary, until Carl recovered from his stroke.

The sun was low on the horizon, making the clouds bleed with fiery intensity over the towering live oak trees lining the highway. By the time she reached Ten Bears's tiny hut, it would be full dark. She hated climbing that steep path to his house at night, and the sky smelled of rain—the bad kind. Nothing like a flash flood to spur a girl on.

Great.

A flickering light far ahead on the left caught her eye just before she spotted the red stain and a limp furred body sporting a massive rack of antlers in the opposite lane. She hit the sirens, because headlights shouldn't be looking out from the middle of a field and bobbing up and down.

Picking up her radio she hit the button as the car behind her disappeared into the distance. "Dispatch, T-2 . . . I mean, *T-1,* southbound on 377, at mile marker . . . aw, hell, someone snapped it off . . . let's say about fourteen miles out of town, rolling code. We've got a 10-50 . . . deer flip with possible injuries."

Maggie's voice was calm and professional. "Dispatching an ambulance now, Sheriff, and calling for backup. I just saw Dave's trooper car pull in at the Branding Iron. Want me to notify Texas Highway Patrol and wait for them to reach him, or should I just call the restaurant? You know how bad the radio reception is before a storm. I'm probably going to lose you in a minute."

"Copy that. Call the restaurant. Good catch. I'll secure the scene and set some flares. It's almost dark and on a blind curve. Oh, and see if y'all can dig up a number for Sam Kerchee and call him. Apparently, he finally broke down and bought a cell phone. If he needs medical assistance, get T-6 over there, stat. If not, then tell him I'll be late for our meeting. T-1 out."

She parked well off the road, leaving on her lightbar to warn other drivers, then sprinted across the highway and down the embankment—sniffing carefully as she stepped through the knee-deep grass and weeds for the distinctive dusty scent of any of the variety of rattlers that lived in the region. It was hard to smell anything over the deer musk and blood that hovered in the still air, but she fought past the hunger the rising moon caused. Tonight she had to be a cop first, a werewolf second. Company would be arriving soon and she couldn't afford to get distracted.

"Hello? *¿Hola?* Can anyone hear me?" Cara couldn't see any bodies in or around the vehicle as she walked toward it and couldn't decide whether that was good or bad. But then the sound of shallow, ragged breathing and a small whimper made her turn her flashlight away from the black SUV to the nearby brush. There, nearly hidden in the mesquite and cactus was the pale, red-stained arm of a child who must have been thrown from the vehicle. In seconds, Cara was by her side, checking her for injuries.

Still clutching a soiled pink Care Bear in one hand, the girl, who appeared to be about seven, opened her eyes slightly and tried to focus. "Mommy?"

She touched the girl's blonde hair lightly and moved the flashlight around, looking for broken bones or deep cuts. Other than a variety of scratches and embedded cactus spines, she seemed remarkably healthy. "No, honey. My name's Cara, and I'm a dep—the sheriff. Y'all had a little accident. Were you driving with your mommy? Was there anyone else in the car with you? What's your name?"

The girl nodded and tears welled as she finally noticed the uniform and badge. "Brittany Foster, ma'am. Me and Mommy are going to Grammy's house." The light twang in her voice had a regional flavor that said she lived somewhere nearby. Her little chin started to quiver. "Where's Mommy? My leg hurts." The thick, wet scent of her fear was giving way to ammonia panic. Not good.

Cara kept her movements light and calm and took a quick sniff of the leg. Then she scanned the ground for any evidence of fire ant mounds or other wildlife that might have bitten the girl before replying. "You just got some cactus spines in your leg, Brittany. You've had that happen before, haven't you? I've got some tweezers in the car and we can fix you right up. Y'all just stay right here, don't move, and I'll go get your mommy. Okay? You keep—what's your teddy's name?"

A sniffle and a nod said Brittany understood. "Mr. Bear. He falls in the cactus a lot, but he never cries when Mommy pulls the stickers out."

Pulling a small penlight from her utility belt, Cara turned it on and handed it to the girl. "Well, Mr. Bear is very brave,

'cause I know those spines can hurt. Now, you stay right
here in the light and make sure Mr. Bear doesn't get scared
while I go get your mommy. I want you to listen for sirens
for me, okay? They're going to come and put your car back
on the road so y'all can get to your Grammy's house."

Brittany nodded and started to play with the flashlight,
turning it toward her surroundings. Cara hated leaving the
girl alone, but she had to find the mother. The SUV had finally stopped rocking on its roof. She played the bright
beam of the flashlight around the wrecked vehicle, searching for the driver. The pungent odor of dripping antifreeze
and gasoline made it impossible for her to smell the woman.
"Ms. Foster? Can you hear me? Please answer if you can
hear me."

No sound other than punctuated hisses from drops of hot
fluid on the engine block met her ears. One entire side of
the vehicle was buried in a mass of young mesquite trees,
making it difficult to see. She crawled down on her belly
under the branches and played the light around—

There she was!

Cara shook her head slightly in the small space. She was
also thrown from the vehicle when it flew off the road. The
car must have flipped and landed right on the woman . . .
well, actually not much more than a teenager, and a mirror
image of the girl. She was alive, but unconscious and bleeding badly from a cut on her forehead. And the roof of the vehicle was resting right on her pelvis and legs. "Motherf—"

A tentative voice from the darkness made her cut off
what she was going to say. "Mother? Cara? Did you find
Mommy?"

She wiggled backward, ignoring the multitude of
mesquite spines that ripped at her hair and shirt, thinking
desperately. "I sure did, Brittany. But she's sort of stuck, so
I have to help her out of the car. You just stay right there,
'kay? Don't come over here, because there's antifreeze all

over the ground. It'll make you sick." If she acted quickly, there was a chance to not only save the woman's life, but also to ensure she didn't wind up in a wheelchair for the rest of her life.

She'd never tried to use her Sazi magic to lift an entire car. She was barely alpha enough to lead her pack and hold the members in an emergency. Still, it would only have to be for a few moments until she could drag the woman out from underneath.

Or . . . hmm, maybe the reverse would work better.

She walked around to the back of the vehicle and inspected the terrain with the flashlight. Yes, that could work. If she braced her back against the massive live oak butting up nearly to the rear bumper, she could lift the entire car and then use her magic to move the woman.

But there would be a witness. There was no way she could pull this off without the girl seeing, and humans didn't know the Sazi existed.

To protect and serve.

Cara played the light over the woman's still, barely breathing form. There was no escaping her duty. She had to risk it. "Brittany, honey. I need you to turn off the flashlight for a minute, 'cause it's making it hard for me to see. Can you do that for me?"

There was a long pause and she knew the girl was getting scared again. Her voice was barely audible and trembling a little, obviously wondering what was happening and why her mommy wasn't talking. "Okay." The light went out and she breathed a sigh.

"Now, this door is going to be really hard to get open and it's gonna make a lot of noise. But you need to trust me. Just ignore what I'm doing and you keep listening for the sirens. Tell me if you hear them, and I'll have your mommy out in just a second."

The girl's voice was getting panicked again, rising and

falling with a singsong, breathy quality. "Cara? Mr. Bear is scared of the dark."

She was going to have to make this quick, or the girl would come over looking for her mom. There was no way she was going to let her see her trapped under the car. "Um, do you know any songs, Brittany? Sometimes singing in the dark helps . . . *bears* that are scared. Do you know the song about the spider climbing the water spout?"

Cara braced her back against the trunk of the old oak and spread her arms wide enough to grab both sides of the car, digging in her fingers with enough supernatural strength to bend the metal slightly. She had to keep hold of the frame. She couldn't afford for the bumper to shear away, causing her to drop the vehicle back on the woman. With a barely audible grunt, she dug in her heels and began to lift.

"Uh-huh. Grammy has a CD with lots of songs. I know all of them."

Forcing her voice to remain calm was the hardest thing she'd ever done as the vehicle began to move. "Okay, then why don't you sing it for me? I don't remember the words too well. But I'll join in and then your mommy can, too."

The girl's pure, clear soprano filled the night. "Eensie weensie spider, climbed up the—"

Cara forced her mind away from the song to concentrate on keeping the vehicle level. It was trying to fall forward to its heaviest point—the engine. But she couldn't let that happen. She forced her elbows to lock so the roof wouldn't shift or fall over onto the woman's chest. She felt her muscles ache and then begin to burn as she lifted the entire vehicle a fraction of an inch.

"—washed the spider out! Out came—c'mon Cara. You said you'd sing with me."

Sweat rolled down her forehead and she panted out a few words. "Finish it once for me first. 'Kay?"

"Oh, okay." The sullen tone in her voice vanished when she started over from the beginning.

Inch by inch the SUV rose from the ground as Cara's heels dug in deeper. The oak bark cracked, and sharp branches splintered under the force, cutting through her shirt and wedging into her back. Now her neck muscles were starting to spasm and she wanted to scream from the exertion. When she thought it was high enough, she pressed outward with her magic, searching for the woman with senses she couldn't explain. Power swelled and flowed, a subtle wind that touched every surface—caressed the blades of grass, each flower and leaf until she touched a leg. She knew it was a leg, but even after years of training, she still couldn't explain *how* she could sense a body among the surrounding rocks and branches.

She let the woman fill her mind until every nuance of her body was memorized. The world disappeared as she surrounded the woman with magic, felt the almost sensual tingle as she became one with another living, breathing being. She grieved at the damage to the woman's legs and went an extra step—one she hadn't planned—and mended the fractures, attached torn ligaments, and let blood flow again through undamaged veins.

Then, as she felt her arms failing and her legs buckling, she lifted the woman's form—pulled it from beneath the twisted metal and floated her a few feet, to safety.

Seconds later, gravity won the battle and the vehicle slipped from her hands, crashing down to the ground loud enough to make Brittany scream, turn on the little flashlight, and start to run crookedly toward the tree. "*Mommy!* Cara! Is Mommy okay?"

Cara took a moment to catch her breath before hurrying toward the girl and stopping her from limping around the back of the SUV. "Your mommy will be okay now. But she's hurt, so I don't want you to see her until I wake her up. But I promise you she'll be fine. Now, you take my big flashlight and give me the little one." She removed the penlight from the girl's hand and gave her the large flashlight. With four D cells, it was heavy enough to force the girl to concentrate to keep it steady.

Tears were flowing freely down the girl's scratched, dirtied face, and she looked up into Cara's face with desperation. "Mommy's okay, isn't she? Daddy got hurt once and he never came home. I don't want Mommy not to come home!"

Cara heard a car door slam from behind her squad car, although she hadn't seen headlights or heard it arrive.

A pleasant baritone spoke from the darkness. "Your mommy is going to be fine." The girl pointed the flashlight up and smiled when she saw a man wearing a Texas Ranger white hat and uniform walking toward them. She didn't ask a single question, but just ran over and hugged his leg and walked away to sit down on the ground, telling Mr. Bear that everything would be fine now.

Cara lowered her voice to the lightest whisper and shook her head in amazement. "Y'know, Ranger Kerchee, that's just weird how you do that magical persuasion thing. I didn't even see you drive up, and I'm supposed to be the Alpha around here."

He smiled brilliantly, softening his Comanche-born Roman nose and high cheekbones. "Yeah, you're the Alpha, but I'm a Wolven agent. We're *supposed* to be able to sneak up on other Sazi. And if you'd stuck with the program instead of running off to the police academy, maybe you could do *that persuasion thing*, too."

"People here would say you're a *brujo*, you know, for the way you can make people see things that aren't there. A witch."

The humor dropped away from his face. He glared at her and crossed arms over his chest. The white hat couldn't hide the darkness—the death—in that gaze. "And people would say *you're* She-Hulk." Cara flushed and glanced at Brittany, only to find that she was frozen in place, mouth open as though to speak, unseeing of everything around her. Damn, he was good!

His voice hissed into the darkness. "What in hell did you think you were doing, Alpha Salinas? I could have your *life* for the way you've fucked up this accident scene. You think nobody's going to *notice* there are marks on the ground and on the roof that match up with that woman's legs, or see your torn shirt and bark in your hair? You think your colleagues are *stupid*? Think they won't ask questions—investigate? Maybe even question the girl or find your fingerprints . . . or finger *dents* on the SUV?"

Cara absently ran her fingers over the normally tight bun at the back of her neck to discover it was disheveled and did indeed have bits of bark littering it. She had no excuse and she knew it. He was right. She'd overstepped her bounds—risked her entire pack, their entire kind in fact, with exposure. The Wolven agent had the right, and the authority, to take her life on the spot. It was their way. All she could manage was an embarrassed shrug and a whispered, "She would have been a cripple, Will."

"And you think she didn't *deserve* that fate? She risked her own life, and her child's, by not wearing seat belts. Have you measured the skid marks in front of that eight-pointer yet? She was doing at least ten over the limit. What gave you the *right* to change the future she brought on herself?"

She looked up then, met his eyes—accepted whatever fate he would give, and told him the reason, the one truth in her life. "To protect and serve."

He emitted a sound that shouldn't be produced by a human throat: the angry, frustrated cry of an eagle denied a dinner. He stalked away, leaving her unable to breathe for a moment. Was he really going to let it go? Would she live to see morning?

He grabbed the buck by the antlers with one hand and pulled the heavy animal to the side of the road as easily as if it were empty skin. As sirens began to fill the air, he turned to her with his face set in cold stone. "Keep your mouth *shut* and don't make any excuses or statements about anything. I'll fix anything strange after the reports are filed. But the three of us *will* be discussing this tomorrow at lunch. Plan on it being a *long* lunch."

The three of us? She opened her mouth to ask, but he suddenly wasn't there. He was just . . . gone. But then she heard a sound overhead and realized he'd turned into animal form and flown into the darkness. Brittany was again quietly singing to Mr. Bear. When she looked behind her squad car, there was no sign of another vehicle.

Damn, he's good.

ADAM MUELLER LET his foot off the accelerator when a flare came into view on the side of the road, causing the car behind him to close rapidly before the driver finally hit the brakes with a quick squeal of rubber. The flashing lights in both emergency lanes and the smear of red on the road ahead started his adrenaline pumping. He automatically slowed even further and started to scope out the accident scene.

"Adam? What's happening?" Vivian Carmichael's voice from the backseat was thick with sleep. "Are we there yet?"

He glanced in the rearview mirror to catch her gaze. "Nope. Not yet. Looks like someone hit an animal and flipped. Only county mounties and state patrol on the scene, so we must not be near the city yet."

She snorted slightly and turned deeper into her pillow. "Well, for God's sake, don't stop and offer to help. You're not a cop in this state, you know—and we're on vacation. I'm sure they can manage without you. Let's just get there and find a hotel room. I'm sick to death of sleeping in this truck's miserable excuse for a backseat."

A slender young woman in uniform stepped into the road, put out one hand to stop him, and started to wave an ambulance forward. He turned his face just slightly toward the backseat, because he couldn't seem to take his eyes off the deputy. "They're moving out the ambulance, Viv. It'll just be a second and then we can go."

She just grunted and covered her head with the pillow to shut out the bright red lights that filled the truck's cab. He couldn't figure out why the uniformed woman held his attention so completely. She was certainly gorgeous . . . had that whole Jennifer Lopez thing going on, except more heavily muscled and curved. But no . . . that wasn't it.

There's something about the way she moves. The woman turned when someone in the field shouted at her, and he noticed the back of her uniform was ripped and covered with bits of leaves and bark. Adam abruptly wondered what she smelled like . . . and whether she would taste salty from exertion. But before he could open the window to catch her scent, she'd turned back around and was waving him, and the growing line behind his truck, into the opposite lane to go around. Her movements showed annoyance, bordering on anger, but it didn't appear to be directed at anyone in particular.

He slowed briefly as he passed her, turned on the interior light, and their eyes met. He nodded as he would to any other officer on duty—with a sense of comradery, but it was more difficult to pull his eyes back to the road than it should have been. A shiver raced through him because her eyes had been those of a predator.

And there was nothing he liked better than a dangerous woman.

Chapter 2

THE DARKNESS IN the woods was absolute, forcing Cara to use her nose to find her way. The clouds overhead had an oppressive weight to them and the scent of rain taunted her dry tongue. She wouldn't mind if a few inches fell. The crops could use the water, even if her backpack, and the clothes inside, would get wet.

Maggie had been able to find a phone number for Sam and learned he wasn't injured or sick, relieving her mind a little. Since, by the time she was done at the accident scene, it was later than she'd planned. She pushed herself along the familiar trail even faster, her claws digging deep into crumbly limestone as she climbed higher up the steep hillside to the stone-and-grass hut the elder Kerchee called home. She couldn't afford to be distracted, but too many things roiled around in her mind. The rescue team *had* asked questions—ones she couldn't, didn't dare, answer. They'd accepted her calm statements about tearing up her shirt in the mesquite bramble, but there had been more than one raised brow of disbelief. Still, they were pleased enough about the condition of the woman and child that they'd let it drop. But what would the reports say? Who was the third person that Will was bringing to lunch tomorrow, and would she wind up being the main course? What would happen to her pack if she was put down?

She nearly missed the sharp bend at the top of the cliff during her mulling, but caught herself at the last moment. Perched on an outcropping where no sane person would live, the little hut managed to withstand the harsh weather and still look new, even after the more than twenty years she'd known the old Comanche shaman. There was no arguing that the view from the cliff edge was stunning though, especially in spring. It was the sort of landscape painters trekked for miles to use as inspiration. Cara was sorry she wasn't arriving in daylight. She'd have loved to see the stark white cliffs covered with wildflowers. They'd been especially beautiful this year, turning the barren land into a kaleidoscope of color.

Still, I wish he'd put a damned road up here.

She was huffing a little by the time she scented the buckskins she knew were stretched out on frames on the back porch. Allowing herself to revel in the scent, she paused to catch her breath. For the tenth time since she'd stripped and turned into her wolf form, her mind started to wander, this time to something a little more pleasant and, as such, more disturbing. What was it about that guy in the black truck that she couldn't get out of her head? He'd just caught her eye for a second, like every other rubbernecker in the line had done, but that one look just kept nibbling at the back of her mind—

"Welcome, Sheriff Salinas. Congratulations on your promotion." She let out a little yip of surprise because she hadn't even noticed him, nearly invisible as he was behind a massive turpentine-scented juniper. That was twice tonight she'd been caught flat-footed.

She shook her furred head before sitting down on her haunches. "I hate it when you do that, Ten Bears! I'm supposed to notice *you* first, not the other way around. You really know how to embarrass a Sazi. And I'm only the *acting* sheriff since Carl had that stroke. The voters will decide whether I go back to being chief deputy in November."

Sam Ten Bears Kerchee chuckled low and stepped out from behind a tree. "Yes, but in your heart, you know how you wish the citizens to vote." His prominent nose and broad mouth bore a strong resemblance to Will's, but his shoulders were stooped with age and his face deeply wrinkled. He walked like a man decades younger, though, without limp or cane. The moonlight broke through the clouds for a moment, making his eyes twinkle merrily. "And while I should apologize for startling you, there are so few people I'm still able to surprise at my age. Any small thing amuses me. But please pass along my sympathies to Sheriff Howersen's family for his illness." He swept his hand gracefully toward the hut, suggesting she precede him. "Now, come in before the rain. I know you prefer to use the back door."

She wagged her tail and huffed lightly, trying not to indulge the thought of holding the title beyond the next morning. Every day she expected to receive the call from Joslyn saying Carl would be back at work tomorrow. Instead, she stood up and stepped past Ten Bears onto the porch, latching onto his final line, not that he'd be fooled. "Only because you insisted on building this place so you have to put one foot off the cliff to get in the front. Have y'all *ever* used that door?"

He chuckled as he held open the door, letting the subject drop. "Not as often as in my youth, I admit. Still, Will appreciates the door location. He often flies in from Austin to visit, now that he's working there. He's a good grandson."

They fell into their usual routine. Ten Bears helped her off with her backpack, and pulled an elegantly painted rice paper and black lacquer screen from under his twin bed. He carefully unfolded and erected it so she could shift forms and put on her clothing in private. She watched his silhouette step to the other side of the hut and fill two mugs with hot water from a nearly whistling kettle on the two-burner propane camp stove.

"I saw him tonight. Will, that is." Cara concentrated on her human form and felt the transformation begin. It was never easy for her, even after so many years. Some alphas could shift from form to form without a second thought. Boy, not her. Shifting into wolf form wasn't too bad—mostly it made her jaw pop for a few minutes and her toes tingle where the nails turned to claws. But the shift back to human became like the deep ache of old joints on a cold wet day, combined with a sinus headache from a slender muzzle shortening to her normal nose. She had to take a deep breath and blink a few times before she could concentrate enough to complete her thought. She knew Ten Bears would wait for her to finish. He always did. "But you probably already know that."

She coughed to clear her throat and stretched her arms high over her head to ease the muscle spasms. She heard the slow clinking of a silver teaspoon against the ceramic mugs and smiled. The real silver was one of the few luxuries Ten Bears allowed himself. The thought was pleasant and soothing after the mad rush to get here.

"There are disturbing things going on in both the Sazi and human worlds, Carlotta. It's true I've had many visions lately, and know of your encounter with my grandson. I didn't call you here tonight merely to share your company over tea."

She paused, her hands still behind her back hooking her bra, trying to imagine what things the Sazi police force would need to be involved with in her state. There were only a dozen Sazi families in the entire state of Texas, and a mere eight members of her far-flung pack shifted with the moon. "Do these *disturbing things* involve my pack? Is one of us in danger?"

The old Comanche didn't answer. He just kept stirring, apparently waiting for her to finish dressing so he could look her in the face. Her mother had always said being around Ten Bears was like trying to watch the blossom on a flower unfold. It always did, but you never saw it happen. Since he was fully human, he couldn't rely on scents to tell him what she was feeling or thinking, and he kept his own emotions enough in check that Cara couldn't smell anything over the strong scent of his homemade wild rose hip and clover tea.

She hopped out from behind the screen, still putting on the last moccasin, her curiosity strong enough that it should be visible in the air. Ten Bears held out a box of tissues as she approached the small wooden table. She gratefully took one. A few snorts and sneezes cleared her sinuses and she carefully folded the tissue and tucked it in her pocket. He didn't have trash pickup and there was still a burn ban in effect.

Next to the steaming, oversize pottery mug on the table was a small bag of mixed dried herbs and she smiled in relief. The bag smelled strongly of sage and pepper, along with things she couldn't easily identify. She'd never been foolish enough to question the contents for fear of insulting him. Clutching it to her chest briefly like the lifeline it was, she tucked it in her pocket. "Thank you, Ten Bears! I don't know that it'll last for a full month, but I'm grateful for even this small amount. Are you out of supplies? Do you need some money for more? I know you've always made my tea for free, but I don't mind paying—really. I'd pay nearly anything to keep getting it. This is the first remedy that's actually *worked* on my condition."

Ten Bears pulled the spoon from his mug and tapped the liquid off on the rim before setting it carefully on a folded piece of paper towel. He fixed her with a piercing gaze. His dark eyes were a little more cloudy than the last time she'd visited. He really needed to visit an eye doctor to get those cataracts checked. "You were very merciful to save that woman, Carlotta. While I may not say why or how, your kindness will be returned tenfold in the near future."

Cara breathed a sigh of relief. If Ten Bears said it, that's what would happen. While he wasn't a Sazi seer in truth, because he was full human, his gifts had served her pack well for many years. "Thank God! Could you maybe tell Will that when you see him next? I'm pretty sure he was ready to put me down on the spot."

His head cocked slightly, and the thick, sweet scent of his confusion and curiosity slapped her nose just as a roll of thunder sounded overhead. In seconds she understood why he was bewildered. "And how would my vision help you avoid your punishment, Sheriff? You made a choice, knowing the consequences. Wrong done for pure motives is still wrong. Does the *reason* for a crime matter when you're arresting a suspect?"

A leaden feeling in the pit of her stomach began to grow. She hadn't received a Wolven punishment since . . . well, since she began training to become a Wolven agent. She still had to cover the scars when she wore shorts. "Are you saying I'm still going to be punished? Will I—" She coughed and took a sip of tea before continuing, her fingertips tapping on the rim. "Will it be bad?"

He shrugged. "My visions haven't included any image of you where you didn't look whole. They have been of larger events. But that doesn't mean you weren't in pain." He picked up the silver spoon again and stirred for no apparent reason. "Pain is something we all must face—young and old, Sazi and human. There is pain that can kill, and some we only *wish* would kill us."

She frowned and leaned back in her chair with her arms crossed over her chest. Another flash of lightning was followed by the dull thumping of rain on the grass roof. "You're being unusually obtuse tonight, Ten Bears. Why don't you just say whatever you're going to? What are the larger events that involve me and my pack?"

He fixed her with a stare that seemed to bore through her, and his scent was the hot metal of determination, which blended with the dusty rain from outside. "I will be going away for a time, Cara. I've been invited to be the head dancer at the All Nations Powwow. It is a great honor . . . one I'm not certain I'm worthy of." His nervousness was evident in his scent, which was unusual.

A laugh boiled up out of her, easing the creeping dread that had been threatening to overwhelm her. "So all these predictions of doom are just because you're going away for a few days and won't be around to tell me the future? I'm a big girl, Sam. I can run my pack until you get back. When do you leave? Do you need a ride to the airport?"

He shook his head, but his mood didn't lighten. "As my fathers did before me, I will walk to the great gathering. It has been many years since I've undertaken such a journey, but my totem has made it clear that such a vision quest is necessary. I will gather more herbs for your remedy while I'm there, as well, so it will be many weeks before I return."

"You're *walking*? Where is this powwow?"

"It will be held in Albuquerque this year and it will take several weeks to make the journey each way. Will bought a map for me with the route marked. But because I will be gone for so long, I felt I should tell you—" He paused, his emotions chasing and crawling over each other for prominence in her nose. A wistful sort of sorrow finally won, which made her rear back a little in surprise. "I have come to care for you during the many meals you have shared with me, Cara. You remind me much of my daughter when she was young. I often found it difficult to bear the knowledge of her . . . *pain* in a murky, possible future—especially if I knew it would happen in *any* possible future. I made many journeys when I was younger."

The lead was back in her stomach and had been joined by flutters that made bile rise in her throat. "So, you're telling me you accepted the invitation to the powwow because something bad is going to happen here . . . to *me*? Something you don't want to watch?"

He nodded and a buzzing filled her ears. "Something I cannot stop. Still, great pain can blossom into great joy, if you allow it." A warm smile eased the years from his face, and he reached across the table to pat her suddenly clammy hand. "You, and your pack, will be tested in the coming days, Cara. I believe you're strong enough to bear this challenge, or I wouldn't leave. But true strength is sometimes marked by knowing when to let go—and that will be *your* greatest challenge. You live for your pack, and they for you, as it should be. But very soon, your vision will have to expand to encompass the whole of your kind, rather than just your own pack."

Cara shook her head, trying to wrap her head around the strange, cryptic words. "I don't understand, Ten Bears. Expand how? If not my pack, then . . . *who*?"

"That, I cannot say. But from now until I return, you must always consider the consequences to the whole of your people. You must not fail when the danger makes itself known. You must not fail, and *you* must not fall."

She rested her elbows on the table and leaned forward with a strangled sound that was close to a scream of frustration and rising panic. "Please, Ten Bears. If I mean anything at all to you, *please* just tell me. What's going to happen?"

He sighed. It was a rasping, tired sound that made her wonder if he would ever return from his journey. She'd never seen him look so worried, and *defeated*. Lightning flashed outside the window and the skies opened to flood water down on the roof so loudly it hurt her ears.

Nothing could have prepared her for what came out of his mouth next. Thunder and lightning arrived as one in a cacophony of sound and motion, but it was his words that made her heart nearly stop in her chest. "In the coming weeks, Cara, several of your pack, your *family*, will die in terrible, bloody agony—and you must be the one to knowingly send them to their deaths."

Chapter 3

THE AIR RUSHING past the truck window was too laden with wetness to dry Adam's sticky skin. But the scents of clean air, wildflowers, and trees were so intense it was worth enduring the summerlike heat—well, at least to *him*.

"Can we *please* roll up the windows and turn on the AC? This humidity is ruining my hair." He glanced over at his passenger. As usual, Vivian looked model perfect, without a honeyed blonde hair out of place, much less *ruined*. But that was probably because of the copious amounts of mousse and hair spray she slathered on.

"I'm getting accustomed to the sights and scents down here, Viv. That's sort of the purpose of this early recon, don'tcha know. I need to be able to describe it to the pack when we get back to Minneapolis. I'm not even sure why you wanted to come with. I can't imagine you'll be one of those volunteering to move to Texas."

She lowered her sun visor and removed an imaginary spot of lipstick from the corner of her mouth before turning her head and replying in a sultry manner. "It seemed a good way to spend a little . . . *alone* time with our newest pack leader."

The absurdity of the statement struck him and, despite his intended goal not to offend her on the trip, he barked out a surprised laugh. "My god, is *that* what all this has been about? The dozen phone calls over the last week, telling me how much you *needed to get away*? The barely there shirts you're about to fall out of? You're bucking to be the alpha female of a new pack!" He shook his head with mixed amazement and annoyance. "I've spent three days on the road with you, trying to figure out your angle. But this . . . this one didn't occur to me." Adam tapped one finger on the steering wheel and shook his head in tiny little movements. He had no doubt she could smell his annoyance and couldn't help himself—he had to raise his sunglasses onto his head to see her reaction.

Although a consummate actress, he'd taken her by surprise with the blunt assessment, and she reacted with more honesty than she'd planned to in scent and body language. She wasn't nearly as offended as embarrassed to have been found out. "Well, you certainly don't have to make it sound so . . . *conniving*. What's so horrible about wanting to spend time with you? We used to spend a *lot* of time together."

His chuckle was bitter, and he hoped it cut her as deep as she'd cut him two years before. "Oh yah. We did. Right until the day you realized I wasn't going to challenge Josef for his position, no matter how hard you pushed me. It grated on you every single day that I was happy to remain his second in the pack, didn't it? So what—you think now that I've been told to lead a dozen families down here by the council, I'm going to be the new alpha?"

Her voice was smug, and her peppery, sickly sweet scent said conniving wasn't too far a stretch from the truth. "You *are* the new alpha down here. That's what Josef announced to the pack."

"Well, Josef can say whatever he wants. But the reality is that there's already an alpha in place down here. We're joining an existing pack of red wolves, and I can't see any reason to upset the applecart. And after what happened last fall. . . . Well, let's say I'm in no hurry to run the show *anywhere*."

For a moment, her voice took on a trace of the old warmth and she reached out to touch his hand. But the power that tingled his skin no longer stirred him. It was just ordinary Sazi magic—without the intoxicating sensuality it once held. He was almost sad about that.

"It wasn't your fault, Adam. Tyr wasn't right in the

mind. You couldn't have predicted he'd take such a small thing so far."

He yanked away from her touch hard enough that he had to overcorrect to put the truck back in the lane. Right now, he didn't want anyone to touch him, because there was no point in trying to make his life, and his choices, all better. It was hard enough for him to imagine running a pack again, after screwing up so bad. "Not so small a thing. There's no point denying it, Viv. I'm the only reason my pack leader's son is dead, a dozen families are being sent out of Minnesota in exile, and the humans might discover the secret of the Sazi."

THE PUNGENT SCENT of gasoline overpowered even the fragrant bush near the pumps as Adam filled the second tank of the truck. He tried not to watch the dials spinning as another hundred dollars drained from his wallet. He'd hoped the prices would be better closer to the gulf coast, but no such luck.

Viv was still sulking with her arms crossed and her foot tapping hard enough to put a permanent dent in the floor mat. The lavender flowers highlighted by the late morning sun were a pleasant respite from her icy glare. He wasn't sure why he expected anything different from her, and wondered what had compelled him to ignore his first instinct to travel alone. But hey—if he wanted to punish himself, he couldn't think of a better way to do it. Her transition from whining to sullen and back again since their little conversation a few hours back was punishment enough for five men.

When the handle finally clicked, he turned off the switch and slid the nozzle back into place. Once the cap was on again, he paused to deeply inhale the sweet scent from the bush. He was just turning when a voice sounded next to his ear and he suddenly, without warning, couldn't move a muscle.

"Smell sort of like grape Kool-Aid, don't they? Mountain laurels are native to these parts, you know."

He reacted instinctively, pushing back against the power that engulfed him, struggling to free himself. But the pressure on his body was incredible—as though an invisible hand was squeezing, compressing his flesh against his bones. There was no doubting there was a Sazi behind him, one powerful enough to withstand his best attempts to move. Even Josef had to struggle a little to hold him still, but this . . . his effort had all the effect of throwing a bucket of water against the Hoover Dam. Laughable and futile. So he stopped trying and remained still.

"What an *unexpected* surprise to see you here in Santa Helena, Mr. Mueller. Especially since you had strict instructions not to show up until the council gave you the go-ahead." The words were quiet, no more than a whisper, but there was slow death in the tone. He still couldn't see the man's face, since he couldn't even move his eyeballs, and there was no scent to guide him. Nothing at all, which meant his assailant was with Wolven, at a minimum.

He found himself turning, although he wasn't the one in control. But the movements were so natural and delicate that no human, even if standing right next to his truck, would be able to tell that he wasn't moving of his own volition. Viv had all the liveliness of a store mannequin, which shouldn't be possible if the same person was holding them both. But she was absolutely still in the cab, except for the slow movement of her chest. The slight smile on her face was belied by the panic deep in her eyes. It was obvious she was trying to fight the hold, and was failing just as he had. But unlike him, she would wear herself out fighting, rather than conserving her strength in case she needed it later.

While the voice hadn't brought any recognition, the man's face certainly did. Adam's eyes would have widened if they could have. It wasn't often an average Sazi came in contact with the council representative for all of the werewolves in the world. No surprise he could hold them both. Hell, Lucas Santiago could probably simultaneously hold the entire Minnesota pack and make them play hockey against one another. For decades he'd been the alpha male of one of the largest wolf packs in the world, in Boulder, Colorado. Gossip claimed he was second in power to nobody but the Chief Justice.

Adam felt his body lean back against the truck and his arms cross over his chest in just the way he would do himself if chatting with a friend. With a nearly audible pop, he felt the magic loosen around his head and throat. *Just* his head, while the rest of his body was trapped as securely as if embedded in concrete.

"Now then, Mr. Mueller. Would you care to explain yourself?" That same light, quiet tone was combined with mild curiosity on Santiago's permanently tanned face. He didn't appear angry, but then—who really knew what he thought?

Adam had to cough more than once to get any moisture back to his mouth so he could speak. He lowered his voice to a hoarse whisper, knowing the other man could easily hear him, but keeping to neutral words in case any humans overheard. "My greetings to you and your family in Boulder, sir. I mean no disrespect, but I'm confused. I was *instructed* to come down here and recon the area for my family."

The man's brows raised and he pursed his lips in interest. "Really? Well, that certainly is worth discussing in more suitable surroundings." Meaning more *private* surroundings. "I'm staying at the La Vista Motel at the other edge of town, Room 118. I'll expect you and Ms. Carmichael to be checked in in half an hour. Room 117 is available."

"But we're already staying at the Super 8—"

Santiago turned and walked away without removing the magic on either of them, nor responding to his statement. Instead, he turned his power up a notch until Adam's skin began to sting and burn like he was rolling on hot sand. He got the point. It wasn't until the elder man's rental car disappeared from the parking lot and another two minutes had passed that Adam could move again.

After he finished paying for the gas and returned to the truck, Vivian was still rubbing her arms to ease the pain. He fought the urge to do the same thing.

"Who was that?" she asked, once he was seated behind the wheel once more and had started the truck. "What did he want?"

"Lucas Santiago, the council rep for the wolves. He's never visited our pack and damned if I know what he's doing in Texas. I only recognized him because Josef has a picture of the two of them in his office."

Vivian's voice was approaching panic. She never did deal well with confrontation when the threat was real. "We need to get out of town. Right now. Go somewhere he can't find us."

He found himself chuckling at yet another absurd thought. "Jesus, Viv! He knew our names, for crying out loud! You saw his car leave while we were still statues. He wanted us to know that he could find us, kill us without even trying, pretty much anywhere if we tried to skip. I don't know what the hell we did wrong, but I'm sort of fond of breathing, don'tcha know, so I'm headed to the motel like he instructed. How about you? You want me to drop you at the bus station? Think you'll make it a dozen miles before he crushes your windpipe from the comfort of his room?"

Her voice lowered to a whisper and she started to rock slightly under her seat belt. "I don't want to go. I don't want to talk to him, Adam."

Part of him felt sorry for her, but mostly he was annoyed at her cowardice. And she wanted to be a *pack leader*. What a laugh. "Oh, for God's sake! Get over it. You're an alpha werewolf. You'll heal from anything short of death. The man can't be a psychopath and be on the council. They don't put up with that shit. Hey, if we screwed up, we'll get bloodied a little. That's part of life. Hell, there's no saying we're not *all* going to have to fight for our position in this new pack, so get used to the idea. Now borrow me a pen so I can write down the room number before I forget."

Vivian didn't respond, which was fine with him. She did hand him the pen so he could write down the motel name on the back of an old envelope, then followed him quietly to gather their things at the hotel. The new place was a few blocks over and they checked in, as instructed, next door to Santiago's room. She twitched a little when Adam knocked at thirty minutes on the nose, and her scent was thick with ammonia. But she didn't bolt.

Santiago answered without raising his voice, "Come in."

They walked through the door and Adam took in the surroundings at a glance. The decor pretty much mirrored his room, with turquoise paint starting to peel on the plastered walls, and obvious wear fraying the edges of the floral print curtains and bedspread. Viv's room was little better. She'd been assigned an adobe pink room that she'd quietly proclaimed hideous. It seemed surprising to find a council member staying in little better than a dump, considering there were better accommodations in town. Adam realized the older Latino was on the phone, and from the muffled voice on the other end of the line, he was talking with Josef.

Relief flowed through him and the air suddenly felt a little cooler. *Good. That should settle the issue.*

"I appreciate your time, Alpha Isaacson. I'll let you know what I decide." Santiago pressed the button to end the cell phone call and closed the cover with a nod of acknowledgment to them. "Please have a seat. I'd like to ask you both a few questions. I'd appreciate it if you'd wait until I'm done with one of you before the other jumps in. But first, you probably should know that I won't be questioning you as your council representative. There's a new person representing the wolves on the council."

Adam glanced at Viv, but she didn't grasp the significance of the statement. Maybe it was the cop inside him, but the question just popped out of his mouth. "Then can I ask in what capacity you'll be questioning us?"

The older man's mouth twitched a bit and he leaned back in his chair—obviously one borrowed from another room or the lobby, since it didn't match the two they sat in. He crossed one ankle over the other knee and clasped his hands over his stomach. "You can. I've taken over as head of Wolven for the time being." He motioned with his eyes to a file folder on the bed. Adam hadn't looked at it until that moment, but the words, "Mueller, Adam David" on the label surprised him. "I understand you were an agent before you joined the Minneapolis police. A good one, according to your records."

That took *not good* to a whole new level. "So, our being here was a Wolven matter?"

"*Is* a Wolven matter," Santiago corrected blandly, which shook Adam to the core and fluttered his chest a bit. Despite what he said to Viv, there *were* worse things than death in the Sazi world, and getting worked over by the head of Wolven was definitely on the list. "Let's start with a simple question, Mr. Mueller. Why are you here? Start from when you heard the announcement from the council. What did that announcement say?"

The tone and wording was familiar. He'd been on the

asking side too many times, with too many suspects. And there was no way Santiago was going to give up a bit of information about his conversation with Josef. He might as well just relax and answer the questions. He had nothing to hide.

He took a deep breath, licked his tongue across his teeth, and leaned back into the chair. "Two weeks ago, our pack leader, Josef Isaacson, called a surprise meeting of the pack—"

"Well, it really wasn't a surprise to all of us." Viv interrupted with her usual running commentary. "I'd heard rumors o—" A cool wind of raw power raised the hairs on Adam's arm and he glanced at Vivian to discover she had been cut off mid-word and was now frozen in place. He fought not to chuckle at the elegant simplicity of the Wolven chief's solution to interruptions.

"You were saying, Mr. Mueller?" Adam pulled his eyes away from his pack mate and met the eyes of the other man, who was now holding a notepad and pen, waiting patiently for a reply.

"The surprise," he began, with a significant look at Viv's frozen form, "was that Josef asked for a *full* meeting, including human family members. He doesn't do that often. I arrived early, to help set up the chairs, and Josef called me into his office to discuss the situation, in case reactions got out of hand."

Adam waited while Santiago finished scribbling and asked a question. "So you both expected there might be problems when people learned the council had voted to split the pack?"

He snorted and shook his head angrily, remembering his initial outrage at the sheer audacity! Leaning forward aggressively, he spit out a reply with clenched fists. "Hell yah! Wouldn't *you* be concerned about problems when people discovered they were being uprooted from their homes . . . exiled against their will?" The moment the words left his mouth, he was sorry and embarrassed. He really didn't expect Santiago to answer, and didn't need to antagonize the man. He closed his eyes, took a deep breath, and leaned back into the lumpy cushion. It took long seconds before he could relax his fingers and respond calmly. "Sorry. I didn't mean to imply . . . I mean . . . yes. We expected there could be negative reactions."

If the older man was annoyed, he hid it well. His tone remained calm and measured. "And what did you . . . or should I say, what did the *pack leadership* do, to address the concerns of your people?"

He shrugged. "What *could* we do? The council's word is law. Josef explained he'd done his best to change the council's mind. He told us all how he'd had long meetings with the wolves' representative on . . . the—" His brows furrowed as the realization hit him, just as the other man's raised significantly. "Actually, what he told me was he talked to . . . *you*."

More scribbling on the pad gave Adam a moment to watch him. He couldn't smell anything over the secret Wolven cologne that masked the scent of emotions, but just watching his body language revealed a growing anger. But he didn't know who it was directed at. "He mentioned me by name?"

"He did. Can I ask who our representative is, and how long you've been running Wolven?"

Santiago ignored the question. "Was anyone else in the room while you were discussing this?"

He shook his head. "No, sir. Josef doesn't have an alpha female, at least not a permanent one."

"Did Alpha Isaacson discuss his efforts to change the council's mind with the pack?"

Adam thought back, trying to remember. "I don't think so. Not unless it was after I left."

The pen paused over the pad, and Santiago locked eyes with him. "You left the pack meeting before it was over?"

"Yes sir. I had to go on shift. I didn't think my watch commander would find the reason *acceptable* if I was late."

Santiago nodded and actually gave him a small, lopsided smile that went all the way to his eyes. "No doubt. So, who brought up the idea of you coming down here to . . . what did you call it—*recon* the area? Was it at the public meeting, or in your private discussion beforehand?"

He glanced around the room to see if there was a water pitcher. It was getting a little close in the room, both from the humidity and Santiago's crackling power, which raised the small hairs on his neck. Even being on the other side of the room didn't help much. He was almost afraid to stand up for fear of getting shocked.

As though reading his mind, the other man put down his pen. "There's pop in the fridge next to the bathroom. You might as well get us each one. Hope Coke's okay. It was all they had in the machine outside."

Adam stood up and eased past the other man, glancing sideways at him a little nervously when he said casually, "And yes, it is humid today. It's not just me."

After pulling three cans from the tabletop refrigerator with a fake wood door that didn't want to seal when closed, he tried carefully not to think about anything at all. When he handed one can to Santiago, he was surprised to discover there was no ache when their skin touched. He'd managed to swallow all that power, leaving only the light scent of ozone—the calm after a storm. There was now no sense at all that the other man was anything more than an ordinary human. That took more talent than he could even imagine.

After setting down the third can next to Vivian's motionless arm, he popped the top on his and looked squarely at the Wolven chief. The silvered temples of his dark hair seemed out of place with the smooth, unlined face—as though the gray had been painted on a much younger man. He might as well take the bull by the horns. "If you can read minds, sir, why are you bothering to question me?"

The answer was both chilling and reassuring, leaving Adam to wonder what to do or say. "I can't read every mind—you're just one of the lucky ones. And I'm questioning you because not every word that appears in a person's mind winds up on their tongue. I wanted to hear what you had to *say* before I decided what you had to hide. More luck for you—I don't think you're hiding anything. Oh, and you might as well call me Lucas. I try to stay on a first name basis with my agents. But back to the question—reconning the area. Whose idea?"

My agents. Was he being reactivated? Why? Was it a good thing or bad? Adam shook his head to get his mind back on track. "Well, it was sort of both of ours. I don't remember who brought it up first. When he said the council had appointed me as the new alpha, I said I'd never been to Texas. He said the same, and we wondered how we'd know who to pick to go, or whether we should ask for volunteers. He said he felt like he was picking cattle to go to auction . . . meaning slaughter, and I think at that point, we both made some . . . well, some pretty . . . um, *disparaging* remarks about the council in general and their heritages in particular." Might as well be up-front at this point. Lying would lead to a bad place if his thoughts were an open book. He shrugged ruefully. "No offense."

This time, Lucas actually grinned. "None taken. Especially since I wasn't part of the vote. But I have heard the tapes of the meeting, so I do know what was and wasn't said to your pack leader. I need to do a little thinking at this point, and I have a meeting to attend."

Adam stood up. "Then we should be going. If we're not supposed to be here, then we'll just—"

But Lucas waved him back to his seat. "You stay. You're going with me to the meeting. But, Ms. Carmichael, I'd like you to wait in your room until we return."

Vivian let out a heaving blast of air as he released his hold on her. It was as though she'd been holding her breath for the full conversation. She started to rub her arms again. "That'll be fine. Um, don't feel like you have to hurry on my account." She stood and literally leaped for the door. Adam could see her hands shaking lightly as she closed it behind her, but then again, she'd never met anyone from Wolven. She probably had no idea that powers like Lucas's even existed.

Once she was gone, Adam waited while Lucas tidied up in the bathroom, trying to imagine what sort of things were in store for him. "Is there anything I'm supposed to do at this meeting?"

"Hard to say." Lucas's voice was muffled from behind the door, but Adam got the impression his inclusion in the meeting was an impulse on the Wolven chief's part. "The alpha down here hasn't yet been informed about the council's decision." He stepped out of the bathroom, rubbing his damp hair with a threadbare blue towel, and met Adam's dropped jaw with a wry smile. "We'd hoped to break it to this pack slowly—let them get used to the idea like your pack did. But two alpha wolves arriving in a town this size has probably already been reported to the alpha, and you never requested permission to enter the territory. Coming with me to meet with her might be the only thing that keeps you and Ms. Carmichael alive to see tomorrow."

Chapter 4

EVEN THE SMELL of her sister Rosa's award-winning green chile couldn't get the knots out of Cara's stomach as she stood rigidly next to the sink, watching out the window for Will and his *guest* to arrive. Rosa had grumbled but complied when ordered to close the restaurant for the day so there would be a place to meet with the Wolven agent. Cara just hoped her big sister wouldn't return to find little bloody bits of her strewn across the patterned stone tiles.

God, wouldn't that piss her off! She hates to mop the floor.

The black humor abruptly made her laugh, but it sounded hollow and stark in the empty room. Once again, she checked her watch and then reverently touched the small *medalla de oro* at her throat. It wasn't quite noon. He'd said *lunch*, but she didn't ask what time, so she'd arrived early, hoping to get it out of the way and done with—whatever *it* might be. She said a small prayer that her family wouldn't suffer for her mistake.

The sound of a car door slamming behind the building started her nerves jangling again, so she bent over the bubbling pot on the stove and inhaled the spicy, savory scent, trying to center herself while she waited for the door to open. A sip of tea helped, too. Not only did the herbs alleviate her symptoms, but it was also wonderfully calming.

Will Kerchee walked through the back door without knocking. He'd visited often enough to be nearly family. He, too, checked his watch as he looked around the room. A variety of emotions erupted in the air around him, telegraphing his confusion.

"Afternoon, Cara. I thought I'd be the last one here." He shrugged and closed the door. "I'm glad I'm not. This way we have a chance to chat before Lucas gets here."

If Cara hadn't already been holding onto the counter to breathe in the chile scent, she would have fallen over from the sudden bonelessness in her knees. There was only *one* Sazi by that name who Will might invite to a meeting—the head of all the wolves was going to *execute* her.

"So—" she said through a fuzzy brain that couldn't seem to focus—"I *am* going to die today. I . . . I didn't expect to be . . . scared." She looked up at him with tears beginning to well and watched him wince from the ammonia panic that rushed from her pores. "Does that make me a coward, Will?"

He stepped closer and put a comforting hand on her arm, pulling her forward to help her into a chair. "No. It doesn't. Everybody gets scared, and you earn a lot of brownie points with me for admitting it. But remember we don't know anything for certain, Cara. I know I seemed mad last night, but the truth is I would have done the same thing in the circumstances. That's why I let it go. But I had no choice. I had to tell Lucas. He's the head of Wolven now— my boss—and he was already coming to town to meet with you. He'd have known something was up if I'd tried to lie to him when he cornered me and asked me about local news."

That stemmed the tears, and curiosity began to beat at her. She'd never actually met Lucas Santiago, but he was legendary, both for his compassion and his ruthlessness. "He was coming here to see *me*—as the Wolven chief— before any of this happened? Why?"

Will gave another of his fluid shrugs that told more than words could that his wings weren't far beneath his skin. "Honestly, I haven't a clue. They only tell me what they think I need to know. But something big is happening, and it looks like you've fallen into the middle of it." He reached out to ruffle her bangs like he would to a kid sister. "I promise you I'll be here for you, though. I'll do everything

I can to reduce your sentence. Maybe you'll just lose a strip of hide."

She nodded shakily but actually felt some of the tension ease from her. "Yeah. I've had that done. It's not pretty, and it hurts, but anything I can heal from is infinitely better than H and H."

Will nodded and filled a water glass before sitting down across from her at the table where the staff normally ate. "I've known Lucas for years, and he's not one to overreact. The parabio isn't fond of killing alphas in the worst of circumstances—actually I like the thought of him as the chief in that regard. Fiona has a temper on her. She'll do a head-and-heart execution without much more than the word of the field agent. But Lucas is a detail man. He'll pore through the file and consider every alternative first."

"Glad you approve." Cara and Will both looked up, startled, to see a casually dressed Latino leaning in the open doorway, looking amused. She was definitely going to have to get her ears checked, but at least Will hadn't noticed him come in, either.

Will didn't so much redden as darken, all the way down to his collar. He stood up in a rush and stepped back, nearly at attention. "Sorry, Lucas. Didn't mean to tell tales out of school."

The older man waved it off and stepped in the room, his sweeping gaze taking in every corner. "No. It's good to hear what my agents think of me from time to time. Keeps me centered." He flicked lightly glowing golden eyes to Will as he grabbed a chair, spun it around, and straddled it. The worn, nearly white jeans stretched taut enough to reveal heavily muscled thighs. It made Cara realize he wasn't just an administrator who'd be sitting in a chair while running the agency.

He gave a small snort and shook his head. "Jeez, would you loosen up a little, Kerchee? We've known each other too long for you to believe *all* the press about me. I mean . . . the *bad* stuff, sure—but all that good, honorable, warm and fuzzy crap?" His face remained serious, but his eyes were twinkling.

From the corner of her eye, she caught Will's grin just as raw, powerful magic flowed in a wave from Lucas and swirled around her. It made her skin itch and her throat tighten. She rubbed her fingers together, trying to get the feeling back in them, waiting nervously for those eerily bright eyes to lock on hers again.

"Ms. Salinas, I've spent a good part of the morning considering what to do about your actions last night. I understand why you acted as you did, but it was still wrong. Under the circumstances, however, it would do more harm than good to inflict a suitable punishment, so I'm giving you a pass this time." He gave her a long, dangerous look. "*Don't* do it again."

Cara let out the breath she'd been holding. She would've said something to reassure him that she understood, but she was interrupted by the sound of the restaurant door opening.

A delighted low tenor from the doorway made her turn her eyes away from Lucas, but she couldn't see around his broad shoulders without tipping her chair. "Well, I'll be damned! If it isn't the *terror from the sky* himself! How you doin', Cloudsfall? Been a long time!"

She finally half-stood so she could see the speaker and their eyes met. The word shot out of her mouth before she could stop it. "You!"

"You!" Both words hit the air at the exact same moment as the driver of the black truck from the previous night stopped mid-step and stared incredulously. He was a *wolf* and a powerful one to boot! So why didn't she feel like growling? Normally, other wolves felt like a threat to her.

"Glad you two have met." Lucas nodded and flicked his

finger, urging the new man to step closer. "That'll speed this along."

"No, we haven't . . . I mean—" She fumbled her way around the thought, unable to take her eyes off the newcomer. He was taller than she'd imagined him to be, and his skin was a little darker than the truck's dome light showed—but it appeared to be a tan, because his neck showed hints of lighter skin. Still, the unruly black hair that made her want to run her fingers through it, and the vivid blue eyes were the ones etched into her memory.

Again his words came out at nearly the same time, completing her thought. "We haven't really *met*. She was just there, with the ambulance."

She smiled and nodded, surprisingly pleased he would remember. "And you were in the black truck."

Lucas cleared his throat, and she realized that she had been staring for long seconds, not saying anything. Just memorizing his face. She flushed guiltily and sat back down.

Will grabbed a chair and, like Lucas, turned it around and straddled it. He leaned his arms on the top ladder-back rail and grinned at the new man, while occasionally flicking his eyes to watch her. "Well, you certainly seem to have made an impression on our local alpha, Adam."

Adam. That was a nice name. But then she realized that Will was teasing her as much as he was the new man and shot him a nasty look. Adam must have noticed her annoyance born of embarrassment because his nostrils flared. Then he stepped forward and reached into his front pocket. He pulled out some change and removed a quarter. He tossed it on the table in front of Will with an evil smile before returning the other coins to his pocket.

"Make it out to Adam—best wishes. Need a pen?"

His words had an accent, but she couldn't place the location. Will suddenly smelled embarrassed and reached out and slapped the quarter back across the table so hard it went off the edge and bounced on the tile with a melodic ting. "Fuck you, Mueller."

Tension filled the room between Adam and Will—not so much dangerous as testing. Cara was pretty sure she was wearing the same confused expression as Lucas, but he was the one who asked first.

"Is there something going on I should know about, gentlemen?" There was a warning rumble to the words, and another flow of magic, which stopped just short of touching either man.

This time, Adam flushed lightly and shook his head. "No, sir. Just a private joke."

"That's going to *stay* private. *Right,* Adam?" Will's words had a hard edge, the sort that spoke of adventures better left in the past.

He nodded once and sighed. "Right. Sorry, Cloudsfall. I shouldn't have pushed that button. How about we start over?" He held out his hand, but from his expression and scent, Cara could tell he wasn't sure if he'd taken the joke too far.

She'd never heard Will referred to as *Cloudsfall* before, but being both Native American and a raptor it made sense to her. And, it was obvious the three men were comfortable with the name. But she felt a little at a disadvantage. She'd thought she knew everything about Will, only to discover a brand-new past history with strangers.

After a short hesitation, Will held out his hand and shook Adam's, then released and closed his hand into a fist. Adam did the same and they bumped knuckles like old buddies. "Just as much my fault, man. I should have remembered you get testy when I tease you. Oh, and you need to call me *Will* from here out, too. Sam and I switched lives a few decades back."

Cara's jaw dropped nearly to the table! Sam? Will and

Ten Bears had switched *lives*? A few *decades* back? That would mean when she was a little girl. . . . Had it been *Will* who'd bounced her on his knee?

Um—

Adam laughed lightly and sat down next to Cara. He tried to make it casual, but his scent was both anticipatory and excited. He smelled of mingled pine trees and lemongrass. Was it cologne or just his underlying scent? Either way it was a warm, soft tang she could get used to. She had to work to smell it over the peppers and cumin rising from the bubbling pot on the stove. He was also a powerful alpha—not in the same league as Lucas or Will, but just the amount that bled from him made her skin tingle.

She forced herself not to stare at him, but she did notice the dark stubble on his strong jaw and amazingly long lashes before she pulled her gaze away. He didn't look at her at all after that first time. He kept his attention completely on Will. "So, Sam's your grand*father* now? Wow! How cool is that? No wonder you're in uniform. He had quite the career behind him. I know you're really good at illusion magic and persuasion, so making people believe was probably no big deal, but was it hard to pass the Ranger test without the background?"

Will pursed his lips and shrugged. "Nah. We switched when he was still on the Dallas force. He got pretty smashed up during a high-speed chase and decided it was time to hang up his shield. People gave me a lot of slack when I showed back up, thinking *he* was having post-traumatic stress—so, I had time to study and learn the ropes. And, of course, I already had my Wolven background. It wasn't that big of a deal." He turned to Cara and apparently noticed the look on her face. Or maybe it was her scent. Even she could smell her own confusion. "Hell! That's right. You didn't even know about that, huh? I guess I never thought to mention it. You were still a kid when it happened. Do you even know how that works? You're an alpha, so you're probably going to have to consider it one of these days yourself."

Cara shook her head, and Adam spoke up. "Actually, I don't know much about changing identities either, other than it happens. Feel free to enlighten me."

Will raised his eyebrows toward Lucas, who nodded. "Okay, so I've done the father-son, grandfather-grandson thing a bunch of times. Different people do it their own way, but I prefer to stay within my own family. I didn't really have to do as much in the past as I'm forced to now—because photographs and fingerprinting didn't used to exist. You could disappear into the landscape and *become* someone else just on your own word. Lots of people did that during the gold rushes or after the Civil War. Any time there's unrest, it's easier. Now, I'm sure you know the reason." He paused, apparently waiting for a nod, but Cara could only shrug and shake her head. Will sighed. "The major problem is that Sazi age a lot slower than humans. Yeah, we all tell our kids that alphas live a couple extra decades, but often that can be seven or eight decades, even for the lesser alphas! People like me and the *parabio* here—" Will jerked his thumb toward Lucas, causing Cara to raise a finger with a question.

"What's a *parabio*? You called him that before, but it's not a Spanish word."

Lucas quirked one corner of his mouth in a half-smile. "It's actually a Comanche term. Comanches were among the first democracies, in case you didn't know. They elected their leaders from within, and bloodline didn't matter. If a warrior was seen as being worthy—leading the charge in battle, giving good advice to others, having the respect of the tribe, and such—they became *parabio,* or great leader. Will knows that I was once the equivalent of a *parabio* for my tribe. Good leaders listen to their people without prejudicing their views beforehand. But that's beside the point here. Go on, Will."

Will was nodding as Lucas spoke. "Yep. Anyway, me and Lucas have lived for centuries. People can't grasp what it means to live decades or centuries longer. Mostly, our appearance is the issue. Dick Clark aside, being eighty and looking thirty sort of freaks people out. Take that a step further, and looking like thirty when you're a *hundred* and eighty will earn you pitchforks and torches on your doorstep. We Sazi seem to stick at about thirty for a really long time, then stick at forty for a really long time, and so on. Now, I just keep looking like me, so I'm one of the lucky ones. It really saves on the illusion magic to just gray my hair and move a little slower, before stepping into the life of a younger descendent—because, well . . . all us injuns look alike, ya know—" The wink was what got her and she finally laughed along with the others. But when he continued, she was forced to look closer at Lucas. "Now, the *parabio* here, he takes another route. His illusion magic is exceptional. He can even change his freaking *scent*. So he becomes an entirely new person."

So did that mean the person she was looking at, smelling, sensing across the table *wasn't* really Lucas Santiago? Or did it mean that Lucas Santiago wasn't real at all? She had no doubt she suddenly reeked of sweet, thick curiosity. Who was the Wolven chief? What did he look like in his "real life"?

Adam cocked his head. "But how would that work? You can't just magically appear as a new person in today's world. There are birth certificates and passports, fingerprints and retinal scans, plus lots of other things that can identify us from birth. How in the world could you just up and *become* a new person?"

Lucas gave an enigmatic smile and raised his brows. "I've had *lots* of time to practice creating identities. There are loopholes in any system, and Wolven keeps up with all the new tricks. Real people with real lives die every day—in accidents and natural disasters, war and murder. Sometimes, *miraculous recoveries* aren't as miraculous as you think, and the person the police recovers isn't that person at all. But that's enough of that for now. I think it's time to get started. We'll start with introductions since it's fairly apparent not everybody knows everyone else—at least as well as they'd *thought*." The phrasing was significant and both Will and Adam shifted uncomfortably in their chairs. "Rather than have you each introduce yourselves, I'll tell you what *I* want you to know about one another. Then you can take it from there later."

He swept his gaze around the table. "Ladies first, I suppose. This is Carlotta Salinas, acting sheriff of Tedford County, and the alpha female of the Texas pack. The Salinas family is Tejano, meaning they homesteaded in Texas while it was still a Mexican holding. Her family sided with the Republic of Texas and fought against Santa Ana, and she and her pack still hunt on land that is part of an original Spanish land grant. Her strong points are speed and minor healing talents, and her negatives are a quick temper and a tendency to see only the trees, but not the forest."

Cara bit her tongue when he said that. A week ago, she probably would have objected—and strenuously, but Ten Bears had said the exact same thing last night.

Have I really been so rigid and shortsighted?

Santiago continued. "She's a Mexican red wolf in animal form. Regular red wolves are endangered and presumed extinct in Texas, so they keep to private hunting grounds and don't mingle much with other packs." He seemed to be addressing the comments about her and her family's history to Adam, but she wasn't certain why.

"Both of you seem to know Will Kerchee, but before he was Will Kerchee, he was Sam Cloudsfall Kerchee, and be-

fore that, was . . . well, let's just say one of those closest to
Chief Ten Bears of the Comanche. He became a Wolven
agent when I met him during the Civil War, and has been
one ever since. He's an eagle on the moon and the term *terror from the sky* probably isn't a bad thing to consider him.
Stay on his good side, because understand he can take either one of you in a fight and, quite possibly, *both* of you at
once."

Lucas paused as though he'd heard something, then
stood and walked to the window to look out for a moment.
He shook his head, tiny little movements that said something was bothering him and flared his nostrils next to the
window opening. But she couldn't smell a thing from him
and he didn't elaborate. No doubt he was wearing the Wolven cologne. He opened the refrigerator next to the door
and pulled out a small glass bottle of Dr Pepper, then raised
one inquiring eyebrow at them. "Anyone else want one? I
haven't had one of these for ages. I didn't realize they were
still making the Dublin formula."

Adam and Will both raised their hands, so she did as
well. Rosa was absolutely addicted to the sugared soda.
"They still ship them locally, just not out of state." After a
questioning look from Adam, she explained, "Dr Pepper
was founded in the town of Dublin, here in Texas, and
made a deal with a local company for sugar for the soda.
But when they started to ship nationally, the sugar plant
couldn't keep up, so they switched to corn syrup like
everyone else. But they still make some of the old formula.
It tastes a *lot* better!"

She was impressed that Lucas could palm two bottles in
each hand without straining. He had bigger hands than
she'd first thought. When he sat down, it was as though he
were full human. He'd managed to completely mask all of
his power, somehow pulling it inside himself until he was a
blank slate. "All you need to know about me is that I'm

presently known as Lucas Santiago. Up until a few months ago, I was the alpha male of the Boulder pack, and the council representative for the wolves. That's all changed and, before you ask, no I won't tell you how it all came about, other than it was a choice I made for a variety of reasons. Now, your present council rep is Nikoli Molotov, the Alpha of Chicago. But if you have any problems in the next few months, I'm the man to talk to, even though I'm presently the Wolven chief. I've replaced Fiona Monier for the time being. She's my second. But *I'll* be taking personal responsibility for all agents in Texas and South America until further notice. That means you'll report to *me*."

Will looked as taken aback as she felt, and there was some underlying text that Cara couldn't just let sit. "I'm afraid I'm confused, Chief Santiago. You said *all agents*. But I've never been in Wolven. I never finished the program."

He smiled, but it was a baring of teeth with no humor behind it. "Welcome to the future, Sheriff Salinas. Your promotion in the county hierarchy was your graduation. I'm making you a reserve agent. Your field supervisor—and yours, too, Adam—will be Will."

Adam didn't look nearly as confused as Cara felt. He nodded, but smelled frustrated, as though he'd suspected something and had just gotten verification.

"I wondered if that's where you were leading with the *my agents* comment earlier. I have to presume there's a reason why you're doing this. I haven't been in Wolven for quite a few years, but reserve agents were only activated when there were bad things—*really* bad things coming. You gonna tell us what's up?"

Lucas shook his head but met Adam's eyes calmly. "Not yet. It's a very complicated situation. I can tell you there's a lot going on in the world right now. Individual events may or may not be connected. That's what I'm here for—to look at the whole forest. I'll be asking each of you to look for specific trees. And, that leads me to your introduction. Adam Mueller is a former Wolven agent. He was partnered with Will briefly when he joined the agency. Presently, he's a fourth-grade patrol officer in the Minneapolis police out of the very rough Franklin Safety Center of Precinct 3. His good points are brute strength and the brains to back them up. Negatives are a tendency toward inflexibility and not listening to advice." Cara watched the small muscle at the back of Adam's jaw clench, but that was the only outward sign of any concern at the comment.

"He's second in command of the Minnesota pack, which is unfortunately one of the largest in the world. I say *unfortunately* because the pack hunts in a relatively populous area, and last fall the increasing number of wolves was noticed—by the humans, during a regular pack hunt organized by Mr. Mueller. They are sending wolf biologists to Minneapolis to start a study."

Cara felt her eyes widen. Her hand flew to her mouth as she let out a small gasp. This time, Adam clenched his fists and jaw simultaneously in the corner of her vision. But he met her gaze and the intense blue eyes were filled with both pain and pride as Lucas continued. "Naturally, what the humans notice, the council notices. We're living in a world of less and less space, people—and unless we want to blare our existence on the front page of every newspaper in the world, the council *must* take action when things like this occur." He dipped his head toward Adam with a carefully blank expression. "You understand I normally wouldn't mention your role in this, but the circumstances demand it." After a brief nod, Lucas looked at both her and Will in turn. "And just so you know, Adam's been cleared of any formal responsibility for the incident by the council. It's not to be brought up in conversation with pack members."

Lucas tapped one finger on the wood and looked at each

of them. "You realize I can't bring any of this information to the average Sazi. It's one of the reasons I just activated both of you—putting you in the *need to know* group."

Cara nodded in full understanding. The die-off of red wolves in the region was why her own pack had become so very secretive. She tried desperately not to look at Adam. *Madre de Dios!* How would she feel in his place . . . if it had been *her* wolves who had been noticed by the outside world during a casual hunt? Would she have the courage to sit here, facing down potential detractors, with the same composure? "Of course. So, what happens now?"

Lucas took a sip of soda and tapped on the table again. His power began to leak out of him again, as though it was a nervous habit. The pins-and-needles sensation started again in her fingers. "What happens now is that the council has decreed that two dozen pack members, and their families, from Minnesota will be split off and transferred to other packs in less populated regions. Adam Mueller will, quite possibly, be one of the new alpha males." He paused and locked his eyes with hers. "The Texas pack is the destination for half those families."

Chapter 5

ADAM WATCHED AS the young Texas alpha took in the implications of what Santiago said for a long moment. He didn't expect the sudden explosion of sound and motion as she pushed back her chair, stood, and let out a bitter laugh. Her scent was filled with too many things to sort, but anger was right up on top.

"Y'all have *got* to be kidding! You can't double the size of my pack in a day—with complete outsiders!"

Lucas apparently expected the reaction, because he nodded once and swept his hand toward her chair, suggesting she sit back down. "We can and will, Ms. Salinas. The council has considered the situation thoroughly. We fully understand—"

Carlotta didn't return to her seat. Instead, she stepped back and leaned against the counter, making her service revolver shift against her hip. Her arms crossed over her chest and she shook her head in annoyance. "No, I don't think you understand at all. What you're proposing is complete and utter horseshit. It won't work."

Adam's skin began to sting from the sudden surge of power that swept past him to dance right at the edge of Salinas's aura. She winced, but didn't back down. "You're treading on very thin ice, Alpha Salinas."

Her eyes flashed and it nearly made Adam smile. "You can take a strip of hide from me with your power if you want, sir, but it won't change the facts. You said I'm known for not seeing the forest for the trees. Well, let me tell you something—you're so far outside the forest, there *aren't* any trees. Y'all might be trying to avoid exposure of our kind with this plan, but what's actually going to happen is an *increased* chance we'll be found out. You don't understand how this part of Texas works."

Lucas's eyes narrowed and the golden glow in them ratcheted up a notch. "Alpha, you really need to sit down and—"

Cloudsfall held up his hand with a thoughtful expression. His scent revealed both curiosity and concern. "No, Lucas. Wait. I think I know where she's going with this. You really need to hear her out, because it's something that should have occurred to the council—or at least to you."

The older man flicked his eyes sideways and sighed like

a balloon leaking air. Then he stood up, turned his chair around, and sat back down. He leaned heavily against the chair back, causing a loud creaking sound that punctuated the sudden silence. The power around him dampened a bit as he picked up his bottle, took a sip, and then motioned to Salinas with it. "Alright, I'll listen. Remember I don't have the power to change the council's decision. But, if you raise a good enough argument, I can take it to the Chief Justice and see if the matter can be reopened."

Carlotta looked surprised at his sudden willingness to listen to her. No, actually she seemed more *stunned* and was struggling to collect herself—her jaw was moving, but nothing was coming out and her scent was confused. Frankly, Adam was a little surprised himself at the turn of events. Apparently, his old partner's opinion had higher value to Santiago than he'd imagined. The phone rang suddenly, but apparently had been shunted directly to the answering machine. Salinas stopped to listen, so he took the moment to have a sip of pop. She was right that it had a very different taste than regular Dr Pepper—smoother and strangely, *less* sweet. He actually liked it quite a bit and took another long drink.

A nearly unintelligible male voice was asking for directions on the recorder. Apparently, she didn't feel the need to pick up the phone because she shrugged and returned her attention to them.

She took a deep breath after a sip of something vile-smelling from a cup next to the stove, and blinked a few times. "Okay, then . . . thank you for listening. I'm sorry I swore like that, but I'm a little on edge today. That's not an excuse, but . . . well, there you go." She shrugged and then plopped a massive metal ladle into the pot on the stove and stirred the boiling goo—the scent of peppers, garlic, and cumin billowed into the room. Then she returned to her seat. He couldn't help but notice her leg brushing by his as she did, and found that he didn't mind the contact at all, nor the warm scent of honeysuckle, ripe peaches, and rain that rose from her skin every time she moved.

"Anyway, I think Will understands where I'm coming from, and I'm trying to figure out a way to explain this without seeming like I'm being prejudiced or anything. First, I want to make it clear that I have no objection to a few families joining our pack. That's not the issue. But y'all can't move that many people from another state into this region without drastic consequences!"

Santiago's face was completely bland when he replied. "Why not?"

She raised her hands in front of her helplessly and looked around as though searching for something. "God, I don't know if I can explain it!" After a few seconds, her gaze returned to Lucas's and she raised one finger in the air with a smile. "Wait! Yes, I *can* explain it. But y'all will have to bear with me for a second." She stood without waiting for his response, lifted the telephone off the nearby wall, and carried it back to the table. "I'm going to call my sister on speakerphone, but I don't want her to know you're listening. Y'all can't say *anything*—don't even cough—or this won't work."

Lucas started to open his mouth, but Cloudsfall raised one finger to catch the older man's attention, smiled, and nodded. "Let her, Lucas. I know where she's going and if she's right, you'll learn a lot more this way."

Carlotta lifted the receiver, dialed a number, let it ring twice, and then hung up. As she noticed the scent of his curiosity, she shrugged. "Private family code. She'll know it's me calling now." This time, she hit the speakerphone button and pressed speed dial. She put a finger to her lips and there was a small part inside Adam that wished it was his own finger touching there. He intentionally moved his leg, rest it against her knee, and was pleased when she didn't move away.

A woman answered in a frustrated contralto. "It's about time you called! *Chingado,* Carita, it's been *insane* here all morning! Next time, y'all need to find another place to hold your meeting, or at least give me time to get out of town!"

Cara raised her eyebrows at him significantly, but he didn't understand, so he just shook his head and shrugged. She put a note of confusion in her voice. "How come, Rosa? What's up?" She paused for a moment, then continued as though she'd had a flash of understanding. "Oh! They've been calling you, huh? Sorry I've got you on speaker. I'm cleaning up from the meeting."

"No big. You're on speaker, too. This is my first chance in an hour to change Felix's diaper. Yeah, they've been calling, and calling and *calling*! I finally stopped answering, and then they started to call my cell phone. 'How come the restaurant's closed, Rosa?' 'Why's Cara meeting with the Texas rangers, Rosa?' 'Who are those new men in town, Rosa?' Ay ay, ay, like I'm a mind reader or something! Paco said the rumors are at full tilt. Down at the donut shop Mara hinted I got closed down for a bad health inspection, and then Betty at the bank called to ask if it was true about the Rangers finding drugs under my floor boards. *Drugs,* Cara!"

Cara winced at that, heaving a sigh that would be heard over the speaker while her sister swore in more than one language in the background. "Okay, okay! I get the point, Rosa! No more pack meetings at the restaurant during business hours. Everybody's just leaving. Will says hi."

"He better not have eaten all my chile! I know how he is. For a bird, he's got too big a stomach." Lucas had to cover his mouth so he didn't laugh and Cloudsfall silently flipped his middle finger at the phone. "I need to sell that chile—especially now that I'm going to have to convince people I don't have rats and cucarachas."

"Okay, I get it, Rosa. We didn't eat the chile, but we did drink a few of your sodas. I'll buy you more. I've got to get back to work now. I'll call you later."

"Yeah, yeah. And you *better* stop by the paper and make sure there won't be any reporters showing up tomorrow to ask stupid questions. It's bad enough people seeing the sheriff and Ranger trucks hiding behind the building, but I don't even know who the attorney from Colorado *is*, so I don't want to hear a bunch of questions I can't answer."

That brought all four of them to attention and even Cara's jaw dropped. "What did you say, Rosa? Who said anything about an attorney?"

Adam could almost hear the shrug. "Hmm . . . old Mr. Gomez, I think. You remember—he had that grandson going to college up north of Denver, who got picked up for a DWI? It was years and years ago, but he swears someone there at the restaurant looks like the man who prosecuted his boy. If y'all were having any other meeting but a pack one, I wouldn't even mention it."

Lucas started to swear silently and shake his head in angry frustration with two fingers rubbing the skin just above his eyebrow while Cara fought to end the call. "Okay, Rosa. I'll call you later. Really got to go now."

"Okay, hun bun. Don't forget you promised to come over tonight and help me wrap tamales for Gloria's Quinceanera party and look at the dress she picked out. The kids have been looking forward to it all week. They keep complaining how they never see Tia Cara anymore."

That made her smile and it made her whole face light up. "You tell Gloria and Raul I'll stop by after dinner, and give the baby a kiss for me. But . . . it might be a long day, so don't let them wait up if it gets too late." She didn't look at any of them, but she suddenly seemed very tired; weary—as though the weight of the world were on her shoulders.

"Eh. Paco wouldn't let them anyway. Tomorrow's a school day. Don't work too hard, Carita. You know how I worry. Call me later, sweetie."

She pressed the cut off button and waited, her lips moving as she counted to three silently, then picked up the receiver, probably to be certain there was a dial tone. "So," she finally said after a long pause, resting her forearms on the table and meeting the eyes of each of them in turn. He might be imagining it, but she seemed to pause longer on him before returning her gaze to Lucas. "You see now why a dozen families from Minnesota can't just suddenly appear down here? There are only *two* newcomers in town today and I'd be surprised if you haven't already had your whole genealogy mapped out on the high school blackboard. A major move like you're proposing would have tongues wagging across four counties and people sniffing all over the place. You gotta understand, the demographics in this county are over forty percent retired. These people have nothing better to do with their time than speculate about anything and everything. At the very least, the people selected will have to have some ties to the area."

Adam watched as Cara nodded her head toward him, without actually meeting his eyes. But she still didn't move her leg from where their thighs were pressed almost intimately along the entire length. "Now, Officer Mueller here is actually a pretty good pick, because there are Muellers who homesteaded in Fredericksburg—a couple of counties away. There's a big German population there. I could come up with a creative excuse for him and possibly one or two others to move down, but a *dozen?*" She shook her head, causing a few stray, wavy dark hairs to come loose from the tight bun at her neck. "Nope. There's no way."

"Call me Adam, please . . . sheriff." The sentence came

out a little softer than he'd planned, causing a half-smile, but no comment, from Cloudsfall.

She looked at him then and her scent took on the light dusty scent of embarrassment. "Oh, of course. And I might as well be Cara, if we're going to be . . . um, *working* together." As though an afterthought, her leg finally moved away from his with a small jerk and she looked away to glance at her watch.

Lucas was staring at his nearly empty bottle while running a slow finger around the rim. The resulting tone was like fingernails on chalkboards and it was all Adam could do to stop himself from reaching out to grab his hand to stop the squealing. Finally, after what seemed like an eternity, Santiago stopped and reached behind him to pull a worn leather wallet from his pocket. He removed a pair of twenties, placed them on the table, returned the wallet, and then leaned back in his chair. Crossing his arms over his chest, he looked around the table slowly, making sure he had all their attentions—as though there was any doubt.

"Okay, here's what we're going to do. Adam, you and I are going undercover . . . in a rather unusual fashion." At the trio of startled expressions, he elaborated. "See, I probably *was* the prosecutor for that man's grandson. I did a stint in both the DA and County Attorney's offices—*as* Lucas Santiago. So, my cover here is blown anyway. It won't take people long to notice the Minnesota plates at the motel, either. Will is right that I should have remembered how people gossip in a tiny town. I grew up in one, but apparently have become forgetful after living in a city so long."

He stood up and walked to the metal wire shelves next to the massive multi-burner stove, and started looking for something. He continued to talk with his back to them. "I own an interest in a number of properties in Boulder. Mostly, they're pack businesses, but not all of them. My wife and I have been talking about my retirement from my practice, since I've already been the pack leader up there too long as it is. People are starting to comment on how well I'm holding up to my insane litigation schedule. It wouldn't be a stretch to convince people I was thinking about moving to Texas . . . or at least, considering investing in potential future growth down here."

Adam could see where he was going with the idea. Investors can ask stupid questions and promise about anything. People are happy to spill their guts for the potential of financial gain. That was why so few people reported being scammed by professional con men, making his job more difficult. He found himself nodding while staring at Lucas's broad back and thought of something. "So, is that my cover, too? I don't know if I can pull off acting like an investor. It'd be too easy to find out I'm just barely making it on my salary. One call to my bank would have my loan officer rolling on the floor at the question. Plus, I haven't had anyone die in the family recently to fake a windfall."

Lucas turned around, holding a short stack of white foam containers with lids. He shook his head with a smile. "Nope. You're just going to be you . . . with a bit of a twist. Your story is you've gotten burned out, which isn't that unusual, considering your beat. I presume you already gave notice after Josef gave you your orders?"

"Yeah, but I haven't said anything about being burned out to anyone. I just told Reggie—my partner—that I needed to find better money. He nearly offered to walk with me, but his wife is about to have twins. I'm single, with no kids, so I'm more flexible." He wasn't even sure why he said that last part, but it didn't hurt anything.

The Wolven chief returned to the table, put down the stack of containers—causing an odd look from both Cloudsfall and Carlotta—and took his chair again. "No problem there, on either side of the question. You found some information on an offshoot of your family . . . pick something logical. An old bible in the attic or some such, with information about a black sheep that got disowned. It happened all the time in the last century . . . trust me. You drove to Texas to meet up with your buddy Will, taking along an old girlfriend and discovered—" He swept both arms outward and smiled with something approaching wonder. "—*paradise*! Texas is *amazing*! It's peaceful, the people are terrific, and the worst crime in town is the occasional cattle rustler. It's everything you've ever dreamed of, but just didn't know it. You are going to draw on every acting lesson you've had in your life this week, Agent. You're *in love* with Santa Helena and are going to tell every person you meet just that."

"Actually, that's not true at all." Cara's voice was matter of fact, sounding very much like a cop. She leaned back in her chair and crossed her arms over her chest, causing the badge on her pocket to flash sunlight in his eyes. "There's crime here—lots of it. Meth, both labs and users, is bad all over the county, we're the back door for illegal immigration heading north and I'm fighting a losing battle with keeping the San Antonio gangs from recruiting in the schools. It's not just picking up estrays and truants down here. I'm understaffed, underfunded, and overworked. I turned off my radio for the meeting, because my dispatcher knows she can call the restaurant to get me. But if I turned it on, you'd probably hear the same codes you're used to hearing back home—robberies, domestic violence, drug busts, and even the occasional murder."

A light dawned in Adam's head. "Okay, so let's go a different route. I'm just here visiting Will, but suddenly am swept away—seeing a place that can still be saved. A place where I can make a difference and help it *not* become Franklin Street." Lucas and Will both smiled, but Cara looked uncertain, so he added in total seriousness, "You wouldn't want to see the beat where I work. It'd make you *welcome* the San Antonio gangs into town." She looked startled when both Will and Lucas nodded in agreement. He was getting into the idea of going undercover again. It had been a long time. "Okay, yeah. I can do that. But—" He shook his head and grimaced a bit. "That might be too much of a stretch for Vivian. She's not that good an actress, and no matter how much money she gives the theater guild she never will be."

He noticed a confusing mix of scents from the sheriff and turned to see her staring at the side of his face with near sadness, mixed with anger. She shifted her eyes when they met briefly and smelled suddenly embarrassed. He'd thought it was just that she didn't like the plan, but could it be she was jealous? That's sure what it smelled like. But he hadn't considered whether she was attached, either. He hadn't noticed a ring, and now her hand was tucked underneath her arm. Would it piss him off to find out she was married? He realized with surprise that it just might.

"She doesn't need to be," Lucas said with a serious expression. "She's going back to Minneapolis with me in a few days . . . whether or not she realizes it. I don't know her very well, but I know her *type*. She couldn't exist in a small town any more than a wolf could live underwater. No, we want Ms. Carmichael to act just *exactly* as we know she will. While you're waxing ecstatic about the town, she'll be making snide remarks and being a general pain. By comparison, you'll be a breath of fresh air to those who love living here and, at worst, you'll be looked at as naive by those who feel they're trapped. That's all fine."

Cara cleared her throat and raised a finger. His eyes dropped automatically, before he could even register the motion in his brain. No ring. "But won't people ask questions when she moves back down here—*especially* if she made rude comments?"

Adam shook his head, possibly too vigorously. "She

won't *be* moving back down here. I decided that when I learned on the way down she was trying to push her way in as alpha female. I told her in no uncertain terms that there was *already* an alpha female. I won't stand for any power plays. Besides, after meeting you I know me and my pack members will be in good hands."

LUCAS AND CLOUDSFALL wore the same startled expression that was probably on her own face. "You heard right," he continued with a single nod, "I don't plan to be the alpha male down here. But if you're in need of a second, I'm your man."

Lucas sighed. "I figured you'd probably say that, Adam, but I'd ask you to reconsider. Your people are going to need *both* an alpha female and an alpha male for a time. If you later want to step down, that's fine. But Cara might not survive leadership challenges from some of the Minnesota pack, so—" She felt her eyes widen at that but she didn't comment as he closed his mouth suddenly and pursed his lips. She didn't know much about timber wolves, but a *lesser* wolf could take her out? That was a little scary.

Then he started to tap one finger in the air. "Actually, you know what? I'll need to check with Charles for verification, but I think there's precedent to make some temporary changes to the rules down here. When the bears moved out of Bavaria to join the Siberian group early in the last century, there was so much infighting that the council set up a *no-death* period. No challenges . . . leadership, mating, or otherwise would be to the death, until the people became properly integrated and *every* challenge had to have a Wolven official present, just to be certain there were no . . . *accidents*."

"That would be a *great* idea!" Cloudsfall said with a smile. "I can tell you that it's going to get pretty ugly down here when this pack finds out. They're likely to wind up drinking too much and saying things that'll get them killed by the Minnesota people."

Outrage flooded her and the noise that escaped her would have been considered rude in most circles. She didn't care, though. "*Excuse me?* That's not saying much for my people, Will! You're making them out to be pissy and petty, and they're not!"

The Comanche Ranger snorted and shook his head with chin dropped and eyes bordering on insulted. His power rose until it nearly singed the air. "You gonna tell me Paco doesn't have a mouth on him after a few tequilas, Cara? Get *real*! People down here are used to it, but trust me when I say that the lowest of the people moving down here are bigger dogs than Paco—and he'll get his ass kicked. I'll bet there's not a single member of the Minnesota pack who can even *get* drunk." He looked at her with cold sureness. "Other than you, Cara, there's not a person in this pack who's not going to wind up on the *bottom* of the combined puppy pile."

After Cara was able to close her dropped jaw, she looked around at the three men with horror. "Is that true? Are y'all planning on moving down people who are going to completely eliminate my pack structure? If so, then Will's right. My people will probably fight and *die* before they're willing to be turned into the kicking dogs—omegas to a bunch of outsiders." Could this be what Ten Bears, or whoever the hell he was, had referred to? Was she going to be forced to send her people into a losing battle with other Sazi? No. She was their alpha and would protect them before she'd send them into danger. "I *demand* a say in who comes down—their powers, their abilities and . . . *cultural attitudes*. Like it or not, human prejudice is an issue, too."

She leaned back after her little diatribe, fingernails digging into her palms. She struggled to keep her face blank, her body appearing loose and confident, and her emotions minimal. The silence was deafening and the lack of scent from both Will and Lucas was unnerving. But Adam was bleeding enough emotion for all of them. He bounced from excitement to anger to worry and fear. It was a heady combination of smells that nearly made her sneeze. He didn't say a word, but Cara could tell he was annoyed by how the muscle at the back of his jaw was flexing and how he was struggling to keep his magic in check. It roiled the air around him like an electric cloud. Still, she couldn't hear his teeth grinding, so that was something.

After a few tense moments where everybody tried to ignore the heightening energy and battle scents, Lucas nodded. "You're right, Alpha Salinas. You deserve a voice in who comes down here. The council didn't discuss the issue, but I'm sure Councilman Molotov would agree. I know *I'd* want to debate the matter if I were in your shoes." He paused and took a slow breath, obviously thinking hard. He slapped his open palm down on the varnished wood tabletop. Even though it was done lightly, Cara jumped. "Okay, here's what we're going to do. In a few minutes, we're all going to walk out the front door, visible as the sun. We're going to be laughing like old buddies who have just had a friendly lunch. If anyone is on the street that either you or Will recognize, Ms. Salinas, you're going to invite them over and introduce us."

"Introduce you as . . . *who*, sir? An investor? An attorney? A friend of Will's?"

Lucas nodded. "All of the above . . . well, mostly anyway. From now on, though, until this is done we're all on a first name basis. Lucas, Will, Adam, and Cara. That's the only way it'll work. Here's the story on me. I'm an attorney from Colorado who's getting close to retirement. I know some mutual friends of Adam's from Minnesota. I ran into him at the motel and he was on his way to lunch with Will, who he came down here to see. Will invited Adam to the friendly lunch he *already had* scheduled with you, Cara. Now that I've met you all and heard all the great things the town has to offer, I'm interested in investing and think my *mutual friend* of Adam's would be interested, too." He turned to Adam and pointed a finger at his chest. "Who in your pack has the most ready cash, or already has investment properties? We'll need to involve them."

Adam pursed his lips briefly. "Probably Mike and Sheila Kassner. They've got a string of art galleries in the cities and do some rental renovations on the side. He's loaded but is getting fed up with his partner in the gallery, a family member—not part of the pack. He's actually one of the people who offered to come down."

Cara furrowed her brows at Adam's statement. She couldn't quite figure out what he meant by a family member who wasn't in the pack. How was that possible? She nearly opened her mouth to ask, but it wasn't important. What *was* important right now was getting the stories straight. Curiosities could wait. "So, what am I supposed to do besides introduce you guys?"

Now Lucas turned stern again. He looked at both her and Adam critically. "You and Adam will be spending as much time together as possible for the next three days—making up a list of potential candidates for this pack. Adam, I know that volunteers were your *preference* for those who came down, but the reality is that Cara's right. The transition from city to small town is going to be difficult, and Sazi abilities are critical. You'll need to think of your pack as a whole. Which members could start new businesses down here that might prosper, what businesses are *needed* here that wouldn't be seen as an intrusion by the locals? Where to house them, etcetera."

Cara cocked her head a bit as the phone started to ring in

the office again. "Why three days? What's going to happen then?"

Lucas opened his mouth to reply when an intentionally loud voice came over the answering machine's recorder. "Cara, it's Maggie. You're needed."

Adrenaline rushed through her. She stood up in a rush without excusing herself and headed into Rosa's office. It was a damned good thing Maggie had raised her voice, since she never would have heard it normally from underneath the invoices and packing slips stacked on top of the machine.

"You there, Sheriff? You're not answering your radio."

Sheesh! She really needed to talk to Rosa about fire hazards like covering up the vents on an electrical appliance—especially one this old. She picked up the receiver and tucked it into the crook of her neck while she removed the multihued papers to find the off button so the conversation wouldn't get recorded. Ah. There it was. "Sorry to keep you waiting, Maggie. What's up?"

"There's trouble down at the hospital, Cara. Billy spotted a white van, just peeking out of the brush off Little Coffey Creek Road. He thought it might be a *coyote* dropping off illegals, so he radioed for backup and took up a position to watch."

Oh, God! Here she was, sitting in a stupid meeting while some of her people might be—"Were shots fired? Is anyone down?"

She heard Maggie's sigh of relief. Even though she seldom showed it, being the dispatcher—hearing horrible things happening and knowing she couldn't go help—was a huge strain on her. "Thankfully, none of our people. But by the time Rick arrived, Billy noticed vultures were starting to circle. They found three bodies—cause of death unknown. They looked recent, probably no older than last night, according to Billy, but it was obvious animals had gotten to them. I guess it was pretty messy with claw and bite marks. They're at the hospital now and the coroner's been called. Rick found papers on them and checked them. The IDs are fake, and there was a whole stack of blank ones in a compartment under the driver's seat. So if Will's still there with you, you might mention it. I've called it in to Immigration and Customs Enforcement, but you know how long it takes to get anyone down here."

"Copy that. Thanks, Maggie. I'm on my way." She hung up the phone at the same instant she flicked her radio back to life, and walked back to the other room. "Duty calls I'm afraid, gentlemen. We're going to have to put off this warm and fuzzy meeting for now." She pointed at Will. "You might want to come down to the hospital with me. We've got three dead illegals with claw and bite marks. No cause of death yet." Dipping her head to Lucas, she added with a note of apology. "I'd invite y'all, but there'd be questions."

Lucas nodded and Will stood up with a glance at his boss. "I'll drop by the motel later and fill you in if it's a Wolven matter." He motioned to the items on the table. "By the way, what are those containers for?"

The older man grinned broadly. "I don't know about anyone else, but the smell of that chile has been driving me insane since I walked in, and now that I've been told not to touch it . . . well, I can't resist." Cara let out a brief laugh and he continued. "I figured I'd buy one for each of us—since I doubt your sister would have much cause to object that way. Anyone else interested?"

"Oh, *hell yes*!" Will exclaimed with a similar grin. "Rosa's right that I can down a whole pot in one sitting. I think I've been really good, sitting on my hands over here."

Cara dropped her chin and shook her head with amusement, but noticed Adam didn't leap to his feet at the offer. Well, maybe he wasn't big on Mexican food. "Sure. Why not? She'll yell and gripe at me tonight, but won't pass up the money, either. It's way too much, though, so I really should get you some change. But the safe's locked and I don't have any cash on me. Can I bring it to you later?"

Lucas shook his head with pursed lips. "Don't bother. She's out a whole morning's receipts. I should probably *add* money, not get some back."

She couldn't really disagree with that, so she just took the containers off the table and walked over to the stove. In a few seconds, they were full and she passed one out to each—even to Adam, who looked up at her with surprise. She shrugged. "Maybe you'll like it. I know Rosa would be insulted if y'all didn't at least *try* it."

Will stepped toward the back door. "Be right back. I just want to put this in the car before I forget."

The radio was buzzing with the locations of her deputies as she wiped down the stove where some of the chile had dripped—Billy was back on the road to check out a reported rattlesnake in someone's front yard. Elliot was back out at the Garcia house again. When would Miguel ever learn not to get pushy with Estelle when he'd been drinking? She handed him his dick time and again when he started to bitch at her. They'd never actually hit each other, or someone would have to get booked. But they yelled and screamed enough that the neighbors kept calling 911. She couldn't blame them.

Tim was at the pawn shop on a possible stolen property report. Nothing else was out of the ordinary, thankfully. While she busied herself with quickly cleaning up their trash so she could leave, she heard both amusement and the rumblings of an order when Lucas said, "I'd suggest you say something appropriately complimentary when you meet Cara's sister tonight, Adam. It would be a good way to start the blending process."

She swung around sharply before she reached the trash

can, a bottle of pop in each hand and what probably resembled horror on her face. "*Tonight*? But tonight I'm—"

Lucas completed the thought. "Spending the evening with your sister. I know. That's the point of all this. As I said, you two—" motioning at her and Adam in turn— "will be spending a lot of time together in the next few days. While you were on the phone, I explained the rest of the plan to Adam and Will. As soon as you're off shift, you'll drop by the motel and pick him up, then take him to meet your sister and her family. He'll explain things. Afterward, you can start to work out the details of this move. Now, we all have work to do, so let's get moving. Adam, you're with me."

He picked up his container and walked out the door without another word, leaving her to stand there, looking shell-shocked. An equally uncomfortable Adam stood and followed Lucas out the door with a shrug and an apologetic smile. But although his scent mostly matched his uncomfortable look, a light citrus scent of happiness followed him out the door.

Chapter 6

SOFTLY BEEPING INSTRUMENTS blended with the low lights and antiseptic scent in the hospital room. Cara stepped closer to the bed, being careful not to make any noise that might wake up the occupant. Livid bruises on the woman's pale skin reminded Cara vividly of the previous night, but the fact that the patient was in a regular room, rather than intensive care made it all worth it. All she'd wanted was to see the slowly raising chest and peaceful expression for herself. She'd just turned to leave when she heard an accented voice that was sleep-filled and hoarse.

"Yo're *her,* aint'cha?"

Cara turned around and smiled gently at the lightly frowning face. "How're you feeling, Mrs. Foster?"

A pause, combined with an uncomfortable scent. "I'm not married. Yo kin call me Missy." The accent spoke of bayou country, somewhere deep in Louisiana. "Yo're that sheriff ma girl was telling me about, ain't ya? Yo're *Miss Cara*—the one what called the ambolance?"

"Yep. I'm Sheriff Salinas . . . Cara. I'm so glad y'all are doing better, Missy. Brittany's a terrific little girl. It would have been a shame if she wound up without a mom . . . or worse." She didn't want to excuse the other woman's actions. The girl could have been killed, and these hospital bills were going to follow Missy Foster for years to come. One minute is all it would have taken to buckle up.

Missy nodded, barely perceptible amongst the white sheets that seemed to envelop her small form. The machines attached to her continued to beep softly. "I've thought 'bout that . . . *a lot*. Pretty stupid o' me not to strap her in. Mama's been reminding me just how lucky we was." She stopped and then stared up strongly at Cara, her gaze intense and filled with . . . *something*. "But it wasn't all *luck*, was it, Miss Cara? I remember things—not all of it, mind yo, but enough. It ain't natural, me being alive, is it?"

Cara forced herself not to show any surprise, but it was an effort. *Madre de Dios!* Could she have remembered her lifting off the truck? She didn't dare talk about it, but she would have to check up on Missy for a few days, see just what memories she had. Pasting a smile on her face, she replied lightly, "Heaven was watching over y'all, that's for sure."

Again Missy nodded, but her eyes kept that same intensity. "Yes'm. God works in mysterious ways. And yo don't gotta worry, Miss Cara. I won't tell no one. Not never." She reached out a hand, lifting up the tubes attached to her skin with white tape that nearly matched the color of her skin. Her eyes filled with tears. "I can't tell yo how grateful I am to have a 'nothah chance to watch ma baby grow up. I won't mess it up—I promise."

Cara took the woman's hand in hers and blinked back tears as she squeezed lightly. Missy's scent made it clear that she wasn't kidding. Citrus and hot metal, tinged with wetness said the woman was both grateful and determined to straighten out.

They remained that way for a moment, just holding hands, until Cara heard a man clear his throat in the doorway. Will's voice was flat, but his scent said he was a little choked up, too. "We really need to get to it, Cara."

She nodded, released Missy's hand and turned toward the door, leaving the woman she had saved to go attend to those she didn't get to in time.

"THIS IS NOT good." Will's hushed voice spoke the understatement of the year as she stared with horror at the mangled body only partly covered by a white sheet. The scent of the man's blood couldn't cover up the other scents—coyotes and vultures had feasted on the body, but before that had been . . . *Sazi* who'd fed. On a human. ¡*Madre de Dios*!

"No shit," she replied with an equally quiet voice. "But pathology wasn't my strong suit at the academy. What do you think the coroner's going to say? Is there any chance they'll think the three men killed one another?"

Will shook his head, his expression grim. She watched as he tried to find something to do with his blood-covered examining gloves, moving his hands around without touching anything. Finally, he stripped them off and tucked them in the front pocket of his pants, inside out.

"Not even a chance. Look at the lividity of the abdomens on each of them. It's obvious they died on their stomach and the blood pooled. You already saw the back. It was talons that severed this man's spine and cracked his skull. To me, there's no other plausible cause of death. But the most disturbing thing to me is the parts that were taken before death—the lips, cheeks, eyes, and liver. Damn! The screams must have been horrible. Someone must have heard, even being that far out in the sticks. No, a raptor did this, and from the different radius of openings, there were more than one. We've got some rogue shifters out there attacking humans. This is definitely a Wolven case, but I'm not sure how to handle it since so many people have already seen the bodies . . . and who knows how many saw the actual event?"

"So what do we do? Someone's going to come in any minute to prep them for the autopsy and there are too many people in the hallways to just walk them out of here." She opened her senses fully, her mind working furiously on an explanation for being here without having signed in, in case anyone walked through the door. The reception nurse knew they were in the building, because she'd asked after the Foster woman to learn her room number.

"I wouldn't worry too much about that. I've already got aversion magic surrounding this room. I did that when we walked in. Nobody will want to get anywhere close to the door until we're gone. But actually, now that I think about it, isn't Bob Sloan still the coroner here?"

When she nodded, he continued, the cool scent of relief pushing his fear and anger to disappear into the overhead fans. "Good. He's an excellent G.P., but forensics aren't *his* strong suit, either. This is going to look like an animal attack to him . . . no doubt in my mind. He'll probably slap a label of *death by misadventure* on it after a cursory examination and call it good—especially since they're probably not from local families, who might want a full autopsy and lab work. At worst, he'll attribute the skull punctures to a bobcat or javalina."

She found herself nodding unconsciously, agreeing with Will's assessment. "You know, I hadn't thought of that . . . but you're right. While the punctures are large, had I not been able to *smell* that raptors attacked the men, I wouldn't have even thought of it. And by the time Immigration and Customs Enforcement shows up, the cause of death will be unrecognizable. Okay, let's just wait and see what happens on this end. Since it's probably not going to be reported as a homicide, it'll just quietly disappear into the files."

"No, they're not homicides." Will's eyes flashed angrily as he stared at the mangled body. "But they're definitely *murders*. And it's our job to find out who did it."

Chapter 7

"MAN! SLOW DOWN for a second. I need to take a break." The mid-afternoon sun was baking the limestone underfoot and the still air burned when he inhaled. Even in the shade it must have been a hundred degrees. Adam's tongue was lolling out as he struggled to draw in enough breath. It amazed him that Cara still looked fresh and ready for anything. He didn't think he was out of shape at all, but being in the heat in animal form was like . . . well, like wearing a fur coat in a tanning bed.

He plopped down unceremoniously in the shade of a tall bush and lowered his muzzle to his front paws, trying to slow his breathing so his head would stop pounding. He smelled her approach first, sweet honeysuckles and peaches that cut through the chalky dust that had already coated his fur. He opened his lids a crack. Cara's bright white muzzle pointed down under concerned golden eyes.

"You okay back here? Heat getting to you?"

"No, I'm not okay. My God! How do you stand this temperature? Is it like this all the time?" He closed his eyes again, shutting out the intense light. He longed for a lake to jump into, or even a tall glass of cool water, or . . . lemonade! Yeah, that's what he should be doing right now—drinking lemonade in front of an air conditioner. But, instead, he was running over rocks in the desert heat, getting cactus spines in his pads, and searching for a freaking attack bird!

She flicked her gaze behind her and then sat down on her haunches. "Actually, I hate to be the bearer of bad news— but this has been a fairly mild spring. It's not even ninety out here. That's a little below average for recent years. It just feels hotter because the rock reflects the heat. You'd think that being white rock, it would be cooler. But it's not." She stood up and shook herself, flinging bits of dust and rock from her fur. "We don't need you to get heat exhaustion, though, so you might just hang out in the shade for a few minutes, or walk back to the car for a drink. You may not realize it, but you've actually climbed quite a bit in elevation."

He raised up his head in surprise. "We have? I thought Texas was low and flat."

A sharp bark was followed by a quick swing of her tail, causing the sunlight to highlight the white tip. He'd never seen fur of her color before—russet with black underlay, even though her face was solid white. It was a really striking effect. "Hardly. You're in the hill country, our limited version of mountains. Santa Helena is eighteen hundred ten feet above sea level, and right now you're probably sitting at close to two thousand. By the time we get to the top of the cliff, it'll be about twenty-two fifty. What's Minneapolis . . . a thousand?"

He shook his head with effort and it started to throb again, so he rested it down between his paws once more. "Not even. I think it's about six fifty."

Wind rushed over him, combined with the peculiar spicy scent of feathers and he heard Cloudsfall's—no, make that *Will's*—taunt from above. "Wussing out on us, Mueller? Daylight's burning, man." The volume rose and fell as he circled around them, looking for a place to land.

Adam pulled back his lips from his teeth and growled low, glaring up at the massive eagle. He was just about to make a snide remark when Cara did instead. "Leave him alone, Will. The heat and elevation are getting to him. I don't feel like carrying him back to the car if he passes out, and I doubt you want to walk naked over the cactus to do it either. If you want to do something productive, why don't you fly back to the van and grab the water jug? I was so riled up after arguing with Billy that I forgot to put on my backpack."

A pause and a flap. "Shit. Forgot about that. Okay, be back in a second." With another swoop of feathers, which stirred a brief, delightful breeze, Will disappeared into the distance.

"Will's a fast flyer," Adam said with a nod. "He'll be back in less than a minute."

Cara dropped to the ground nearby, taking advantage of a small patch of shade next to a boulder and started to clean her muzzle with the side of one paw. He abruptly noticed how long her lashes were when she blinked and sneezed lightly. "I know. We've had races in the past—him in the air and me on the ground."

That deserved a twitch of ears. "Really? Who won?"

She huffed out something very close to a laugh. "It depends. I sliced and diced him the first time on level ground, so he changed the terrain to make it tougher on me. Then I did the same back to him, making him fly through canyons with strange air pockets. I had to pore over weather maps for our last race to find just the right spot. So far, we're even—two wins each, one tie."

He looked at her with a new appreciation. Will was damned fast and if she smoked him bad enough for him to pick the next course, that was . . . well, impressive. Adam wasn't quite sure what to say about it, so he picked a different topic after a few moments of silence. "For what it's worth, I thought your deputy was an ass. My watch commander probably would have laid him out if he'd mouthed off to him like that. Hell, I thought about it myself, except my paws don't bend into very good fists." It had been a great idea of Lucas's to show up on site in wolf form so Cara and Will could say the three of them—Lucas, Vivian, and himself—were all tracking dogs, sent to look for more bodies. It hadn't taken hardly any illusion magic to make them all appear to be German shepherds to the asshole deputy.

She moved one forearm in a close approximation of a shrug. "It doesn't matter. Billy's just . . . *Billy*. He's not a bad cop, overall—but he's got some serious issues about working under a woman. He thinks we all ought to be chained to a stove or popping out babies. He was livid to the point of resigning when the governor appointed *me* to fill Carl's slot until he's back on his feet. And I gotta tell you . . . I was just as surprised as everyone else. Hell, I can't remember hearing about a governor doing that unless the sheriff *died,* and even then . . . well, he normally doesn't get involved in local stuff. But when the letter arrived, I expected Rick Seguin's name to be on it. He's got the name recognition. The Seguin family goes way back. There are towns and streets named after his ancestors. I still don't know why I got tapped." She paused and looked at him, almost apologetically. "Family background means a *lot* down here, just so you know 'cause . . . my argument's got nothing to do with, well, *y'all*. I don't want you to think—"

He waved it away with a word. "Don't. Really, I was a little annoyed at first, but once you got your sister on the phone, it made perfect sense. It's a lot like the neighborhoods in my beat. Everybody knows everybody, so new faces stick out like a neon sign. It means I'll be spending some time at the library, looking up old surnames to see if I can match up the rest of my people."

She nodded and lifted her nose to a slight breeze that made the tiny leaves of the tree he was under flutter lightly. "Try the museum first. It's a really good one and the curator knows the history of just about every town in the hill country. She's just the sweetest thing and has a mind like a steel trap. But be careful, 'cause she's a tricky one. She'll try to pull every ounce of information out of you. That's *why* she knows the history of every town!"

He'd just opened his mouth to reply when he heard the flapping of wings overhead. Adam wondered what someone would think if they saw an oversize eagle flying across the landscape carrying a gallon jug of water with a bowl tied to the handle. When Will reached them, he reared back and tilted his wings to hover briefly before lowering the jug to the ground with a series of short flaps. He reached down with his beak and removed the short rope attaching the jug to his leg.

"Lucas said to take ten. Vivian's having altitude sickness symptoms, too. I'll fly up to the top of the bluff and see if there's anything worth taking a closer look at from the ground while you guys hang out. So far it looks like the perps made a clean getaway. Not a track, a drop of blood, or a feather in sight and I've been looking hard." He flapped once, just to keep in the air as he circled around them.

Cara nodded, her eyes tracking his slow flight. "Sounds good. I'll stay here with Adam until he's ready and then we'll head west, toward the cliff face. Oh, y'know, you might check out Ten Bears's cabin. With him on his way to the powwow, someone might have decided it was a good place to hide out."

Will twisted his head in mid-flight and gave an almost imperceptible nod. "Good point. I'll head there next. Don't worry about waiting for me if you guys give up or Lucas calls you back. I can fly to my car later. I have to get back to Austin before shift tomorrow anyway."

With a hard flap and a piercing screech, he rose a dozen stories in seconds and was nearly out of sight before Adam could take two breaths. Both he and Cara stared at the water jug greedily, but neither made a move toward it. His dry tongue screamed for a taste, but something held him back.

And I know what it is.

After a hanging pause he finally gave up. "So, who does the honors? I guess we might as well get used to being naked in front of each other if we're going to be pack members. I can't open a screw top jug with my claws."

Cara nodded. "Pouring's a bitch, too." He was getting accustomed to her Southern accent, that made *pouring* sound like *poe'in.* Another long pause and then she snorted lightly. "Okay, we might as well do this. Now *I'm* getting a headache. Just promise not to gawk at the scars on my leg. I don't feel like using extra magic to hide them and . . . well, they're part of who I am."

She stood up and shook once more, before he could reply, and then transformed slowly, rising up to her feet until she was fully upright. Golden skin with curves all in the right places replaced the fur with definite alpha-level speed. He hadn't realized how much of the same russet flowed through her hair, now loose and shoulder-length around her heart-shaped face. The sun highlighted the red strands until they were the color of expensive red wine. He found himself staring at her for a long moment and getting more excited than was appropriate. She sneezed and snorted several times, as though her nose was plugged, but seemed to get over it quickly.

Moving his gaze down didn't help lessen his arousal any as she knelt down next to the water jug, opened it, and started to pour water into the bowl. Her breasts were full and nicely formed and her waist slender. And her hips . . . they were just perfect, firm and muscled. The skin just begged to be stroked, slow and easy.

What would she do if I turned human right now, slid up behind her, grabbed those hips, pulled aside her hair, and nipped the back of her neck?

It was probably a damned good thing he'd remained in wolf form . . . and was lying down.

He dropped his eyes lower. Okay, that fixed his little erotic image. Ouch! She wasn't kidding about the scars on her leg. Two narrow strips had been carved nearly all the way down the thigh, and had never properly filled in. He could only think of one way that could have happened.

"Had a strip of hide taken, huh? Who'd you piss off?"

She sighed. "*Two* strips, if you'll notice." She reached forward with bowl in hand but then her nostrils flared—probably catching his new, muskier scent. Well, he couldn't help it with her kneeling there, looking all naked and gorgeous. But it made her stop and blush lightly before she placed the bowl down in front of him. She didn't comment, but she did turn her back to him before raising the jug to her own lips. He kept his eyes on the rocks, watching a long line of tiny ants crawl toward the base of the bush. But what he *wanted* to do was watch the muscles play under her skin, follow beads of sweat rolling slowly down, see her chest move as she swallowed, and—

Damn! Get a grip, Adam!

He fought down his attraction with effort, and lapped up the entire bowl. He kept his eyes on the ground as she leaned over and filled the bowl again while he continued to drink. She paused and her scent filled his nose. Oh ho! He wasn't the only one aroused. Wow, did she smell good— sweet and sultry, spicy and . . . *hot.*

Magic washed over him in a wave as she turned back to her wolf form right next to him. He could feel her warm breath in his ear and it made him shiver, despite the heat. Maybe this new pack wasn't going to be so bad, after all.

He raised his head from the bowl, licking the last bit of water from his muzzle. She was standing so close that if he lifted his head too fast, he'd hit her jaw. They were frozen for a moment, each of them just breathing slowly in the hot shade. Her neck was right there, almost inviting him to nip the skin, feel the fur brush across his tongue. A shudder passed through him as he imagined what she'd be like under him . . . but then he pushed the thought away. Not the right time or place.

Pulling his head back a bit, he rose to his haunches and locked eyes with her, just inches from the tip of her nose. "So, what'd you do?"

It took her a few seconds of staring blankly at him but she finally blinked, startled. "What?"

His lips pulled back in a quick, amused pant. "What'd you do to earn two strips of hide out of your leg? It must have taken some . . . *skill* to piss off someone that bad."

His casual tone broke the spell and she blinked a few more times before stepping back to her own patch of shade.

"Long story, and sort of . . . *personal.* Let's just say Fiona and I didn't agree on the things I should do to become an agent in Wolven. It's why I never finished training."

Damn! Fiona Monier did that? He'd never found her to be a particularly difficult woman to work with, although he knew a lot of agents complained about her. "Okay. Sorry. Didn't mean to bring up bad things."

She shook again and carefully picked up the handle of the jug in her teeth—placing it next to the boulder in the shade. It wasn't a bad idea. While it probably wouldn't help much in keeping the water cool, at least the plastic jug wouldn't explode. "No big deal. But if I'm going to be forced into the agency again, I can't say I'm sorry it'll be working for Lucas. He seems decent enough. At least he listens."

Adam stood up and found his head wasn't pounding anymore so he could nod without pain. "Fer sure. I don't know much about him, either, but I trust Clou—I mean, *Will's* instincts. If they've known each other as long as Lucas claims . . . well, that's good enough for me."

Cara paused and then looked at him, her thick antifreeze scent of curiosity beating at his nose. "Could I ask . . . I mean, about the coin? Why was Will so mad at you?"

Shit. He knew that was going to come up. With a light kick of his front leg, the pale blue bowl flicked across the ground, neatly clearing a small barrel cactus to land right next to the water jug. "Sorry. Not my story to tell. You'll have to ask him. But actually, I think it's sort of cool. I don't know why he gets so annoy—"

A woman's scream suddenly filled the still air, coming from the direction of the cliff face. Without even thinking, he found himself racing toward the sound, with Cara at his heels. Ignoring the cactus spines that slammed into his feet from below and the spiked branches of the trees that tore at his fur, he surged forward, only to be passed by as though standing still by the smaller red wolf.

What he saw when he broke through the last batch of trees was a massive owl, equal in size to Will in every way, pulling at a small, dark-skinned girl who was screaming and shouting at the bird in an unknown, guttural language. It seemed to be trying to lift the girl into the air by the arm.

And it was wearing . . . *gloves* on its talons.

Chapter 8

THERE WAS NO time to lose. There was no time for Cara to do anything at all but react. The giant owl had managed to get a sufficient grip on the girl's arm, and it was taking off, flapping hard. But it was rising slowly because of the burden it was carrying, so there were still a few precious seconds to change the situation.

She raced forward and threw herself into the air . . . but only came back with a mouthful of feathers from the bird's tail. Something was very different about the taste of the feathers, and the scent. She just couldn't put her finger on what, but she was careful to spit the feathers into the center of a spiky agerita bush so she could check them out later.

Losing the tail feathers in the gusting wind was enough to throw the owl off balance, but now it knew it was being pursued and put extra effort into gaining altitude. A hard flap made it and the screaming girl rise by a dozen feet, and there was no way Will could get back in time.

Looking around, she saw one hope. It was tricky and Adam or Will might wind up scraping her off the cliff later, but it was all there was time for. She turned around and raced back the way she came, nearly running into Adam as he arrived.

"Cara, wha—"

She spun around and got her bearings and then ran back toward the cliff, throwing an answer over her shoulder. "No time to explain. But be ready when I bring down the bird!"

She was pleased he didn't ask any more questions. He just nodded and followed her. The girl was doing her best to pry open the owl's talons, using pressure points near the center of the foot as she might do to a chicken. And it was working—the bird almost let go and had to readjust its grip in mid-flight . . . giving Cara the split second she needed.

Pushing herself to run faster than she had in years, she streaked toward an old, weathered mesquite tree, growing from the ground at the angle of the constant winds near the bluff. She clawed her way up the trunk of the tree, forcing her way through the spiked branches, which ripped into her skin with brute force. The tip of the tree loomed before the bird was in position. But like a motorcycle on a ramp she couldn't stop. She jumped forward the last few feet, landing hard on the branch. It bowed under her weight and then, as she'd hoped, sprung up again like a diving board at the pool.

Digging her feet into open air, she hurtled forward, searching for the bird. It took every ounce of her concentration to ignore the fast approaching cliff face, but it was worth the effort. The owl was too busy trying to rise away from Adam's powerful leaps from below to notice her attack from the air. She slammed into the bird with enough force to send all three of them careening toward the rock wall.

"Catch the girl!" She screamed the words without seeing if Adam was in a position to do so, but she prayed he was. While a five-story drop might shatter her bones or the owl's, they would heal. It could easily kill the human. She tumbled through the air, clinging to the back of the bird with teeth and claws, trying desperately to avoid the owl's snapping beak and powerful wings as it tried to unseat her.

Her stomach lurched as they abruptly dropped toward the ground and it took her a moment to realize that Adam was standing on a tall rock, only his back legs still touching. He'd managed to grab hold of one of the gloves on the bird's talons with his teeth. He was pulling with all his might, steadily dragging them toward the ground, while trying to avoid injuring the girl held in the other talon. But the owl wasn't to be denied that easily. It relaxed both feet and the gloves dropped off, causing Adam and the girl to tumble off the boulder to the ground.

Cara bit at the owl in a frenzy, but couldn't get through the thick layer of feathers to do any serious damage to the huge Sazi bird. And then they started to rise again. Without the extra weight of the girl, she realized it would be child's play for the owl to fly up and scrape her off against an overhang.

Apparently, Adam thought of the same thing. "Jump! It's going to slam you into the cliff."

She wished it could have been a graceful, intentional leap, but she didn't know how. Her gymnastics coach had never anticipated a need for her to dismount an owl while in wolf form. All she could do was let go and allow gravity to take over. She slid off the bird's back and tumbled once before getting her bearings again. Adam leaped out of the way, and they both winced in unison when she hit the rock and the shock crumpled one leg with an audible *snap*.

A fast-moving shadow and a whoosh of air was all the notice either of them got. Then Adam was on the ground, screaming as the owl's talons raked through fur and skin. Blood splattered across the white caleche limestone, filling the air with the smell of fresh copper pennies. The pained howl both terrified and angered her. Lucas had said Adam was a powerful fighter but now he seemed to be out cold. She could still hear him breathing—but raggedly, with a faint whistling that told her his lungs might be punctured.

Ignoring the pain that shot through her as she jumped down onto her wounded leg, she rushed to help. White flowers erupted in her vision with each step as she surged forward with fangs bared.

But her help wasn't needed. With a piercing screech, she watched as a second bird dove into battle. Will had arrived and was streaking toward the ground with talons bared. The owl spotted him and twisted at the last second, forcing Will to turn in midair to make a second pass.

"Get Adam to safety, Cara! I'll deal with this asshole."

Something white flashed from the corner of her eye. She remembered what Will had said about there being more than one. "Look out, Will! I think there's another one coming." He spun his head almost completely around while still aiming toward the owl and barely dodged a well-placed grab for his left wing. She could feel a sudden flow of stinging magic from Will, but the owl shrugged it off as though it were nothing. He tried again, this time aiming for individual body parts, which made sense. If he could hold one wing, it wouldn't be able to maneuver and would fall. That time, it almost worked, but again the bird shrugged off the magic and kept attacking.

She leaped up on one low swoop and grabbed the owl's leg with her teeth. It was enough to distract it and her weight made it drop a few feet. Will grabbed onto the owl by the chest while tearing at the neck with his beak. It screeched and clawed and tried to break away.

Part of her reveled in the taste of its blood, and she desperately wanted to bring it down, rip it into shreds—fill her belly. But she couldn't give into the need the moon was forcing on her. She wouldn't stoop to their level. No, they needed to capture one of the birds—find out its identity and why they were attacking humans. Will might win a battle with two birds, but she doubted he'd worry about keeping them alive.

What they needed now was help. She raised her muzzle and let out a low, long howl, hoping Lucas and Vivian were within hearing distance. A quick glance ensured that Adam was still breathing. But she didn't see the girl, and wondered what Adam might have done to hide her. A few sniffs was all it took for her to find the girl's position. She was tucked into a small crevice in the cliff face, staring out at the battle with an open mouth and eyes showing too much white. There was so much blood, hate, and anger in the air that she couldn't learn anything more than that she was fully human and not from around here.

Damn.

Another opportunity at the owl presented itself and her mind returned to the battle. She leaped again and caught the owl's other leg, this time higher up, and tasted arterial blood. She shook her head, growling and forcing her teeth in deeper while Will ripped at the wings. But even then it wasn't enough. The other bird . . . no, make that *two* birds—one golden eagle and a second owl—arrived and began to dive at *Adam*, ripping at his still form, forcing them to choose between the battle and letting him die.

She let go of the owl and hopped on three legs to Adam's side, leaping at the birds to force them away. He might not be pack yet, but he was still a wolf and a friend of Will's. She stood over him, crouched, with teeth bared, the pain in her foreleg only spurring her on. Her position effectively blocked the way to the girl as well and the birds all fluttered and swooped around, trying to decide what to do, while avoiding Will's constant attacks.

At last Will broke off and landed right next to her. He made a brave show of their small number . . . or maybe it wasn't a show at all considering what Lucas had said about him. Maybe he hadn't been trying as hard as it appeared, although she couldn't imagine why that might be. "Leave now and we won't kill you outright here and now. If you turn yourself in to your flock leader for the deaths of the humans, and show good cause at a Wolven inquiry hearing, you might survive. Otherwise, I'll track you down and take you in to answer for your crimes here. I've tasted you, smelled you. You can't hide."

The golden eagle swooped once more and let out a sharp sound that was close to a crow's caw. His deep voice bore an accent—not quite Mexican, but definitely from one of the South American countries. "The good cause for killing the humans was . . . we were *hungry.* Your laws mean nothing to us, Sazi, and you won't find us so easy to harm again. Eat worms, little fledgling!" The eagle circled the wounded owl as it flew crookedly away, and never looked back, apparently not in the least concerned that Will might follow.

Cara watched as the sizeable bald eagle beside her lowered his head and the scent of his anger burst into the air. He lifted his wings slightly, as though to give chase, but a clatter of small rocks behind a stand of mesquite was followed by Lucas and Vivian. She was panting from exertion, but Lucas looked ready for anything. It had startled her when he'd changed form at the motel before they came here. He didn't seem a large enough man to transform into the massive white wolf which dwarfed both Vivian and Adam. Of course, everybody was larger than her. Timber wolves just . . . well, *were* larger than red wolves. She'd gotten accustomed to it since meeting the visitors.

"What's going on? Where's Ada—" The voice from the lovely, sleek black-and-silver wolf, who made her struggle not to growl, cut off abruptly when she spotted her pack mate's still form. She faltered and took a shaky breath. "Is he—?"

Cara shook her head. She had a difficult time pulling her eyes away from the vicious wounds the talons had inflicted. They reminded her far too much of the ones that had ended the lives of the men she and Will had just viewed. "But he needs to get to a healer . . . fast. I'm not quite sure how he's still alive even now."

"Adam's tough. He's been through worse. He'll heal eventually on his own, but you're right . . . we don't have the time for that. People have noticed him, and he has to get back to Minneapolis for his last two weeks on the job." Will's concern made her turn her head. She had to raise her head until her neck popped to see his face. He'd turned back human and apparently had given himself the illusion of wearing clothes, for which she was thankful. No matter how calm she'd tried to appear before Adam, she still wasn't completely comfortable being naked around strangers—especially ones who found her attractive.

Vivian had approached and was now sniffing Adam's face. Cara was a little befuddled at the woman's scent. There was no worry, no fear. In fact, if Cara didn't know better, she would swear the wolf was wearing Wolven cologne. But whatever the Minnesota wolf was thinking or feeling was going to remain a mystery.

"Agreed." Lucas's firm voice startled her back to the situation. "We need a healer, and I think Cara's our best shot in the time available." He turned his head and caught her eye. "I know it's one of your lesser talents, but I presume your mentor showed you how to focus the magic of another alpha or pack member to increase your power?"

The hot wind gusted stronger. She could tell because her open jaw got filled with dust. She coughed and looked down at Adam, and then back up into Lucas's lightly glowing golden eyes. "Um . . . no. It makes sense to me that it should be possible, but I never had a . . . what did you call it? A *mentor*?"

This time, both Will and Lucas looked surprised, but Will was the one who asked a question. "You were a known healer in Wolven academy and were never assigned a mentor to train your talent?"

She was spared answering when the sound of pebbles disturbing in the background made all heads turn toward the cliff face. Shit! She'd completely forgotten about the human! Naturally, the girl was trying to quietly escape . . . and who wouldn't want to flee three talking wolves and an eagle who had just transformed into a naked man.

"I am *such* an idiot!" She said it low, but of course everyone heard. "Adam and I were trying to protect the girl from the birds. I completely forgot Adam hid her in the crevice."

Lucas lifted his nose into the air and sniffed, then turned angry eyes, but not to her. They focused on Will as the girl abruptly froze in place. Again, she could feel her skin stinging from the wave of magic flowing from the white wolf. Even Vivian took a few steps back to get out of the direct path of the energy. "You encountered the birds we were here to find and didn't follow them, Agent? *Why?*"

She felt compelled to come to Will's defense. "There were three of them, sir. Each one must have been very powerful, because he couldn't hold any of them with magic. They started to attack Adam and . . . well—"

Will's voice sounded proud, but pained. "Thanks, but I don't need you to protect me, Cara. You're right, Lucas. I should have followed them, no matter what the potential consequences might be. I might have captured one, or found their hideout."

Lucas stopped and shook his furred head. With a breath of magic, he was just suddenly human again and fully clothed in the same outfit waiting back in the car for him. There was no blurring of form or time lapse. He was just . . . *poof* . . . one minute wolf, and the next an elder, silver-templed man with warm brown skin. Wow.

"No. You're right, Cara. If there were three of them with equal abilities to yours, Will, then you did the right thing. Wolven can't afford to lose any agents to grandstanding at this point. We need every agent in the field to use caution."

He stepped over and squatted next to Adam, taking in the wounds with a glance. Then he stood and walked over to the girl and looked her over just as carefully. She looked young, probably no more than fifteen, but that might have been because she was short. Her straight black hair was braided and reached the middle of her back and her face, frozen while looking over her shoulder to check their positions, was pretty, with a broad nose and full lips and skin a little darker than Will's. The clothing was . . . unusual— perhaps even a party costume. The long skirt and top were obviously handwoven wool in a colorful geometric pattern. The sandals on her feet were likewise handwoven, with tiny bells and colored beads mingled in the sturdy green-gray fibers.

"All right," Lucas proclaimed after a few seconds of thought and a deep sigh. "So, we have two problems here. We need to get Adam healed, and we need to question the girl about what happened to the men you found. I can't think of any other explanation for her presence here." He turned his eyes to her. "Cara, you and I will work on Adam. Will and Vivian will talk with the girl. Remember that she's seen some strange things today, so treat her with kid gloves. I doubt we can come up with any plausible explanations for talking animals, so don't bother to try. Will, I know you've got a basic understanding of most of the common languages so just get what you can and keep her calm and focused."

Will nodded and replaced Lucas at the girl's side as he released his hold on her. As the elder man approached, Cara knew she was going to have to become human again to do hands-on healing. "Sir," she said in a quiet voice once Will and Vivian were leading the panicked, babbling girl to a rock to sit. "My illusion magic isn't the best, and if I have to concentrate on healing—" She let the thought trail off, hoping he'd get the point.

"Understood, Agent." He raised his voice slightly and turned his head while pointing to a lichen-encrusted boulder, which had fallen off the cliff in a long-past time. "Will, give us a little more room over here. Maybe walk her around behind that rock?"

Will nodded and he and Vivian, still in wolf form, moved toward the spot. She winced internally. It wasn't quite what she'd been hoping for, but it would have to do. Lucas chuckled lightly. "Don't worry, Cara. I knew what you meant. But it reminded me I didn't want the girl to watch the healing process. She's already seen enough. I'll make sure you're wearing clothes by the time Adam revives, and I'm fully mated to my wife. I won't even notice you."

That made her look at him because the scents of his love for his wife—cinnamon, nutmeg, citrus, and warm sugar, were so compelling that she abruptly wondered what it would be like to feel like that for another Sazi. She'd only heard of a few true matings, but they were seldom happy ones. One person mated to another . . . magically compelled to forever love a person who might or might not ever love you in return. It was a terrifying prospect. Alpha males often had multiple women mated to them—women who were devoted as slaves, while the men enjoyed the freedom of variety. It hardly seemed fair. But to be the woman who captured the absolute devotion of a male of Lucas's power . . . she couldn't even imagine it.

Cara nodded. "Thank you, sir." As she was taught from her childhood, she concentrated on her human form and willed her body to shift. It wasn't as fast a process as normal, and it hurt like blazes, because her healing magic needed to first mend the bones in her broken front leg in order to make it a human arm again. She was breathing hard and sweating, halfway between forms, until she felt a warm energy surround her. Magic filled her and the pain washed away in a rush of cool golden light. In seconds, she was human again, without the accompanying stiff muscles and stuffed head. She also appeared to be fully clothed, wearing her uniform—probably because he'd never seen her in anything else.

Cara glanced at him with what was probably shock on her face. He shrugged and knelt down on the bloody white rock next to Adam's mangled form. "Looked like you could use a little help and we need to speed this along."

She lowered herself to her knees, her body betraying her eyes as coarse sand and pebbles embedded in her knees hard enough to make her wince. She might *look* like she was wearing clothes but it was, after all, only illusion.

Adam was breathing, but it was ragged and still whistled lightly when he inhaled. She could feel the fluttering of his heart when she gently touched his fur. There was so much to do, even though she could see his body trying to heal. But the gashes which opened his flesh were wide enough to see bone, crisscrossed his body. They would leave nasty scars if she wasn't careful. Unfortunately, she wasn't a trained physician, so she could only add to his own abilities and hope his body knew what to do. She raised her eyes from the cursory inspection that bloodied her hands and made worry and near-panic fill her. She'd never tried to save a Sazi's life. Not like this. "I'm not very good at this, sir. Maybe it would be better to call someone in—"

He rested a hand lightly on her shoulder and stared at her with calm eyes. "There's no time. You know that. But healing magic is instinctive. You'll know what to do once you start. At worst, my wife Tatya is one of our finest healers and I'm mentally connected to her. I'll have her instruct you through me if you need it. But I'd like to get some sense of your abilities, so let's see what *you've* got first. If you look like you're having trouble, I'll step in."

She nodded tensely, closed her eyes, and let her magic flow outward. Healing two people in two days was more than she'd done in a very long time, but maybe it *was* time to start pushing herself again. She'd gotten out of shape in more ways than one. Her magic surrounded Adam, felt the outline of his body, touched every hair . . . memorized the curve of each claw and the shape of his ear. Pressing inward, the wounds appeared before her in the blackness like a jigsaw puzzle waiting to be assembled. She heard a noise and it startled her for a moment, threatened to pull her back to the baked, sunlit day. But then she felt a golden light fill her mind, overlain on the darkness.

"Concentrate." Lucas's voice had taken on a new timbre. There was a confident, almost feminine quality to it. "I can feel the ability in you. You think it's a minor talent, but it's stronger than you believe. Bind to your patient, let him fill your consciousness. Become one."

The words sparked a memory. She *had* bound to the Foster woman, but for some reason she was hesitating now. Why?

"Don't question reasons or motives," said the warm voice now inside her mind. "Just let go and make him whole. Trust yourself."

Was that it? Was she not trusting her own abilities? That wasn't fair to Adam. He'd given himself to save another, just as she would. She had to give him her best, no matter what the outcome.

With a breath of thought, she gave herself to the magic. Letting go of her conscious mind, she let warmth fill her and then sent it into him. An answering spark grabbed onto her magic like a lifeline, pulled her so suddenly and completely into the wolf on the ground that it took her breath away.

If healing Mrs. Foster had been a pleasant, slightly sensual experience, then touching another Sazi—an unattached alpha male wolf—was erotic enough to make her entire body swollen and tight.

"That's normal," said the voice, which had manifested and was now floating in the darkness as the image of a slender woman in a physician's white lab coat, with ice blue eyes and pale, almost ghostly hair in a ponytail that reached her waist. This must be Lucas's wife Tatya. She laughed lightly. "You're allowed to enjoy the process."

Cara could barely think through the sensations that were pounding her body with the need to touch, and be touched. Her skin ached and she could feel wetness between her legs when she shifted. A gasping whisper escaped her. "I can't concentrate. I can't do this."

"You don't have to concentrate. Just trust the magic—give yourself to it." A pause then, and as though reading her panicked thoughts, "Don't fear this, young alpha. Fear can ruin him; even kill him. I can feel he's very weak. He doesn't have much longer. He needs to draw on your healing magic and, through you, on Lucas's power. You're merely the conduit until you're better trained. Reach out to him, find his mind—bring him back to consciousness. Then his body will do the rest."

She nodded as she stared at the concerned doctor in her mind. She knew Mrs. Santiago was correct. She couldn't afford to let her own fears of intimacy with a stranger kill a fellow Sazi. "What do I need to do?"

Tatya began to fade as she spoke. "Touch him. Let your hands roam the wounds. Your magic will know what to do. Seek his mind and pull it to you." She disappeared, leaving only a spot of golden color that surged forward until she was surrounded by it, filled to brimming with energy and light. "Capture his heart and keep it safe until you can find his mind. Please hurry—"

Even as the voice faded, Cara could feel Adam's heartbeat slowing, his breathing getting more labored. He'd lost too much blood and couldn't manufacture enough to fill his heart with the wounds still open and bleeding. Setting

aside her fears, Cara threw herself into the magic like a
swan dive off a cliff. She lowered her hands to his body,
nestled her face in his neck ruff until she could smell fur,
fresh pine and the tang of musk over the metallic scent of
blood. She reached out with magic and mind, calling his
name out over the ravaged landscape of his body. "Adam!
Where are you?"

Cara let her hands roam his body, healing flesh, muscle
and bone. The golden glow kept her mind fresh and alert,
despite the aching pleasure that wracked every inch of her
body, threatening to take her to climax. As her hands moved
to his belly to close a wound that was nearly wide enough to
spill his intestines onto the ground, she felt a small answering pleasure as she brushed his sheathed cock.

Maybe there's another way to find him.

She'd never tried to actually *use* one talent, the heredi-
tary curse of her family. It was an ability some women in
her ancestry had used to become wealthy and powerful.
But to her, it was something to be shunned. She'd used
every method available to tamp it down—keep it from ruining her life as it had her *madre*'s. But with Adam's life at
stake, she had to use everything in her arsenal. She reached
out for the moon, felt the growing thread of power of it just
behind the sun. She opened her scent glands to the moon
magic with a mental command and felt even Lucas's hand
on her shoulder tense. He might be mated, but it was difficult to ignore the scent of an alpha wolf fully in heat. She
dropped lower, until she was touching the full length of
Adam's wounded body, and then put her neck next to his
nose until he couldn't help but draw in her scent with each
breath—the scent of a female Sazi ready to be bred.

She poured more magic into him and felt his body start
to rouse. Everywhere she touched, flesh healed and awakened with pleasure. She let herself drop into his magic until they were one. Now she could see his mind, exhausted

beyond belief. Even the scent wasn't enough. Gritting her teeth, she knew what she had to do and accepted what the consequence might be. She reached forward and clamped her teeth deep into his furred neck and growled. A shock of awareness flowed through him from the new sensation—pain and pleasure combined, and he suddenly focused on her presence, turning to her in her mind and fixing glowing eyes on her with an answering growl.

Adam. I'm waiting.

Cara slowly moved out of his mind, willing his consciousness to follow her up to reality. He hesitated, so she bit him again, this time harder and released more pheromones. Finally, ancient instinct overcame his wounds and the weariness and he followed—not tentatively, but in a frenzied, heated rush that made her retreat in panic. This was the danger of her condition—men lost their minds and turned into full animals. They wouldn't stop until they accomplished their goal. Every male in the area would fight and forcibly mate with her again and again until she was pregnant . . . or dead.

And she knew she would likely let them. Her *mami* Maria had welcomed them into her body without logic or reason. Cara still remembered waking up as a child, seeing *Mami*'s battered and bruised body, the memory of the night still so fresh in her mind that she wept as she prayed in the flickering light of the candles at the altar in her bedroom, asking to die rather than do it again. But she *would* do it again, every month. She remembered her sister, who was born as the result of such a night, telling her how Cara's father, Jorge, had arrived, called from far away by Maria's scent. She'd mated to the powerful alpha male and they married.

Maria had tried desperately to be true to him. But while he worked hard to make sure she was hidden away each moon, and fought the males when they would arrive, her mother often found a way out to take on the full pack. One month, the males got too rough and she didn't come home. It wasn't long after before her father started to train her to take over the pack, even though she was only a child of twelve and Jorge, Jr. was just six. While the men of the pack were horrified at their actions and remorseful beyond words at their inability to stop themselves, Jorge could never quite forgive them. They'd killed his wife. Rather than go on a rampage and slaughter them all, he moved to Houston, leaving Rosa to finish raising Cara and Jorge, Jr. The pack second, Paco, was put in charge until Cara came of age to take over. While she and Papi talked every week by phone, he didn't visit often.

Because of what had happened to her family, Cara'd struggled against the condition as she reached puberty— kept herself away from men who might cause any reaction. Tried everything she could think of to change her scent. But nothing had worked, and she struggled against the heated looks and scents of the males in her pack on the moon, felt her own body nearly succumb. She'd only been able to avoid couplings by her speed and magic. She'd finally broken down in tears while dining with Ten Bears one night. Thankfully, he'd understood and found a mixture of herbs that had allowed her to live a relatively normal life for these past dozen years.

So this was the first time she'd given into the sensation, the first time she'd experienced going into true heat. She had one moment to feel terrified before the wolf inside roared into her consciousness and . . . exhilaration filled her. Muscles awakened and an intense need filled her to the brim, turning her mind to fire. Her eyes were still closed, but she didn't need them. The scents and sensations that surrounded her were so intense that every twitch of an arm or a toe brought amazing images. There were males here, one so close she could taste his scent on her tongue. She would have them all, but him first. His magic reached out to her, flowed around her body until every hair stood on end. A low whine escaped her, encouraging him, and his answering growl caused spasms low in her body. The male snuffled his nose into her hair and fought his way to his feet until he was standing next to her. She no longer noticed the press of rock into her palms and knees as his hot breath seared her cheek, and his leg bumped hers. No, not with fur. That wasn't right. She willed the thread of magic forward, felt him shift forms until it was skin that brushed hers, not fur. But his mind was still the animal's. He snuffled again and began a series of slow licks along her neck that shattered the last shred of her resistance. She was ready.

Before anything else could happen, she felt something struggling to pull her away from the warm body next to her, just before the male's teeth had time to close on the nape of her neck—to hold her still long enough to spin and mount her. She was already in position with head bowed, neck bared toward the hot, frantic breath, awaiting the feel of his weight. Her body was responding to the male's increasing musk, swelling and lubricating. She needed more stinging of his magic . . . of his body, needed to feel him inside her . . . to finish. She fought the magic that held her from the male. But she gasped and her eyes opened wide when someone grabbed her shoulders, sinking fingers into her flesh deep enough to hurt. She felt herself lifted up bodily and was shocked awake when she hit the cliff hard enough to smack her skull.

"*Cara*! Come out of it! You need to get out of here." Lucas's voice was rough and his eyes too bright. "That was an incredibly stupid thing to do. Even *I* might not be able to hold him in full mating frenzy."

She came fully back into her mind, realizing what had nearly happened . . . what she'd nearly *caused*. She crawled backward along the rock wall, away from the pair of wild-eyed males—one lunging against the magic that held him back. Lucas didn't have an erection, but his nostrils were flared, and his fists were clenched so hard the knuckles were white.

She shook her head frantically, fighting the need to go back to them. She knew if she did, they would give in. They would take her as she needed to be taken. She turned her nails inward to bite into her palms, forcing her mind to clear.

Her voice still sounded thick with the hunger that boiled her blood, even though her human mind understood he was right. "It was all I could think of. It saved his life."

Lucas nodded an acknowledgment, but still pointed toward the car. "Just get out of the area and figure out some way to get rid of that scent until we can get you back to the motel and my bottle of cologne. Use the rest of the water jugs to bathe if you have to. Avoid Will if you can. He's a raptor, but I'm not certain he won't be affected, too."

Adam lunged against Lucas's magic. He broke free enough to let out a low, needful howl. Cara turned and ran to her truck and . . . hope. If she wasn't mistaken, the solution was in the glove box. She prayed she'd been as tired as she remembered the previous night. The narrow, winding deer trails through the cactus and mesquite quickly took her away from the cliff. Lucas was still managing to keep the illusion of clothing on her, but that didn't stop the many spined plants from reaching out to rip at her hair and skin.

Another frenzied howl and an angry eagle's screech, both sounding closer than before, cut the air as she reached the rock where she and Adam had rested earlier. Her steps faltered and she fought not to turn around and return to those who chased. Opening her glands was a double-edged sword because now her body wanted them as much as they wanted her.

But then a flash of light caught her eye. The sun had shifted enough that the water jug was no longer in the shade. It was enough to remind her why she was running. She grabbed it on the fly, feeling the heat of the water as it splashed inside the opaque plastic. It wasn't boiling, but it would have to do.

She finally felt a measure of safety when she reached the truck and there was nobody following in sight, scent, or hearing range. The first thing she did was retrieve the keys she'd buried under a nearby yucca, and pour some hot water on an old oil-stained rag hiding under the front seat. She wiped the sweat, and hopefully the *scent*, from her skin. Then she opened the rubberized toolbox in the truck bed and put on her clothing, marveling at how close Lucas had managed to make the illusion to her actual clothing. It was only when she moved quickly that the two didn't mesh. Grabbing an empty, discarded McDonald's cup on the floor in the extended cab, she opened the glove box, prayed—and then nearly wept in relief. The plastic baggie with the herbal tea from Ten Bears was still there. No infusers in the desert, though, so she'd have to do it the old-fashioned way. She reached into the baggie and extracted an amount close to a teaspoon.

Then again, better make it a tablespoon *today.*

After putting the herbs into the cup and pouring in about half the remaining hot water, she put the lid back on and placed it on the dashboard to steep in the sun, rolled up the small gaps in the windows, locked the doors, and put her service revolver on the seat within easy reach. She stared out the window at the seeming calm of the hill country landscape, feeling the heat of the sun seep into her skin. It was only a matter of time before they made it back here, and she tried not to think about what would happen if Lucas couldn't hold Adam back—or even lost his own battle and joined in the chase. Reinforced steel and bullets might not be enough to stop them.

Worse still, as another spasm of pleasure between her legs made her gasp, she wrapped her arms shakily around herself and realized she might not even *try* to stop them.

Chapter 9

"WHAT IN THE hell happened to me?" Adam sat in a thinning band of shade next to the cliff face next to Lucas, staring with horror at the vicious gashes and bruises on his naked body. He looked like he'd been in the middle of a gang war and *felt* like he'd been hit by multiple trucks. His throat was raw and dry, as though he'd been screaming, but his mouth was filled with the sweet taste of peaches and sugary musk. Everything was fuzzy—the last thing he remembered was taking off after Cara to where a bird was attacking a young girl.

Said girl was now sitting on a rock nearby with her back to them, speaking in an unknown language. He could tell from Will's frustrated expression that he wasn't the only person who didn't understand what she was saying.

"Trust me . . . you don't want to know the details." Lucas's voice sounded tired; weary enough to have been in a pitched battle for days.

He looked around again, noticing they were missing a person. "Where's Cara?"

Lucas let out a harsh sound, too bitter for a laugh.

"Hopefully back in her truck by now, with the doors locked and the windows up."

He furrowed his brow. The older man's words held some deeper meaning, and it seemed like Adam should remember what he was talking about.

He'd just opened his mouth to ask when Will's voice made them both turn their heads. "Lucas, I could use some help over here."

Lucas nodded and rose to his feet easily. Must not be as exhausted as he appeared. Turning his head, he looked Adam up and down. "Stay here if you're not feeling up to moving around yet. You've been through a lot. But let's give you some clothes so we don't spook the girl any more than necessary."

With a whisper of magic that smoothed against his skin he was suddenly wearing clothing . . . the simple jeans and top he'd worn when Lucas first saw him at the gas station. He watched Lucas walk the short distance to the others. After a few moments, Adam tried to brace his back against the cliff to push off and stand up, but his muscles screamed enough that he settled for rolling over, getting his knees under him, and clawing his way painfully up the craggy cliff face until he was unsteadily on his feet.

Man! What sort of wringer have I been through?

He limped over to where Lucas was now listening to the dark-haired girl with a thoughtful expression.

"No," he said, addressing the comment to Will. "You're right. She's not speaking Spanish, but there's something about the syntax . . . I remember it, but it's been a *very* long time." He held a finger up in the air and his expression brightened. "Wait! I remember now. I think she's speaking a form of modern Mayan—maybe Yucatec or Hooashtlaan. That's spelled H-u-a-x-t-l-a-n, just so you know."

The girl suddenly smiled and locked eyes with Lucas. Adam was surprised she wasn't hyperventilating after being attacked by a giant owl and hearing wolves talk. But who was he to argue? After all, she might have some Sazi in her family. The girl broke into a long, rambling speech, which Lucas listened to with concentration etched on his face. But then he shook his head and held up a hand to stop her. The scent of the girl's frustration combined with a near pout that nearly made Adam smile. Lucas said one word, "Maa," and then flattened his palm and moved it downward at an angle. It was a common gesture to Adam, one he'd used more than once to get the speaker of a foreign tongue to slow down so they could be understood.

She nodded and closed her mouth, but followed Lucas's every movement with bird-bright eyes.

Lucas ran fingers through his hair and kept his hand on top of his head for a moment. "It's probably a very good thing that you used a little persuasion on her so she'd think all of what just happened was a bad dream, Will. But eventually, we'll need to find out more, since the birds are key to this mess."

Ah. No wonder she's so calm.

The older man paused and blew out a slow breath. "Wow, but it's been a long time since I've spoken Yucatec. Okay, let's start slow." He fixed his eyes on the girl's face and spoke a series of guttural tones, ending it with an upward tone that marked it as a question. *"Baa ash k'aa waa aleek?"*

She repeated the words, ending on a flat tone. Her smile put happiness so plain on her face Adam didn't even need to scent the air to find the citrus.

Will moved his head toward Lucas. "What happened? Did you ask her about the van?"

Lucas laughed. "Hardly! All that said was 'hello.' Mayan doesn't have a single word of greeting like English. I said something close to 'What do you say?' Remember that I'm speaking barely remembered Yucatec and she's speaking some modern version of a different dialect. You'll have to be patient. This is going to take awhile."

Vivian, now back in human form and appearing to wear a T-shirt and shorts said, "Would it be easier to ask her yes or no questions then?"

Again Lucas chuckled. "It would if Mayan had a concept of 'yes.' There is no such word. Most likely, she'd just repeat the same question back to me. I wouldn't know if she was answering or just clarifying the question. No, it'll probably be easier to find a translator once we establish a few basic things. But that will take time, too. The only person I know . . . or actually, *knew* who spoke Mayan recently . . . died."

For a moment Lucas looked profoundly sad, but his scent held an incredible variety of emotions, from joy to anger, sorrow, fear, and all points between. After a second, he shook it off and returned to the situation at hand. He looked at the girl again and then pointed a finger at his own chest. "Lucas *een k'aa-abba.*" Then he turned the finger so it pointed at her. "*Beesh aa k'aa-abba?*"

Again she sighed, and a wave of profound relief rose into the air from her pores that highlighted, rather than dulled, her natural scent of salt water and fertile silt. Her words were sprinkled with sharp, abrupt sounds. Adam was glad Lucas seemed to be able to follow it as she spoke slowly and clearly, gesturing often and pointing her own finger at her chest. She followed the words with a smile after putting her hands almost daintily back to her lap. "*Aahutziri een k'aa-abba . . . oosh Ziri. Haach kee-eemak een wo-ol een k'aaholteekach*, Lucas."

"*Bie shan taen.*" He turned his face and said to the three of them, "Her name is probably spelled A-h-t-z-y-r-y, if I remember the translations right. It's pronounced like she said it, *Aahutziri*. But we can call her Ziri. She's happy to meet us . . . well, *me* at least. Okay, what would probably be easiest is to find out where her home is. That will tell us at least where the people in the van likely came from."

"*Too-oosh aa k'-aah,* Ziri?"

Adam watched as she slowly responded for what seemed a very long time, while Lucas nodded. Mayan must be a pain to learn, and he wondered how Lucas had come upon the language, and when—to have learned an ancient version.

Lucas nodded and was about to tell them what she said when she laughed lightly and said one more thing that made Lucas laugh as well.

He was smiling when he turned to them. "Ziri lives in a small fishing village near Teenek in Veracruz. That's on the east coast of South America, below Brazil."

Will nodded. "Okay, okay. Yeah, I drove through Veracruz once, during an assignment. But most of the people I met spoke Spanish. Doesn't Ziri?"

Lucas asked in both Spanish and Mayan. She gave an apologetic look, held up her thumb and first finger very close together and said, "*Poquito.*" That was one word Adam knew. He had to say *only a little* pretty often on Franklin Street.

"What made you laugh?" Vivian asked.

"She said I talked like her mother's father. Her grandfather. He probably still speaks an older version of Mayan."

A sudden wave of fatigue made Adam lean against a nearby tree, only to have more of those blasted spines dig into his skin. He was starting to really dislike mesquites. He flinched forward with a muttered swear and Lucas noticed. "Okay, Adam's wearing out. Let's move this back toward the cars. Cara's probably wondering what's happening to us and we all need to get some water—especially Ziri. No telling how long she's been out here. The area's remote enough that the van could have camped here a week before the men died."

"If Cara didn't use all the water to bathe in." Will's frustrated mutter made Adam wonder again what had happened earlier, but Lucas just shrugged.

"If she did, she did. We'll have to wait to get back to town in that case. I'd rather she was clean of scent when we arrived. I had a hard enough time holding both of you back from following." He nodded toward Vivian. "I appreciated your help, by the way. If you hadn't turned human and grabbed Will's leg before he made it into the air, Cara might not have gotten back to the truck safely."

Vivian glanced at a trio of deep scratches in her arm. Adam hadn't noticed them until she did. She cringed lightly. "Poor thing. I don't envy her. I met one other woman like her, when I visited the pack in Alaska, so luckily, I recognized the scent. Yeah, that sort of thing might be fun for a month or two, but I just couldn't let Agent Kerchee follow her—not like that."

Hearing words like *scent* and *follow* caused flashes of memory to flood Adam's brain and he froze in place, remembering . . . the feeling of Cara's body on his, the exquisitely erotic pleasure as her hands slid through his fur . . . stroking with magic and skin. The phantom sensation of her teeth biting his neck made him reach up to his throat. Yes, there really was a crescent of dimples marking his skin. He recalled the intoxicating taste of her sweat, and the scent of . . . *something*—filling his nose, powerful enough to turn his mind to jelly and make him want to . . . to—

He shuddered at the thought of what he had wanted to do. There had been a moment when his mind shut off and he didn't care whether she was willing, or her form. Was it more than just a depraved fantasy? Could he actually have wanted to . . . *mate* her . . . with or without her permission? Had some sort of animalistic hunger he didn't know he was capable of forced Lucas to magically hold both he and Will so they wouldn't chase her down like a pack of neighborhood dogs? No wonder the man looked exhausted!

"Good God!" The revulsion of the thought was enough to raise bile into his throat.

"Finally remembering it, huh?" Will's voice was coupled with a firm hand on his shoulder as he swallowed back the bitter taste. "Don't beat yourself up too much, Adam. Cara did what she did intentionally to save your life. Lucas said you were fading fast, and it was all she could think of to bring you back. She told me about her . . . *condition* once. Going into heat like that runs in her family. Sam made her some sort of medicine that keeps it under control, so it's not normally an issue."

"So we really were going to—" He couldn't even finish the thought.

Will nodded. "Hunt her down like a pair of hormone-crazed rapists?" He sighed, clearly just as embarrassed and disgusted by the revelation. "Yeah, probably. Hell, think how *I* feel. I've known her family for three generations. I was in the living room with her dad when she was born. Thank heavens Lucas is mated. No way would your pack mate Vivian have been able to hold us *all* back. I can't even imagine what it's like for her, being the alpha, on the full moon. Maybe it helps that they're all family, or that she's the only alpha here so she can hold them off. But after the integration . . . *jeez*. You might want to consider only bringing down mated pairs if you've got them."

Adam shook his head in frustration, borne of shame and worry. "Yeah, that's definitely a consideration. But I'm more worried about the rest of today. If it were me, I'd be treating both of us like we had rabies. I'll consider myself damned lucky if she doesn't shoot me on sight."

Chapter 10

"AFTERNOON! I WAS starting to wonder if you were going to make it back before I went home, Sheriff. If you hurry, you can probably still make it into the meeting."

The tinny words from behind the speaker set into the bulletproof glass in the entry area were accompanied by Maggie's bright smile. Cara put her hand on the doorknob and waited until she heard the buzz that released the lock. She had no doubt her confused look appeared a little snarly around the edges. "Meeting? Did I miss a memo?"

Maggie waited until she opened the door and closed it firmly behind her before answering in her more natural alto in a voice that sounded pleased in a motherly sort of way. "Nope. Just serendipity that paths crossed, so Rick grabbed them for a general chat. There haven't been many meetings since Carl left, after all."

Cara hung her head and let out a small growl. She shouldn't have expected any different, but she was getting damned sick and tired of Rick just up and doing shit like this. And she was even more tired of people like Maggie making snide comments, inferring she would never live up to Carl, even though the older woman probably didn't realize that's what it sounded like.

"Oh, and Yolanda's still back there, too. She said she had filing to catch up on, but I think she's been waiting to brief you. Your phone's been going nuts all day."

Yikes! That's right! How many appointments had she missed this afternoon to go into the desert and search? She couldn't even remember what she'd had on her calendar. But that could wait. Right now she needed to attend the meeting and bring everyone up to date on her search. She forced a smile and hoped it seemed natural. "Could you buzz her and see if she can hang around for a few more minutes? I really need to brief Rick and might as well say hi to everyone else."

It appeared to have worked from the sunny reply. "Sure thing, Sheriff."

Cara glanced at the dispatcher's desk as she started to walk between the short row of desks where half of her deputies did their paperwork. A stack of large, glossy papers was strewn across it, nearly covering the multi-buttoned radio unit. "Are those the new posters for the lobby? About time they got here."

Maggie followed her gaze and shook her head in shared frustration. "Yep. People laugh when they read the posters out there. Expired dates for *upcoming* programs, addresses changed with magic marker on existing ones—do you know Bob from juvie mentioned today that the one for the abuse shelter still has the old area code on the phone number? I hadn't even *noticed* that one. I mean, it's been what—two years since they split the county and gave us the new code? I figured as soon as Dave gets here to take over for me, I'd grab the stapler and just get 'er done. Otherwise, it's going to be another week before I can stay late, and they make us look more than a little stupid."

"Well, if it helps any, I *feel* more than a little stupid today." She said the words seriously, but Maggie laughed.

"Hell—I feel stupid *most* days. Consider yourself lucky if you only feel it today." She winked and picked up the office phone. Her finger hovered over the button for Yolanda's desk. "Now, y'all better get into the meeting before they all slip out the back door and hit the road."

Walking down the short hallway to the squad room didn't give her nearly enough time to process everything that had happened today. But she absolutely had to get her mind back on work for the few minutes she had before she was thrown back into the world of magic and danger, where she had to try to figure out why Sazi birds—wearing *gloves*—would try to kidnap a young Mayan girl and kill three men.

She didn't even *dare* think about Adam and the whole integration issue she still had to deal with tonight. She couldn't decide who'd been more embarrassed when they'd shown back up at the crime scene—where she was locked in the truck, wearing earplugs to protect her hearing in case she had to fire the cocked sidearm pointing out the window crack at them. Apparently, Lucas had brought them all back to their senses, but neither Adam nor Will would meet her eyes, even after the elder wolf had convinced her they were all sane and calm.

The tea had worked. None of the men showed any hint of arousal when she stepped out of the truck cab. No, the general, unspoken reaction was to ignore what had happened, along with scents of humiliation all around. She was actually grateful for the careful avoidance of the issue from the men, but then along came Vivian.

She'd treated Cara with the worst sort of condescending pity, shaking her head and tsking, while patting her head like a toddler who hadn't made it to the bathroom in time. Then she started murmuring things like "It wasn't your fault," and "Oh, you poor thing." After the emotional roller coaster she'd been on, it had been all she could do not to reach forward and snatch out a few handfuls of honey blonde hair.

Rick's professional baritone cut into her thoughts from inside the squad room. "There's an AMBER Alert from Oklahoma City, which came across the wire about an hour ago. One Clarissa Evans, age twelve—blonde, blue eyes, last seen in jeans and a striped red top. Suspect vehicle is a black Chevy Cavalier, about twenty years old, last seen headed south. The information is in your packets. Maybe some of you could stop by places on the way home to give a heads-up and check the parking lots at restaurants. You know the drill."

He paused, noticed Cara standing in the doorway, and tipped his chin in acknowledgment before continuing. "Dave, you're on prisoner detail tonight. Have the trustees pick up the trash in the exercise yard before it gets too dark and if there's time before lockdown, let's see about getting the holding tank washed down. That DWI we picked up at lunch couldn't hold his liquor." He ignored the muttered swearing, but elaborated a little. "Sorry, but the shop wants to take a look at that electrical problem you've been having with your siren switch before you take it out, and Kevin called in sick again. He just can't shake that flu." He turned his head and stepped back a pace, then picked up his coffee mug before sitting down in a chair against the wall. "Glad you stopped by, Sheriff. Anything to report?"

Cara walked into the room, trying to appear more calm than she felt. *Stopped by*—as though she'd been strolling the streets, chatting with people about nothing, like Carl had done every afternoon for the last five years, instead of fighting for her life. She looked out over the small squad of men and women, some in uniform but most in street clothes. Two rows of four, seven men and one woman, with a wide variety of scents and emotions. The third row of tables hadn't been used since she'd been with the department. She tried to remember the last time all of them had been in the same place at the same time, but couldn't.

Maybe Maggie was right. Perhaps she wasn't cut out for this job.

She used to sit out there with them, but now spent most of her time behind a desk, shuffling papers while David drove her patrol. She didn't shuffle well. As much as she hated to admit it, she'd *enjoyed* searching the crime scene today. A quick scent of anger's jalapeño peppers and the burnt metal of frustration rose from Billy when she looked his way. It said he hadn't forgotten her stinging words, when she sent him back to the office after questioning her *ability* to search for clues at the scene—not whether she should take the time, but whether she was capable. She'd threatened to write him up for insubordination, which would be his third strike this year. The first two had been from Carl for similar comments to Maggie, who outranked him by a grade, and a third would probably ruin any chance he might have to hire on with a metro force. She should formally reprimand him, put him on report. But there was no way she was going to doom the county to his presence forever. If he couldn't hire on elsewhere, and she couldn't find anyone to fill the slot . . . no, there had to be another choice.

Maybe I need to look into sending him over to Austin for counseling. She was pretty sure the department still had a cooperative agreement for HR stuff. It wasn't something Carl would do, but if Billy just weren't so damned prejudiced, he'd make a good cop. It'd be proactive and would be another nail in the asshole's coffin if he didn't straighten up. Then she wouldn't feel bad at all about pulling the trigger—figuratively speaking.

Rick coughed loud enough to get her attention and raised one brow at her. Oops. Apparently, she'd been lost in thought a little too long. She shrugged and offered an apologetic smile. "Sorry. Was just trying to figure out where to start." Now she had to be careful with her words. Lucas promised to remove the blood evidence at the scene, and she had no doubt he was capable of it. But there were footprints of the girl, and eventually Ziri needed to make her way back to her village. Lucas promised to question her quickly and then get her back into the human evidence chain if it was required. He seemed to be well versed in Texas law, which was a relief. She didn't want to have to argue about her duties to her job.

Cara cleared her throat and scanned the faces patiently watching her. "I'm sure Rick has briefed you on the incident from earlier today." As usual, Stephanie was busily reading her packet while chewing on the bottom of a pen, but still glanced up and nodded with the others.

"The dogs provided by Ranger Kerchee managed to track down a lead. We found footprints a few hundred yards from the crime scene, heading toward the bluff, but couldn't find anyone hiding in the trees or crevices. One set of prints was about a size four, and aren't very deep, so we're probably looking for at least one child or small adult. We'll need someone out there tomorrow to make casts of the prints. Rick, I'll let you pick who. I've got photos already . . . they're in processing. Keep an eye out tonight for unaccompanied kids or unfamiliar families at stores or walking on back roads. Since there's no way to tell whether the person who left the scene was a witness or involved in the deaths, treat unknown persons as armed and dangerous."

She desperately longed to tell the people she worked with what they were *really* up against. But while one or two might be able to handle the knowledge that Sazi existed, most of them would probably lose it—and wind up shooting every animal, and half the humans, in the county that came within a yard of them. No, it was best just to keep them alert.

Rick cleared his throat and pushed his hat further back on his head, revealing a stubborn cowlick of auburn hair. He was about the only person in the department who actually wore his hat as part of his uniform. Everyone had one, but most only put them on for official occasions—or when it was raining. He told her once he started wearing it during his first assignment in another state when the police chief told him to "shave off that damned hair or cover it up."

She glanced over at him when he raised a finger. "Actually, Cara, we don't have to worry about taking casts. The autopsy results came in while you were out. Doc Sloan said it was an animal attack—probably while the men were sleeping. He said the bites were consistent with a large predator, like a big cat, so we might keep an eye out for a mountain lion or jaguar that might have wandered out of another state."

Elliot spoke up from the far corner—not his usual seat, and when his eyes scanned the other officers quickly, she noticed he very intentionally didn't look at his own row. Billy, Stephanie, and David were all in that row. He smelled frustrated and embarrassed, with just a hint of anger.

I'll have to talk with him very soon. See if he's having problems with someone.

"We used to have cougars around here. My granddad used to talk about them taking his goats. Might be they're coming back."

Cara nodded and fought to keep the relief from her face for a moment, before realizing she didn't need to. It was perfectly acceptable to be relieved there wasn't a killer loose in the county—at least of the human variety. Still, she shrugged, hoping her face conveyed she was skeptical. This might be a good way to impart some information without seeming to. It could keep her officers safe until they caught the shifter killers. "We didn't see any cat prints out there, and the dogs didn't act odd. But I suppose anything's possible. Make sure if you hear any strange noises while you're out in the field, to look *up*. Remember that cats like to go for the head and neck. Who's on area-wide patrol this week?"

Stephanie raised her hand and Cara pointed at her. "Good. You're certified with the tranquilizer gun. Keep the case in your squad car. I doubt a cougar or jaguar would approach the town, but just in case, I'll let Maggie know that if anyone calls in a missing pet report or actually spots a cat, she's to call you." The older woman's ebony hand started to scribble notes on her sheets again. Cara abruptly wondered again why Steph remained working here. She was good enough to go to a much larger area and didn't have any ties to the region. Most of the other deputies were either fresh out of the academy and putting in road time before rotating to something bigger, or lifers who would never leave the county. But Deputy Dion was an anomaly, not that she was complaining. It was sort of nice to have an experienced, competent officer to train the newbies.

She pointed a stern finger around the room and gave an order she hoped wouldn't kill anyone. But she couldn't afford *not* to give the order, in case anyone ever checked. "*Don't* shoot to kill unless your life is in danger. Remember that both cats are threatened in the state. Let Stephanie tranq the animal and call it in. Parks and Wildlife will take it from there. They'll relocate the cat to a more remote area. And let's not forget there were others in the van who walked away from the scene. There might be an orphaned, *traumatized* child out there, alone or with someone. Let's not let down our guard." She paused to let the thought sink in before looking around again. When Ziri showed up, any remaining memories about the birds would be seen as traumatic stress of seeing the others die. "Any questions?"

Nobody raised a hand so she nodded at Deputy Seguin. "I'll let Rick finish up then. I'll be in my office for another hour or so. If anyone owes me a report on a case—" She stared with raised brows at Billy, who was behind about four reports, "Now's the time to get them to me." At least he had the good grace to fidget, although his face and scent were still angry. Paperwork wasn't his strong suit, but he eventually finished it. "Oh, and Rick—see me before you go." She tried to keep her tone light, but she noticed a small frown before he stood to take her place. Good. Maybe he'd get the hint.

Still, despite her simmering anger, she nearly collapsed

against the nearest wall when she reached the hallway. Nobody had asked any questions she couldn't answer and Will had been right about the autopsy. Her legs suddenly felt like jelly and a buzzing filled her head from sheer relief. It was all she could do to walk to the end of the hall, which opened into a second office area in front of Carl's office.

She stared at his name, hand-painted under the gold star. It was still his post. She had to remember that. But it was hard not to want to dig her fingers deep into the pie and claim the job. Do things her own way. Despite her better judgment—despite the pettiness and annoyances, she longed to see her name on that glass. She could do it. She knew she could, if only given the chance to shine. And shine she would. Squaring her shoulders, she strode into the room, ready to face whatever the job could throw at her.

A split row of desks with computers was surrounded by ancient, industrial gray metal file cabinets. Various drawers were open and Yolanda Marquez was kneeling in front of an open bottom drawer, struggling to stuff in one more manila file folder. The small growling sound that filled the air as the drawer nearly bent on the guides made Cara smile, but then Yo usually made her smile. Other than her sister Rosa, Yolanda was probably her best friend in the world. They'd always wound up as lab and locker partners in school, held their Quinceaneras on the same weekend, attended police academy together, and had lunch at least once a week. So far, the new working arrangement hadn't changed that. She hoped it never would.

"Hey, Yo. Thanks for sticking around."

She replied without turning around. "No prob. I've been keeping busy."

Cara looked around at the various open drawers. "So I see. What's up?"

Yolanda spun around and plopped her tail on the floor, causing her utility belt to splay over her ample hips and ride up. "What's up is that we need to allocate some budget money to buy more filing cabinets or find some off-site storage. I'm just flat out of room to store open files."

The words popped out of Cara's mouth before she could stop them. They were Carl's words, repeated from the day she'd arrived at the department. "Then I guess we need to *close* the files." Yolanda flipped her the bird, and Cara fought not to laugh. But Yo was right. They'd been out of room for files for years. But Carl was stingy with money, because the county commissioners were stingy with money. "Maybe this year we can do something about that." She was mulling to herself, but realized she'd spoken out loud when Yo's eyes lit up.

"You really mean it? You'll make a budget line item for cabinets?" She stood in a rush and nearly bounced across the room, smelling like sweet tangerine flowers. "Eee! I'll polish your badge, shine your shoes—heck, I'll buy you lunch for a month if you'll do that!"

Then Cara did laugh but followed up with mock sternness, with one hand on her hip and the other shaking a finger at her. "Huh-uh. No bribing the sheriff. *Ba-ad* deputy."

Yolanda's full lips and large eyes always made Cara think of a sad puppy when she did her infamous pout. She'd used it on her parents her whole life, and even Carl hadn't been immune. She'd been the only one of Cara's friends in town to have gotten a private phone in her room, and her Quince party had been spectacular—the talk of the town, which had probably forced her parents to get a second mortgage on the house. But they couldn't deny Yolanda anything she asked for when she used the sad puppy pout. She also got more raises than her length of service at the department probably allowed. Thankfully, with Cara constantly riding her not to get greedy, it hadn't gone to her head.

"But—" Cara continued, now really considering the

idea, "*You* get to figure out how many we can fit in and where to put them. You know the commissioners are going to go all Spanish Inquisition on me when I ask, so I'll have to show them a workable plan that doesn't disrupt the office. And I don't have *time* to rearrange the office on paper a dozen times. The preliminary budget's due at next month's meeting."

Yolanda looked around the already cramped room—and Cara bet she had suddenly realized her lofty goal might be further away than she planned when she sighed. "Oh sure, pop my pretty balloon." Another sigh, and then she shrugged and turned professional, stepped behind her desk, and grabbed a stack of papers. "Eh. I'll work on that later, when I'm not so tired. But we really need to talk about your schedule tomorrow. You were already tight, and I had to use a crowbar to fit in everything you canceled this afternoon. I'd suggest copious amounts of caffeine and a pair of those expensive running shoes instead of your Wal-Mart tenees."

Cara let out a small whimpering sound and swept a hand toward her office. "We might as well sit down and be comfortable."

A KNOCK ON the door made both her and Yolanda look up, startled out their deep conversation. A quick sniff told her Stephanie Dion was on the other side. The clock showed that more than an hour had already passed. Damn it! She was late to pick up Adam to go to her sister's house and she hadn't even talked to Rick yet. But Yolanda hadn't been kidding about her schedule. "Just a second," she called out and then returned her attention to Yo. "Okay, so it's Commissioner Watkins at eight, Mr. Martinez at eight thirty, and then the Nguyen extradition hearing at nine to start?" She raised hopeful eyebrows.

Yolanda shook her head and lowered her face to her hands with a near-sob. "No, no. It's the commissioner at eight, and the *hearing* at eight thirty. The county attorney will tell you whether you're needed to testify. If so, then you *call me* and I'll reschedule Mr. Martinez, who's at nine."

Cara leaned into the high-backed leather chair and thumped her head against the padded headrest several times. "Write it down for me . . . *please*! With the details like calling you. I'll pick it up when I come in tomorrow." Even though the task was well within Yo's job description, she sweetened the pot. "I'll even buy you an extra helping of peach cobbler at the café next lunch."

She grinned. "I thought you said no bribery."

"Oh, that only applies to bribing your *boss*. I'm allowed to reward my hard working staff—so long as it doesn't cost the *county* any money." They both burst out laughing at that and Yolanda stood up and walked to the door.

"Far be it from me to turn down Rachel's cobbler! But I'll expect it to be a la mode for all the extra goodies you want."

Steph must have heard Yolanda approach the door, because she cracked it open enough to poke her head inside. "All done? I just need a minute, Cara. I know you're busy."

Again her eyes flicked to the clock. "No problem, but a minute's all I've got. I'm already late for an appointment. What's up?"

Stephanie held open the door for Yolanda to exit and then closed it carefully behind her. That was unusual for the deputy, who normally just stood in the open doorway to say whatever she needed to. There were few secrets in a department this small, so something sensitive enough to talk about behind closed doors was worthy of Cara giving her full attention when the woman sat down across the desk from her.

She started in without any preliminaries, but that's one of the things Cara liked best about her. The scent of roses filled the room. Cara found it amusing that not only was it Steph's natural scent, but she put on rose-scented lotion every day, which enhanced the rich, sweet smell. "First, you should know that Rick already left."

Cara clenched fists and gritted her teeth to prevent the string of swear words in her head from escaping. Steph nodded. "Yeah, I figured that would be your reaction, after you said you wanted to see him. Didn't say a word to anyone either . . . just walked out the door after the meeting." She moved herself side to side to get more comfortable in the chair that Yolanda had vacated. "Another thing you should know is that everybody is talking about your meeting with Will and two other men at Rosa's restaurant today."

This time, Cara didn't feel the need to hide a strangled frustrated sound. "*¡Madre de Dios!* Can't I even have a simple lunch with a friend anymore?" She turned off her "sheriff" persona and appealed to the colleague and . . . *friend* she used to sit next to at the tables. "Really! Would anyone have said a word if I'd done the same thing when I was just a deputy? C'mon, Steph. You know I'd tell people if it was a case or something. Will just wanted to introduce me to a friend who was visiting."

The woman shrugged and then nodded in a way that said Cara was stating the obvious. Her bright white teeth flashed for a moment when she reached out her tongue to lick across her bright pink lipstick. "Oh, I know *that*. That part was easy to figure out. No, I'm more interested in the friend than what you and Will talked about. I wondered whether you were interviewing him. Is that what the meeting was about? You don't have to tell me, of course, but I'm really curious."

The question caught her cold and she reared back in surprise. "Interviewing him? For *what*? I don't have any positions open and certainly don't need any help at my ranch. Besides, he lives in another state—he's just visiting."

Stephanie waggled her head and curiosity grew in her scent. Cara fought not to sneeze. Roses and sickly sweet antifreeze should be banned as a combination. "Maybe yes, maybe no. Someone down at the beauty parlor saw Minnesota plates and caught wind that the guy's a cop in Minneapolis."

Cara shrugged. "Sure. That's how he knows Will. So what?"

The other woman smiled knowingly. "Well, you remember I've got a cousin who's with the St. Paul PD? I asked him about the guy, and it turns out he's top notch—decorated from here to Sunday *and* he just put in his notice." She tapped a polished burgundy nail on the chair arm. "We could really use someone of his caliber if he's thinking about moving down here."

Damn, Steph was getting to be a little too good of an investigator. Cara was going to have to start watching her step around the woman. Simultaneously projecting calm and confusion was a little difficult, and she hoped she managed it. It was probably better to stick to half-truths. "Once again, I don't have any positions—even if he *was* interested in moving. I'm only sitting in this chair until Carl comes back, so that empty desk next to yours is where you'll find me in a few months."

The next words out of Stephanie's mouth were sarcastic, but in a friendly teasing sort of way and she moved her head from side to side while making little quotation marks in the air. "Oh, puleeze! *I'm only sitting in this chair until Carl comes back.* You can do better than that, Cara! The office is running smoother than it ever has and you know it! The guys might not like the changes you've made, but in my opinion it's about damned time people started treating law enforcement in this county like a *job*. The guys are showing up on time . . . in *uniform* and making chatter on the radio. Two months before you slapped that demerit in

Billy's file for failure to report, would he have called in that van?"

Cara shrugged one shoulder, not committing the truth to the air. The department had been going to shit under Carl's rule, and although she was loath to speak badly of a man in a hospital bed, the whole place was turning into a real police department since she'd taken control. She was going to hate to see all the improvements go away when he returned. *If* he returned.

Stephanie nodded and raised one finger into the air triumphantly. "Exactly! He would have considered it to be too much trouble and have just stayed away from that route for a day or so, until someone else spotted the vultures circling." She shook her head in annoyance. "He's quite the piece of work. I hope you fire his ass one of these days." A pause, long enough that Cara nearly felt the need to make some noise, but then Stephanie continued, and she was up to something—the roses had bitter overtones. Apparently she'd been working on this next little speech all afternoon and felt a little guilty. "And, actually, you *do* have a position open. It's just been on the books so long that you've probably forgotten about it—or maybe you never knew Carl was trying to fill it."

That one really did floor her and she could feel her jaw drop. "I *do*? What position?"

Stephanie's smile was sweet enough to rot teeth. "Truant officer." She let it sink in for a long pause and then continued. "Remember when the school district increased in size two years ago when they built that new subdivision between here and Junction? Well, they applied for permission from the state and were approved. But Carl couldn't find anyone and finally gave up. It doesn't pay as much as a deputy position, and not every cop likes kids. But this Officer Mueller is apparently great with kids. He was the coach for a bunch of Boys' Club–Police Department teams–basketball, hockey, and a couple of others. He's donated free time to shelters and even helps out with the D.A.R.E. project."

Truant officer. She started to tick off the benefits in her head. Local surname, good record, likes kids. Wow. Would that be a perfect fit, or what?

Stephanie continued. "And I don't know if you've ever looked at the job description, but the truant officer is a reserve deputy. Anything bad-bad happens, and you can call him up. We'd have a spare hand . . . a *real* cop with experience. According to Darnell, his beat was one of the worst in the city. He's seen everything and might be good eyes and ears in the field for drug stuff. Billy and Tom aren't really up to snuff on anything other than finding meth labs. But Mueller has seen it *all*—crack, heroin, ecstasy, and every gang under the sun. No way would our local kids be able to put anything over on him. As a bonus, if Carl does decide to retire, he'd be a shoe-in for your old slot."

Cara found herself nodding thoughtfully while staring at the wall over Stephanie's shoulder. "I think I have some reading to catch up on." She turned her eyes to the liquid brown ones opposite her. "Where did you say I could find out more about this position?"

Stephanie stood up with a brilliant smile. Now, oranges and roses . . . that was a better combination. It reminded Cara of the time she went with her sister to the Tournament of Roses parade. "I'd start with the files from when Carl started looking. Yo probably has those. Then, if you happen to wander by my desk, the statute book is in the outbox. The pages listing the duties are marked with a paperclip—just in case anyone happened to need a copy."

She turned and walked to the door. Her head swung around when she reached for the knob and she winked. "I hear he's quite the piece of eye candy, too. He's the wrong flavor of the month for me, but there aren't any rules about sheriffs and truant officers that I could find."

Cara could feel a blush creep up her face and the older African-American woman laughed. "I guess you've already noticed. You go, girl! Have yourself a little fun. You spend way too much time being the tough one."

She was almost out the door before Cara remembered. "Oh, one more thing, Steph—"

The woman paused, turned, and leaned on the jamb with the knob still in hand. She raised her brows to confirm her attention.

Cara decided to keep the question casual, but she'd been in the row Elliot had avoided. "You and Ruiz having any problems? He was acting a little strange in there."

There was a pause and while Stephanie's face remained studiously blank, her knuckles on the door knob tightened. "Nope. I haven't noticed anything odd." She paused. "That all?" No twitches, or sweating, but the scent of black pepper burst into the air and tickled Cara's nose.

She's lying. But why?

She shrugged, not letting on, or pushing it—for the moment. "Yep. Just wondering. Thanks for letting me know about Rick and finding the info on the position. I'll check into it."

The sunny smile returned in a flash. "Good luck. Hope it works out."

When the door closed, Cara grabbed a sticky pad and wrote herself a reminder to talk to both Billy and Rick privately. Maybe what was up with Elliot had to do with one of them. After sticking it firmly on the bottom of her center drawer, the first place she always looked when she sat down, she shut down her computer and turned off the desk lamp.

While it would be easy to get wrapped up in looking over the files Steph mentioned, that would have to wait for another day. But she couldn't help but admit she was sort of excited about discussing the idea with Adam on the way to Rosa's.

Try as she might, she couldn't keep another random thought from flicking through her mind. *Or am I excited about seeing him for another reason entirely?*

Chapter 11

"AW HELL." ADAM looked sideways at Cara as the scent of frustration and mild anger rose from her. Up until that second, she was fine . . . discussing the possibility of a job he might actually be interested in down here. He'd never heard of a place where there was an actual attendance officer, who drove around the county picking up kids and issuing summonses to take them to *court* for being out of school. Some even wound up in *jail*, alongside their parents, for repeat offenses! Wow. Apparently, Texas took their mandatory schooling laws pretty seriously. But he liked kids and constantly struggled to get more of them to stay in school. How many hours had he spent in outreach programs, trying to convince boys as young as ten of the importance of an education? Maybe this wasn't such a bad system—getting them to understand what they might later face if they didn't straighten up. It was at least worth looking into more.

Cara stopped the pale gold sedan at the start of a driveway leading up to a low-slung adobe house. She tapped her fingers on the steering wheel and bit at her lower lip nervously.

A few cars were tucked under white aluminum carports and a scattering of bikes lay on the grass. Adam looked at the seemingly innocuous scene and couldn't figure out what might be worrying her. "What's up? Is there a problem?"

"It looks like she's invited the whole damned pack over. I'd really hoped to introduce you to Paco and Rosa a little more privately." She tapped and fidgeted for a few minutes more, and her emotions were all over the place. Finally, she sighed. "Okay. How about you just follow my lead for now and we'll sort everything out later."

She didn't elaborate any more than that, so he just shrugged. He'd hoped to wrap this up quickly and get back to the motel in time for the hockey playoff game. He'd been looking forward to it all day because the motel room had a good television with cable. But pack business came first. "You're the Alpha. Whatever you say."

Nodding once, she pressed the accelerator again and slowly pulled up to the house. Adam was glad he'd chosen a mixed outfit for tonight—new black jeans over polished cowboy boots and a cream colored polo shirt. It tended to blend at any occasion, from ball games to high-end mixers by the pool. Cara had changed out of her uniform before she met him at the fast-food restaurant, and he was glad she did. The simple, sleeveless white top was tied at the waist and flashed enticing hints of smooth golden skin, while the faded jeans were tight enough to hug every curve. She'd even threaded a white ribbon into a complex french braid and applied a hint of makeup, both of which softened her features, transforming her enough that he'd never guess her occupation if he didn't know.

While a part of him was amused by the small-town game—meeting "unexpectedly" in a parking lot and leaving one car after casually chatting through the windows—he understood it was necessary to keep people from talking.

His every movement was under scrutiny and Lucas had been firm about creating the right impression. Cara knew the people, so she made the rules.

He watched her close her eyes and take another deep breath as she turned off the car, obviously steeling herself for what lay ahead. The tangled mix of emotions was too much to sort, so he didn't try, and he could hardly blame her. He'd been just as much of a wreck before the pack meeting back home.

Adam reached for the door handle, deciding to give her whatever time she needed before facing her pack. But before he opened it, he turned his head. He'd never actually said the words and knew he had to. It had been chewing at him all afternoon. He reached out and touched her arm, the first time since he'd gotten in the car. It wasn't a surprise that she twitched a bit and stared at him with eyes too wide. "By the way . . . before I forget—*thank you*. I wouldn't be alive right now if not for you." He squeezed her arm lightly before pulling back and unlatching his seat belt. "I just wanted you to know."

Before her dropped jaw closed and she could think enough to respond, he opened the door and got out, closing it firmly behind him. A deep breath he didn't realize he'd been holding leaked out of him. He'd never been good at acknowledging things, but risking her . . . well, at a minimum, her *life* to save his—no, that couldn't just sit.

A shout of "*¡Que chulito!*" followed by laughter and a baby's delighted squeal inside the house made him glance up and smile. It was always nice to hear happy sounds inside a home. He'd heard enough screams and cries to last a lifetime. A crunch underfoot and he lifted his boot, wondering what he'd just ruined. It looked like a *nut*. He reached down to pick it up. Sure enough, it was a small crushed pecan, still in the shell. That was when he noticed that there were dozens, maybe *hundreds* more of them hiding among the blades, some old and blackened but many as fresh as the ones on his counter at home. He looked up at the towering trees overhead, wondering how many nuts they produced every year that people would allow this many to remain to rot on the ground.

He felt Cara's presence next to his elbow. Her scent was warm, but still filled with a variety of emotions. "Do you like pecans? We get a ton of them from these trees every year. There are plenty more down by the river, too, if you're the enterprising sort."

He twisted his head and his shoulder brushed against her bare arm, sending tingles of magic through him like an electric shock. She must have felt it, too, because her eyes widened and her breath hissed inward. "Oh yeah. Pecans are my favorite snack." He realized after they were out that the words sounded far too intimate, the tone low and smooth, hinting of much different things—but those big brown eyes of hers kept sucking him inside and making him forget where he was.

Her tongue flicked out and ran around her lips and he could smell her nervous anticipation. He watched the fading sunlight flash off the dark pink, cherry-scented gloss and wondered if it would taste fruity, too.

"You've got a smudge." She didn't move to stop him as he reached forward and wiped his index finger along the edge of her mouth, removing the nearly invisible bit that was outside the edges of her lips. Her eyes followed the hand as he brought it back to his own mouth and lightly sucked off the flavored coloring. Yep . . . cherry, and definitely worth a longer taste. He leaned toward her, and he could hear her heartbeat speed up until it was thudding hard enough he should be able to see her shirt move. Her scent grew, became unmistakable—the same as when she'd been pouring water earlier, and her nostrils flared, catching his increasing musk. He'd just lifted his hand to slide it behind her neck when the screen door slammed, making them both jump.

"¡*Dios Mio*! What in the world are you doing standing out here staring at the trees, Carita? And who's your friend?"

Cara let out a small yip and flushed guiltily. She blinked several times and swallowed hard. "The . . . trees, yeah. That is, Adam's never seen—" He smiled encouragingly and stepped slightly in front her, walking toward the woman on the porch with his hand out.

"Hi, I'm Adam Mueller. I'm—"

Cara quickly moved in front of him, now in more control. "He's a cop friend of Will Kerchee's, here visiting from Minnesota. He had lunch at the restaurant with us." She turned her head toward him and raised her brows with a warning look. "Adam, this is my sister, Rosa Ruiz."

Ah, that's right. I'm supposed to follow her lead.

He took more time to look Cara's sister over. The resemblance was obvious, but there were differences, too. Rosa's face was a bit broader, more round, and her body shorter, without the long waist Cara had. She still had a good figure for a woman with multiple children, but there was a little excess weight around her belly. "A pleasure to meet you, Rosa. I was just telling Cara how much I like pecans." He gestured upward. "These are really beautiful trees. I'd love to have nuts in my yard just fall for the taking."

Rosa let out a little snort, but there was pride in her eyes. "Yeah, you say that now. But wait until they're beating the crap out of your shingles and you have to dig them out of the gutters and rake 'em up every other day so they don't kill the grass."

This time, Cara let out the snort and he got a sense how similar their movements were and how warm a relationship they shared by the teasing tone. "Like you've picked up a rake or climbed a ladder since Gloria and Raul got old enough for chores."

Rosa fought not to smile. Her eyes twinkled merrily even though her voice was stern. "Kids need to learn responsibility. Besides, they get to eat the pies *and* keep the money they earn from selling the nuts in town. In wet years, they make a better salary than *we* do. They've got it pretty good and don't you believe otherwise."

The door slammed again and an excited boy rushed toward them. "Tia Cara! Tia Cara! You're here!"

Cara scooped up the boy of about six or seven as he leaped toward her, and spun him around in a bear hug before easily supporting his weight with his legs and arms surrounding her so he was face to face. He had darker skin than either Cara or Rosa, large brown eyes, and straight black hair that was neatly trimmed. His natural scent was a combination of pecans with a peppery hint of sage. He was already bordering on handsome and when puberty set in— yeah, his parents were going to have a handful with this one. He knew how to blink those long lashes and work a grin to get women to absolutely melt. Cara obliged with a soft smile and a burst of cookie spice scent that nearly made Adam laugh.

"Hey, *mijo*! You been being good? I hear you won a ribbon for a report about weather. You going to be a scientist when you grow up?"

Rosa reached forward to ruffle his hair. "Yep. He's a good boy—and a smart one. Well, y'all catch up and hurry inside so Adam can meet everyone. I've got beers and a pitcher of margaritas ready."

Raul nodded his head vigorously as his mother stepped back onto the porch and disappeared inside the house. His voice held the same light southern twang. "Yep. I'm gonna study icebergs at the north pole."

Adam pursed his lips. "That's pretty ambitious. It gets awfully cold up there, don'tcha know."

The boy turned his head, as if noticing him for the first

time. His nostrils flared and Adam realized he was already catching a scent. Pretty young to be getting symptoms, but not unheard of. His answer was well worded and serious. It made him sound much older. "Sure, but wolves can stand the cold better than humans. And it's important. Know what? The ice packs are *melting*. If people don't study them now, we might not get a chance later."

Adam nodded and crossed his arms over his chest, finding the boy's knowledge on the subject engaging for someone his age. Maybe he should see if Kevin would be interested in corresponding with the boy. After all, he just got back from the Pole himself. "So do you think the greenhouse effect is causing it?"

Raul's thoughtful expression showed that he not only knew what the term meant, but also had an opinion about it. He shrugged, nearly losing his grip on Cara's shoulders. "Dunno. The shows on TV say so, but people in books Teacher gave me think it's a natural cycle. I think the only thing they know is *nobody* knows."

Cara smiled and bounced him once to get his attention. "This is Adam, by the way, Raul. He's a friend of Will's. You remember—the Ranger who comes to the restaurant?"

His mouth opened into an O and his eyes got wide. Suddenly, he turned back into a normal little boy with the attention span of a gnat, as though a switch had been thrown. "You're a Texas Ranger? Know what? That's the other thing I want to be when I get big, after I get done with the icebergs, and before I buy a ranch and raise cows. You talk funny for a Ranger."

Adam shook his head and laughed as the boy's train of thought derailed. "Nope. I'm not a Ranger. I'm a policeman in Minnesota. Have you ever heard of Minneapolis? Do you know where that is?"

He nodded. "Sure. We have a map on the wall at school. That's the state with lots of lakes and that big mall. Teacher said there are lots of bugs there, 'cause of the water, but we have different bugs here that like the heat. Bugs are really cool. I want to study them, too. Know what? Mama took me to the mall in San Antonio last week to buy Gloria's Quince dress. I like the mall 'cause they have an arcade."

Cara chuckled and Adam nodded, uncrossed his arms, and leaned back against the tree trunk. "Yep. We have the Mall of the Americas—the largest one in the world. It's probably a little bigger than the one you went to here. But I'll bet your sister's dress is as pretty as anything we have there."

Raul nodded his head vigorously. He squirmed to get away so Cara lowered the boy back to the ground. "Ooo, yeah! Know what? It's pink with this *biiig* skirt, like on the Cinderella video! And she even has a crown, but that looks more like Belle's or maybe Snow White's. She keeps it in a box in her closet." He tugged on Cara's hand, trying to drag her toward the door. "C'mon! I'll show you."

But she pulled her hand out of his with a laugh. "How about you run inside and tell Gloria we're coming. *¡Vamos!* We'll be right in." She winked and he grinned again before turning and racing into the house, yelling his sister's name.

"Cute kid," he said with a nod toward the house. "And your sister seems nice. She's full human?"

Cara nodded and stared at the house. "Yeah. I'm the only one in our family who turned. Both Rosa and my brother Jorge are human, but their kids will probably turn because Paco—that's short for Pasquale—and Sharon do. That seems to be how it is here—it skips a generation. Does that happen in your pack, too?"

"Mostly. Sometimes we'll get two alphas who'll have another Sazi, but it's hit or miss. A lot of our families are enrolled in the breeding program just so they can have kids at all." Cara nodded, seeming to understand what he meant, but didn't offer any comment. Did they even have a breeding

program here? That was something he probably needed to
find out. The program back home was a big deal, and cou-
ples were on a long waiting list for available Sazi babies, because only full humans or alpha females could carry a
shifter baby to term. The moon magic often caused miscar-
riages, and there weren't nearly enough suitable women to
go around who were willing to be surrogates. If the pack
here could have children as powerful as Raul, it might help
him decide which families to bring down.

He paused and had to raise his hand to his brow to block
the sun that had lowered enough to be right in his eyes. But
the sky had turned an amazing color—filled with oranges
and reds down low, with purples and blues higher up.
"Wow, is that a sunset!"

She turned her head and watched the sky with him.
"Yeah. We get ones like this a lot. You ought to see what it
looks like right after a storm. I've got pictures of the windmill on my place with sunsets that are unreal. Sometimes I
frame and sell 'em in a little shop in town."

That perked his ears. "You like photography? I've just
started—"

Rosa's voice called out of the closed screen door. "Hey,
you two! Get your fuzzy butts in here. Paco's about to turn
on the game and these tamales aren't going to wrap themselves!"

Adam flicked his eyes to his watch. It *was* time for the
game! He'd nearly forgotten—again. That was becoming
a trend that both worried and interested him. "Yeah, I
would like to watch that, unless you planned to have a pack
meeting."

She shook her head and moved a bit, waiting for him to
step away from the tree. "No, let's keep this casual tonight.
The whole pack isn't here. It's one thing to tell Rosa and
Paco—people would expect that, but telling just a few
would tick the rest off." Her eyes moved to his shoulder

and she twirled her finger in a circle with a frown. "Spin around for a second."

Adam furrowed his brow but obeyed and felt the light slap of her palm between his shoulder blades, brushing downward. He turned his head and looked down to where Cara had stomped on something on the ground. "What's up?"

"No big deal. You just had a scorpion on your back. I got it."

He felt his jaw drop as she lifted her foot to reveal a small, thoroughly squashed yellowish brown insect with a long tail and stinger. His skin abruptly crawled as he scanned the rest of his clothes. It suddenly felt as though there were a hundred more of them under his shirt. "A *scorpion* is no big deal?"

"Nah. You get used to them. They're bark scorpions—live in the trees. They're not aggressive and the sting isn't much worse than a honeybee's. Spray on a little window cleaner and it fixes it right up as fast as we heal. We've got bunches of biting things down here that bother me more than scorpions. Fire ants are a pain in the butt."

She started to walk up the few steps to the porch and he found himself following, shaking his head, thinking about the implications. "We've definitely got a lot to talk about before my people move down." He said the words quietly, so nobody inside heard.

With her hand on the screen door handle she replied in a near-whisper. "True, so let's try not to stay all night, huh? I've got a really busy day tomorrow, so we need to get as much as we can discussed and leave time for me to get a decent night's sleep."

Oh, that was just too good an opening to pass up! Yeah, she might get annoyed, but he didn't think so based on what he'd seen so far. As she pulled back the door to step inside, Adam leaned next to her ear, chuckled lightly, and whispered. "You just let me know what time you want to go to bed. I'm yours to command tonight."

He was rather pleased to smell that embarrassment wasn't the *only* emotion to rise from her when she instantly blushed.

Chapter 12

"SO? TELL US about him!" Rosa's words came out in a low whisper as the four women leaned over the kitchen table, shredding cooked beef roast with a fork and surrounding it with corn meal before wrapping the works in wafer-thin corn husks.

Her niece Gloria was standing at the counter, showing them samples of party favors, being careful not to get anything too close to the food. Cara had already seen the dress and *wow*, Raul had been right—she looked like a princess. She didn't even complain much that the dress was pink. White was hard to find in the stores unless specially made, and pink would make Papi, a native Salvadorean, happy. It was hard to believe she was nearly fifteen. Sometime during this past school year, both her body and mind had transformed into an adult's. It seemed only yesterday she was parked in front of the television, watching *Sesame Street*. But now her long dark hair, hazel eyes, and knockout figure were probably turning enough boys' heads that Cara hoped Rosa had already talked to her about sex.

Like her mother, Gloria kept her voice quiet, but there was no mistaking the hint of girlish awe. "Omigawd, Tia Cara! Adam is *totally* hot! *Please* tell me you're going to bring him to my party! Can you just imagine the look on Mary Rode's face if I danced with someone *that* fine at my Quinceanera?"

Gloria was now holding out a picture of a white and pale pink balloon arch and waiting for compliments, so Cara obliged, while being very careful not to answer the question about Adam. He would probably be around for the ceremony, and if he became the alpha, he would definitely need to become one of Gloria's *padrinos*, but whether she would *bring* him to the party . . . well, who knew? She put a bunch of enthusiasm in her voice, so hopefully nobody would notice she ignored the question. "Pretty! Y'all have done a *terrific* job planning this!"

Of course, seeing all the favors, from invitations to decorations, reminded her she needed to run to San Antonio and pick up her own contribution to the event—the *medalla de oro*. The solid gold religious necklace that would set her back nearly a full paycheck. She was just happy she'd put aside a little out of the last few checks so she could afford it.

Rosa raised her eyebrows and her voice held a hint of disapproval. "You just keep your mind on boys your own age, *mija*, and don't you worry about what Mary Rode thinks. What would Antonio say if he heard you lusting after a man twice your age? You'd end up walking into your own party alone! You just leave Mr. Mueller to Tia Cara."

Cara struggled not to blush as she reached for another handful of sticky corn meal with one hand, and a few jalapeno slices with the other. Apparently, Rosa knew full well what she'd interrupted.

"*Sheesh*, Mom! It's not like I was planning to rip off my dress and throw myself on him. It's just a *dance*."

Rosa snorted, not budging an inch. "Yes, and dances lead to other things. Remember he's a wolf . . . and an *alpha*. You can't hide attraction from a wolf's nose, so you just get it out of your head right now. Your *papi* is going to have a hard enough time letting you start to date after the Quince without smelling you chasing after older men. Don't do anything that would make him change his mind—that's all I'm saying." She made a small dismissive gesture with the back of her clean hand. "Now, go take that stuff back to your room before something spills on it. Then you can watch the game for an hour before bedtime. Oh, and check on Felix and Raul before you sit down. They should be asleep, but let me know if Raul is reading under the covers again. That boy is going to go blind if he keeps trying to read with that little penlight Luis gave him."

The turmoil of emotion scents that rose from her niece told Cara that Gloria wanted to stay in the room to continue to argue the point, but she knew better than to push her mother right now. She had far too much to lose this close to the party. She gave a great, heaving oppressed teenager sigh that made Rosa roll her eyes and shake her head, before stomping out, taking the stack of samples with her.

Rosa sighed and passed another wrapped tamale to Cara, who stacked it in the pan. Her fingers moved in almost unconscious harmony with the other women. Of course, since they met to do this nearly every other week, that wasn't a surprise. It was a tradition *Mami* started and she and Rosa kept up after losing her. And when Sharon and Penny joined the family . . . well, it had turned into a way to keep in touch and keep the pack a functioning unit. "*Anyway* . . . tell us about Adam, Cara."

Sharon and Penny had been fighting to keep from smiling during Rosa's lecture to her daughter, but now they didn't bother to hide the slightly lecherous looks that said they'd been thinking the same things as Gloria. "There's not much to tell. He's a friend of Will's. He's visiting. Oh, and he's the Second of his pack in Minnesota."

Sharon leaned forward to take a sip of her margarita through a straw. Cara could never figure out why she salted the rim, only to drink through a straw. After the fragrant tequila mix lowered in the glass significantly, she raised her brows. "So, is he with Wolven, too? Is that where he knows Will from?"

Cara nodded and lowered her voice even further. Hopefully, the game in the next room was loud enough that he wouldn't hear them. "I think that's how they met. Oh! And that reminds me. I don't think it's a secret . . . at least nobody told me it was, so I think I can tell you. But *I'm* a Wolven agent now, too! That was part of what the meeting was about. The old council rep for the wolves, Lucas Santiago, is in town and was at the lunch, too. He's the attorney from Colorado you mentioned, Rosa. He's the new head of Wolven and is recruiting all over the country."

Jaws dropped around the table and Rosa let out a small, excited squeal before quickly catching herself with a hurried hand over her mouth. She switching to silent bouncing and then reached across the table and grabbed Cara's hands, squeezing them with shaking intensity. The bright citrus of pride and happiness swept through the room, and it occurred to Cara that she hadn't really let it sink in with all the other things going on. A light gloss of tears formed in her eyes as she smiled, because only Rosa truly understood what it meant to her.

"Omigawd, Carita! I'm so *proud* of you! You've wanted that since you were tiny, even when Mami was still with us. I was afraid . . . *really* afraid you were going to pine away with a broken heart when you walked out of training. I mean, I don't blame you after what that woman did, but it hurt me so bad to see you like that. I know you're happy now, and made a life for yourself . . . but *Wolven*! Oh, hun bun! Tell us *everything*!"

Questions fired from all three women. "What changed

their mind?" "Are you going to have to travel?" "Ay ay ay—and what about your *job*? Can you do both?"

She answered them as best she could, since she didn't know everything herself. Sharon was the first to raise her glass with pride. "To Cara, and to the status it brings our pack! Oh, and to Lucas Santiago, for being smart enough to pick her!" Cara laughed and raised her glass. Penny followed and then Rosa. Suddenly nobody cared that they'd have to scrape dried corn meal off the glass stems afterward as they clinked them together and took a sip in celebration.

A rousing yell from the other room was followed by whoops and general laughter, causing all of them to look up. A few seconds later, Paco swung open the slatted door, which separated the kitchen from the rest of the house. Cara was reminded abruptly why Rosa had been so attracted to him. He was darkly handsome, with expressive dark eyes and sculpted features that could probably put him on magazine covers if he tried. She found herself comparing his looks to Adam's and realizing something startling. She never thought she'd find a man with blue eyes and a light skin attractive, but here she was, comparing him to every man she knew, from guys she'd dated in high school, to her own brother-in-law.

Thinking of him made her wonder about the laughter in the next room. He was the Second in a big pack. Surely he was good at meeting people. Still, she'd have to ask how he was getting along with people before Paco left the room.

He took a sniff and raised his brows after kissing Rosa on the top of her head and reaching for the refrigerator handle. "You girls must be having some fiesta in here! I didn't know invitations and balloons were such exciting things to talk about."

Rosa put her hand on Cara's shoulder and said with pride, "Cara made *Wolven*, Paco! That's what the meeting today was!"

Her Second looked at her in astonishment for a moment and then grinned broadly, a pair of Corona bottles in his hands. "No shit! That's awesome, Cara! Hey, we'll really have something to celebrate on the moon—you're getting the backstrap for sure this month. Only the choicest deer steak for our rising star."

It occurred to her then that the word *would* spread like wildfire through the pack, and she really wasn't sure she was supposed to have said anything. "Okay, but look, guys—I'm not even sure I'm supposed to have told y'all. Keep it secret for now, huh? Let me find out more first and then I'll make a general pack announcement." She looked around the table in turn, and they each nodded.

"Yeah, that makes sense." Music on the television made Paco's head turn. "I'd better get back. Otherwise, Eddie and Jorge will wind up in here, and start asking questions about the scent."

Cara nodded then raised her chin in appreciation. "By the way, thanks for changing the channel. It was nice of you to watch the hockey game with Adam instead of the NBA playoffs."

Paco shrugged. "Hell, I haven't seen a Stanley Cup game in years. I've never really understood hockey, and Adam is answering stupid questions for us. Nice guy and smart. I finally understand what that frigging blue line is for! Besides, you know how I feel about the middle games of the NBA playoffs."

Cara shook her head and let out a small chuckle before reaching for her glass again. "You're not going to go on again about how they're *fixed*, are you? I'll bet you wouldn't dare say that to a player's face." She took a sip, feeling the smooth tequila push the salt off the rim into her mouth to dissolve on her tongue.

He jutted his chin defiantly but didn't raise his voice. It told Cara that while he was still in control, if he put down a

few more beers, he was going to start to get obnoxiously
opinionated. She'd have to get Adam out of here before
that happened. She loved her brother-in-law, but Will was
right about him.

"I might. When's the last time you saw a four-game
sweep? Years! That's because all the playoffs are going to
six or seven games now, and *that's* because fans have to
buy the tickets in advance! People get pissed if year after
year they don't ever get to see a game in their hometown.
And I mean . . . c'mon! When the Bulls are having a year
like this one and they trip all over their feet like they did
the other night? Nope, I know damned well they're going
to win tonight and it'll go to game six. At least with the
Stanley Cup, I don't know the outcome."

She shook her head, and so did Rosa. It was no use trying to change his mind. He was firmly convinced he was
right and when he got convinced—"So, real quick, how's
Adam getting along with the others—Chris, Jorge and . . .
Eddie?"

She was more than a little worried about Adam meeting
Eddie and had wanted to stay in the room to watch the in-
teraction, but Paco had shooed her into the kitchen. Since
Cara had never watched a game with the male pack members, it would seem really odd to do it today without ex-
plaining why.

Paco understood the underlying question about his twin
brother Eduardo. "I haven't noticed anything. Adam did
give him a little raised eyebrow when Eddie said he was
going to spend the weekend in Dallas because José had
called to ask him to *vamos a coger viejos*. I guess Adam
must speak some Spanish, because he got a surprised look
and stared at Eddie for a few seconds. But he didn't smell
aggressive and let it go, so I think it's okay."

Shit! She hated it when Eddie went bar hopping in Dallas. It always led to trouble. "Damn it! I really wish he

wouldn't, Paco. You know how I feel about him hanging out at the gay bars with illegal immigrants. I mean, I know he can't get or give diseases, and he carries his ID, but what if he breaks skin on someone during sex or gets picked up in an ICE raid? Can't you talk to him?"

As usual, he brushed off her concerns with a wave of his hand, which nearly sloshed beer onto the floor. "Eh. You worry too much, Cara. He's been seeing that one *mayate*, Juan Carlos, up there—the bricklayer from Zacatecas he met at Bamboleo's for a couple months now. The guy has a real green card, and he always lets Juan Carlos be the *activo*, the top, so that'll never happen. Let's face it, it's not like there's much chance of him finding a stable relationship down here. When we decided to accept his lifestyle so he could remain with the pack, we had to accept the things that go with it."

What he said was true, but how would the newcomers from Minnesota deal with hunting with a gay male wolf—especially one who spent his weekends with *mayates*, Mexican immigrants who might or might not have crossed the border hiding in a trunk? Were there other gay pack members? She just didn't know, but it sure had been a shock to this pack when Eddie came out of the closet. It had taken a long time for him to be accepted by his own *family*—over a dozen full moons before the others wouldn't snap at him for standing too close in wolf form. That definitely needed to be one of the topics of discussion with Adam. It hadn't even been on her mind when she'd discussed cultural attitudes at the restaurant . . . at least, she didn't think it had been. But so many things were about to change, for all of them. Maybe this needed to be the first thing.

"Yeah, but that was before he started hanging out at the bars up north, Paco, and before I became sheriff. And now that I'm in Wolven—I just don't know. Maybe . . . well, maybe it's time to look at it again. It's not just a question of lifestyle anymore because those bars might get *raided*. Hell, the H-E-B grocery in San Antonio got raided last week, in broad daylight. Even if not this time, then what about next time or the time after?" She shook her head and looked down at the now perfect square of corn meal she was idly playing with. "I need to think about this."

She noticed Rosa start to nibble at her lower lip and saw why. Paco's face had gone dark and the sharp jalapeño of his anger was stronger than the peppers in the bowl right in front of her. "No, *we* need to *talk* about this. That's how this pack works, if you remember."

He'd opened his mouth to continue when a loud knock on the screen door was followed by voices in the next room. Oh, great! More people were arriving. It sounded like Joe and Tara. Now a full half the pack was here. Rosa got a startled look on her face and stood up in a rush. "Paco, I need to talk to you outside . . . *now*."

She didn't wait for a response. She just bustled out of the kitchen, her plastic *chanclas*—flip-flops—clicking against her bare heels like a telegraph machine, leaving the other four to look at each other in surprise. Cara flared her nostrils, trying to get some sense of the emotions her sister left behind, but got nothing other than surprise, with a touch of worry. Paco got an odd look on his face, and Cara knew why. While he might appear to be the tough-as-nails head of the household, it was Rosa who actually ruled the roost. He followed out silently but Cara heard him pause for a moment to welcome the new guests and offer them a beer . . . just as soon as he came back inside.

The mood at the table took on a decided downward spiral. Penny picked up her glass, emptied the remaining green liquid, and then silently started to attack the spiced meat again with a fork. Sharon's face remained studiously blank, but it was pretty obvious from her scent that she was curious about what was happening.

That made three of them.

BLOOD DRIPPED FROM Adam's muzzle as he yanked again, trying to get the deer in his mouth unstuck from where one hind leg had become wedged in the crook of a tree. Finally, he walked around behind the deer and simply freed the still-warm hoof and then lightly leaped over the antlers to begin to drag it again. The taste of fur and meat on his tongue nearly made him want to stop and eat, but no. He was pretty sure he couldn't.

It must be a test. That's the only thing that makes sense.

Why else would the events have happened as they did? Paco and Rosa went outside and talked about a lack of food for the guests in his hearing range, while Cara continued on in the kitchen as though nothing was happening. Rosa had made it very clear to Paco that if they fed the guests, it would use all the meat in their freezer and there was still another week until his paycheck. Paco had told her they would worry about that later, but now it was dinner time and they had to be good hosts.

The only thing he could figure is that Cara wanted to test him to see what sort of pack leader he'd be. No Alpha would allow his people to go hungry. It just wasn't *done*. Surely she would know of the problem through the pack mind-link. Josef knew what any of his pack was thinking or worried about at any time. He might even be watching Adam this very minute. So if Cara hadn't done anything yet, either Paco and Rosa were being punished—which didn't seem likely, or it was a test of *his* resourcefulness.

No problem. He was up to the challenge.

He could see the lights from the house in the distance

and figured he hadn't been gone long enough to be noticed. The timing had been the critical part. He couldn't just announce he was going for meat—that would be insulting to the hosts. So he'd waited until someone was back in the bathroom before announcing he had to go, too, and would just wander outside. He'd stripped, shifted, and scented a nearby deer before the screen had finished slamming. Oddly, many of the deer were wearing ear tags, as though in some sort of experiment. So, he'd avoided those and searched for one without. The whitetail buck he located wasn't very old, but was heavily muscled. The antlers were uneven, larger on one side than the other, but that wouldn't affect the taste, which was amazingly sweet. He certainly couldn't fault the quality or quantity of game here. His pack members would be thrilled if hunting was as good every moon as tonight. As a bonus, this should be enough meat to not only feed the crowd tonight, but also to put a little *extra* in their freezer.

Always make sure you leave your people better than you found them. He never could find any fault in his mother's logic, so he continued to live by the words.

Cara and the other women were still in the kitchen when he dragged the deer the last few feet to the back door. Now, how best to get her attention? He could simply go around, get dressed and walk through the house . . . but then the others would smell the deer blood. He could call out for her to open the door, but someone other than her might do it instead. No, this would probably be best handled with magic.

He hadn't done this in a very long time—but maybe that was the point. He closed his eyes and concentrated, pressed outward with his magic, finding the tiny air cracks around the closed door. While he *could* send his magic through solid objects, it sure was easier without barriers. An awareness came over him, stronger even than the sense of his own pack. He could feel the presence of three wolves in the room. One aura glowed and pulsed right at the edge of his magic, brighter than the others. He reached forward just a little more and touched it, and found himself pulled inside smoothly, with the ease of slipping his hands into well-worn driving gloves. New intensity flowed back along the thread of magic, making him shiver in the darkness. His eyelids began to heat from the surge of energy and he didn't dare open his eyes for fear the glowing would attract attention from the window.

In his mind, he could see Cara raise her head and suck in a sharp breath. One of the other women—Sherry, Sharon, something like that—looked at her quizzically. "Something wrong, Cara?"

He could see the other two women at the table through Cara's eyes, and wondered if this was how Josef viewed the world. It was a strange, but intoxicating feeling to be attached this way . . . very much how his first hunt was while Josef was out of town *that* night—the night when he didn't listen to the others and chose a new hunting ground. It was the night the pack was seen.

He heard Cara's voice, but it echoed inside his head, as though he were the one speaking. "I . . . I thought I heard something. But I'm sure it's nothing." She shivered and tried to brush away the magic, rubbing her skin as though she'd walked through a spider web.

No! Damn it, he wasn't doing this right, apparently. He pushed forward harder, ignoring the strangeness of the sensation, and allowed more of his magic to attach to hers. She started violently and nearly dumped over a large pottery bowl filled with some sort of sticky batter. Again, the other women looked at her strangely but continued working. This time, he added a thought—*I need to see you outside, Cara,* pushed along the stream of magic. He didn't know if she would hear it, though, so he enveloped her with his magic, pulling backward toward the door gently.

He felt her nostrils flare and her skin heat from the connection. She pushed back her chair with shaking hands. "Didn't you feel that?" The two other women looked at each other and then looked around carefully before shrugging.

"I didn't feel anything. Did you, Penny?"

The other woman shrugged a second time, but Cara was already on her feet. "I'm going outside for a second. Tell Rosa I'll be right back."

Finally! But just to be safe, he kept light pressure on the thread, reeling her toward him even as she walked the short distance to the door. It wasn't until she was outside and off the porch, standing in the darkness that he finally released her. Suddenly, *not* being connected felt strange, but that was normal. He'd felt disoriented for the better part of a *day* after disconnecting from his own pack after the hunt.

She found him in the darkness of the trees with her nose and was walking his way with a worried scent.

"What's going on out here, Adam? Why are you in wolf form? Has something happened?" Her voice was a harsh whisper laced with the adrenaline rush of a radio call of shots fired.

He stepped aside, revealing the downed deer. "I just wanted to report *mission accomplished* without the whole house knowing. I presume this was what you wanted me to do, right?" The look on her face and the intense scent of confusion that rose from her told him he'd been way off base. "So, from your dropped jaw, I'm guessing this *wasn't* a test?"

"A *test*? Gee . . . wow. I really don't have any idea what you're talking about. I mean, it's a gorgeous deer, but—"

He sighed and sat down. "Okay, how about you run around and grab my clothes off the front porch and I'll explain my dim-witted logic here after I dress."

It wasn't until she sprinted around the front of the house nearly too fast for his eyes to follow that he heard it, a low, soft swooshing . . . like wings riding the air currents over-head. He would normally dismiss the sound as an owl or other night predator, if it wasn't for the fact that the shad-owy wings that soared through the dimly lit patch of grass were as wide as the porch. His stomach lurched as the air rushing past smelled distinctly like . . . *Sazi*. Specifically, like the owl who'd nearly killed him this afternoon.

Was the house being watched? He hadn't smelled any-thing when he was hunting, but then he'd been concentrat-ing on the game. Cara's aura suddenly touched his and he realized it was because she'd caught the scent, too. When she was cranked up, her magic was formidable.

"Should we follow it?" Her voice was low and angry, ap-parently wanting a second crack at the bird. He realized he did, as well. He glanced up at where she was scanning the sky, just as he was. He shook his head. While his eyes were exceptionally good in the dark, Will had told him back at the motel there wound up being *three* birds before they'd chased them away.

"Not tonight. I don't even think it knew we were here. But if it did, then we can't afford to leave the others alone to hunt down one. They've already proven they think inde-pendently and can strategize. Still, I'm betting they're stay-ing close by, since this house is only a few miles from where we found Ziri—as the owl flies. No, I think we need to stay alert, but not alarm anyone. I'll talk with Lucas in the morning and see if we can tell your pack about this. Ex-tra eyes might really help, and we need them to be on their guard, in case Ziri wasn't the only target."

He watched her clench and unclench her fists and then let out an exasperated breath. "You're right, of course. But I hate to leave my family alone, knowing there's danger. Paco's a good fighter, but these things are way out of his league. Maybe I should stay here a few days. I've got some vacation time—"

He touched her hand with his nose and she looked down with worried, angry eyes. "There's always something, Cara. The world is full of danger. If you stay here with your sister, what happens to the rest of the pack? And what happens to the humans in town? There's no evidence that the birds have targeted anyone other than those in the van. Ziri didn't know why the men in the van were attacked, or why they came back for her. She didn't even know the men, they were just *coyotes*, driving her north to a supposed job in California so she could help support her family. Lucas knows she's hiding something, so he's still working with her—but it might have nothing to do with the birds. Maybe it was a personal grudge that has nothing to do with us or even Ziri. We just don't know enough to change our habits yet." He paused, seeing that her anger was dissipating, even though the worry remained. Then he raised one front foot and lightly touched her hand. "I know you're worried. I would be, too, in your place. But for the moment, I think we just need to be our normal selves—if we stay visible and vigilant, we're doing all we can."

She nodded and a small smile was followed by a burst of cinnamon and citrus. "I keep forgetting you're one, too—a cop. It's nice to know someone who understands the frustration. But, you're right. There's nothing we can do tonight without more information." She shook off the tension like shedding rain from her fur. "Let's get you cleaned up and I'll have Paco start the grill." She turned and walked toward the back door but paused and looked over her shoulder. "And then you can tell me whatever possessed you to go out hunting tonight."

Chapter 13

"SO YOU REALLY haven't bound your pack to you? I've never heard of that." Adam scraped his fork around the small blue plate to pick up the last bits of fruit and crumbles with obvious enthusiasm. "This is amazing cobbler, by the way. I haven't had peaches in *years*. What brand is it?"

She laughed lightly and added his plate to hers as she stood up before taking them over to the sink. "No store-bought in this house. But I admit the peaches are frozen. I bought a bushel over in Fredericksburg last summer 'cause I'm a sucker for cobbler. Or, when I'm feeling ambitious, warm peaches and pecans in caramel syrup—sort of like a Bananas Foster, over homemade ice cream. They're one of my weaknesses, and they really grow sweet ones here."

She returned to her chair, which was close enough to Adam's that their knees brushed, and pulled the county map back to the center of the kitchen table so they could both see it. A small yawn overtook her, even though it wasn't that late. They'd left Rosa's house around nine, after a terrific barbeque—nearly equal to summer fiestas on the moon. The pack had been really impressed by Adam's willingness and, she had to admit, his *ability* to bring down a deer that large by himself, when it was still days to the moon. But his reasoning for *doing* it—well, that had been a little . . . strange.

She shook her head lightly as she pulled pen and paper back to her after wiping a few stray crumbs from the polished wood. "I guess I haven't heard of a pack leader binding his members, either. That just smacks of Big Brother too much for me. Why would it be necessary? Down here, we all want the same thing—to make the pack happy and strong. Does your Josef not trust the members to further the interests of the pack?"

He furrowed his brow and didn't answer for a moment, so she let him think while she looked again at the map. Little foil stick-on stars were scattered over the surface, marking the homes of her pack members. They were mostly clustered in small groups around the edges of Santa Helena, with one or two in town. But there was one star miles away, in Houston, and another near the border of Mexico. They were part of the overall pack, but seldom hunted with the group. As alphas who could control their change on the moon, they had that option.

While there were plenty of homes available for the newcomers to live in, the trick was not to make their presence too obvious to the locals. That new subdivision was pretty big, so a couple could probably go there—

"I guess I don't have an answer for that." The words were accompanied by a frustrated shrug. "It's all we've ever known. The pack in Chicago does the same as Minnesota, and so does Alaska. But I'm certainly willing to consider other options for down here . . . when in Rome, and all that. I'll talk to the people we pick when I head back north."

"Well, the ones that are going to do best down here will be independent thinkers anyway. The people here, humans and Sazi alike, are pretty tough. There's lots of agriculture—raising goats and cattle, plus seed crops like millet and thistle, so you have a lot of farmer and rancher families in the area. Of course, there are service businesses here, too, but I don't know what *new* ones would survive. There's not a lot of cross business between counties. You might look around town tomorrow and see if you have any ideas. I know the chamber of commerce and economic development committee are actively looking for new business moves—offering incentives and grants. That might benefit us."

"Well, the one thing I noticed you *don't* have here is a discount department store. Maybe a Target?"

She snorted abruptly. "Hell, we'd love to get a Wal-Mart or K-Mart or, sure . . . a Target down here. But they've all turned us down. We're not large enough, population-wise, for their rules."

Adam's smile held a touch of mischief. "Yeah, but before . . . you didn't have one of the vice presidents of the whole company in your pocket. Minnesota is the home base of the Target chain, and our second female, Cherise, is one of the VPs in new development. She might be able to . . . *bend* a few rules. In fact, I can pretty much guarantee it. It's why she was installed in the position. The local stores are considered pack businesses for hiring our members."

The thought of that stopped her cold. That could solve the entire problem! It was a new business that would certainly be welcome and provide jobs to locals. Bringing in a home management "team" was pretty common, and while there might be a few grumbles, nobody would really fuss about a sudden increase in outsiders from the same state. "Yeah, you definitely need to put that on your *must do* list when you get back. That's . . . um, just *wow*!" She looked back at the map and hopelessness was replaced by elation. One random idea could actually make this whole thing *work*! Something moved against the sensitive hairs on her cheek when her jaw dropped and she smelled that a bit of cobbler was stuck to the skin. She reached out her tongue to flick it away, but it was too far, so she raised her hand.

It stopped in midair, her wrist held in a firm grip by Adam. His touch nearly burned every time their skin met, and she couldn't help but gasp at the intensely warm sensation that flowed up her arm. His gaze had gone dark and serious and she couldn't seem to pull her eyes away. "Don't."

That one word brought shivers, and the sudden pounding of her heart increased when he leaned closer. It was the

scene in front of Rosa's all over again. She waited, trans-
fixed, as his aura surged over the top of hers, teasing her
skin and raising goose bumps. By the time his lips touched
her cheek, she couldn't seem to breathe. His tongue flicked
lightly, removing the crumbs, and the scent of pine trees
and sweet musk filled her nose, turning her mind to putty.
She found herself turning slightly to meet his mouth and it
was waiting, frozen in place, when she did.

His grip on her wrist tightened just a bit as his lips
brushed hers, and paper rustled from his other hand reaching forward to ease behind her neck. She'd expected the
kiss to start slow, but it didn't. There was near desperation
in the way his jaw worked against hers, his tongue circling
and exploring as he pulled her head tight against his. Beard
stubble tickled her chin as he twisted his head slightly.

He tasted of peaches and sugar but, underneath that, was
fur and fresh deer. She realized she'd never actually kissed
another Sazi . . . at least a wolf. There's been that one cat in
Wolven academy, and while he was an excellent kisser,
among other things, it had been casual—this *wasn't*. Her
hands started moving of their own accord, pulling away
from his grasp to explore his neck, his hair, while he turned
his tongue into a hot wire from her mouth to her stomach.
Damn, he was a good kisser!

She lost track of time as his mouth worked over hers before moving to suck on her lower lip hard enough to make
her groan. He went to her jawline next, tiny little feather
kisses accompanied by magic and tickling, sandpaper rough
hairs that flowed shivers across her skin. By the time he'd
reached her neck and ear, he'd pushed back his chair and
lifted her over to straddle him. She could feel the swell in
his pants through her own thin jeans and a sudden spasm
down low pulled a sharp hiss from her.

"Damn, you smell good." His words came out a husky,
growling whisper and his hands tightened on her waist.

"So do you." The growl was apparently contagious because it was in her voice, too. And she wasn't lying . . . he did smell incredible. His musk was increasing and she couldn't help but roll her tongue against his neck. The sharp, sweet taste caused shivers to turn into a pulse that swelled her skin and turned the air around her to fire.

Things started to happen too quickly to follow—his hands under her shirt, unhooking her bra, while she tugged his shirt out of his jeans. The shirts disappeared in a few seconds, nearly breaking the chain of her necklace, and suddenly there was skin against skin, while his mouth moved from one breast to the other. He nipped and sucked at her nipples, grinding those coarse hairs against her sensitive skin, while she cried out, dug fingers into his shoulders and pushed herself down to rub his erection against her. She growled and lowered her head to his neck, biting sharply into the skin. She rubbed her hands along his chest, her healing magic finding each closing wound and smoothing dimpled scars into smooth, perfect skin once more.

Another growl rose from her, and he answered with one of his own. But this one was different and his magic pushed inside her violently . . . pulled at her wolf and called to the moon. He started to snuffle against her neck and then ran his tongue slowly up, from shoulder to ear. The reminder was abrupt. A sudden panic filled her mind even as her body soared higher, encouraging his hands and tongue. He said she *smelled* good!

¡Madre de Dios! It was happening again. The tea should last longer than this. It always had in the past.

"Adam . . . we have to stop." She fought to get the words—closer to whispered pants—out, because part of her didn't even want to say them. And she was glad he didn't stop when she asked. He continued to flick his tongue against her hardened nipples while raising his hips to press against her. It felt so good. God, it felt good, and she wanted him inside her. Her hands reached toward his belt buckle, and he moved her backward on his legs to give her room before returning his hands to smooth against her spine, trailing magic like tiny electric fingers that caused another series of contractions inside her. She watched with horror as her own desperate fingers undid his buckle and started on the zipper even as she tried to pull back.

She swallowed hard, fighting the need. She was really going to do this if she didn't fight harder. There would be no protection from whatever he wanted, and however often he wanted it. She was alphic, and could wind up pregnant or . . . worse. In desperation, she yanked his head backward with both hands, using his hair as a handle. His eyes were fully glowing with a deep, almost violet light, and he growled again, baring his teeth. Only a flicker of humanity was still in those eyes. He was nearly lost to his animal. "Adam! Listen to me! It's happening again, and you have to help me stop. I'm going into heat. We can't do this . . . not like *this*."

His biceps flexed, trying to pull her against him again. His low, rumbling growl made her breathing still. His muscles were so smooth and solid and her body ached to feel them surround her. Hot tears welled in her eyes as *Mami's* battered face came to her mind again. She understood now . . . knew what the prayers had meant, and why she'd been so afraid, and looked so . . . *hopeless*. "*Please*, Adam!" Tears began to flow down her face, even as she released him and buried her face in his hair. "I do want to do this with you someday, but as *humans,* not . . . animals! I don't even *know* you yet!"

Cara's body, or more precisely, the wolf *inside* her body, fought for control and her tears wet his hair as she sobbed, knowing what was going to happen. His hands were between them, loosening her zipper, even as her own hands had finished opening his. His cock strained against the fabric of his underwear, pulsing against her hands as she ran fingers along the length of it. It would feel so good . . . she needed him to ease the aching.

She surrounded it with one hand, squeezing lightly as heady musk filled the air. But then Adam paused, his fingers just inside the elastic top of her pale blue silken panties, brushing the already slick hairs.

A violent shudder overcame him and his hands moved back to his sides. When she looked down, they were clenched into white-knuckled fists and a fine trembling vibrated his muscles. She leaned back, her hand still involuntarily resting against his crotch, and looked at his face. His eyes had stopped glowing and were filled with understanding and . . . horror.

"Not like this." He repeated the words shakily with a low rumble still threading through his voice. He shook his head, as though trying to clear the need from his mind.

The wolf in her railed against him stopping. She growled again, ending with a needy whine, and waited for a response. But he gritted his teeth and refused with a firm shake of his head.

"*Please*—" The word had double meaning and she hated the desperate tone from the two halves of her mind. Stop. Don't stop. Each equally needy and praying he'd listen.

He took a slow breath and then released it, while she sat on his legs, naked and hungry for his touch. "We need to calm you down. That's the first step." He grabbed her wrists, pulling them up and away from his open fly. "I know this isn't your fault. Will and Viv explained it to me back at the motel. So I know you can't just step away and let this go. Even if I walked out, you'd go out and find someone else, and you might hurt *him*." She knew it was true, even as the words left his mouth, and the thought of it sickened her enough to make bile rise into her throat.

He held up her arms so her hands were in front of her

face while she swallowed hard and stared at him with desperation, not daring to speak.

"Can you lock your fingers together for me?"

She nodded yes, but then her hands refused. They turned in his grip and began to stroke his hands while the wolf opened her scent glands wider. He closed his eyes and let out another shaky breath. "Shit, woman! You could make a fortune bottling that stuff. I feel like a teenager locked with naked cheerleaders in the shower room right now—not sure where to start first." Another breath and a sharp head shake. Then his eyes met hers again. "Fuck. Okay, let's try again." He moved her wrists so her hands were resting on his bare shoulders. The wolf liked that and began to knead the muscles while he groaned.

He raised his hands between her arms, being careful not to brush against her breasts. His face twitched from time to time as she pressed against his crotch, trying to encourage him, even as she fought to keep from doing it. "Okay, this is something my mom used to do to us kids when we were little—on nights the wolf got too hard to handle."

She couldn't help but laugh. Even the wolf found it funny. It took him a moment to get the joke, but then he chuckled. "Not quite what I meant to say." He placed his palms flat on her cheeks, and then began to stroke the skin on the sides of her nose with his thumbs, applying a light downward pressure. He pushed his magic in a flowing wave that tingled every hair like an electric current.

The first, almost lazily slow, caress made her eyes open wide as a shock of sheer pleasure clenched her body enough to hurt. The second movement of his thumbs froze her in place as intense waves of warmth swelled her skin. On the third stroke, her fingers dug into his shoulders and she threw back her head, crying out as a violent orgasm swept through her body.

The tingling contractions and out of body sensation must

have lasted for the better part of a minute, while she ground herself against his crotch with short, frantic movements and dug fingers into his neck. It really *did* feel like her heart stopped for a long moment in the middle, just like she and Yo used to read about in novels. It was easily the best climax she'd had in her life and that made meeting his eyes all the more difficult after. But when she could catch her breath, and see again through the dancing white lights that had erupted in her vision, she had to ask. It took two tries before she could get the words out, but she *had* to know. "Your *mother* used to do that?"

Adam's face was stunned and his hands frozen in place where they'd been before she pulled away and screamed. His scent was embarrassed beyond belief, and his voice horrified at the implication. "Well, certainly not with *that* effect! It made *us* fall sleep! I was pressing along where your whiskers are in animal form. It's supposed to be calming." He lowered his hands, not quite sure what to do with them now, as he flushed and laughed. "Wow . . . well, I suppose it did still solve the problem."

Yeah, solved one but started another. She loosened her grip on his shoulders and looked around as heat rose into her face, searching on the floor for her shirt. But it wasn't on the floor. One of them had flung it across the room, where it was hanging from a cabinet pull next to the refrigerator. She glanced at him again, obviously uncomfortable with bare chest and open jeans. He was still erect, probably painfully so, but she didn't know what to do about it without making things worse. Would even standing up start things rolling again?

Adam noticed where her eyes fell and shrugged, then pushed her backward gently with his hands safely on her jean-clad hips, until she was on her feet off to the side. "I'll live. Guys get used to this sort of thing, don'tcha know. Just don't ask me to try to zip up or walk for a few minutes." He chuckled again nervously and pulled his chair forward until his legs were underneath the table. She couldn't see where her bra wound up, but she quickly retrieved the shirt and buttoned it while he put his elbows on the table and dropped his forehead into his hands with a groan. "Oh, and you might want to brew up some of that tea you mentioned this afternoon and maybe open a window. That scent is making me want to do some pretty strange things."

She hurried to do just that, because with his head down on the table, every muscle in his broad back stood out in sharp, defined relief. Even now, she fought the urge to run her tongue up his spine between the ridges of muscle. She had to close her mouth after she realized she was actually drooling on the floor.

Yeah, definitely time for a cup of tea.

Chapter 14

ADAM KNOCKED ON the door of Lucas's room, the early morning sunlight not quite breaking over the treetops yet. A light breeze pushed a scent across his nose that smelled remarkably like Cara. *Uffda!* Everything smelled like her this morning. He couldn't get the scent out of his head. Dew, peaches, and honeysuckle musk, like some seductive wine that made him drunk with the barest whiff. He'd spent the whole damned night dreaming of her—his mind working through a dozen scenarios where they didn't stop. In some, he'd taken her right on the tabletop; in others, he carried her upstairs to her bed. In a few, they'd run outside in their other form, letting the night air thrill across their fur as they—

"Come in." The voice from behind the door startled him enough to make him flinch and for the hundredth time, he had to shake the images out of his mind. All the better reason to talk to Lucas.

Adam opened the door and found Lucas seated at the desk, a dozen files open all over the room. Ziri was in a chair next to the bed, watching cartoons on television with rapt interest, even though the sound was off. There was still plenty of noise from her crunching down a bowl of Corn Flakes. The scene made her look like every other kid on a Saturday morning—if you didn't look at her clothing too closely.

"Do you have a second? I need to talk to you."

The visual contrast struck Adam as funny while he waited for the other man to reply. Lucas was barefoot and wearing faded jeans and a well-worn yellow shirt with his name, the word *coach*, and a snarling wolf emblazoned across the back, while wearing a Rolex and chewing on the end of an expensive, engraved fountain pen. He circled an item while waving Adam to a chair. "Clear off a place to sit and grab some coffee. I just need another minute so I don't forget what I wanted to tie together in these files."

The coffee was the same brand as he normally bought, so he poured some in the surprisingly nice mug from the motel tray and added some cream from a miniature white pitcher. Either the motel did room service, or Lucas had already been down to the little restaurant on the corner to snag real cream. He sipped and watched the television with Ziri, who turned to him once when a commercial came on and smiled. She pointed to herself and said, "Ziri."

He nodded and did the same. "Adam."

She repeated the word several times, making it sound more like *Aah-dome,* but it was close enough and he nodded.

Lucas closed the folder in front of him and turned around. He smiled at Ziri and said something in Mayan, with a much smoother, conversational tone than in the desert. He must have gotten some practice over the evening. It made her nod and move to the other side of the room and spin the television on the turntable away from them, so Lucas could sit down next to him and they wouldn't get distracted.

Adam raised his brows and gestured toward Ziri with his head. "Anything new?"

Lucas let out a little frustrated sigh. "Not enough. She definitely saw something out there, but I don't know if dragging it out of her will do anything more than traumatize her. I'd rather find the information some other way if I can. I made some calls and found a small resort near her village that was willing to send a runner to let her family know about the accident, and that she's okay. I'm thinking we might want to keep her housed here for awhile. Sending her back would be an insult to her family, and I'm not willing to send her forward to her original destination. I can't take her along when I leave, so that leaves here."

A thought occurred to him. "Any idea how old she is?"

Lucas nodded. "She's fifteen, although she doesn't look it. She's the oldest child, which is why she came here to find work. It's probably a good thing she didn't understand what was in store for her. Those birds probably saved her from a sweatshop where she'd earn pennies, or winding up in some pimp's stable."

He certainly agreed. "Cara's sister, Rosa, has a daughter just Ziri's age. The father works for the post office, and Rosa has a part-time restaurant so she's able to say home with the kids a lot. If Ziri just spoke a little English, or even Spanish—"

"Actually, I've been working on that." He raised his voice. "Ziri."

She turned her eyes to Lucas, and struggled not to flick them back to the brightly colored animation on the screen. "Can you understand what we're saying here?"

"A leetle . . . yes?"

He answered in Mayan and she went back to the program. "I've been spending time touching her mind, trying to implant words and some syntax. Sort of like a mental Berlitz course. She can carry on a simple conversation right now, but it'll be better by the time I leave. I'll talk to Cara about placing her with the sister until I get back. Good thought." He paused and then went serious. "So, what can I do for you, Adam?"

He swallowed hard and took another sip. "I . . . I think the council needs to find another alpha for down here. I don't think I can . . . *work* effectively with Car . . . Alpha Salinas." He tried desperately to keep his mind blank as to the reason and watched the other man carefully to see how he reacted.

Lucas's face remained studiously blank. "Ah. Well, then you'll be happy to know that Cara dropped by this morning on her way to work with the same request."

She did? His jaw dropped and the coffee cup nearly fell from his hand. Rather than happy, Adam discovered it made him angry and . . . *hurt*. Didn't she think he had any control? Or was she questioning his ability to be a good pack leader? He noticed Lucas watching his reaction and pulled himself together, nodding sharply once. "Oh. Good. Then it's settled."

The other man smiled slightly and raised up his cup. But before he took a sip, he said, "Not really. I told her no. She has my bottle of cologne, and that should help block her scent for the time being."

Relief mixed with horror, and blended with . . . what? He didn't know and he couldn't even think to reply.

Lucas continued on as though he hadn't reacted, dropping

the subject completely and moving to a new, or rather, an *old* topic. "Oh and, I've been doing some thinking since then about our discussion here yesterday. And doing some checking around, too. I was just about to make a call to another agent. I'd like you to listen in because it directly affects you." He reached out and put down the cup, then picked up his cell phone and pressed the down arrow until he reached the number he wanted. After three rings, the call was picked up by a man with a medium baritone. "Yeah? What's up, Lucas?"

"Can you catch a flight to Minneapolis today, Tony? I need your particular expertise to find out whether someone is telling me the truth about some questions I asked."

Adam could hear the muffled reply of the man—presumably agent—named Tony. He must be new, since nobody by that name was with Wolven when he was an agent. "Hell yes! Anything to get away from these damned hundred-year-old files. The paper falls apart in my hands. Haven't you people—and I use that term loosely—ever heard of microfiche or scanning?"

The chortle was nearly a growl, as though Lucas was indulging the man . . . barely. "Yes. And we dismissed the idea. Tapes can be stolen and so can data. File folders with brittle paper are more difficult to slip in a jacket pocket without anyone noticing. And it's tough to fit even a single page of parchment the size of the Declaration of Independence in a sock, if you know what I mean. Now, when you get to Minneapolis, you need to seek out the pack leader, Josef Isaacson. He's your mark."

"Mm-hmm. And am I there for interrogation or enforcement? It's getting harder to get guns on a plane on short notice. That'll cost you big bucks."

Adam's eyebrows rose, but he didn't comment. Since when did Wolven members need to use guns on pack leaders? And when did agents start dictating their own pay?

Lucas shook his head, as though the man on the other side of the call could see him. His voice was confident and commanding, with a hint of danger around the edges. It was as though he wore a different persona when talking to this agent. "No guns. I don't want you to do anything to Josef if you discover he's lying. He's out of your league, and I don't want him put down without council orders. I just want you to *overhear* a conversation between him and his Second, Adam Mueller, from two weeks ago. That's *Adam* . . . M-u-e-l-l-e-r. Write it down. It was a private meeting, in Josef's office, and they were discussing splitting the pack. I'm getting two different stories on what happened and so far, I'm believing Mueller." He nodded to Adam with that, and ignored his dropped jaw at the conversation. What in the hell was being discussed here?

"Don't let Isaacson know what you're doing. Specifically, I want to know whether he told Mueller to come to Texas this week. Oh, and if you can find out whether he later had any conversations with a Vivian Carmichael— leggy honey-blonde and all around scheming alpha bitch— I'd like to hear about that, too. If he does make you, keep him in place until I get there in about three days. Alive, but wounded is fine."

"Should I take Bobby along with me? He's in a mood for . . . *wounded.*"

Lucas appeared surprised and pursed his lips. "Agent Mbutu's in Chicago? Are he and Asri—?" He let the statement hang, as though not quite sure what to say.

Tony chuckled just as Adam smiled at the name. Damn. Robart Mbutu! He didn't know anyone named Asri, but he remembered the African chemist fondly. They'd shared a love of chocolate—even though the python agent could never fully enjoy candy because he tasted each ingredient separately, rather than as a whole. "Nah. Nothing like that. But his lovely wife doesn't do morning sickness very well.

Asri . . . *suggested* he take a hike for a few weeks, so she didn't slice him up by accident—accidentally on purpose, in my opinion. He'd *hoped* the second trimester would be better, but . . . not so much."

A burst of laughter from Lucas sounded both delighted and pitying. "Yeah, I wouldn't bet on that. The dragon women of Komodo weren't ever known for looking fondly on their mates until the eggs were safely underground. Morning sickness lasted all the way through the pregnancy. But don't tell him I said so. He's the one who wanted to *breed*, so he can find out the reason why there aren't many snakes or dragons anymore. Yeah, do take along Bobby. There's nothing Josef can throw that he can't handle. If you can hook him into the vision, that would be even better. Then there'll be no question if the council wants corroboration. Just don't make a scene or take anyone out. I don't want any loose ends with the pack or the public to clean up when I get there."

The other man's voice had a questioning tone. "You're on the a la carte menu now, you know."

"We'll discuss it when I get there. Just get moving and call me when you've got him in a secure location." Lucas pressed the end button without another word, or waiting for a response. Then he flipped down the cover on the phone and looked at Adam with raised brows.

"So, you might be winding up with the Minnesota pack, depending on what the council decides after hearing the evidence. Will that be more to your liking?"

He couldn't decide what to say or do and Lucas let him take his time. Finally, he fought his way around to the main question. "Did I just hear you put a *hit* on my pack leader? For crissake, he's going to know what you just said through the pack connection!"

Lucas nodded and took another casual sip, apparently

choosing to ignore the roiling scents that rose from Adam enough he nearly choked on them himself.

"Not a hit. Not yet. And no, he won't have a clue what's coming. Let me give you a little background and bring you up to date on what your *pack leader* has been up to lately." He grabbed a file folder from the bed and tossed it into Adam's lap. "This is a statement I took last night from Vivian. After a little . . . *gentle persuasion*, she admitted Josef sent you down here for the express purpose of killing you. I'm not quite sure why she thought she'd be safe from the same fate, but she was pretty convinced of it."

Adam was busy reading the statement, written in a bold, masculine hand that seemed to fit Lucas's personality. The words she said Josef called him—*traitor, motherless cur, murderer*—spun in his mind.

"The council didn't order you to be the Alpha here. They gave full authority to the pack leaders to make the final decisions. And Josef never talked to me, nor any other council member. I asked. No, you were sent here to die and, in fact, have been cut off from the pack for over a week. It's why you've been irritable and depressed. You've been pining for your pack mates. Fortunately for you, though, he had no way of knowing how lenient Cara is about strange wolves in her territory. I really didn't know either, until I met her." He sighed and shook his head. "But if Vivian wasn't lying . . . and I doubt she could . . . then he expected you to be slaughtered for coming here, either by Cara or me. He knew I was coming here and had ordered everyone to stay away until I met with Cara's pack."

Adam heard an almost eerily calm tone in his voice that betrayed none of the emotions swirling through his head. "He blames me for his son's death, and for the pack split. I'd suspected that, but he swore otherwise and I could never tell when he was lying, because of his natural scent."

Closing the file didn't remove the words from his mind. He wasn't pack anymore. But he could swear he could still feel them, in the background. Were they only memories? Is that why he attached to Cara so completely and . . . *desperately*? And what did that mean for the other pack members who would be cut off before coming down here?

Lucas's voice was sad. "I'm starting to think Josef's gone completely insane over Tyr's death. It's happened before and, if so, then he's a danger to everyone up there. Tony Giambrocco is a new turn—an attack victim who is gifted, or some might say *cursed*, with hindsight. He'll be able to tell me, and the council, everything that went on behind closed doors as though he was there."

That perked Adam's ears. "You have a *seer* in Wolven now? And he can see the past? Wow, would that speed up case resolution!"

Lucas laughed with a trace of bitterness. "Yeah, but he doesn't come cheap. He has no loyalty to the Sazi, and trying to rein him in with discipline only serves to make him more stubborn, so we have to pay him better than the competition. He was a freelance assassin as a human, working for the Mafia and is a lone wolf—unable to be bound to a pack because of his mate. He's quite possibly the only three-day wolf to ever become an agent and certainly the only one with a per job fee arrangement. But he's not in Wolven just because of his gift, so don't piss him off when you meet him. He's turned bullets into a whole new kind of obstacle on the Wolven training course—one that's even impressed a few council members."

A Mafia hitman seer who works for Wolven because it's the highest bidder? Bobby Mbutu married and about to become the father of *dragons*? "This sounds like the plot of a bad reality TV show. You sure you're not bullshitting me?"

Another laugh, but this one was amused. Lucas relaxed back into his seat. "You ought to hear what's happening in the *council*. It's a whole new world in Paris. But that's beside the point. For the moment, what I need you to do is work with Cara for the next two days and give me a list of people to bring back." He raised a hand to stop Adam's protest. "Just deal with it, Agent. If you can't stand to be in the same room together even after the cologne . . . and I *don't* want to know the details, then make the plans by phone. But I want a firm list of twelve families ready to take back with me by five o'clock on Friday—and you need to start making a decision . . . do you want to come back to join this pack or not? If you say yes, then you're off the list to take over Minnesota if we need to replace Josef."

Adam took a deep breath and nodded. Cut and dried, just that simple—at least for Lucas. But for two packs, the decisions he and Cara made could change the lives of a dozen people forever. "If you have to put Josef down, there's a chance that neither pack will follow me as Alpha. They're the same people, and they're loyal to him."

Lucas shook his head lightly, with tiny movements. "People will follow any good leader, Adam. But leaders make mistakes. It's how you *deal* with those mistakes that determines whether they'll trust you enough to *keep* following."

"How did *you* deal with it? Making a mistake, that is. If you've ever made one." The sound of frustration playing through his voice was clear, even without the burnt metal scent he knew the other man could smell.

He'd expected a laugh or anger for daring to ask. What he didn't plan was the weary, almost sad sigh. "Made one? Hmm . . . *which* one? There've been too many to count lately. You'll find yourself asking questions there aren't any answers to—should I have stepped in sooner? Should I have gotten involved at all? Did I make it worse, or better? What could I have noticed that might have made the difference?" He shrugged. "But you don't have time to second guess. All you can do is look around you, listen to your people, make your decisions, and move on. Oh, and watch your back when you have time. Outliving your enemies is a key element of leading."

Watch his back. He never thought he had to do that alone—believed his pack, his *family*, would *help* watch it. "That reminds me! Cara doesn't bind her pack, but Josef does. Do I insist, or let my people pine down here? What do you do in Boulder?"

The shrug didn't really help to answer the question. "Boulder was lightly bound . . . not like Josef does. We're aware of each other, but there's no strong tie. I'm severed from them now, and so is the Alpha who took over for me." A small smile and a shake of his head didn't really telegraph any particular emotion, and his scent was still blocked. "I never really planned to stay for as long as I did. Time sort of got away from me."

He looked lost in thought for the barest of moments and then shrugged again. "So, I guess there's no good answer. There are advantages and disadvantages to binding, and the *level* of binding, for a pack leader. Cara's pack is also family. They see one another every single day. There's probably never been a need. But with the new members coming down . . . well, that's something she and the new Alpha Male are going to have to work out. Your people are more aggressive than hers. She's going to have her hands full. I think it'll make her grow as an Alpha, but it also might be too much for her. She might wind up the Second or even the Omega eventually. That's the way of packs. I think Raven Ramirez, who will be taking over the Boulder pack, is considering full binding. He might pull it off, since that pack is splitting, too."

Boulder is being split, too? So this really wasn't just retribution against his pack for one mistake? Adam remembered Raven, the previous second in command of Wolven.

Yeah, he would be a good pack leader. Strong, confident, easy to talk to. Lucas kept talking even as he nodded to himself.

"Things happened up there that might not have if I'd been attached to the members. But I can't allow myself to believe it was a *mistake* not to fully bind them. It was a choice I made with what I thought was good information."

The older man picked up his coffee cup again and started to put it to his lips before realizing it was empty. He set it back down and looked at Adam with world-weary eyes. "Still, don't be too certain your members will pine down here, either. Pick the right people, and they might consider the structure down here . . . liberating."

Lucas's voice filled with determination. "Remember that sometimes people don't recognize freedom until the chains are off and they have something to compare the chains to."

Chapter 15

"SHERIFF? DO YOU have a minute?"

Cara stopped on the bottom step of Tedford County's century-old limestone courthouse and looked up and behind her. The county attorney, Jeff Stone, was hurrying toward her, his arms laden with files. He nearly lost his grip on the oversize trial case in his hand and Cara reached out to steady it.

While she'd known Jeff for years, she made the play of keeping her tone professional, mostly for the benefit of other ears on the square. "I've got *just* a minute, Mr. Stone. My calendar is insane today. What can I do for you?"

He looked at her with chagrin and the dry heat of embarrassment rose over the top of his normal scent, which always reminded her of canned limeade. It was probably the slightly cardboard hint that did it. Apparently, he was flustered enough he forgot to play the game. "Yeah, and I know that's my fault, Cara. I really thought we were going to need your testimony today. Sorry to make you sit through that whole hearing for nothing."

She shrugged. "Occupational hazard. At least the judge ordered the extradition. That's one more bed I've got available in the jail."

"Mmm-hmm. I saw the state correctional board turned down Carl's request to add new beds. What are you going to do now?"

A little frustrated noise leaked out of her before she could stop it. "They aren't *new* beds. That's the frustrating part. They're right there now, sitting open. But they're *allocated* for female prisoners." She knew she was stating the obvious, especially to Jeff. "We don't *have* any female prisoners. Why not use them for the men we do have? I'm getting tired of shipping them to out of county jails. The gasoline alone is killing our budget."

Jeff shrugged. "Ah, the mysteries of logic in our state capital. Well, I'll try to do my part and push for early hearings on extraditions, like today." He let out a little laugh. "Maybe you need to stop arresting so many people."

She returned the laugh. "I'll take that under advisement. That all you needed? 'Cause I really have to get." She tapped her watch face to emphasize it and he got a startled look on his face.

"*No!* I mean, could we sit for just a second? I really do need to talk to you, but my arms are killing me. It's important, or I wouldn't ask."

He shifted the files around again and she sighed. She really did have to get back, but after checking her watch again, she realized she still had ten minutes to make her next appointment. It was only a two minute walk back to the office—one minute if she hurried, and goodwill with the county attorney's office was never a bad thing. Nodding once, she scanned around the courthouse square, then pointed to the seldom-used gazebo, covered with ivy, that was only a few steps away. "How about over there?"

"Sounds good." He joined her in the short walk. Cara nearly reached out to help with his load of files, but there was such a fine line between helping out and insulting him that she didn't. As much as she hated it, there was still a very strong male-female tradition in this county, and insult came quick and stuck hard.

Cool dampness closed around her as they entered the open structure. The scent of growing plants and rich soil made her forget the muggy heat just a dozen feet away. A few black mud dauber wasps had built nests in the upper reaches of the gazebo, but they weren't at all aggressive like the red ones, or yellow jackets. A quick flip of her hand toward one made it fly lazily in the other direction. Jeff ignored them entirely. "Okay, here's the thing," he said once he'd placed his burdens on the slatted bench next to him and removed his cream-colored cowboy hat. "I'm missing some cattle—I think."

She knew that the Stone ranch was one of the largest in the region, and missing cattle was a very big deal, but she shrugged because it wasn't her business. "Why tell me? The Cattle Raisers Association agents are paid to handle that. I know you've worked with them before. I haven't picked up any estrays lately, if that's what you're wondering."

He shook his head. "The TSCRA guys can't help. They've already been out to the ranch. There aren't any tracks in the fields or even foot prints. My ranch manager hasn't checked all the ear tags yet, and we haven't finished branding the spring calves, so he told me to call back after

I was done. But I *know* they're missing, probably close to a dozen of them. See, I found *blood*."

"So . . . *what*? You think someone is slaughtering them on the spot? Right there in the fields?" That might well turn it into a case for her department. Rustling was one thing, but killing them would be destruction of property.

He ran fingers through his thick sandy hair and then pushed his metal-rimmed glasses higher on his nose.

"Yes . . . no. I don't know for sure. There's not *enough* blood, if you know what I mean—that's the problem. There's too much for a simple barbed wire cut or a coyote taking a calf or two, and Hank and I checked the animals for healing wounds. Nothing. But there's not enough for a full-fledged slaughter. It looks—and I know this sounds stupid, it's why I haven't made out a report yet—but, it really *looks* like something just swooped down, cut them up a little, and then carried them away. And *please* don't laugh and ask me about alien abductions. The ribbing from my wife is bad enough."

Cara's mouth went dry enough that a startled cough escaped her. It was the word *swooped* that did it. Had the birds—? She remembered Jeff raised Red Brangus, massive Brahma-Angus cross cows. The birds were certainly strong enough individually to lift a heifer, and two could probably manage a full grown bull. How much blood had those talons pulled out of Adam with just a few swipes? Her heart started to pound and she had to lick her lips before she could continue. "Which field was it? Is it part of your regular acreage?" The J Bar S spread was north of town, the opposite direction from the van, which would drastically increase the range they'd been considering. Or could there be more than one flock?

Jeff shook his head. "No. It was on a leased parcel, down near Little Coffey Creek. It started to happen a month or so ago, and we decided to move the cows back to the main ranch last week. But I can't keep 'em there for long. My whole west pasture will wind up overgrazed and covered in mesquite by auction time. I'll have to throw some straw as it is and with the drought, there's not much to be had. So anyway . . . could one of your deputies maybe . . . I don't know, maybe take a look around out there? Is that allowed without a report? That new guy at the TSCRA will get pissed if he hears I stepped over his head and filed a report with your office. He's really territorial and I don't need that sort of grief. You'd think for the amount of dues I pay, I'd make the decisions, but—"

That would answer so much—especially the mention from the birds that they attacked the van because they were hungry. If the cattle were moved, and the deer kept to the undergrowth where talons couldn't reach . . . which they no doubt would if they spotted a bird the size of a freaking hang glider, there wouldn't be any other game big enough to feed a full grown Sazi, except maybe feral hogs. She found herself nodding almost absently, because who would report *hogs* disappearing? They were a nuisance to most everyone in the county. She met Jeff's eyes as a glimmer of an idea came to her. She needed to start making some calls. "Sure. Tell you what—I'll do it myself, off-shift. Then nobody else will catch wind of it. If I find something that points toward a rustler, I'll call the Association. But I'll need a key to the gate."

The cool ozone scent of relief and gratitude burst into the air. Jeff pulled a key ring from his pocket as he spoke. "I *really* appreciate this, Cara. You have no idea. If you want, I can have Hank meet you out there to show you the blood spots we found. He covered them with rocks so the fire ants wouldn't eat up all the evidence." He handed her a small padlock key and his business card. "Leave me a message if you find anything, or if you want one of us to walk the fence with you. Oh, and you might want to take a shotgun with you. There was a whole nest of rattlers down by the creek when we moved the cows. We didn't bother to kill 'em since the cows were going anyway."

She nodded again, even though rattlesnakes didn't worry her nearly as much as the alternative. *Oh, I'll be taking along a shotgun all right, but it's going to be loaded with* silver *shot.*

IT WAS AFTER six by the time Cara finished a series of phone calls to game and cattle ranches around the region. Damned if there hadn't been a rash of disappearing animal occurrences, from cows and ranched whitetails to goats and even tagged exotics—elk and axis deer. But there hadn't been enough at any one location for people to put in a report. A call to the state park over at Devil's Sinkhole revealed that camper disturbance reports of feral hogs was way down this year . . . to the happy relief of the rangers. Her question of, "When did you start to notice?" showed that everything seemed to have started around March.

Why March? She tapped her pen on the yellow notepad in front of her, and took another sip of wretched orange soda . . . the last thing available in the machine. She really need to talk to someone about getting some decent selections in the break room, or at least getting it stocked more often.

Was it just sheer chance that a flock of birds had happened on her county during some sort of weird Sazi spring migration, or was there more to it? Did Sazi birds even migrate? She added a note to her list—*Ask Will about migration and food.* Just from looking at the number of missing animals, even if she counted some as escaped or natural deaths, there were *way* too many for such a short time. Her own pack only downed one or two deer a month on the moon. But the animals missing counted in the *dozens!* And she'd only called five or six ranches south of town.

Her phone rang and she reached out to answer it absently, going so far as to put the receiver to her ear before realizing it was her cell phone. She shook her head and tried to focus as she opened it and answered. "Sheriff Salinas."

The voice started her heart pumping and she felt a flush rise into her cheeks. "Um, hi. It's Adam. Did Lucas talk to you today . . . um, that is, *again*?"

Shit. So, he knew she'd stopped by and talked to him. Well, that made sense, she supposed. But it didn't help the churning in her stomach. "About that . . . I really want you to understand *why*—"

He interrupted hurriedly. "It's okay. Really. You don't have to explain. I found out when I stopped by to ask Lucas the same thing."

Oh. She didn't know quite how she felt about that. Did he have different reasons? Did he not like her pack or . . . "It's just that I didn't think I was being—"

He completed the sentence, with the exact words she was going to use. "*Objective* enough. Yeah. Me, too. Some days it sucks being a pack leader." A sad sort of chuckle found its way past the light static on the cell. "So, anyway . . . did Lucas get hold of you before he left?"

Left? "Lucas is gone? Why? What happened?"

"Yeah, that's why I thought I'd call. When you said how busy you were going to be . . . and, well . . . it's not the sort of thing you leave a message about. There's trouble back home—back in *my* home, Minneapolis. Lucas sent in a couple of other agents, one who has hindsight, to find out why I was sent down here. Apparently, *you* were supposed to kill me."

She felt her eyebrows raise until her forehead skin wrinkled tight. "I *was*? What on earth for? I didn't even know you."

"That was the point. I guess Josef expected that you'd react like *he* would when a strange wolf appeared in your territory without permission. But when the other agents showed up . . . do you remember Bobby Mbutu? Did you ever meet him?"

She nodded, still in a little shock about the idea that someone would think she'd *kill* another Sazi for just driving through town without calling first. Then she remembered he couldn't see the nod and blurted out a few sentences with a breathless quality. "The chemist? Sure. Agent Mbutu is one of the instructors at the academy. He nearly broke my ribs when he wrapped around me after I miscalculated him during sparring. But it's *hard* to watch both ends of a twenty foot python. He took up most of the damned ring!" She stopped abruptly. Why the hell was she babbling like this? It wasn't like her. "Oh . . . sorry. Didn't mean to change the subject. So anyway, what happened?"

He didn't even seem to notice. His voice sounded tired; weary, filled with no small amount of anger and shock. "All I've got is bits and pieces, but from calling and talking to Mom and David . . . that's my younger brother. . . . Bobby and Tony, the agent with hindsight, showed up and Josef declared war—without any provocation at all. Like he knew they were coming or something. Josef used the pack binding to force our lesser wolves to attack the agents when they walked in headquarters. I don't know what the hell he was thinking! I mean, Bobby might spend most of his days in a lab coat looking into microscopes, but he's no slouch in a battle, and I guess this new guy is a hell of a fighter."

"My God!" Her voice conveyed all the horror that had instantly chilled her blood. A pack leader openly attacking Wolven agents?! "Is anyone—" She couldn't even complete the thought. How could someone *not* be dead in that scenario?

Adam's voice took on a sad, soft quality. "Yeah. Three of our pack members, including Vivian's younger sister and our omega. I guess a healer had to be brought in for Bobby's partner, Tony. He managed to take down Josef, but got pretty messed up in the process. Lucas didn't seem too concerned about him, though. Said he's been through worse. But Lucas took the first flight out, about two o'clock, with Viv. The whole pack is in shock and I've got to get back. I know we were supposed to—" His voice sounded unsure suddenly, and she knew why.

"Oh! No, of course you have to go back. I mean, your pack leader is dead and you're the Second—"

"No, no! Josef isn't dead . . . at least not *yet*. Tony took him down with gunfire, but Lucas specifically ordered him not to be killed, so he just wounded him—but I guess it was one *hell* of a wounding, because Josef is still critical and he normally heals really fast. The healer had to put him under to remove all the silver bullets so they didn't poison him. Bobby told her to keep him that way until Lucas arrived. But it's a pretty fair bet what's going to happen, don'tcha know. So—" There was open air for a long moment, enough that she wondered if he was going to continue. She'd just opened her mouth to fill the void when he spoke again. "I guess I need to know from you whether I should *stay* there."

Whether he should stay—A buzzing filled her head like a hive of angry bees, and she couldn't quite pull her thoughts together. "I . . . that is—"

"Look, you don't have to answer now. I have to leave my truck at the airport in San Antonio anyway, so I have to come back at least for that. But the move is still on. I asked Lucas about that specifically. I have no idea what the fall-out is going to be from this. There are going to be plenty of people up there who'll blame *me* for everything that happened today." He paused and let out a growl of frustration before she could ask the obvious question. "It's a long story why, but trust me. And with everything happening down here with the birds and . . . oh! Before I forget, Lucas stopped by your sister's house and Ziri's going to stay with them until he can get back here."

"With *Rosa*?" She stood up in a rush, fast enough that her chair tipped over and hit the wall. Her first instinct screamed *no*! It was too dangerous. Her family could be a target. "Of all the stupid . . . *chingado*! What was he *thinking*?"

Adam's voice filled with chagrin and she could almost see him wince in her mind from the crashing sound. "Um, I'm afraid that's my fault. I suggested it. I know we didn't talk about it first, but I thought that since Gloria is the same age . . . and hey, Ziri can speak a little English now! Lucas taught her. He couldn't just leave her alone and . . . well, *someone* has to protect her until we find out more about the attack." His voice softened and filled with something close to pride. "You did a pretty good job protecting her before, after all."

Cara let out a small snarl over the line as she turned around to stand the chair back up. She had to replace one of the casters that had fallen out of the guide before sitting down again. He was trying to manipulate her. The annoying part was he was succeeding. She started taking slow, deep breaths while she drummed her fingers on the chair arm and considered the alternatives. Adam didn't interrupt.

Her reply, when it finally came, was filled with both exasperation and resignation. "Okay, fine. I guess there's no fixing it until he gets back. But I really wish he would have tried harder to reach me. I don't have a number for him and I found out a bunch of information about our feathered friends."

His voice filled with sudden interest, combined with no small amount of relief. "Yeah? Well, I'll be seeing him tomorrow around dinnertime. I don't have his number either, but is it something I can pass along? I could call you and tell you how he wants you to proceed, or have *him* call you . . . if you'd rather."

Did she want Adam to call—to keep in contact? She realized she did and, after all, she needed to report the information to *someone*. She fought to keep a smile off her face and wasn't sure if she succeeded in keeping it out of her voice. "Sure. That makes sense." She told him everything—from the meeting with Jeff to the calls to the ranches. "And it's not like anyone is going to miss the feral hogs. They get massive. . . . I've seen 'em as big as three hundred pounds, and the males can get really aggressive. But that's a lot of meat, just to feed three birds. It got me to wondering, ya know. So I figured the next step would be to go out the property and poke around a little. I'll see if Will can go with me, just to be safe and then we'll—"

"I want to see you."

"—head on over to the park and talk with the rang . . . what did you say?" It had taken a moment for his words, soft and quiet, to sink in.

"I want to see you. Before I leave tomorrow. It's just . . . even if it's just some coffee at the donut shop—if that's okay." Something threaded through the words, but she couldn't quite put her finger on it.

She suddenly wished he was face to face, so she could see his expression . . . catch his scent. She found herself replying before she even realized it. "Okay. So, what time's your flight?"

"Nine thirty. I figure an hour to get through security and two hours to get there . . . at least according to the motel manager. So, how about five thirty? Is anything open that early?"

She chuckled lightly. "You picked right. Just the donut

shop. It's open at five. I'd say we should make it five straight up, since you'll be hitting rush hour in San Antonio. You might need a little extra time on the road."

"Good. Okay then, it's a date." She didn't correct the term and wondered if he noticed. He paused long enough that he just might have. "Good work on the investigation, by the way. I can see why they tapped you for your post."

That made her smile. Not many people commented on her job. It was nice to hear from time to time, especially from someone who knew the difference. "Thanks."

"Go home and get some sleep, Carita. Sweet dreams." She didn't have time to do anything other than pick up her dropped jaw from the name before he hung up the phone.

Yeah, I'm pretty positive my dreams tonight are going to be at least interesting.

If she ever made it to bed, that is.

A WHITE PANEL van was parked at the entrance to the ranch, the running diesel engine causing puffs of black smoke to drift through her headlights before disappearing into the darkness. The painted banner on the side read, Santa Helena Fine Furnishings.

I could have sworn Tío Luis was going to drop off the table tomorrow. God, would this day *never* end?

She got out of the car and walked over to the truck. The man inside rolled down his window as she approached, and the scent inside made her mouth water. He must have just had dinner. "Is there any chance we can do this tomorrow, Tío Luis? It's been a really long day." Technically, he wasn't her uncle, but Paco's older brother, so her brother-in-law. But he'd always been so much older—even his children were older than her. And she loved him just like an uncle. He'd always been there for her, giving her all the guidance that her Papi would have if he'd lived closer. He wore the gray in his hair and the lines on his dark face proudly. He wasn't alphic and was starting to show his age.

He stared at her critically for a moment. "You haven't eaten yet, have you, *mija*?"

She shrugged. "I had some chips and a soda at the office. I'll be fine. I'm just really tired and want to get to bed."

Luis held up a small white container printed with Chinese symbols. The heavenly scent of fried rice, spiced beef, and vegetables made her stomach growl enough to be heard over the engine.

"Yeah, you'll be *fine*. That's what you always say. Good thing I know you well enough to have brought enough for two." He smiled and winked at her and it made her laugh.

"I'll get the gate."

It only took a few moments for them to move in the new coffee table, the final piece in the set she'd been buying for close to a year. She stepped back to admire the whole set. "It really does look as awesome as it did in your showroom."

He was busily plumping cushions and adjusting pillows as though it were still in the showroom, and then ran a slow hand over the back of the couch. Every piece of furniture he got into his store was babied until it made it to the right home. She tried to remember how many sales he'd turned down during her life, fearing the furniture wouldn't be treated properly. It was as though he was running a shelter for furniture instead of animals.

"You need to make sure you oil the table, *mija*. This dry climate is murder on good hardwood. This doesn't have—"

"Varnish on it," she completed. "Yeah, I know. Just paste wax. I just oiled the end tables last week, Tio Luis. You haven't let me forget since I brought in the first payment."

He smiled finally and sat down, patting the cushion next to him, and opened one of the containers next to the plates she'd brought from the kitchen. The next hour was filled

with eating terrific food and talking about silly things—
from the antics of his grandchildren to *Prima* Carmen's
latest diet and the plans for his float in the Cactus Days parade next month.

He shook his head and swallowed another bite of lo
mein noodles. "Psh! *Cactus Days*! The city council has
gotten way too politically correct. There's not a thing
wrong with calling it Tequila Days, just like it's been for
the last two centuries."

She shrugged. "Well, I guess they don't want to promote
drinking now that they're going in with the other counties
to advertise in the travel magazines. And it *is* the cactus
that founded the town."

"Yeah. The *blue agave* cactus! You know, the one that
makes . . . *tequila*. Santa Helena was for years the only
place this side of the Mexican border that grew all the mak-
ings of top-notch tequila."

"Until the *federales* burned it all up during prohibition in
the '30s. I know. And then . . . no more tequila. There's
only the one big one left in the town square, so why bring it
up? I think the name change isn't such a bad thing. It cut
way down on the DWIs at the carnival last year. Nobody
felt compelled to live up to the heritage."

He threw down another shot of pale sapphire liquor and
then brought a forkful of rice halfway to his mouth. His
scent turned into a confusing mix that clashed with the
spices in the food. "You can't hide from your heritage,
Cara. You shouldn't ever *try* to run from your beginnings—
nor be ashamed of them. You have to hold up your head
with pride and stare down those who would take it from
you. People here forget that sometimes, and it makes me
sad. I'm just thankful that you've always run this pack with
pride. I heard you talking with Raul the other day, telling
him the stories of how our people came to be here and how
we've always protected the people of Santa Helena. How

when the *federales* wanted to burn down the distillery—the whole town, the Sazi chased them off. You've never forgot our beginnings, *mija,* and that's good." He glanced at the small altar in the corner and dipped his head. "Your *madre* is proud of you, just as we are. I know she looks down and smiles for you not changing our ways and diluting who we are." He took the bite and chewed, nodding with fervent eyes that told his pride as much as his scent did.

Diluting. Was she about to do just that? Was there any way to make a bunch of timber wolves—Adam and his people—*familia,* without betraying all the red wolf Sazi who had come before her? She threw back another shot of tequila, closed her eyes, and tried not to think about anything at all.

But the image of Adam's strong jaw and broad chest wouldn't be banished. The vivid blue eyes haunted her long after she closed the door behind her uncle and chased her into her dreams.

Chapter 16

ADAM LEANED BACK in the plane seat, his thoughts too muddled to even be bothered by the acceleration as the jet took off, right on time. He hoped his bags made it onto the cart he'd watched being loaded, since he'd dived through the door at the last second after sprinting out of security.

While San Antonio's version of rush hour was laughable compared to home, he hadn't exactly gotten started on time. It was a good thing they'd set an earlier time to meet, or he would have missed the plane altogether.

A small smile crossed his lips. *It was worth it, though.*

The cheerful Vietnamese couple who ran the donut shop had ignored them totally as they sat at the back table and talked about . . . things. He'd just planned on talking about his people moving down, but it had evolved into a *real* talk—about morals and values and reasons for doing things. Even though they'd had to use a lot of euphemisms and roundabout terms, the information still came through. He'd learned why she left the Wolven academy and couldn't really blame her. Not everyone was cut out to handle the executioner side of the job. You can't force a person, even a Sazi, into killing when they believe it's the wrong choice, but Fiona had tried. One hide strip was imposed for refusing, and the other because Cara had taken her complaint to the Chief Justice, instead of going through proper channels. Of course, he'd sided with the Wolven chief because agents have to be able to take that last step, whether or not they *like* it.

If anything, Adam found he respected Cara *more* for taking her lumps and walking away, than if she'd stayed and caved in against her beliefs.

The safety video flickered on the screen at the front of the plane, but he'd flown so often he didn't need to look. Besides, he was enjoying remembering.

The time had slipped by so quickly, filled with too many cups—coffee for him and tea for her—and far too many warm, sweet donut holes, which the little smiling woman kept adding to the basket between them. They'd talked of packs and photography, plus movies and favorite meals . . . in the kitchen and the field.

"Here's your snack, sir. Would you care for something to drink?"

Adam looked up, startled, as a smiling flight attendant in a trim blue uniform placed a cardboard box on the tray in front of him and looked down, waiting for a response. "We have coffee and tea, or perhaps a soda?"

Another smile turned the corner of his mouth as he looked over the offerings on the narrow silver cart. "I think I'll have tea. Yeah, hot tea would be great."

He steeped it until it was about the same color, but it wasn't the same kind of tea. It didn't have the same odd, bitter flavor, but it was enough to remind him of the taste of her mouth when he'd kissed her—on impulse but very intentionally.

In the dim, quiet alley behind the shop, he'd pressed her up against her white truck with the gold and black star on the door. Her eyes went wide and a little panicked when he tightened his hands on her waist, right above her utility belt, but she didn't stop him except to weakly protest with nearly whispered words, "Adam, I—"

That's all he let her get out before he closed his mouth over hers and inhaled the scent of her. It wasn't the thick, nearly visible scent that drove him mad like the previous time. She'd used the Wolven cologne that Lucas gave her, but he could still smell the intoxicating scent of woman and wolf, pheromones that smelled soft and nice, and she tasted of sugared tea.

It lasted far longer than he planned, but time seemed to slow down until there was a crystalline sharpness to the moment. Their mouths and tongues had worked in comfortable unison—neither pushing for more than what it was. He memorized her body with his hands, every muscle and curve from shoulders to thighs and allowed her to do the same. But it was their magic that was the truly spectacular part. It swirled over and through them, raising every hair on his body with an electric breeze that took his breath away.

More than anything, it had told him what he needed to know. There was more between them than simple lust, born of instinctive needs neither could control. They related to each other on any number of levels. He *liked* her. But he also knew that he was the *cause* of her condition, or at least an accelerant. That was a bit of a worry. By the time he'd finally released her, her breathing heavy and eyes glazed, the scent was starting again. He left before it filled his mind—before his body refused to let him get into his truck.

Still—He took another sip of tea and patted his shirt pocket, feeling the thin cardboard through the fabric. *It was definitely worth a few miles over the speed limit and some frantic clock watching.*

He had her card, along with her cell number, and he would be back . . . even if just for one day, and one *spectacular* night. Oh yah. Definitely a night, followed by a leisurely breakfast in bed. He'd decided there was something here worth coming back for. Now he just had to find out if there was anything left back home that could still change his mind.

"READY TO GO to lunch, Cara?" Yolanda's voice cut through the fuzz that had been filling her mind all morning. Cara looked down to see she'd drawn another series of doodles on the budget allocation form. *¡Madre de Dios!* She could make another copy of the form, but how embarrassing was it going to be to call back Commissioner Hawkins to ask him to repeat everything he'd talked about for thirty minutes this morning? Some days she really wished the office was bugged so she could listen to the tapes. She vaguely remembered something about changing grocery wholesalers for the prisoner's meals, which was really important, but didn't know how it came up or the result. No, she'd been too *preoccupied*. Even now, she could still taste coffee on her tongue at odd times and Adam's magic had left phantom sensations that tingled her skin.

She blinked a few times, shook her head and smiled at her friend. "Sure."

It wasn't until they reached the little Chinese buffet at the edge of town and sat down with their plates and tall glasses of iced sweet tea that Yo said, with seeming casualness, "So, you gonna tell me about him, or am I gonna have to beat you bloody?"

Cara froze, the lo mein noodles hanging limply from the chopsticks halfway to her mouth. Then she let out an abrupt roar of laughter that would have turned heads if there had been any people in the room. No wonder Yo had chosen a back table in the overflow dining area!

Her friend grinned at her wickedly as she replied, "That obvious, huh?"

She snorted as she dunked her egg roll into a dish of hot mustard and lowered her voice to a near whisper. "*Ay, ay, ay, stupida*! I might not have your nose or ears, but I've got *eyes*! You've looked like a crushing tweenie for two days now!"

It was a gentle reminder that Yolanda knew about the Sazi, without being too obvious. Even the pack didn't know she knew, but sometimes Cara needed to talk to someone who wasn't right in the mess. It was fine to talk to Rosa about most things, but who was there to talk to *about* Rosa—when she'd been so depressed and angry after Papi left and made Cara's life a living hell? Or when Rosa refused to discuss problems she might have with Paco or Eddie? No, Yo had always been there to talk about things, little ones and big ones . . . way back to when she'd helped pick up the pieces of Cara's sanity after her first change at thirteen. When other girls were getting their first bra or period, she was trying to rule a wolf pack, and failing badly.

Yo had handled it well, taking in the concept of werewolves with a shrug—as though Cara had announced she was adopted. And she was an amazing sounding board, with good judgment . . . though lately Cara hadn't been talking about pack things because life had been quiet. But nobody knew the personalities in her pack as well, inside and out, and this might be a prime opportunity to discuss the Minnesota situation. She kept her voice low because the restaurant had started to fill with the regular lunch crowd. "Truck fodder," she said, and Yo nodded sagely. It was old code, saying the topic was too hot for public ears and they needed to eat quickly and then drive around town talking in the truck. On bad truck fodder days, Yolanda would drive so Cara could scream or cry without risking their necks. Thankfully, today wasn't one of those days.

They ate even quicker than normal, anxious to get done and paid. When they were safely in the truck with the air-conditioning blasting on the road out of town, she finally started to talk—about Adam, and the council's decision and, with some reservation, about the birds. They were all tied together and she couldn't think of any other way.

Yolanda took a slow, deep breath and then shook her head once. "Wow! That's . . . you've had an interesting few days, Lottie." How long had it been since Yo had called her something other than Cara or Sheriff or Chief? That nickname went way back to grade school and was reserved for their closest moments. "So, everything comes down to Adam, and whether you two end up in bed? Doesn't it all come down to that?"

Cara shook her head after an incredulous look sideways. She flipped on the blinker and slowed the truck before turning on the county road that would meander through thickets of live oaks and fields of wildflowers back toward the other end of town. It was their typical route and would get them back before the end of lunch.

"*What?* No. How could it? A dozen families, Yo—a *dozen*—are going to join the pack. Some rogue birds are killing people in my territory. How could everything I just told you possibly come down to whether or not we . . . well, whether or not I like him?"

Yolanda sighed with a long-suffering *how could you figure out this stuff without me* tone and ran fingers through her no-nonsense dark bob. Her natural scent of daisies and mums became laced with hot metal frustration.

"Okay, let's go through it. A dozen families are joining the pack. Yeah, there are housing issues and integration issues. But like you said about the Target store, that's easily solved. But if *Adam* winds up Alpha Male, what will the men think? Will they follow a *gringo?*" She held up a hand when Cara's mouth opened in automatic protest. "Ah-ah-ah. Don't you tell me you hadn't considered that! You know Paco, and Eddie *and* Luis. They might spout all the right words, but they're as racist as any guy in a pointy white hood and you know it. Paco's your Second and if Adam doesn't wind up the Alpha, that'll be where he sits instead. You're about to cut off your own *cuñado*'s dick, strip away your brother-in-law's pride; his identity. Go ahead . . . lie to me and tell me it's *not* why you didn't tell the pack about the council's orders the other night." She snorted and took a sip from the bottle of water they'd picked up at the gas station. "C'mon, let's hear it. I can't smell a lie like *they* can."

And she couldn't, because Yo was right. She clutched the steering wheel harder, instead of beating her head against it like she wanted to, and let out a small frustrated scream. "*Chingado!* What the hell am I gonna do? Adam's in Minnesota right now, but he'll be back—along with the others. I've got to talk to the pack, make them understand that we have no choice. But how the hell do I do that?"

A small chuckle beside her said she wasn't looking at everything, yet again. That was one of the best things about Yo. So many things occurred to her, all at once. The whole problem just *popped* into her head, complete with answers.

But Yolanda's answers were seldom what she wanted to hear. The truth was usually hard and bitter, matching the scent that filled the cab.

"It's time to face the music, Lottie, and you know it. It's what you've been preparing for since that first hunt with the adults—since the first time you had to defend your right to rule against the men. *You* are the Alpha, not Paco or Luis, or even Sharon. Yeah, they *elected* you, as such, but wolf packs aren't a democracy . . . no matter how much you want to play that game. You've got the brawn and the magic to turn them into quivering puppies. The election was for show. So it doesn't matter what they want, just like the council doesn't care what *you* want—'cause you're just a puppy to them."

Another sip of water while she waited for Cara to absorb the words, just like usual. "Your problem is you don't want to confront anyone, don't want to make waves. Just like you hold your tongue down at the office, even though you want to—and *should*—knock heads some days. Just like you didn't want Rosa, or *Adam*, to know how much you want to screw his brains out. No waves, no fuss . . . but no *cajoñes*, either. For the hundredth time, you really gotta get over that."

She didn't comment on that, but Yolanda didn't expect her to. It had been a long-standing dispute. "So, try to figure out how to tie the birds into that scenario. What do *they* have to do with Adam, Miss Know-it-all?"

Her friend shrugged, as though it was incredibly obvious, not taking any offense at the sarcastic tone. "Easy-peasy. The birds are the birds. They would have been here in either event. But you *didn't* follow them, track 'em down, and make them pay for their crimes . . . and that bugs the shit out of you. It bothers the *cop* in you. You stayed with Adam, stood over him . . . protected him, and then walked past every single iron-clad rule in your world to save his life. Face facts, Lottie. You opened your glands to bring him back—you did what *killed* your mom, what you swore to me on her *grave* you'd never allow yourself to do. You're tied to him and you *like* it. You think about the birds, and up pops Adam. You talk to Will, and up pops Adam. The investigation is part of the relationship . . . all tied up in a neat little package with his picture on the paper. You let him kiss you because you wanted him to. How much you want to bet me you'll tell him about your research before anyone else?"

She'd shut off the truck under a low hanging tree at the entrance to a field of bluebonnets and Indian paintbrush, letting the truth of the words wash over her as she watched the wind make patterns in the blooms. Her words came out as a whisper. "Fuck. I already did, Yo. I didn't have Lucas's number, and he was going to see him later today—"

"Pfft! You could have found the old man's number with one call, and you know it. Give it up, girlfriend. You're hooked and you're in deep shit. Just get over it and accept the facts."

God, maybe she should have let Yo drive after all because she just wanted to turn into a blubbering mass in the corner. A solemn, nearly flat tone invaded her voice, the resignation before the enevitable. "So, what do I do about it?"

She felt her friend's hand on her arm, and the rush of warm cinnamon and sugar into her nose from the comforting smile. "It isn't a death sentence, Lottie. I know it's scary, and way more so in your case. But just admit you liked Adam pushing you against the truck and running his hands over you while he kissed you . . . in that absolute stillness right before the dawn. No cars, no birds—just the two of you letting loose of your fears." The words caught Cara by surprise. She hadn't gone into that much detail. But Yolanda just shrugged and gave a little smile. "Uh, hello? I moved a week ago, remember? Duh! You were necking about ten feet from my bathroom window. Why do you think I asked?"

The laughter that bubbled out of Cara was so sudden that it nearly gave her a headache. Had she subconsciously remembered that when she parked behind the shop? *¡Madre de Dios!* How insane was that?

"You were such a puddle after he left—you sat in the truck without starting it for almost twenty minutes with a goofy look on your face—that I nearly came outside to check on you. So I can say with complete authority that you are *toast* when it comes to that man, and you need to stand up to your pack about him. Yeah, Paco will get a little miffed about it, but he'll get over it. Adam will have to prove himself, but he'll get over it. And you need to stand up on your hind legs and be a *woman* . . . which is about ten times tougher than being a man." She raised her brows and crossed her arms over her chest. "So, you asked for my advice, and here it is: You get your ass out there, find those birds like the awesome cop I know you are, and you sit your pack down and lay down the law. Then you call your man and tell him to get his sweet butt back here so you can strip him naked and have your way with him."

"Yolanda!" If her friend could smell emotions, she would find that humor was right underneath the embarrassment that flushed her face.

A broad smile flashed white teeth that nearly matched the paint job. "Hey, I just calls 'em as I sees 'em." But then the grin fell away, as though being sucked off, along with all the color in her face. Fear, bordering on ammonia panic, swept away the cookie spices. She was staring over Cara's shoulder and when her arm pulled away from her chest, the finger she pointed was trembling just a little. "But speaking of seeing 'em, is *that* one of the badass birds?"

Cara turned in her seat quickly, just in time to spot a massive owl sailing past the driver's window, probably the

one she'd injured as it was missing feathers on its leg. She
tried to imagine how Yolanda saw it, since she'd never gotten accustomed to the size like Cara had with Will around.
It had a wingspan nearly the length of her extended cab,
extended bed truck and was carrying a full grown hog in its
talons, already limp and bloody. It was flying parallel to the
road they were already on and the tree overhang would
hide the truck from the air if she didn't raise a dust cloud.

"Shit. Grab the binoculars from behind your seat and then
buckle up, Yo. We're gonna go do a little *bird-watching*."

Chapter 17

OTHER THAN THE extra cars parked in the lot outside the
private health club that served as pack headquarters, the
scene looked absolutely normal. But David, who had picked
him up from the airport, warned him he was going to be
shocked.

"So, how many Wolven people have showed up so far?"

His little brother turned the steering wheel and drove
down the line of cars before pulling into a slot. Adam recognized most of the cars—about a dozen pack members
were already here. There was a black SUV with Illinois
plates and two rental sedans he didn't know. "Just the original two agents and the council guy who's running the
force now. I don't know if they're sending anyone else.
Everyone's being really closemouthed. Mom was here earlier, but she couldn't handle the scene. Tommy and Jill and
a couple others have been cleaning up blood all morning,
so it might not be as bad as it was earlier. Remember that

steakhouse drive-by a while back? How there was blood and glass *everywhere*—floor, ceiling, walls . . . even splattered across the flowers?"

Adam nodded. His brother was on the local force, too. They'd both been working the same shift that night. "Yah. That bad?"

The laugh was brittle enough to make him wince as David turned off the key and unbuckled his belt. "*Waay* worse. When I left to pick you up, Roberta was on her way to the store to buy about a dozen pails of Kilz—the oil-based kind. The drywall soaked up the blood and it's going to stink to high heaven even after scrubbing. Personally, I don't care how much bacteria the stuff kills. . . . I mean, Tommy said it's good shit, he swears it worked when the sewer backed up in his laundry room last fall, but I think we're going to have to tear out a few walls in the reception area. I can't even imagine how the pack is going to respond next week on the moon. We're going to have a lot of freaked out wolves, smelling the blood of so many pack mates."

They were out of the car, walking toward the entrance when Adam stopped. David took a few more steps and then paused as well, waiting.

Maybe it was spotting his brother tense, or the scent of mild fear that drifted to him. But, like a small child who doesn't want to leave the safety of the covers to close the closet door, he wanted to enjoy the scents of *home* for just a minute before entering hell. He closed his eyes and inhaled deeply. It had rained the night before, and the air was cool and wet, filled with ozone and the scent of pink and yellow tulips, which had burst out of the planters around the front door. The smells were so very different than down in Texas, where purple lupines were a unique dark blue and daisies fought for the attention of his nose, and the air felt as though it would burn his lungs with each breath.

A distant siren made his ears perk and his brother likewise turned to the sound, not quite consciously. There hadn't been any sirens while he was in Santa Helena, except for the testing of the fire engines each morning. He was surprised to realize he had found it more than a little refreshing and even now, his muscles tightened as a second car joined the first toward a distant problem. Maybe he *was* getting burned out, even though it had never occurred to him.

"You ready?" David asked the question calmly, a hand on his jean-clad hip just above the chain that was always attached from his belt loop to his wallet. The scents of concern and understanding flowed from him.

Adam squared his shoulders and nodded. "Let's do it."

Even though David had done his best, there was no way to truly prepare for the sights and smells that hit him as he walked through the door. Multiple eyes turned as he opened the glass door that bore deep cracks and a scattering of bullet holes. They'd been covered by masking tape so they weren't obvious, but it was amazing to him that there wasn't any yellow tape blocking the door to climb under, nor familiar uniforms taking photographs of the scene.

It was the *lack* of things he noticed first. The comfortable leather couch was gone, and so was the grand old corner table, made of mahogany and marble. In their place were two of the white plastic patio chairs normally scattered around the swimming pool in back, and the small table from Josef's office down the hall. The walls were damp to his waist and the paint faded from scrubbing. But it was the smells that got him most . . . worse than he'd expected. Fear and pain, blood and bile that even ammonia cleaner couldn't mask. Over it all was the drowning deep scent of sorrow that covered everything like a dark shroud.

"Adam! Oh thank God you're back!" Jill Taylor dropped a sponge into a pail of foamy, pink-tinted water and threw

herself into his arms. She began to sob, clutching his back
with desperate intensity while her husband Tommy looked
on, appearing as though he'd like to do the same. Instead,
he raised his chin in greeting and set his jaw while blinking
back wetness angrily.

"Sorry you have to see this, Second." His voice cracked
enough that he stopped, refusing to give in to the urge to
break down.

Adam held Jill, petting her short blonde hair like a child,
while he nodded grimly back to Tommy, his friend for so
many years and the pack's Third. He and Jill had been one
of the families he'd considered taking down. "I'm sorry
you had to *live* it, Tom." And he was. He should have been
here, should never have left the pack in the care of a mad-
man. Tommy's rolled-up sleeves revealed gashes and
bruises, along with one hole with burned edges that told
Adam he'd been among those Josef had used as cannon
fodder against the Sazi agents. Nobody in their pack, save
those on the force, used guns . . . and certainly they didn't
have silver ammo that would char flesh.

David didn't meet the eyes of either of them. He just
walked past Tommy toward the locker room, his emotional
scent lost under others too strong and visceral. He hadn't
asked his brother if he had any healing wounds, and David
had been careful to shower with peppermint soap so he
wouldn't know. Peppermint could hide a world of ills and
part of him wished he could spray it all over the building.

Adam never would have believed this of his pack leader,
even if someone had told him—had predicted it. He would
have laughed at the absurdity.

"Thanks for getting back here so quick, Adam." Lucas's
quiet, serious voice from the hallway made him turn his
head and, strangely, fight back a growl. He reluctantly pulled
himself free from Jill's grasp. Tommy stepped forward and

eased her away, then put an arm around his shaking wife to lead her back to a chair to sit.

He started to follow Lucas down the hallway but turned back to look at the others before he rounded the corner. "Tommy." The older man raised his head. "Why don't you take Jill out to sit in the garden for a little while? I think you guys could use a break."

Tommy nodded gratefully and squatted down next to his wife, lifting her chin to whisper to her and kiss away her tears. Adam left them to deal with it, but he was definitely going to have to talk to someone about getting a Sazi psychiatrist in here to help his people pick up the pieces.

His people. Yah, underneath all his worries and fears of ruling them, he was the only leader they had now. He *would* protect them.

He walked down the hallway, trying to shake the scent of blood that permeated everything. Probably it had been a good idea for someone to remove the bulbs in the hallway. It was one thing to smell the blood, but the dark spatters and dents in the pale peach paint were a little easier to ignore in the dimness.

Lucas disappeared into Josef's office. Adam was a little annoyed that someone would just set up shop in a private office, but then again, it really wasn't Josef's anymore— not if *he* had any say in the matter.

Adam walked in to find that Lucas had planted himself behind the desk. This time he did growl, low and meaningful. The older man raised his brows and nodded before relinquishing the chair to him without a word. What in the world was he doing, growling at the Wolven Chief? Was he suddenly feeling suicidal? Did he *want* someone to kick the shit out of him? He didn't approach the chair, but something in the action by Lucas satisfied whatever was bothering him.

Two other men were in the room, which had been remarkably spared from the battle that raged outside. They
were sitting in the high-backed wing chairs and looked
suitably weary while sipping whiskey from lead crystal
glasses. Adam recognized the slender dark-skinned man
who carried the dusty scent that said *snake* and he dipped
his chin in greeting. "Hey, Bobby. Sorry about all this."

Bobby stood up and took one step before leaning forward fluidly and holding out a hand that looked like a
puppy had used it for a chew toy. "Been a long time, Adam.
And don't worry. We know none of this was your fault."
Adam shook the hand firmly, because Bobby would be insulted at anything less, before leaning up against the desk.
Bobby nodded toward the third man. "You met Tony Giambrocco yet?"

He shook his head and looked Tony over. He was about
Adam's own age, with dark brown hair and blue gray eyes.
It was obvious he'd taken the brunt of the attacks the day
before. A gash from hairline to neck sliced through the corner of his mouth. It was slowly healing and his throat had
obviously had fangs try to tear it out. Tony was likewise ap-
praising him, watching his every movement with eerie
calm. He picked up his glass with a black gloved hand and
raised it in a light salute that revealed a shoulder holster
with a loaded .44 revolver under his suit jacket.

Adam didn't find it difficult to imagine this man as an
assassin. He had that cold, empty look to his eyes that said
yesterday had been all in a day's work. If he saw this person in a crowd, he'd be the focus of attention—the single
threat to be watched. Tony's thin smile didn't reveal a thing
about what he was actually thinking. The only surprising
part to Adam was that he was one of the *good* guys here.
He probably should acknowledge that. "Thanks for your
help yesterday, Agent. Lucas said you tried hard to keep
casualties to a minimum."

Tony smiled with the same black humor he'd expect from one of the guys in the squad room and chuckled lightly. "Well, I kept *deaths* to a minimum, anyway. Bobby took care of those. But casualties . . . no, most of them were mine. I just wish it hadn't taken so damned long to *find* Josef—the fucking coward. He was hiding in the back room, directing the other wolves like puppets on parade. It was pretty clear there was nobody home in the eyes of the first ones to attack us. Once we put him out, the rest of the pack snapped to and stopped trying to kill Bobby and me." He stopped and cocked his head and all the humor dropped off his face. "But you . . . I imagine you would have been out in front of the troops in the same scenario. It's probably best you were somewhere else. I would have seen you as a threat."

A dark smile, closer to a baring of teeth, came to Adam's face as Tony took a careful sip of amber liquid, wincing a little when it apparently stung the wound. "Likewise, I'm sure."

Lucas cleared his throat and they all turned their attention. "Adam, the only reason Bobby and Tony are still here is I wanted them to meet you. You're all agents now, and I'd prefer for agents to start to meet each other in controlled settings. They're on their way to Ziri's village to question her family, via Santa Helena. I'm hoping you have a direct number to Alpha Salinas, so I can let her know they're coming. I think Tony can manage what I couldn't in finding out what Ziri saw."

He reached for his pocket and extracted the card. "I do, and that reminds me—Carita did some research down there and found out some information about the . . . situation." He wasn't sure if the others knew the details, but they must at least know something to be going down to investigate. "Should I give you the intel now, or would you prefer it in private?"

Leaning forward with obvious interest, Lucas smelled

pleased and slightly amused, but he didn't know why. It was then that Adam noticed he could actually smell Lucas, who now revealed an underlying scent of cactus fruit and prairie grass, along with sweet curiosity. And, like at the restaurant, he was keeping his power inside. Actually, he realized he scented Lucas in the outer room, sharing the pain and anger of the wounded pack. It had probably helped him be allowed to walk through the building unmolested, where the Wolven cologne might be a liability when everyone's nerves were on edge.

"No, please go ahead. What did she find?"

Adam told them all about her conversation with the attorney, and how she'd tied it together with the missing animals. "She told me as soon as she can hook up with Will, she's going to check out the property."

Lucas turned his attention to Bobby, who was taking notes in a strange sort of shorthand that was nothing more than squiggles and swirls. It wasn't the sort secretaries used to write—his mother had done some typing for an old lawyer when he was a child, and that was different, though no more legible, than Bobby's. Still, he seemed to understand it, because he was reading back over it from time to time, mouthing words. "Bobby, when you get there, check to see if she's gone out with Will yet. That's Sam Cloudsfall's present identity, by the way—Will Kerchee. He's a Texas Ranger. If Will hasn't been able to fit it in, take an afternoon and help her out. But remember it's her territory and she's a fellow agent. It's her game down there, so if she doesn't want your help, back off. But," He raised a finger and pointed at Giambrocco. "Tony's session goes on with or without her permission. That's straight from Charles. I'll let her know that when I talk to her."

The Chief Justice had ordered Ziri be questioned? This was sounding like a lot bigger deal than he'd first thought. Was there more to this than a simple case of rogue birds?

Lucas stood up and pushed back his chair. "Okay, time for you guys to take off . . . before the other pack members get here. I think they've seen enough of you two for awhile."

Before he could even register the thought in his brain, Adam took a step forward and spoke, the inflection in his voice flat and commanding. "*No.*"

Lucas raised his chin and motioned to the others to obey, as though he was expecting the interruption. Confusion roiled through Adam as he tried to figure out why he stopped Bobby and Tony from leaving. The older wolf must have noticed. "You're not sure why you're feeling so aggressive, right? Trying to figure out why you're counter-manding my orders?"

All he could do was nod, furrow his brows, and try to figure out how to respond.

"You're an Alpha in your prime, and there are unattached wolves nearby. You're seeing me as a threat, even though it's not on a conscious level. Growling at me for being in the center chair, taking the final word on directions . . . that's all the wolf talking. The best thing to do is ride with it. Those who might challenge you for the top slot are going to be aggressive to you now—meet your gaze, snarl, or growl. You'll probably have a few fights on your hands during the next days if you stay."

Adam blew out a slow breath. It made sense and yet it didn't. "But I've never wanted the pack. I've been content to be Josef's Second."

That pulled a laugh from all three men, but it was Lucas who spoke. "You've been content to be Second because Josef *convinced* you that you were—as part of the pack binding. I've done it myself with some of the more aggressive members of my pack. In centuries past, the newly crowned Alpha would simply take on all comers, defeating . . . and usually *killing* the lesser alphas. Leadership challenges are to the death, after all. But that's tricky to explain in today's world, so the council recommends to new alphas that they *first* try to use magic to lessen the aggression of powerful alphas in their pack. But without Josef here, the need to rule is starting to eat at you. And it will eat at others, too." He paused significantly. "But that's not why you stopped them from leaving, is it?"

While Lucas had been talking, Adam had tried to think just what did make him stop the pair from leaving. Yes, there was something to what Lucas said about feeling aggressive, but that wasn't everything. "I need to see for myself." He dipped his chin to Tony. "You can do that, right? You can let me see what *really* happened here yesterday . . . with your gift?"

Tony shrugged. "Yeah. Can't imagine why you'd want to, but I can do it." He glanced around the room as though looking for something. "Here's as good as any, I guess. Bobbo, how about you go sit on the other side of the room. I doubt you're interested in a rerun."

"No lie." The tall African stood up and walked over to join Lucas at the wet bar in the corner.

Tony looked at him again and started to pull off his gloves, tugging to get the tight leather peeled off his fingers. "Okay . . . choose your victim."

"Excuse me?" Adam felt his brows raise as he stepped closer. "What do you mean?"

Lucas responded. "Hindsight is a very unusual seer gift. Instead of seeing random flashes of some unknown future, the seer is drawn into a past scene—through the visceral experiences of a person who lived it. He can touch a person and sift through their memories, then use his gift to project those events to a third party. So, you'll be able to view the events that person lived."

"*View* . . . yeah right," replied Tony dryly after an intentional snort. "Don't expect just a simple viewing. Maybe other seers get lucky and just get visuals. But so far I can't do that. I'm too new at this to do much more than pause, rewind and fast forward, if I can even make them dredge it up. No, you'll be getting a roller-coaster ride of sights, sounds, smells, and sensations. You'll feel every claw tearing your skin and taste sweat, blood, and bile on your tongue. You'll hate it or enjoy it, just as that person did, so pick carefully who you want to be attached to, or you might see a lot more than you want. The victim . . . I mean, *subject* won't notice a thing, but unfortunately, *we* can't pull out of there until they're done with the event. Memories are sort of like podcasts—short loops of time that replay when triggered. Freud would have been fascinated with some of the things I've learned."

"Freud?" Adam couldn't keep the surprise from his voice. "You've heard of Freud?"

The scent that rose from Tony was a blend of amusement and annoyance, a caramel citrus mix, even though his face was a blank slate. "Uh, yeah. Psychology minor, business major, in case you care. Testing the soundness of his theory of unintentional verbal utterances being attached to memories, what most people call Freudian Slips, has become a bit of a hobby of mine lately. *Anyway* . . . the best I can do is fast forward a memory pod, and that's a case by case thing. Oh, and you won't really be sure while it's happening that you're going to survive." He chuckled lightly as he tucked the gloves inside the pocket of his jacket. "I'm your ticket inside the world's most realistic video game . . . no quarters necessary. If I could find some way to market this shit to EA Games, I'd be a friggin' billionaire." The smile he gave had more than a little challenge to it. "Sure you're up to taking a dip in *my* pool, tough guy?"

Adam ignored the sarcasm. He was starting to realize he might not be giving the man in front of him enough credit. Perhaps there was a good reason why Lucas trusted him enough to send him here. He felt his chin dip once, sharply and squared his shoulders. "Whatever my wolves endured, I'll endure. You were both there. Who would be the best person to view through? Someone who was there from beginning to end."

Tony looked over at Bobby, who shrugged. "How about that one wolf who met us at the door?" Tony suggested, "The little blonde with the short hair who's been cleaning up—she was the one who did your hand, right? I know she gave me the claw to the face."

"Yeah," replied Bobby with a skeptical look. "She'd be a good pick, if you've got a strong stomach. But she was probably most strongly under Josef's control, so I'm not really sure how much she'll remember. What was her name again? Jane? Julie?"

"Jill?" As much as he didn't want to, he felt himself stiffen. Jill seemed so terribly traumatized by the event. But maybe that was the point. If she was there the longest—"You're sure it won't hurt her? I don't want to cause any damage."

"Actually, it'll probably *help*." Tony seemed confident, almost casual about his ability and Adam felt himself being persuaded, almost against his will. "I can bury the memories pretty deep when I leave, so it'll be like forgetting the details of childbirth—or so I'm told. Personally, if *that's* what childbirth is like, I'll stay home and send my wife in a cab so she doesn't rip my face off."

Bobby laughed but it had a nearly fearful edge. "At least your wife is human, so she isn't physically capable of ripping off your face. Mine is not only capable, but occasionally *eager*. I think I'll be hiring you to make Asri forget all about it. She's not the forgiving type." He looked directly at Adam and shuddered. "Don't ever knock up a Komodo dragon, kid. The fun isn't worth the pain." He stood up before Adam could ask more about this woman Bobby had tied himself to. He nearly opened his mouth to ask when he realized it would only avoid what was to come. It was so much easier to banter and tell war stories than to walk into the war.

"Speaking of pain, let's do this." Adam's voice sounded flat to his own ears, and it sobered the mood in the room.

"I'll go get her."

Adam could hear murmuring in the corridor outside as Bobby opened the office door, which disappeared when the latch closed again. He realized just how well insulated the room really was and it seemed strange he never noticed it before. After a deep sigh, he raised his hands before asking the obvious question. "So, what now?"

Once again Tony shrugged. "Bobby comes back with the woman, you do the touchy-feely stuff to make her feel comfortable, and she sits down on the love seat with me. I'll ask her one or two questions to jumpstart the memory you want. Soon as I touch her, the game starts. Her eyes will shut—that's my own twist on these sessions, by the way. It's probably not necessary, but it helps the person focus, and other people keep their distance. Now, once that happens, I'll hold out my hand." Tony paused and lowered his voice until it was a warning rumble and pointed one finger at him. His scent became filled with determination's hot metal with a hint of burnt coffee anger. "*Do not*, under any circumstances, touch me *until* I hold out my hand. The last two people who did that got a bullet in the head. They were damned lucky I came to before I pulled the trigger a second time."

Adam fought down his initial response at Tony's scent and words, which was to leap forward and reach for the man's throat, make him show more respect. Wow! Lucas wasn't kidding about feeling overly aggressive. He managed to tense his muscles and remain in place and keep his voice calm, but there was tension at the edges that he struggled to control. "I don't like that. I'd prefer you put your sidearm out of reach."

The smile in reply was a baring of teeth and the words sarcastic with a distinct Italian accent. His scent was calm, but hovered on the edge of hostility. "No. I'm a fucking three-day, who'll be in a trance and will be surrounded by people who have already tried to rip my face off. *Capisce*? I don't think so. Next question."

Behind Adam, Lucas let out a sigh. "Tony keeps his gun during sessions. End of discussion."

What in the world sort of hold did Tony have over the Wolven chief to make him continue to side with him over caution? Adam shook his head and held up placating hands. He was glad they were on the same side, but really didn't want to deal with him ever again.

He opened his mouth, but was saved from responding when the door opened. Jill was nearly shaking as she entered the room and began to rub her arms. No doubt she was feeling the sting of magic from so many Alphas gathered in the same place. Lesser wolves would often avoid pack headquarters altogether when Josef was in one of his moods.

She flicked her eyes up briefly to meet his before lowering them again and ammonia panic flowed in a rising wave. "Have I done something wrong, Alpha?"

The trembling in her voice made him soften his reply and project an aura of warmth and concern. "No, of course not, Jill." He held out his hand and stepped toward her. "There's nothing to be afraid of. I'm just trying to find out a little more about what happened, and these gentlemen said you were there when they arrived. We'd just like to ask you a couple of questions, if that's okay."

She nodded, almost shyly and offered her hand. It was sweating and cool and her scent such a chaotic mess of emotions that he began to sneeze.

"I'm sorry." She winced just a bit. "I'm trying to control them, but I just can't seem to manage it."

"Maybe I can help you." Tony's voice had gone soft and warm, giving Adam even more insight into the man. "How about you sit down here and I'll see what I can do about that. I'm a healer of sorts."

Jill's eyes rose hopefully and then noticed the gashes on Tony's face. A hand flew to her mouth. "Oh my lord! Your face! You're a healer? But you're not healed yet." Shock and sadness drifted to the top of the pile of scents.

Tony only smiled and it reached all the way to his eyes. "Nope. I'm not that sort of healer. I'm a three-day, just like you. But we're *both* going to be okay, right?" He patted the cushion next to him, leaned back into the posh leather, then crossed one ankle over his other knee and put an arm on the back of the love seat. It was a seemingly casual series of motions that Adam realized was carefully planned.

She nodded, shaky at first, but then with a little more confidence. "Yeah. We're going to be okay." She walked past Adam to sit next to Tony.

Once she was seated and looked reasonably comfortable, Tony began. "So, I know we went over this before, but now that Adam's here, I'm sure he'd like to hear it directly from you. About what time of day was it?"

"It was early afternoon. I'd come on shift just after lunch, and had been there about an hour, so I guess around two o'clock."

"There was a—"

"What were—" Adam interrupted, starting to ask the next logical question of "What were you doing when the agents arrived?" when he felt Bobby suddenly appear near his shoulder and a firm hand squeezed the back of his neck. He stopped short when he realized Jill's focus was on him, rather than Tony and the other wolf was shooting him a warning look. He was interfering in a process he didn't

understand. "Sorry. Never mind. Please answer Mr. Giambrocco's questions, Jill. I'll just listen."

Her eyes turned back to Tony reluctantly and Bobby removed his hand. "I'm sorry, what did you ask?"

"There was a bell ringing when we first arrived. What
was that?"

Her eyes lit up. "Oh! That's right, we were just finishing
a fire drill. I'd forgotten about that. It was pretty loud,
huh?"

Tony chuckled. "Yeah, sort of hurt my ears when we
first walked in and we couldn't hear each other very well."

This time, Jill snorted and crossed her arms with a mild
expression of annoyance. "It hurts my ears *every* time. I
mean, I know it's important, but I wish the security company would give us a little more warning before they do it
remotely. I mean, we have people in the *shower* half the
time."

"Oh yeah," Tony said with a laugh as Jill's arms uncrossed and she rested one hand on the cushion near his
knee. "I'd be more than a little annoyed if I had to race outside in a towel just to discover it was a drill." He paused
and dropped his arm off the love seat back until his fingers
were very close to hers. "So, we sort of had to shout to understand each other at first."

She nodded. "Yeah. You know, I didn't think it was any
big deal that you were visiting. Josef is the Alpha, after all.
He gets lots of high-profile visitors. People are checking in
all the time. I took your card—"

"Just as the alarm turned off. It was completely silent for
a moment."

"Like your ears just popped," she agreed with a nod.
"Then I asked you to sit down and picked up the intercom
to tell Josef you were—"

At that moment, Tony reached forward and took her
hand in his. Jill froze, mid-word, and began to shake with

intensity for a moment. Then her eyes closed and she relaxed back into the plush leather bonelessly. Adam watched, fascinated, as Tony's eyes began to twitch under the closed lids. He started to move closer, but Bobby pulled him back. "Don't do it, man. He'll tell you when he's ready."

Tony's voice drifted from the love seat. "Yeah, I'm still here. Just sifting. I got her pretty close to the start . . . just need to fine-tune a bit." More eye twitching and then he reached up his other hand, eyes still closed. "Grab a chair and then take my hand when you're ready. I've paused it right where we walked in."

Adam did as instructed. He rolled the desk chair around to the edge of the love seat and sat down. He closed his eyes and reached out his hand, but paused at the last moment, feeling supremely nervous for the first time since waiting to learn if he'd been accepted into the police academy.

"Haven't got all day, Alpha. Let's do this."

It startled Adam and he jumped, causing their hands to connect. Abruptly, the world dropped out from under him and light filled the darkness behind his closed lids. He heard Tony's voice as though from a distance. *Okay, the ride's about to start. Make sure your hands and feet are inside the car and the safety bar is locked in position.*

Before he could figure out how to respond, a loud ringing assaulted his ears and he winced. He was seated at the reception desk in the next room and the air smelled of tulips and chlorine. Sunlight danced off the crystal vase on the table, filled with pink and yellow blooms. The door swung open and two men walked in the building. As though sharing two brains, Adam both knew the men as Tony and Bobby, but also didn't know them at all. They were strangers, but one smelled of fur, and he felt himself smile. The voice that came from his throat, unbidden, was feminine, but was drowned out in the cacophony of noise.

"Can I help you? Sorry for the noise. Alarm testing will be done in a second."

The tall African-American man cupped a hand to his ear and leaned closer. "What?"

He felt his throat constrict and force words out louder. *"IT'S . . . NEARLY . . . DONE! CAN I HELP YOU?"*

Adam heard Tony's voice again, but it was outside the context of the scene. "Let me move forward a bit. Lots of useless conversation here until the bell stops." Again his head swam as sound and motion rushed by him in a blur. It was enough to make his stomach heave.

The next sensation Adam felt was intense pain—so strong that all he could do was scream, over and over until his throat was hoarse. Another bit of narration didn't help ease it. "Sorry, overshot the mark. But now you know first-hand how Josef turned them against us. We'll go live from here."

When Jill/Adam's eyes opened, the world was overlaid with red and fear and anger were being pressed on her/his mind with a force so intense that it was all Adam could do to keep his sanity. *Kill them . . . kill the strangers!* The voice was low and urgent, pushing at the back of his mind until there was nothing but the need for blood—the need to kill these invaders into her home. For the first time in her life, she shifted without the moon. A tiny logical part of her mind knew it to be a strange and dreadful thing, but there was no stopping the fur from flowing.

"Shit! They're going wolf on us!" Jill/Adam heard Bobby's warning and leaped over the desk before the snake could run. Blood flowed as teeth grabbed a dark hand and began to gnaw. Sweet copper filled Jill/Adam's mouth and the tangy scent of pain and fear made her chew harder on the hand. The blood also called pack mates, who surged from the hallways to join the hunt.

A gunshot rang out just as the snake used stinging magic

to throw her away to hit the wall. A second shot came too quickly to truly distinguish it from the first and Adam heard Tony's voice over the snarls and howls. "Lucas said not to kill anyone, Bobby!"

A sharp snapping sound ended with a yelp. Jill/Adam sniffed at the wolf on the floor. Tabitha, their Omega, was no more. But she wouldn't be the only one to fall. "Lucas isn't here, and there are more of them than us! Do whatever you have to so we can get to the Alpha. He's gotta be pulling the strings! Want me to shift your form so you can move faster and fight better?"

Another gunshot, snarls, and the sound of breaking glass as the dark-haired man that Adam knew was Tony spoke. "Oh *hell* no! These guys might be three-day dogs on the moon, but right now they're fighting like they're on angel dust. There wouldn't be enough left of me by the time I got down the hall to make a decent fur collar on a jacket. There's nobody home in these eyes. I'll stick with ranged weapons, thanks. Toss me your Ruger if you're going to shift and see if you can clear me a path with some of that magic you're always bragging about."

Another wolf joined the fray . . . her *mate*! But no, he was trying to stop her and she couldn't allow herself to be stopped. She bit at his throat and he yelped when her teeth sunk past fur and skin. Part of Jill/Adam's brain rebelled. She hurt her *mate*! That can't be. Must . . . stop. Must . . . must . . . *kill*. The pain was too much, the magic too strong for her to resist. The strangers *must die*!

The man with the gun turned his head, which was all the time Jill/Adam needed. With a leap, claws raked down his face, and the man crumpled into a heap, screaming and swearing. But he rolled out of the way and kicked at her hard enough to cause her to smash into the table. It collapsed into shards of wood and stone and stunned her for a moment. The dark-skinned snake shifted and coiled

around another pack mate until it dropped away, dead. Five
more furred forms emerged from the rear of the building to
attack his multicolored length and he lashed out at them
with power, teeth, and tail. Blood splattered across her
face, and marred her vision until she could blink enough to
clear it. The man with the gun jumped over two snapping
wolves and started to sprint down the hallway. He began to
kick open doors, while shooting at wolves that got in his
way.

Jill/Adam followed carefully, stalking until she could get
a clear attack. *Kill him. You* must *kill him, Jill!* Josef's
voice was powerful and his magic more so. Her pack leader
must be obeyed above all else, and she threw caution to the
wind. When the intruder's foot raised to kick in the door to
the room where her Alpha was hidden, she struck. She rode
him down through the doorway, teeth and claws tearing at
whatever bare skin she could reach. But it wasn't enough to
stop him—nor was the painful surge of magic from her Alpha. She was blown back through the door by the swell of
power, unable to breathe against the press of stinging
magic. The man swore and stumbled, and then let out a primal yell as he pressed forward, twin revolvers firing shot
after shot until the Alpha finally went down in a bloody
heap, unconscious.

The power and pain finally stopped, so abruptly she
crashed to the floor. Jill came to her senses, and her human
form, in a cringing heap in the hallway, hearing the screams
of her fellow wolves fade into whimpers and crying. She
was covered in red and she *hurt*. There was too much
pain . . . too much blood—

Just before the world went black, Adam felt one more
thought cross the woman's tattered mind.

Lord help me . . . what have I done?

"And that's about it until she woke up on the couch in
the back room with the others." Tony's calm voice didn't

hold the horror that it should. There was no anger from him toward Jill, nor the other wolves—but also none of the revulsion or the fury that clawed at Adam's own guts. It made him literally sick to his stomach to have watched people he knew—people he once led—be driven to the edge of madness.

He could sense a small amount of regret in Tony, or was it from his mate? The sensation felt more feminine, and sad, at the carnage he'd been forced to cause, just before the Wolven agent slipped inside himself again. "I'm going to let go now, so I can finish up with her in private. You might find it a little disorienting."

Disorienting wasn't quite the word for it. Adam woke on the floor, heaving up the last of the donut holes and coffee from breakfast, until there was nothing left but bile to be spit onto the bloodstained Oriental rug, which he doubted would ever come clean again.

Nobody spoke at all while he sopped up the mess he made and Jill came back to consciousness. She didn't remember the hindsight session, and found it a little disturbing that time had elapsed in the room she couldn't recall. Still, she *did* seem calmer walking out of the room than when she'd walked in, for which Adam was grateful.

Lucas's voice was soft. "You doing okay after that, Adam? Need to talk about it?"

Adam shook his head and felt his stomach churn again. "Talking about it is the *last* thing I want to do, if you don't mind. It's a bit much to wrap my head around."

Tony nodded and started to slide his leather gloves into place once more. Adam was forced to wonder what it would be like for someone like Tony to be pulled into Wolven crimes so strongly that he lived them. "Understand fully. I'd like to say I'm used to it, but it'd be a lie. Still, at least you know what you're dealing with when it comes time to decide what to do about Josef. We'll take off now, if that's okay, Lucas. I need to crash for an hour or so." The older man nodded and it was just a few minutes later that Tony and Bobby left the room with appropriate closures and then Lucas walked to Josef's bar.

He pulled down a pair of glasses from the shelves. "Name your poison." He turned his head and the filtered light from the Tiffany style shade turned his silvered temple a pale green. "Thankfully, that's not literally. I've already had Bobby remove the poisoned bottles. Josef really *had* lost it."

What the fuck! Shaken, he sat down in the chair vacated by Bobby. "Um, Stoli, I guess. That's what I normally have."

Lucas scanned up and around and then looked down toward the floor on the opposite side of the bar. "Ah. Apparently, we know the target of the poison now. How about Absolut?"

"Yeah. Sure. Whatever." All of this was just too much. "How could I not have noticed he'd lost his mind? Enough to destroy the pack—everything he's built up his whole life? Could Tyr dying really be the cause of all this?"

He wasn't really asking Lucas, just mulling under his breath, but the older man sighed and sat down, pushing the glass of clear liquid across the table, past the ones still bearing a trace of whiskey. Leaning back into the cushions with a confusing mix of scents, he shook his head.

"I wish I had an answer for you. For what it's worth, it looks like a lot of the pack will wind up supporting you in this—if it *was* Tyr. Yes, there are some who think you brought all this down because of your decision that night. But most realize that Tyr challenged you for his own reasons, and having those skiers spot the hunt the night you led the pack was just a convenient excuse to take you out." He took a sip of what smelled like brandy and tapped one finger on the side of the glass. "Something to think about, by the way. Maybe you want to send those who *don't* support you down to Texas. The number is about right to achieve the goal."

That raised his head, nearly frantically, which twitched Lucas's brows. But before he could shout out the "No!" that threatened to burst from his mouth, Adam stopped to really consider the idea. Life here in Minneapolis would go on, and those who were left would probably be glad to have the dissidents . . . those who supported Josef's actions yesterday, gone. And those who went would be happy to be rid of him. He hadn't gone far enough with Cara's pack that they would know the difference, but how far had he gone with *Cara*—? "You said she would have a voice in that decision."

Lucas nodded. "That I did. And those who went down wouldn't have a very good opinion of you. I guess it depends on how your first meeting with her pack went. If you hit it off, then sending down people who hate you might cause friction. But if those people stay up here, *this* pack will suffer." The shrug that followed said everything, and nothing. "Like I said, there are no easy answers. The council's decision was clear. The Alpha in Minnesota would be the one to make the decision. There hadn't been a vote on allowing Cara to be involved. There's no question after this fiasco that you'll *be* Minnesota's Alpha." The soft chuckle was one of both frustration and comradery. "This is going to be one of those annoying decisions you're probably going to regret in hindsight no matter what you choose."

He was spared thinking up a response to that when there was a knock on the door. Bobby had closed it when he and Tony left. Adam turned his eyes to the carved wood. "Yes?"

The door opened smoothly inward and David stuck in his head. Behind him in the hallway, looking both nervous and slightly nauseous was Vanessa Wright, who was always the first to pitch in during any crisis. She was good at it, too, so it was nice she was here.

"Adam? Sorry to interrupt, but I really think you and Chief Santiago need to see this."

He glanced over at Lucas, who raised his brows. They both stood and followed David out the open door and farther down the hallway toward the recreation room. "Nessa was cleaning up the rec room and . . ." David turned his head backward to look at the pale-skinned beauty, a dairy queen pageant winner in her teens, "How about you tell them how it happened?"

She nodded with tiny movements, and the intense scent of surprise mingled with fear. "Well, the mess wasn't really too bad down there, and I figured we'd need somewhere for people to gather later because . . . well, the reception and weight rooms where we normally meet are trashed right now. I was really just straightening it, because a couple of the pinball machines had been shoved around and the couch was against the wrong wall."

Vanessa paused, because they'd reached the room in question. Adam walked in and discovered that one of the wood paneling sheets had a hole in it about the size of his head, just below the chair rail that separated the paneling from the painted drywall. David moved his hand in a sweeping gesture toward the hole while Vanessa continued.

"I lost my balance when I was moving the couch because it got caught on the rug. When I reached out to steady myself, my hand went right through the wall. Now, I've worked at this club since we opened it as headquarters nearly a decade ago, and I *never* had any idea there was a room behind that wall." She turned to Adam. "Did you?"

Adam felt himself rear back and he looked to David for confirmation. His brother nodded. "You *really* need to take a look in there, bro. Josef had apparently gotten himself into some really weird shit." He held out a flashlight for Adam to take.

Lucas stepped forward with him and they both crouched

down in front of the hole. The first thing he noticed was a pale orange light from a computer CPU in standby mode. He turned on the heavy black aluminum flashlight and an involuntary swear burst from his mouth. "Holy shit!"

Chapter 18

"ARE YOU REALLY sure this is a good idea?" Yolanda's voice was a low hiss from inside the cab. She was alternating looking into the binoculars through the windshield, and watching Cara undress. They'd followed the owl until it disappeared into the shadowed depths of one of the canyons where Cara had raced Will.

"Following it is the only way to find out what's happening. There's no road down there. We'd get stuck. But I know that canyon like the back of my hand. I'll be fine." She hurriedly removed her bra and panties before carefully folding everything and putting the clothes behind the driver's seat. "You just concentrate on covering our tracks. Remember, call in the tag on that abandoned car we spotted hidden in the mesquite grove and think of something to buy me a little time." She thought of herself in wolf form and felt magic start to shift her body. Today it didn't feel nearly as painful. She was grateful for that. Maybe she still had a little residual magic from Lucas helping her along.

She heard Yo gasp as the fringes of the magic pressed against her, making her cringe and press herself against the truck door. That was no surprise. Most humans had an instinctive fear of predators, and the Sazi energy that went with it.

Cara shook herself when she reached all fours and she heard Yolanda slide over on the seat until she could see out the driver's window. She heard a sharp inhaled breath. "*Ay Carumba!* Sweet Mary, you really *are* a freaking wolf! That is you, right?"

It occurred to her then that while Yolanda had known about the Sazi in the abstract, today was the first day she'd gotten an actual glimpse into their world. She tried to keep her voice light, but it always came out slightly deeper than her human voice, with a trace of growl. "Yep. I just remembered this is your first time seeing me this way. You okay?"

She nodded, but her eyes showed quite a bit of white. "I . . . I'll get used to it. I think. For the record, though—you're a really *pretty* wolf. I never thought you'd have the same color hair . . . that is, the same color *fur* as your hair."

Cara jumped into the air slightly as a test, forcing most of her weight down on her forelegs when she landed. Her arm had been feeling a little weak since it fractured, and she wanted to make sure she would be able to handle jumping from rock to rock in the canyon. It held, but twinged a little. Still, it would have to do. She looked up at her friend with warmth and let her tail wag once.

"Thanks. Now remember . . . stay out of sight and in the truck. If any of those birds spot you, hightail it out of here and call Will on the phone number I gave you. He'll know what to do." She raised up her front legs and placed them on the window jamb, causing Yolanda to back up a little nervously. "Do me a favor and put my watch on my front leg. I'll try to be back here in thirty minutes."

Yo picked up the watch from the dashboard and reached forward, stopping before she actually touched her. She gave Cara a sideways, suspicious look. "You're not gonna bite me, are you?"

Cara rolled her eyes and raised her nose to the sky in frustration. "*Ay ay ay, stupida*! Would you just put the damned watch on? We don't have all day." The snarl that followed the words probably didn't help. She let out a slow breath and looked at her now nearly panicked friend, being careful to flop down her ears and look suitably helpless. "Sorry, Yo. No, I'm not going to bite you. I haven't yet . . . even when you stole my date for the prom. If I was going to bite you ever, it would have been *then*!" She winked and Yolanda finally laughed.

"Okay, okay. I get the point." She reached forward, no longer afraid, and buckled the watch through the braided leather band, making sure it was fairly tight into the fur so it wouldn't slip off. "But, for the record, Josè asked *me*. I didn't steal him."

Cara lightly dropped back to the ground. "Of course, it was just sheer coincidence that the door to the AV room locked on you both the same afternoon he left me a note to meet him after school."

Yolanda met her eyes with a deadpan expression. "Absolute coincidence . . . that took the better part of a day to set up." She grinned then and Cara let out a quiet snort that wasn't quite a bark. "Now, you'd better get your tail in gear, um, *literally*. Oh, and I figured out our cover. Remember those goats back near where we found the Chevy? I'll tell dispatch they got out while we were checking out the car." The light scent of black pepper drifted to Cara's nose at the creative lie. "It might take a few minutes to put them all back."

"Great idea! Maggie and Bob raise goats. She won't expect us back for awhile." Cara shook herself once more and scanned the sloping hill, searching for the quickest route. As she started down, she heard Yolanda on the radio.

"T-6, dispatch. Me and the Chief are out on CR four-one-eight, northeast of the Rocking L spread. I need a registration check on a gold Chevy Caprice, plate Thomas-Xray-Robert six, four Beta two."

A brief rattle of static caught Cara's ears before the reply. "10-4, T-6. Should I start a second unit rolling to you?"

"Negative, dispatch. No need. Oh, and we're gonna be a little late getting to base." Cara snorted at the faked sound of embarrassment that flowed easily through her friend's voice. "It seems a herd of goats found their way out of the gate while we were trying to get a plate number."

Just before she reached the bottom of the canyon, she heard Maggie's amused voice. "Copy that, T-6. Y'all have fun. Try grabbing a back leg on the kids, and watch out for those billies. They're ornery when you get 'em riled. Oh, and you might be able to lure them with a big live oak branch. They love those. But I'll pass the word along."

The sounds from above faded away as she reached the edge of the canyon fifteen minutes later. She paused to listen and catch the scents on the wind as they flowed through the cool shadows. They'd watched for long enough through the binocs that she was certain the owl hadn't flown out the other end. So, it was still in here somewhere. She just had to make sure that she found it before it found her.

She picked her way among the rocks with care, avoiding patches of loose rock in favor of the bases of massive junipers and boulders. It was during one of her frequent pauses to listen that she finally heard the sounds of feeding—the thick, wet tearing sound like good silk ripping, along with the scent of blood. She eased forward, keeping her body in shadows and the wind in her face. Rounding the last corner finally gave her a view of the owl along with five others! Three were smaller than the one with missing feathers and the other who'd attacked them yesterday. Unfortunately, none of them were talking so she couldn't determine gender or nationality. The turpentine scent of the juniper branches she was peering through contributed to her nausea as she watched the feeding frenzy.

¡Madre de Dios! The viciousness the birds exhibited was

both fascinating and terrifying. She watched as the owls tore at the quickly disappearing hog, the big male's snout now gone so the teeth were exposed in a grisly smile. They screeched and pecked at one another, flapping to keep balance as they fought over each scrap. In the background, she could see an older model gray van, similar to the one they'd found earlier. *But I didn't think there was a road into this canyon.* That deserved more checking, but cautiously. There were far too many of them for her to handle.

Cara eased backward, planning her route behind a series of boulders so she could see better. She crouched, wiggled her hindquarters, and then leaped lightly to her first hiding spot. She stopped as soon as she landed, watching to make sure none of the birds noticed. But then the stinging bite of Sazi magic and a dusty scent from *above* her froze her in place.

The sizzling sound that followed pounded her heart. It was an all-too-familiar noise in this area, and it wasn't a good one. The hissing, nearly whispered words that followed didn't ease her mind any. "¡*Hola*, leetle wolf! You startled me, sometheeng that does not too often happen."

Definitely male. Spanish is his first language, with a South American flair. The greeting was amused and quiet, as though he had no intention of raising an alarm. Yes, a mild citrus scent joined the dusty one. She looked up to find a dark brown rattlesnake resting on top of the boulder in the cool shadows. But this was no ordinary rattler. Its length was easily ten feet and his chest, where it rose up from the rock in a characteristic *S,* was as big around as a cantaloupe.

There was intelligence in the slitted yellow eyes. He had the advantage and he knew it. She could only move backward or forward. There was no side movement available between the cliff face and the boulder. But moving forward would put her in view of the birds, and backward would put her on uneven footing in a slippery pile of caleche. It was why she'd jumped here to begin with. She remembered that a snake could only strike about a third to half its body length, but that was on level ground. Here, he could simply jump down on her and had Sazi speed to boot.

Reason with him? Put on a good show? It was a tough decision to make in only a few seconds. She decided on a combination of them. She kept her own voice to a whisper, but let calm and authority flow through it. "Who are you and what are y'all doing in *my* territory?"

The sizzling sound stopped as he relaxed the long string of rattles in his tail and he lowered his head so it hugged the lichen-covered boulder before easing into the harsh heat. He flicked out his tongue and regarded her for a moment from less than a yard away before opening his mouth, flashing his fangs in the sunlight. She struggled not to back up. "That is none of your beesness, leetle wolf. You'd do well not to ask too many questions."

"People have died. That *makes* it my business. But this doesn't have to involve you, amigo. The birds are the only ones I'm interested in—unless you helped, that is." The unspoken threat hung in the air between them for a long moment.

A light series of short hisses gave the impression of laughter. "Oh, I helped, leetle wolf. I definitely helped. I didn't *eat* the humans as they deed, but they didn't go far after a taste of my venom, *muchacha*."

Had they looked for snakebites among the other wounds on the bodies? She smiled, taunting. "You're bluffing. I don't think they'd let you play. I'll bet they didn't even offer to share that hog down there with you—and it pisses you off." She would have remembered this scent and it definitely wasn't present in the hospital. Sazi snakes and birds sometimes worked together, but the prejudice was always there, hiding just under the surface. Maybe she could encourage that rift.

A burst of fiery peppers in her nose told her she'd been right. The rattling started again and he hissed. "Enough of theesss! Tell me where the girl isss." His S's were becoming more pronounced the angrier he got.

That drew her up short. Is that why he was talking to her . . . they were still hunting for Ziri? Another flash of worry burst through her, but she stopped it quickly. "I don't know what you're talking about."

The snake eased forward, his tongue flicking repeatedly. "You're lying to me, *muchacha.* But perhaps you'd be weelling to *trade.* Geeve me the girl—"

Cara put more weight on her back leg in response to the snake's movement. While she certainly wouldn't reveal Ziri's location for any reason, there might be some value in stringing him along. He paused long enough that she was forced to ask. "And you'll give me *what* in return?"

The snake's eyelids blinked upward and he opened his mouth, revealing the pinkish white maw that was nearly the size of her whole head. He breathed out a slow hiss, filling her nose with the scent of dead, decaying rat and rabbit. "I'll geeve you your *life,* leetle wolf. Otherwise, I weell call my friendsss over to play." He paused and hiss-laughed again. "You wouldn't eenjoy that. But *I* would."

She bared her teeth and tensed. It was time to end this. She was definitely outnumbered. "Go to *hell.*"

"You firssst." He reared back suddenly and she moved, narrowly avoiding the strike as she leaped backward. She turned and bounced her front legs off the cliff face and ran . . . harder and faster than she ever had in her life. She had to get back to the truck to call Will. She couldn't afford to fail.

Cara didn't have to wonder if the snake was following

because she could feel his hot breath on her heels and stinging magic try to hold her in place. She had to pick up her feet quickly to avoid his fangs and prayed that he couldn't jump into a strike while slithering. Faster and harder she pounded over the rocks, not caring about the branches that slapped her face, and the cactus that embedded in her paws. Nothing she tried seemed to be an obstacle for the snake. He flowed over the tallest boulders and skirted the trickiest corners. And with each movement, she had to fight against the web of magic he threw forward like a net, trying to slow her enough to grab her with his teeth. She was weakening and there was still the hill to climb. But when she spotted the truck, she realized Yolanda was standing outside next to it, scanning the valley with the binoculars. *Damn it*! She didn't dare scream a warning, since only silence had allowed her to get this far without alerting the birds. Thankfully, the snake didn't want their help, or she'd already be caught.

On her first leap up the hillside, she felt the rocks under her give way. She scrambled for purchase and felt a moment of panic before her claws dug in. Adrenaline flooded her body and she felt a sudden burst of reserve strength, like a second wind, that pushed her forward even faster. She climbed hard, doing her best to push as many rocks as she could down behind her to slow the snake. When she heard a sharp swear in Spanish, she knew she'd hit him with at least one.

Finally, she saw Yolanda's gaze turn toward them and her friend froze, watching as the massive rattlesnake followed her up the hill. She had to lead the snake away from her friend, but there was no time to shift direction because the snake could see the truck as easily as she could. He might decide a hostage would be a good bargaining chip. Instead, she called on everything in her, forcing her muscles into a blur of movement until she pulled away from the rattler.

She leaped over the top of the slight overhang where they'd parked and issued a command to Yolanda who was surrounded by a cloud of ammonia-scented panic. "Go, go, go, go! I'll keep him busy!"

Dropping the binoculars, her friend obeyed with wide eyes and frantic movements—just managing to get in the truck and close the door before the snake whizzed over the top of the hill.

Cara risked a glance behind her. Her pursuer put on his own burst of speed and, now that he was on level ground, caught up to her when she looked. He threw himself forward and tripped her, sending her into a tumble that would have her pulling rocks from under her skin for a week, if she survived at all. She wound up smashing headfirst into the trunk of an old live oak, hard enough to send leaves scattering down into her face.

"And now, wolf beetch, you're going to tell me everything I want to know."

She shook her head, trying desperately to clear it from the pain and fuzz. The snake was poised over her, smelling of dark glee, his fangs already showing a drop of venom at the tip. Sazi venom could easily paralyze, or even kill, her. And from what she'd heard in Wolven, a skilled snake could inflict a slow, painful enough torture that other agents had revealed every secret in their head.

Shit! She struggled to stand but there was no room to get her feet under her and her legs weren't working right from the tumbling fall. He was going to torture her. Her mind worked frantically while the snake flicked his tongue and waved his upper body in triumph, readying for the first strike. A wild thought crossed her mind. *What if he can't bite me?*

As pack leader, she could hold her wolves from changing on the moon, in case they were in danger of being seen. She could also use her magic to call them back from their fur. Could that work here? She concentrated, forcing every ounce of her will, every bit of her remaining strength, into a single ball of energy inside her. Then, when the snake reared backward, she sent it forward, striking the snake in the chest. She didn't know what he looked like as a man, so she concentrated on the *shape* of a human and pressed a violent wave of magic in and through the snake, forcing him to shift back.

He wasn't expecting an attack like that and couldn't counteract it fast enough. He shifted to human, revealing a slender clean-shaven Latino man with nutty brown skin and nearly golden eyes. He rested on his hips, his limbs flopping uselessly. She knew the arm and leg bones hadn't yet hardened after the transformation from cartilage. It was something she learned while sparring with Agent Mbutu. The snake was now both at his most vulnerable, and his most dangerous. He could use each limb like a separate snake, wrapping them to choke or crush. She memorized his face in the brief moment she knew she had before he could orient himself to shift again. He had a number of healing scars on his torso, reinforcing that he and the birds weren't getting along too well. But then she noticed a black tattoo on his inner forearm. It was in the shape of a triangle with wings, with a wavy line cutting down through the center.

He laughed, his voice deeper than in his snake form. "That was a useless waste of energy, *muchacha*. And one I weel make certain you pay for."

The growing roar of panic in her head as he prepared to shift turned out not to be in her head at all. The man quickly twisted his head until it was completely around like a scene from a bad horror movie. A burst of surprised scent rose into the air, followed by ammonia panic, just before he started to slither away from her. Too exhausted to move, all Cara could do was close her eyes and brace herself as a sparkling chrome truck bumper came racing toward them at breakneck speed.

Chapter 19

ADAM COULD ONLY stare into the hole in the paneling with increasing fury. Pinned all over the walls were photos of girls—dozens of them—some who appeared to be as young as twelve. None of them looked happy. In fact, most of them had a look of abject terror on their face. Lucas tapped his shoulder. "Move that light to the left, over by the file cabinet." He did so, but Lucas pointed up to about head level on the wall. "A little higher."

Adam realized just where he was supposed to stop, because when he reached the right spot, he paused, his mouth suddenly dry. For there on the wall were two photos he recognized. One was of Jennifer, Tommy and Jill's fifteen-year-old daughter. And the other—

Lucas's voice sounded as angry as the scent that rose from him in a choking cloud, mixed with the sharp, sour scent of disbelief. "Now, what in the hell would the pack leader in Minnesota be doing with a photograph of *Ziri* on his wall?"

"I don't know," Adam said through gritted teeth, "But I think we need to find out. Let's get down to the pack clinic and wake that bastard up."

Lucas nodded thoughtfully, tapping his fingers on the edge of the ripped paneling. "First, I think we need to find out the scope of what we're dealing with here. Let's get this out of the way so we can get inside. Since the computer is just on hibernate, we might get lucky and not need a password to get to the files. All we really need is a couple reams of paper and we can have *specifics* to confront him with."

Adam stood and backed away from the wall. "I can handle that. We just bought a bunch of new office supplies before I left. They're in the storage room in the basement." He motioned toward his brother and then toward the hole in the wall. "How about you take care of getting this paneling out of the way while I'm downstairs? Lucas, can you—" He snapped his mouth shut, realizing he'd just about ordered the Wolven chief around like one of his pack members. Lucas wore a bemused expression, rather than an angry one, and the carmelized coffee scent of his anger had a brief touch of citrus.

"No, that's fine. Wolven's role is to be an asset to local packs affected by crimes. What would you like me to do . . . *Alpha*?"

A slow deep breath blew between Adam's lips with the startling realization that he *was* the Alpha now. Whether he stayed here or went back to Texas, he was the Alpha Male of a pack, and it felt really *good*. "It's just that everything is happening so damned fast. This is a major crime scene, but I can't call any of the people I normally would to help. Could you . . . would you *mind* taking some photos of this room before we touch anything? I want credible, untouchable evidence to prosecute his ass before the council. We have some good photo equipment in the cabinet in the reception, if it wasn't destroyed in the battle."

Lucas nodded and waved a hand toward the hole in the wall, and the photos beyond with a disgusted look on his face. "Consider it done. You might also consider checking any of the other computers in the building for signs of . . . *this* sort of crap."

"Will do." Adam raced from the room and the sound of splintering wood followed him down the stairs at the end of the hallway. Just as he reached the bottom of the stairs, he suddenly felt dizzy again, his head swimming and vision fuzzy. He paused and put one hand on the wall to steady himself as a wave of fatigue overcame him in a flash. It passed quickly, but his heart started pounding and he had to struggle to breathe for a moment. *Wow, what was that?*

Shaking it off, he walked down the short hallway to the storage room. He had to look around twice before he found any supplies. Nearly all of the items he'd put down here personally just a few short days ago were missing.

"Yah, there are definitely going to be some changes around here." The words were said almost under his breath as he picked up two reams of laser paper, but they were no less true for having no other ear to hear them. He shook his head and turned out the light.

Halfway up the staircase, his vision narrowed and his heart started to pound in his temples again. This time a sensation of fear accompanied the fatigue, as though from a distance, and a feeling of desperation panicked him.

But why am I panicking? Could he be getting some residual visions from being attached to Jill? He felt his eyes go wide and his breath come in short pants as the reams of paper dropped out of his arms onto the stairs, splitting open and raining paper down to the bottom. He clutched at the slender wooden handrail and tried to call out to the others. But no words would come as fear became terror so great it seized his throat.

Oh, Yo . . . no please . . . you wouldn't! Adam couldn't figure out what the thought even meant, and though he struggled to keep his grip on reality, he felt a tearing sensation deep inside his stomach that was both painful and pleasurable. A swell of powerful emotions—anger, fear, hate, and something even stronger engulfed him just before every bit of his energy was pulled forcibly from his body. A grunt escaped him like something impacted his chest, and the same something then lifted him and threw him through the air. He felt himself falling and knew there was nothing to be done. Strangely, though, as pain filled his body and the world went black, part of his brain accepted the sensation as good and right.

IT WAS NEARLY dark when David held out another stack of papers, still warm from the laser printer. Adam absently tucked them under the pile already in his lap with an incredulous shake of his head that shot pain through his forehead.

He must have winced, because Lucas looked him over critically. "Adam, you look like crap after that fall. You doing okay?"

Adam nodded and took a deep breath, feeling a dull ache radiate through his ribs. It reminded him of getting the flu when he was ten. Every muscle and joint felt stiff and sore. He moved his hand to the back of his neck to rub away a little of the tension. "Marginal. I still feel like a truck hit me. I haven't blacked out like that since I worked a triple shift during a hostage standoff . . . probably a decade ago."

David stood up and stretched his back, which shifted his shirt enough for Adam to finally see the series of deep bruises that covered his torso. "You're damned lucky you didn't break your neck, tumbling down the stairs like that."

He shrugged. "I'll heal. Let's just finish this up before I get so tired I forget to be pissed. What in the hell did Josef think he was doing?" Each page he scanned was worse than the previous one.

Lucas ran fingers through his hair in frustration. His voice held the same furious astonishment that Adam was feeling. "And how many fucking years has this been going *on?* How could he have hidden an operation of this magnitude from *everyone*?" He turned glowing golden eyes to them and lashed out with magic, causing the bulb in the table lamp to flare momentarily. Adam braced for pain, but it stopped just short of hitting either he or David.

"I swear to you there was no *hint* of this, Lucas. You already questioned everybody who showed up at the meeting tonight and nobody lied. We have to face the facts . . . none of us—the council included—ever conceived that Josef was capable of running a child slavery ring over the Internet. But it does explain why he was willing to use the pack to kill Bobby and Tony when they came knocking."

David tapped another series of keys and the printer started to spit out pages again. "And it explains why he had to get rid of you, too, Adam. Having the council pay attention to our pack meant his every move was being watched. He had to get attention away from himself. Killing you and starting an investigation down there would have done it."

Now Lucas started to tap his fingers heavily on the wooden chair arm, nodding in agreement, the scent of his anger no less, but now other emotions added to it. "It's those two pictures that make me wonder most, though. Jennifer said Josef had never spoken a word to her when her parents weren't present. She didn't attend pack meetings and, while she was starting to show symptoms of turning, she hadn't had her first change yet. Was she just a *potential* target? Did he change his mind when she started to smell of fur? And how did he get a picture of Ziri when all that just happened?"

David's voice held frustration when he turned away from the computer screen that had been hurriedly moved from the secret room to the desk here. "I haven't been able to break the password on his Internet e-mail yet, and he hasn't used any of our pack accounts for this . . . business. I'm wondering if he might be trying that new trick that some of the terrorists are using. There aren't any e-mails sent between the parties. They just *start* an e-mail and save it as a draft. Then the other people log on with the same username and make their additions to the information before saving it again. Since the e-mail is never sent, there's nothing to trace—no partners or contacts to find and without the password, or a court order to open the account, we're screwed."

Adam added his thoughts to the mess after picking another slice of pizza out of the box and taking a bite. A black olive slice dropped off the crust onto the top page and he tossed it in the box with the others. "Even worse, there's no way of knowing if Josef is supposed to log on at a specific time to keep the ball rolling. We might be risking sending his contacts scurrying by taking the time to read all this." He picked off a couple more olives and then finished the slice in three bites. Supreme wasn't his favorite, but he hadn't been the one paying.

Lucas sighed. "There's no helping that. Tony called from the hospital. He wasn't able to find a thing. Josef is still in the deep coma the healer put him in, so there's no mind to *touch* right now." He paused to flip the edges of the growing stack of papers and then motioned for Adam to pass over the pizza box. "We've got better code-breaking software at headquarters. I'll get someone there to start on the e-mail account." Opening a new bottle of water, the elder wolf took a long drink before taking the last slice, then looked Adam from head to toe while he chewed. "We might as well call it a night and start again in the morning."

Adam picked up the stack of papers, stood, and deposited them on the desk in front of Lucas, fighting off a yawn. "How do you want to secure the scene? We can't just let pack members wander through here. And everybody has a key to the place."

Lucas nodded. "I'll be staying here. I don't really plan

to sleep, but the couch in the rec room folds out if it comes to it. That'll do, and I'll know immediately if anyone comes in. But I want to get as much information as I can tonight. Charles is pulling the council together for a conference call in the morning, so I can bring them up-to-date. You guys go ahead and take off. Oh, and try again to get hold of Cara before you hit the sack, Adam. I'm a little worried she hasn't returned any of our calls. Not even the *official* ones David left at her work number, pretending to need information on an active case."

He nodded, trying not to let on just how worried he really was at her silence. Adam knew logically that she was perfectly capable of taking care of herself, but something was chewing at the back of his mind. It was probably just his imagination, but he had the feeling something had gone very wrong today.

It wasn't until he and David were walking to the truck to go home that his brother commented on it. There was no particular scent attached to the question, and he kept his voice carefully neutral. "You're worried about her, aren't you?"

Other than his mother, his brother was the one most likely to spot a lie. But an acknowledgment wouldn't hurt. He looked up at the starred sky as he opened the door. They weren't as bright as down there. It was something he'd noticed when he was hunting the deer. He shrugged. "She's tough. I'm sure she's fine."

"It's a damned slippery slope."

He didn't comment further, so Adam turned to him after they were both in the cab and buckled up. "What is?"

David started the truck and turned on the headlights. "It was during that three-alarm fire last fall for me." Adam looked at his brother questioningly as they turned out of the parking lot. He'd just opened his mouth to ask, when David continued. "I knew Bonnie was on shift that night, and when I started to hear calls for ambulances—" He paused and stepped harder on the accelerator to bring them up to speed on the road. "I know a bunch of guys at the firehouse . . . shit, I have friends in *three* firehouses, don'tcha know. But I was only listening for *one* name on the box when they reported the roof collapsed." He turned his head after they were stopped at the red light and had a small smile on his face. "Her hair still smelled like smoke when I asked her out on a *real* date the next day. Like I say . . . slippery slope, bro."

Adam couldn't think of any response, other than, "Fer sure."

Chapter 20

CARA MOANED AND moved the flexible white ice pack to a different bruise, letting the cold seep into her skin to numb it. The timer flicked on the porch light and Yolanda reached over to turn on the lamp next to her feet. She moved her legs on the couch slightly in automatic response and winced. ¡Madre de Dios! Even her *toes* hurt!

"Do you want me to put some more ice in a sandwich bag or something? The doctor said it would help with the swelling. Or will they all be healed before I could make it back from the kitchen? It's just fricking *weird* to see bruises disappearing while I watch."

She opened her mouth to reply, and felt the side of her lip split again—then glared at her friend, who hadn't been much of a friend today. "I cannot *believe* you actually hit me with my own truck!"

Yolanda waved her finger in a teasing way, even though she smelled contrite. "Ah-ah-ah. A goat butted you *into* the truck. Don't screw up the story. And I hit you to save your life. You might have bruises—"

She raised a finger, her eyes still closed as she tried desperately not to breathe deeply. "And cracked ribs. Don't forget about the cracked ribs, because I sure can't."

"*But*," Yolanda continued strongly enough to make her open her eyes. "You are not snake bit . . . or dead."

Cara heard a noise on the front porch and tried to sit up, but Yo waved her back and peeked out behind the curtain cautiously with her hand resting lightly on the grip of her sidearm. She turned her head and spoke in a normal voice. "It's cool. Will's back." She walked to the door and let him in before returning to sit down in the old wooden rocking chair with a low, pitched creak.

Will looked down at Cara over the back of the couch. There was concern in his scent, despite the blank, professional look on his face. "You're looking a little better. That gash on your forehead is nearly healed. We can probably cut those stitches out any time." Then he turned to Yolanda. "*This* is why we don't go to doctors. Don't ever do that again."

Yo shrugged and then shook her head. "Well, when Cara told me you guys heal really quick, I was sort of thinking *days*, not minutes. I mean, I couldn't just leave her out in that field, and broken bones with blood means the hospital in my own sad experience."

He snorted. "You're just damned lucky they took so long to get to you and she woke up before they started doing too many tests." Will reached down and gripped Cara's chin, turning her face into the light. The movement sent sharp bolts of pain through her eyes and she reached up to swat away his hand. "Fortunately, other than the cut, which is going to take some fast talking when you go into work tomorrow, the rest of it you can fake by just moving slow and wincing from time to time for a few days. And if you forget, people will just think you're playing tough."

"Yeah, yeah. I'll heal. Let's all hear it for the amazing Sazi healer. Everybody just ignore the fact I got run over by a freaking *truck* today." She shook her head slightly, winced again, and moved the ice pack to another bruise. But it had warmed to room temperature so she tossed it on the coffee table with a small noise of frustration. "So, enough about me. What did you find out over there?"

Will hooked his thumb at her while looking at Yolanda. "She always this grumpy when she's hurt?"

Yolanda rolled her eyes and smelled of equal parts of amusement and frustration. "*Chinada*! You have no idea. Ever since kindergarten, when she fell off the swing."

Cara nearly laughed, but kept a small amount of annoyance in her voice so she wouldn't totally lose the battle of feeling sorry for herself. "You mean, ever since you *pushed me* off the swing."

Now Yo let out a small chuckle and pursed her lips lightly. "Eh, pushed . . . fell. You only got a scraped knee and still went whining to the teacher. Wuss. Besides, *you* were the one who said Sazi were 'ruthless, but efficient,' if I remember." She raised her fingers to put imaginary quotes around the words. "Using the truck was *both*. I mean, it was a fricking *rattlesnake* the size of an anaconda about to bite you! Well, at least until you turned it human again. But it was too late to stop the truck by then. After all, *I'm* only human."

Will finally gave in and laughed and Cara did the same. She was actually really proud of her friend. It had taken a lot of guts to intentionally aim a speeding vehicle at her best friend, *and* superior officer, without having any idea what the result would be. She turned her eyes to Will. "Did you find any sign of him? Yo says he took off when she shot him in the shoulder as she was getting me into the truck. And what about the birds?"

"Wish I had better news." He leaned back into the plush, brightly colored pillows on the chair. He nodded his chin toward Yolanda but kept his eyes on her and laced his fingers together over his chest. "I found the spot where Yo shot him, but lost the trail when he made it to the rocks. He deliberately started moving through the junipers to hide his trail. Nice job on getting off a shot, by the way. That's no easy thing with an alpha Sazi." He raised his brows with a small smile while Yolanda preened, kissing and waving to an imaginary audience. "I got some blood samples that I'll give to Bobby for testing when he gets here. We might be able to match him, if he's known in our files. Same with the composite of his face and that tattoo."

He must have noticed Cara's curious expression and scent, because he elaborated. "Bobby and his partner are on their way down here, according to Lucas. They'll be here tomorrow. Oh, and they've been trying to reach you all day. It's why Lucas finally called me to come check on you. I know you said your cell phone got busted up during the accident, but you might want to call Adam, so he knows you're okay. I just talked to Lucas on my way over here. There's all sorts of weird shit going on up there and a lot of it has to do with what's going on down *here*."

"Such as?"

He just shook his head. "Call Adam. He knows more than me, and I don't want to mess it up. Anyway, the hog carcass was still there, but other than a few feathers, that's *all* that was there. They broke camp and took the van, but managed to scatter the tire marks with mesquite, so I couldn't even track them. I found evidence of six separate birds, including the two original owls and eagle, so you were right about that. But no snake, other than a few scales on the rocks. But one of the things that concerns me is I found a pair of blue jeans, girls' size six, plus a striped T-shirt. They matched the description of that AMBER Alert that came over the wire yesterday."

Cara felt her heart still for a moment and Yolanda gasped. "You don't think the birds—" She couldn't even finish. It was one thing to kill and eat those men, but . . . a *little girl*?

Will's expression darkened. "I don't know *what* to think. It might be coincidence, but I should at least tell you—" He glanced at Yolanda for a long moment, and Cara could tell he was trying to decide whether to trust her. Finally he let out a small trill and the metallic scent of determination rose from him, "And this information is every bit as secret as the existence of the Sazi—" She'd already proven she could keep the secret for decades, without letting even Cara's own pack know, and she was a fellow cop. Yolanda nodded and zipped fingers across her lips. Will nodded and continued gravely. "But Lucas and Adam discovered that the pack leader up in Minneapolis was involved in some sort of child slavery ring—and it's tied to this area."

Cara's head dropped back onto the pillow wearily. "Oh *fuck!* So, now what do we—"

The telephone jangled in the kitchen suddenly and she let it ring once, trying to decide whether to drag her body up to go answer it. As it started to ring a second time, she sighed and pushed herself to a sitting position.

"Don't. I'll bring it to you." Yolanda touched her shoulder and stood, then quickly walked into the kitchen and answered it before it had finished ringing a third time. "Hello?" A pause, and then, "No, I'm a friend of hers. Hang on."

She walked out of the kitchen holding the portable and passed it to her, mouthing the word, Adam. Cara took the phone and felt a fluttering in her stomach as she put it up to her ear. But she noticed Will motioning to her for the phone, so she passed it to him first, almost relieved.

"Adam? It's Cloudsfall. Hey, I talked to Lucas a bit ago. Really sorry to hear what happened up there. Hang in there, bud." He paused to listen, but the central air unit picked that moment to kick in, and the sound of the fan drowned out Adam's reply. "No, I haven't told her anything yet." Another pause, this time accompanied by a slight smile. "Yeah, well . . . I'll let *her* tell you about what happened. She's fine . . . mostly. She'll heal. Here, hang on a minute."

Will passed the phone back to her and then looked up at Yolanda. "How about I give you a ride back to the office so you can pick up your car? We'll let them *chat*."

Yo nodded and picked up her soda from the table. "Yeah, I really need to get back, now that I know you're going to be okay. We'll talk in the morning, huh?"

Cara nodded and waited, with her hand over the mouthpiece, until Will and Yolanda walked out. The air conditioner shut off just as the door closed and silence closed around her. She looked at the phone once and the butterflies started to churn her stomach again. But she couldn't figure out *why*. Taking a deep breath, she put the phone back to her ear. She tried to decide whether to put a false note of cheerfulness into her voice, but decided against it. There was too much going on to pretend. "Hey, Adam. Cara here." Her voice sounded like she felt, weary and frustrated.

There was a long pause where she could hear him breathing, as though he was trying to decide what to say. "So . . . who'd you piss off this time?" His voice tried for teasing comradery, but a little too much concern leaked in around the edges.

Cara let out a small, sad chuckle. His worried tone was enough to break down the tough walls she'd carefully constructed around . . . well, *everything*. He had the right to know about the pack he might be joining. Plus, if he was going to get annoyed, better it was over the phone. So, she told him—about Yolanda and why they'd been driving on the back road to happen to see the owl. She talked about the pack, and why she hadn't introduced him properly that night at Rosa's. He listened to it all silently, only showing his presence by an occasional acknowledgment of okay, fer sure, or ahh. Then, of course, came the birds and the snake, and Yolanda hitting them with the truck.

"I suppose it was good she missed the *tree,* and she's right that it was probably the only way I didn't wind up dead. I'd been doing fine up 'til then, but then just hit the wall, so to speak. Turning him back took everything I had left. You know a Sazi's in bad shape when she can't even get out of the way of a *truck*. Yo probably wasn't doing more than thirty when she hit us."

She'd hoped that chuckling would lighten the conversation, but Adam went suddenly still—enough that she furrowed her brow and asked. "Adam? You still there?"

He sounded almost breathless when he replied, as though he'd been running for hours. "Yeah. So . . . wha- . . . what time was it you said that happened?"

She tried to figure it in her head, from leaving the restaurant to looking at the watch before she headed down to the canyon. She couldn't remember still having her watch back when she crested the hill by the truck. Maybe it dropped off on the climb. She'd have to ask Will if he spotted it. "I'm guessing, but I'd say around one twenty, or a little later. Why?"

Another long pause allowed her time to drag herself up to a better sitting position and take a sip of diet cola. His voice sounded stronger when he replied, almost matter of fact. "No reason. So, what did Will find?"

She shrugged. "Not much, unfortunately. He couldn't find a trail, but he got some blood that he's going to give to Bobby. You know anything about that, by the way? Why's he coming down . . . not that I mind. He's a good cop and I can certainly use the help."

Whatever had been bothering Adam dropped away, and he started in on his own story, from getting home to seeing the . . . *massacre* site, and talking to Bobby and his partner.

"Um, an *assassin*? In Wolven?" She blinked a few times, trying to process that. "Wow, things have sure changed there. Oookay, well . . . I suppose that's good to know. I guess so long as he keeps his nose clean here." She stopped and snorted. "Oh, who am I trying to kid? That's going to bug the *shit* out of me. I'm going to have to sit on my hands not to go through the posters and find out where he was wanted so I could call them."

This time, Adam did chuckle. "Already did . . . at least as far as finding out he's presumed dead—big shoot-out at an airport between two mob factions that was caught on film by a television crew. I'll show you the clip I found on the web when I get back there. But since all the bodies, including the reporters, disappeared, everything is still an open file. My fingers are turning blue from denim dye as we speak."

Cara let out a laugh and it felt good after everything today. The thing she noticed that lifted her mood more than anything was hearing the words *when I get back there*. It shouldn't matter. But she suspected Yolanda was right. She was toast.

Then Adam told her about the room they'd found, and all her humor dropped away. "Oh my God! Will mentioned this, but he didn't give any details. You found *how* many pictures?"

"Over two dozen." Adam paused and she could almost see him shake his head in angry frustration.

"Have you matched them in with any missing persons' reports yet?" Asking that reminded her about the AMBER Alert, and the clothes Will had found. "We might have something down here on that to help tie things together. Will found a pair of jeans and a shirt in the canyon that matched an AMBER Alert out of Oklahoma yesterday. If you can get a copy of that somehow, you might see if there's a picture of *that* girl on the wall. We might find out if the girls were being targeted specifically, or if the photos were taken *after* the abductions."

There was a trace of pride in his voice that made her feel like preening as Yo had done. "Wow! Great idea! Josef had to have been too preoccupied yesterday morning to do much in the way of adding new things to the wall. He easily could have hidden the photos or transferred the files we've found to a CD or flash drive if he really believed he was in danger. So, if her picture's there, we'll at least know there was *intent*." He paused and then muttered a swear. "Shit! I completely forgot to tell you. One of the pictures Josef had was of *Ziri*. But we don't know yet how long she was a captive before we found her, so that photo could have been taken anytime. You need to keep her under wraps, though. She seems to be a key to a bunch of stuff. That's the main reason why Bobby is coming down. Tony has hindsight, and he's been instructed to use it on Ziri to find out what she saw."

Cara opened her mouth to protest—there was no way she was letting a known killer get anywhere close to the girl, or her family. But Adam cut her off. "I know what you're going to say, but give it up. Tony was ordered there by the *Chief Justice*. That part is going to happen whether or not you like it. But from what Bobby says, Tony can actually be a nice guy. He likes kids and Bobby promised he'd keep things low-key. Nobody wants to traumatize Ziri any more than she is. The only thing Lucas wants you to do is keep the peace and make sure she stays safe."

"I don't like this—" A small growl escaped her and it was probably a good thing Adam couldn't catch her scent.

She was getting damned tired of being told what she would or wouldn't do.

"None of us do, Carita. But think about it—if Ziri saw something vital that she doesn't remember, and it can save other girls—"

She grumbled a small acceptance of the fact and started to pick tiny pieces of lint from the pillow under one leg in annoyance, letting the silence grow as she contemplated him calling her by the same pet name as her sister for the second time now. Part of her liked it . . . maybe a little *too* much. Once she had gathered the lint into a small, furry ball, she deposited it in the empty soda can on the table.

Adam sighed, in probably what he believed was understanding and shared resignation. "Well, anyway, they'll probably be there in the morning. Oh, and they'll be in *my* truck. Again, low-key . . . no rental cars to trace. They'll be driving it down to Mexico after they stop in Santa Helena, to talk with Ziri's family. So, I'll probably need a ride from the airport when I get down there." He let the statement hang as a request, and she struggled not to leap forward with an answer *too* eagerly.

"Oh. Sure, no problem. When do you think you'll be here?"

"Dunno. I should at least stay here for the hunt next week. It'll be the first time for my people without a pack leader."

My people. Sure. Of course he had to consider his own pack first. But did that mean he was staying up there? *Forever?* A knot of . . . something began to form in her stomach and she struggled to keep it from showing in her voice. "Absolutely. You do what you need to do for your pack."

This time he paused. "Things are happening . . . well, really fast . . . for both of us, Cara."

She let out a short snort of air and shifted her hips, hissing in a breath as pain radiated through her back. "No shit."

"I mean, with everything going on . . . I don't know that

anyone is certain how it'll play out. The whole damned world is in flux. So, I figured I'd toss one other thing in the air, just to keep in the back of your mind."

His voice sounded serious, but unsure, so she responded cautiously. "Yeah? What's that?"

She never could have expected what the next words out of his mouth would be. They made her heart race and a thick, wet buzzing form in her ears.

"Minnesota's never had an Alpha Female. But we sure could use one."

Chapter 21

WAS THAT THE doorbell? Adam turned off the shower and listened. When it sounded a second time, he turned the water back on for a quick second to finish getting the soap out of his hair and then grabbed a towel.

"Hang on a second! I'll be right there." He called the words out into the hallway and took a sniff of the air that flowed in around the paneled door. Ah. It was David. He must just be off his shift. No problem—he'd wait for a few minutes. He probably wanted to talk about how Vivian was chasing after him. Adam had noticed it all day yesterday. Yeah, she might have lost a sister, but nothing would keep that bitch from her goal of running a pack. And if she couldn't have Adam, what better way to stay close to the family than with his brother? Thankfully, she was no match for Bonnie in his brother's heart.

Quickly pulling on a pair of underwear and clean jeans, he ran his fingers through his hair and headed to the door barefoot, using the towel to finish drying his arms and neck. He opened the door and was surprised to see not only David, but Lucas and Tommy waiting.

"Hey guys. Afraid you caught me in the shower. I was just getting ready to head down to the club. But I could have grabbed a cab. You didn't have to come get me."

Lucas looked serious, possibly even more so than he did the night before, and all three of the men had such a mixture of scents—none of them good—that Adam was a little taken aback.

"Can we come in? Something's come up." The elder wolf's voice was flat and his eyes were filled with furious intensity.

"Jesus! Something *else*?" He stepped back quickly, adjusting his balance as one damp foot slid a little on the polished linoleum entry. "Sure. Of course, come on in." He glanced into the living room and winced a little at the mess. The suitcases were still strewn on the couches from where he'd dumped them after David brought him home, and a stack of mail and newspapers was spilling off the coffee table. "Sorry the house is such a pit. I haven't really had time to do much other than sleep since I got in."

They walked past him without comment and stepped down into the small living room. Adam closed the door and followed them with the towel around his neck, picking up the suitcases so they could sit. As he put them on the floor next to the hall closet, he motioned with his chin toward the open doorway behind them. "Hey, I've got a pot of coffee in the kitchen that's probably finished brewing by now. Why don't you guys grab a cup while I finish getting dressed."

David nodded. "I could use some caffeine. It was a long night. Go ahead, bro. I know where you keep everything."

Five minutes later, he was dressed and had brushed his teeth . . . twice. There was nothing quite like extra garlic pizza sauce to make his mouth feel like an army tramped through it the next morning.

Everybody was seated around the living room when he stepped back in and he noted David had fixed a cup for him. He sat down in his favorite recliner, took a sip of the sweet, creamy coffee and took a deep breath. "So, what's the scoop this time?"

Tommy and David both turned to Lucas. He dipped his head and closed his eyes briefly, and the anger and frustration that rose from him was tinged with sorrow. "Josef is dead."

Adam nearly spilled the coffee before it got to his lips. "What? But the healer said he'd be fine . . . ready to stand trial in a week or so. What happened?"

"*Murder* happened . . . while our backs were turned. We should have posted a guard at the clinic. You said it yourself—what if Josef was supposed to check in at a certain time? We worried about them scattering before we could arrest them, and didn't think about the alternative— that they might take him out before he could wake up and spill the beans."

"Shit. Did we lose anyone else . . . any of the staff, during the fight?"

Lucas started to tap one finger on his cup and his response both relieved and worried Adam. "No fight. Nobody remembers a damned thing. I talked with both healers and the nurses. It's as though a ghost came in and injected the venom. We're definitely dealing with a pro— no prints, nothing on the video monitors, not a single one of Josef's hairs out of place. It was only the smell that gave it away at all."

The word *venom* grabbed Adam's attention, especially after what had just happened to Cara. "You said *venom*. Did someone smell a Sazi snake when they checked on Josef? Was it rattlesnake venom? Has anyone checked?"

Lucas shook his head, but David raised his brows. "Not rattler venom, but we're not certain of the exact species yet. It is definitely in the viper family, though, possibly an asp. No, the scent that gave it away was concentrated cinnamon oil. Someone was trying to *cover* a scent, so I ordered the body not be moved until I could go through the room. I did a mind-link with my mate, Tatya, and she noticed an odd bruising in one of the wounds. The venom was injected in an existing wound. It's similar to a method employed in another case recently. I'm checking into that angle with the snake councilman, Ahmad al-Narmer. Why did you think rattlesnake?"

He told them what happened to Cara yesterday and how the rattlesnake had been going to bite her to get information. "Of course, that brings up a rather uncomfortable subject to me." He took a deep breath and looked at all three of them in turn. "The deputy with Cara managed to get the snake off her by using the sheriff's truck to *literally* run them over."

Tommy let out a short whistle. "Whoa. Brutal. But I'll bet it worked."

Adam took another sip of coffee and let out a nervous chuckle. "Oh yeah. It worked. Fer sure. But that happened at around one twenty yesterday—" He let the statement hang to see if anyone else would pick up on his reasoning. Tommy didn't react, but then he hadn't been with them at the time. David winced.

Lucas nodded slowly and let out a breath. "She pulled on your magic and you're feeling the result. So, you're thinking you're mated then? That's going to change a few things."

Adam felt panic rush through him and his eyes widened enough that he could feel air cool under the lid. *That* thought had never occurred to him. *I couldn't possibly—* "*Mated*? No! I'm thinking that I attached to her as my *pack leader*. I mean . . . yeah, she drew on me, but it was a crisis. Josef does that all the time. I mean, he *used* to." That was going to take a little while to get used to. Minnesota's Alpha was really *dead*, and the Second becomes the new Alpha.

David and Tommy both nodded, but his brother was the one who spoke. "True. He did that more than once. But we never felt his injuries, bro. You *sure* it's not something . . . else?"

"Jill's mated to me," Tommy added with a thoughtful expression and scent. "She says she knows where I am all the time. All she has to do is think about me and she can almost see me."

Adam shook his head. "See, nothing like that's happening. No feeling her emotions or knowing where she is. No, I think I just got caught in a pack binding. But I don't know what that means. Can it be severed from this side, or do I need to go back down there?"

"Except that Cara doesn't bind her pack . . . or had you forgotten that?" Lucas's voice was calm. He'd put down his coffee cup and now had his fingers interlaced behind his neck. "Have you slept together yet?"

"*What*? No! I mean, it's none of your damned business!" He heard the outrage in his own voice and knew he was overreacting to the questions. But he couldn't seem to help it. His heart was pumping so hard his temples were pulsing painfully.

Tommy looked at Lucas and they both smiled slightly, which pissed him off even more. He let out a harsh breath and held up his hands. "Okay, look. I only brought this up because I tossed out an offer to Cara yesterday. Maybe I shouldn't have, but—"

Now Lucas's expression grew more serious and he leaned forward until his forearms were resting on his legs. "Go on."

"She's having problems with her pack lately and if I bound to her that easily, then others might, too, and . . . well, I offered to bring her up here to be the Minnesota Alpha Female. That is, if you're planning for me to take the pack."

Eyes widened on all three men, and Lucas let out a vicious snarl. "*Goddamn it*, Mueller! You had no authority to offer that. We're trying to shrink the size of this pack, not increase it! Look, the reason I brought David and Tommy with me today is that I wanted to talk to all three of the top alphas to decide what to do. Then you go off, making stupid fucking offers you have no right to, and—" He let out a harsh breath and stood up, his eyes glowing with golden intensity. He started to pace behind the couch and magic crackled in the air, stinging Adam's skin like ants biting.

"David's not one of the top people. He's right in the middle of the pack."

Lucas waved his hand at Adam's younger brother and continued to pace. "I'm too pissed to talk right now. *You* tell him."

David's eyes had dropped to contemplate his fingernails. When he looked up, it was with an embarrassed expression that didn't match the authoritative blue uniform. "Josef couldn't hold me during the fight. Me and Tommy were the ones helping the two agents when the other guys attacked."

Tommy spoke up with a nod. "I was busy trying to hold Jill back. I was afraid someone was going to shoot her. But she chewed up my neck pretty good and got away. I took a bullet for her in the hallway—you probably saw that, but if David hadn't been strong enough, it could have been a lot worse."

Adam took a second look at Tommy. His turtleneck covered the wounds, but Adam remembered them.

Tommy grinned. "Yeah. I mean, it's fine with me, but

she's mated to me. Josef's control must have been something to overcome that. Jill shouldn't be able to hurt me,
ever. She's beating herself up pretty hard over that, but she
just couldn't stop even though she knew what she was doing. And I gotta tell ya—I'm not afraid to use that marker.
It sure as hell is gonna wipe out my *honey-do* list on the
weekends."

He was trying to lighten the mood and, to an extent, he
did. Adam would have laughed as the bright scent of citrus
and cookie spices filled the air, nearly overcoming the boiling coffee anger scent from Lucas. But his main focus was
on David. He'd never thought of his brother as an alpha of
that level. He hadn't seen him in the fray, but he was only
seeing it through Jill's eyes. "You couldn't be held? Even
when Josef was panicked? So why aren't you higher in the
pack?"

His brother let out a harsh breath and then shook his
head with frustration. "I don't want to fight, bro. I just
don't. I mean, I break up fucking gang wars every day—
watch how little kids jockey for position—believing the
number of battle scars is the only way to prove they're a
man. I don't *need* to prove myself, Adam. I don't want to
even now that Josef is dead. I know I'm supposed to want
to, be challenging you and everything, but I just don't."

"Which, of course, is a problem for this pack." Lucas
had finally calmed down enough to not bleed energy and
his eyes had stopped glowing. He leaned his hands on the
back of the couch and regarded the three of them. "David
might be able to hold this pack, but he'd be challenged. Already people are getting wary of him, wondering why he's
been holding back and not climbing. An Alpha has to feel
the need to rule—like you're feeling. But he'd rather stay
where he is, in the middle. Unfortunately, that might not be
an option."

"And I know I probably can't hold the pack," Tommy added. "Not like Josef did . . . and not like *you* could."

Lucas nodded and finally sat down again. His expression when he stared at Adam was still annoyed, but was calming by the minute. "Frankly, I'd rather send you down to Texas like originally planned, along with people who can be trusted. There's more going on up here than we know right now. I found a list in Josef's things that I was sort of surprised to find. It might be a plant . . . intentional disinformation to throw us off. But I'm thinking not. I'm starting to think he was cocky enough after so long of not being noticed that he could afford to do something that stupid."

"What sort of list did you find?"

Lucas raised his brows lightly and waited for a reaction. "An assassination list. You were the first name."

He shouldn't be surprised, but he was. "Was it a very long list? Who *else* was on it?"

David answered. "Anyone who was a danger to him. I was on the list and so was Tommy."

Lucas nodded. "There were a dozen names, and it appears from the memo . . . to person or persons unknown . . . that they were all people who Josef *couldn't* involve in the slaving business because of their magical ability, disposition, or employment. So, we've got a decision to make. As soon as Tony is done down in Mexico, I'm bringing him back here, and have already got a call in to our other seer with hindsight." He snorted and burnt metal frustration rose into the air. "Actually, I've got several calls in for her, but she's not answering. She's like that, though. However, as soon as I can get her up here, we're going to be having hindsight sessions with this whole pack to find out who knew about this. The council's insisted on knowing the extent of the damage, since it could affect us all if the authorities caught wind of it. That's going to be relatively traumatic, and I would prefer that people here *not* be bound during the process so we can limit the damage to the whole pack. I'd like to send any alphas who might be *able* to bind them down there."

Adam was starting to follow the train of thought and it made him sick to his stomach. "But if you send all high level people to Texas—"

Lucas nodded. "You see the problem. There's going to be a group of irritated, unbound alphas that will descend on Texas . . . on Cara's pack of lesser wolves. Even if they're honest, they're going to be in some stage of pining depression or, at least, anxiety for awhile. That's why you're needed there. At least for a time. But, I want to send Tommy, too. His wife needs to get away from this before she has a mental collapse. Tony's memory barrier didn't hold, and their daughter might still be in danger. If we move quickly, and secretly, we might take those who are watching by surprise."

He held up a finger to stop the Wolven chief. "But they're quite possibly looking for *both* Jenny and Ziri. Aren't we asking for trouble by putting them in the same place?"

Tommy answered, his voice and scent filled with angry determination. "That's not going to happen. I won't let anyone take my baby. Even if that means I have to keep watch twenty-four seven until we catch the bastards!"

Lucas tipped his head toward David. "I can make the pack believe it was a fluke Josef didn't hold David. That he didn't dare because he was a cop or some such. He'll, in effect, be undercover up here—able to hold the pack if it comes to it, but without anyone knowing. And I'll be here for awhile anyway. I can run the agency fine from here, and don't have anywhere else to be for the moment. I doubt anyone will be stupid enough to challenge *me*."

Fuck. Just what he needed. "So, that's it then? I pick the

people and Cara gets no say in what happens? She's going to blame me, you know. She already promised civil war if only alphas show up."

Lucas smiled, a baring of teeth that wasn't pleasant. "She won't blame you because you get no say, either. I got approval from the council for a no-death period and, actually, there won't be any rank challenges *at all* for now. I'll pick the people and you'll both deal with the result. The existing pack will remain in the positions they're in to avoid a war. The Minnesota wolves will be newcomers, unknowns . . . just regular pack until everything sorts out up here and you and Tommy will be responsible for keeping them from trying to climb. Of course, *I'll* be the shared enemy. Everyone will hate me in both places, but really—" He shrugged and chuckled lightly. "What's new about that? Everybody *always* hates the Wolven chief. It's part and parcel of the job. Oh, and don't bother asking the wolf rep, Nikoli, for a reprieve. It'll be a waste of time, because he voted against the split to begin with. He doesn't have the stroke in the job yet to change minds."

Apparently, this was all new to Tommy, too, because he was staring with open mouthed shock. "So all of us are going to have to leave our homes and answer to a new alpha, with no say in the matter, and no ability to challenge her? I thought this was going to be a volunteer thing. I mean, I agree with Lucas that *my* family needs to go, but some of the people on that list didn't want to move. And what if this new alpha decides to do the same thing as Josef did? Turn us against one another, I mean. I'm not feeling very trusting lately."

Adam found himself shaking his head. "She won't. Cara's not like that."

Tommy crossed his arms over his chest angrily. "Says the man who's already bound to her. What if you're *already* not thinking clearly? A week ago you were the *first* man to stand up to say this wasn't a good idea and you were going to fight the move tooth and claw. What happened, huh? Answer me that."

He stopped and thought about it . . . really thought, because Tommy was right. He'd been angry and frustrated about the split and, while he felt it was his own fault it happened, he still would have been against it even if Tyr hadn't challenged him . . . and lost. Could Cara be buffaloing them all, like Josef had? Had she brainwashed him somehow into thinking she was perfect? Did the birds back down from attacking *not* because Will arrived, but because she was somehow involved? He met his best friend's pained expression with one of confusion, suddenly not trusting his own actions. "I . . . I don't know, Tom. I wish I did."

Lucas shrugged. "Well, I know. Cara is the sheriff down there because Charles felt she was the best candidate and pulled some strings in the governor's office." He waved off Adam's incredulous look. "Oh, don't look so surprised. Most things, good and bad, that happen to Sazi get there with a little push from the seers or the council—even things you know nothing about for reasons you can't comprehend. The Chief Justice has influence all over the globe, and he was quite impressed with her in Wolven academy. She's strictly law and order and doesn't cave in to popular opinion." He looked around at them all, making sure he had their complete attention. "Charles Wingate has *always* had the best interests of the Sazi people first and foremost in his mind—often to his own detriment. He wouldn't still be the Chief Justice otherwise. The combined council could take him down if it came to it. So if Charles says you can trust Carlotta Salinas to be a good pack leader for your people, then it's the gold standard."

All three men nodded, convinced, at least for now, by the

conviction in Lucas's voice. Adam felt a buzzing relief in his head. He hated to think he couldn't trust his own decisions and feelings. "So, what happens now? The moon is just in a couple of days. We can't be having low-level alphas traveling on the moon."

"What happens now is that you're going back to Texas, and taking Tommy's family with you." Lucas stood up and stretched his back, opening his eyes wide enough that Adam realized he probably hadn't slept at all the previous night. "I'm not unmindful of what Cara said about making waves down there. I'm not just going to pick people at total random. I do think the Kassners would be good picks, for the reasons you cited at the restaurant the other day. I've contacted a few of our better-known Sazi artists. Any gallery started there will be an exclusive outlet for some *very* desirable products. That will set it apart and help it thrive. I also liked your idea about a Target store down there, so I'm going to see what strings can be pulled. Cherise Michaels and I have also already talked. She might well be the next person to go down, at least temporarily, to scope out the area. I'll let you know who else will be coming as soon as I decide."

He pointed at Adam and his scent became all business, better than anger, but less than the warm scents of concern and pride when he spoke about the Chief Justice. "Oh, and you need to check in with your captain at the precinct. He should have just received a psychiatric report that said your retirement is based on burnout. That'll free you up from your last two weeks on patrol, and the council will cover the lost money and emergency travel expense."

Adam shook his head, tiny little movements that spoke his astonishment. Call after call, layer upon layer of planning, just in the space of a few hours. "You've done *all* that shit while I was out cold last night? Jesus, I feel like a *slacker*!"

Finally, Lucas laughed. "Yeah, well, some nights it sucks being the top dog. And I'd love to say I was going to be getting sleep any time soon. I'd be lying, though. But—" and a sly smile turned his lips, "I wasn't hit by a truck yesterday, either, so I could get by on a few hours."

David and Tommy chuckled lightly while Adam felt his face burn. "Yeah . . . well fuck you all. So, how many days do I have to get things together?"

"Oh, you and Tommy's family are going *now*. I'd suggest going and talking to your captain in the next hour or so. By the time I get to headquarters, Vanessa should already have the tickets. She was marked for death, too, by the way, and is still a little panicked about it. She's sticking close to people she can trust—i.e., others on the list. She's a good secretary, but if you want her to go down, too, it might not be a bad idea. She's a low-level alpha and probably wouldn't mind being out of ranking battles for a time. But no . . . with things heating up down there, I want you and Tommy where you'll do the most good. And I want the girls guarded until we can track down everybody involved in this scheme. If Cara hasn't told her pack yet, then do it together. You are the Alpha Male of Texas, as of now. At least, until you hear otherwise."

"And if it doesn't work? What then?" Adam knew the answer really didn't matter. He would be expected to make it work. So, Lucas's response came as a surprise.

"Then you'll come back here and Tommy will be the Alpha down there. Your personalities are nearly opposites. If one doesn't work, the other just might. And I don't deny that the pack here will follow you and . . . well, Cara, too— if it turns out you're mated. I'm going to have my work cut out for me trying to find a replacement up here. There might be some more shuffling from other packs eventually. We'll just have to see."

If you're mated. Uffda. What if he was? Worse still,

what if Cara was alpha enough that some of the others from Minnesota mated to her as well? If she went into heat . . . he closed his eyes, trying not to think about what might happen. The fluttering in his stomach told him that even if he wasn't mated to her, he was getting way too attached.

Chapter 22

THE WINDSHIELD WIPERS smeared the dusty rain into a chalky coating that would take a scrubber to get off. Cara stared into the distance almost hypnotically, watching for some sign of an approaching vehicle, pausing every few minutes to squirt another stream of cleaner with a flick of her finger. She tapped her fingers on the steering wheel in time to Clint Black's latest on the radio and wondered again whether to put the truck in gear and head toward town instead of sitting here at the entrance to the back road to Rosa's house.

They said ten o'clock. Didn't they say ten? Her eyes flicked to her arm, only to remember her watch was still missing, so she checked the dashboard instead. Ten fifteen—but the rain might have slowed them down. The clouds looked darker in the distance and the roads always got horribly slick in the first rain after a long dry spell. All that oil in the roadbase was great in the winter . . . kept the roads free of ice, but a film built up in the summer that was every bit as treacherous as black ice.

She couldn't believe she was allowing this to happen. A known killer was on his way here and she was going to waltz him into her sister's house to interview a child. Although, in reality, Ziri was turning out to be far from a child. She was very much a woman in her own culture. And wow, was Rosa loving having her stay with them! Ziri was an amazing cook . . . good enough that Rosa struggled a little to keep up, but was taking down recipes as fast as she could write. Gloria had taken to the Mayan girl like a long-lost sister. Of course, it helped that Ziri was massively creative, and had a helpful, sunny personality that more than made up for her lack of Spanish and English. She was teaching Gloria how to braid tiny strands of rope with beads into sandals, and had offered to make an authentic waxed flower headdress for the Quince. Apparently, the name of the celebration crossed languages and cultures. Once she showed her skill at dipping fresh flowers in paraffin, Gloria decided on it over the rhinestone tiara. "Omigawd, Tia Cara!" she remembered the girl saying last night, holding up a drawing of the planned crown of blooms, "Isn't this *gorgeous*? Mary is going to be absolutely *green*!"

Headlights in the distance brought her out of her mulling. Yep, it was Adam's black truck all right. She took a deep breath, turned off the radio, and waited as it approached. It was a day later than planned, but even the Weather Channel hadn't predicted this storm system would be so violent. The airports had been shut down for a whole day. Even this morning, flash floods in several surrounding counties had closed roads. It was lucky they'd made it here at all.

She opened her window as the truck pulled alongside her. Bobby's smile was a pleasure to see again. It had been a long time, but he still looked the same—a narrow, angular face, short kinky hair and that ever-present row of brilliant white teeth, ready to appear at a moment's notice. A bright citrus scent burst into her nose when he opened his window and she heard both men laughing.

"Well, Cara Salinas! Look at you—sheriff of the whole county and you managed to make it into Wolven, too!"

She smiled and met his eyes. Well, actually she met his *contacts*, because his natural eyes were red with slitted pupils. She always wondered what he'd done before colored contacts were invented. She knew he was old, even in Sazi terms. Maybe she'd ask him one day.

"Good to see you again, Agent Mbutu. This your partner?" She couldn't keep her voice from flattening, but the other man in the truck's cab didn't seem to mind. He smiled at her and she realized he was actually quite handsome, in a guy-next-door sort of way. But the intelligence that flowed through his blue eyes was what took her by surprise. This was no brutish thug, which made him all the more dangerous.

"Yep, although he's not really my partner—he's actually my replacement. Tony Giambrocco, say hello to Cara Salinas."

He nodded politely and spoke in a medium baritone with no particular accent. "A pleasure, Sheriff. Nice county you've got here. Texas isn't at all what I expected. There are a lot more trees, and the wild flowers are amazing. It looked like a damn jungle when we landed in San Antonio. I'd always heard it was flat and sandy here, more like a desert."

She acknowledged that with a pleased nod. Most every newcomer thought that the whole state looked like the panhandle. "Parts are. But this is the hill country, which is a lot more fertile. Glad you like it." A short silence followed, where the only sound was the flipping wiper blades on the trucks. Shrugging her shoulders, she turned off the switch and heard her voice go flat and sad. "So anyway, we might as well get this over with, huh?"

Bobby laughed. "Don't play the dirge tune yet, Cara. Really, there's nothing to it. You probably won't even notice it happening. Tony's getting pretty good at this."

The other man rolled his eyes and held up gloved hands. "Sheer self-defense. If I didn't get a handle on it pretty quick, my *gift* was going to send me and Sue to the nuthouse."

Bobby motioned to his friend with the fingers resting on the wheel, keeping his eyes toward Cara. "Tony's doublemated to a full human. Weirdest damned thing—she sees what he sees unless he blocks her out."

"And some of the shit I see in this job, I wouldn't inflict on an *enemy*, much less my wife."

He was *mated*—married to a human who shared his magic? "Wow! That's . . . well, that's pretty amazing. I've never heard of that."

Tony laughed, and it softened his whole face. Despite her better judgment, she was finding him almost . . . charming, not at all what she expected from Adam's description. "That's me—one of a kind. But yeah, let's get moving. I'd really like to find a bathroom pretty soon. This maniac behind the wheel must have a five quart bladder. We haven't stopped the damn truck since we left the airport lot."

"Okay, let me turn around and then you can follow me." She paused and then looked at them both, willing them to understand—despite whatever orders they had. "But, even though my niece and nephew are in school right now, *please* remember that my sister is human and so is the girl."

Tony looked at her seriously with what seemed to border on *compassion*. She actually had to take a sniff to believe it. "I understand, and you don't have to worry. I come from a long line of humans. I'm an attack victim, Sheriff. I do okay in this world, but it hasn't been so long yet that I don't remember how to play with real people."

Cara had to pick up her dropped jaw. She'd never met an attack victim before. She'd heard of it happening certainly . . . it was one the reasons why Wolven existed. But very few survived the first change. "Oh. I . . . I didn't know. Sorry."

He shrugged. "Like I said, I get by. Fortunately, I've had some people help me get through it—even if they do have five quart bladders." The words came out deadpan, which made Cara laugh that much louder.

Bobby let out a low chuckle and threw up his hands. "Okay, okay, I get the point. Lead the way, *Agent* Salinas. Let's find Tony a bathroom and then we'll see what we can do about tracking down your flock of birds."

"YOU'RE REALLY MOVING to *Texas*? I mean, I know you put in your notice, but I always thought . . . um, wow!" Reggie Marquez, his partner for over three years, stared incredulously at him from the chair next to Adam's computer station while he cleaned out his desk. Lucas had been dead on the money, once again—even though he'd been a day late. Captain Larkin had received the report, but he took a day to verify the findings. God only knows how that was managed. But the report, whatever it said—and hopefully nobody would ever show it to him—released him from active duty. He was on medical leave for the rest of his time with the department. He just tried not to think about what the black mark on his record would do to his career. But it would let him travel to Texas again, as soon as Nessa could rebook the flights that the storm cancelled.

He'd still suited up in uniform for today, just in case the Wolven chief wound up wrong. Fat chance. He glanced at his partner as he sorted through a drawer. "It all happened pretty suddenly, Reg. It's sort of hard for me to believe, too. But there was a position open, and it seems like a really good fit for me. Do you know I was there a whole *day* and the only siren I heard was the fire department testing the engines?"

"I guess I didn't realize the pressure was getting to you here, amigo. I mean, I know that last neglect case really tore you up, but jeez—you're *good* at this. Even the gang-bangers got respect for you. Are you sure you wanna leave it all behind?"

It was a good thing Reggie wasn't Sazi. He couldn't smell the lie that easily slid through his lips. "Not wanna, Reg. *Gotta*. I put it off as long as I could. But everything in Texas—" he paused, allowing his friend to see warm memories of Cara, and Santa Helena's drowning deep starred sky, play across his face. "Man, it's like nothing you can imagine down there. Like Mayberry RFD come to life, don'tcha know."

Reggie pushed his cap farther back on his head and raised his brows. "Yah, well call me cynical, but I think there's more to it than that. I think you met someone—a sweet little *chica* that makes you not care for nothing but her next smile."

Close. Closer than he probably knew, but Adam shrugged it off with a wave of a picture frame bearing his mother's photo, before stowing it away in the box. He still needed to stop by Mom's house to bring her up-to-date about yesterday's happenings. "I was only there for two days, Reg. Get real."

The slender Latino snorted into his mustache. "Yeah, and I saw Inez for ten minutes in the fucking *grocery store* and knew." He snapped his fingers, causing Charlie at the next desk to raise his eyes from his phone call. "Like that! I chased her all over the neighborhood for two weeks before she'd go out with me. But one look and I was a goner. You saw me, I was like a goddamned Romeo, singing outside her window with my guitar—even writing love songs to her."

"Really *bad* love songs, if I remember. Nothing rhymes

with *orange*, Reg . . . not even *so rang,* no matter how weird you say it. Hell, it didn't even make *sense!*"

He tapped the gold band on his finger before handing Adam the white cardboard cover for the file box that was now stuffed full—full of a past he'd really believed in. Could he believe in anything this much again, down there?

"Love *don't* make sense. That's my point. Shit changes when you find the right one." Reggie paused and said meaningfully, "Shit like becoming a fucking truant officer in backwater Texas after a whole life as a city cop, for example. That's what a woman will do to you, amigo. Make your whole head change. Look at me. Three years ago when we partnered, would either of us have thunk I'd be about to sign a mortgage that would choke a racehorse and be spending my Saturdays shopping for baby strollers—and do you know how much those damned things *cost*?"

Adam wanted to say it had nothing to do with Cara. He wanted to tell Reggie that he was being forced to go down by a council of shapeshifters that didn't give a damn what he wanted. But the truth was, even if he stayed . . . he'd asked her to come up. Didn't that say everything? He sighed in resignation and sat down heavily. "Her name's Carlotta—Cara Salinas. She's the sheriff down there."

Reggie held up one finger and shook it in victory. "Ah ha! I knew it!" Then he lowered his voice and winked. "She's Latina, eh? Well, I always knew you had good taste. But you gotta watch out for them, amigo. They're tough, and they've got tempers on 'em."

"Fer sure. I already noticed that part." A small smile pulled at his mouth.

Reggie leaned forward and clapped him on the shoulder with a low chuckle. It pressed the patch on his sleeve into his arm, reminding Adam again it was the last time he'd feel that slap, or hear his partner's donkeylike laugh when

they rolled up on something so completely absurd that nobody would believe it if it was in a novel. "Well, tell you
what—we'll go have lunch and I'll tell you some things that
will melt her down into a puddle. Then . . . oh, then amigo,
you can find out the sort of lava that's underneath that tough
outer crust."

Chapter 23

CARA STOOD OFF in the corner of the living room, near
the kitchen. Ziri's back was toward her and Tony was sitting on the couch next to the girl, casually sipping a soda.
Bobby had taken up residence in Paco's easy chair and was
trying to talk to Rosa who sat watching Tony suspiciously
in her floral covered rocker.

I shouldn't have warned her. She hadn't told Rosa everything, just that she was a little concerned. But when her sister was restless, she got very controlling. There was nothing
to make her as restless as closing the restaurant for a week,
even if it *was* a well-deserved vacation. So now Rosa was
playing the mother hen and Bobby was starting to get annoyed. Cara turned her eyes imperatively to the cross over
the mantel and said a small prayer this would go well. She'd
been doing that a lot lately. Faith was harder than it should
be lately.

"Really, Mrs. Ruiz. There's nothing to it at all. Tony's
done it to me before and I hardly noticed. He's a seer . . .
he doesn't interact with anything but the past."

"But she forgot! That's the important part. She forgot

because it was bad things she saw. Why take her through it again?"

Bobby let out a heaving sigh while Tony remained coldly neutral. Cara could see that it really didn't matter to him either way. Suddenly, she *could* see what Adam saw—that it would be just as easy for him to put a bullet into all their brains as sip that soda. The scent of his fur was all that reached her nose. No emotions at all bled from him. Bobby finally turned his head toward her and gave her a *look*. She'd seen it before, on other people. It said, *Step in now or I'm going to finish this*.

"Rosa." She said the word softly but with force and her sister looked up with flashing eyes. "Enough. They said it won't hurt her. Watch if you want, but stay out of it. This is business."

Ziri didn't seem at all concerned, but probably because she couldn't follow the conversation well enough to understand. She was still braiding and knotting white strips of twine into an intricate pattern that resembled tatting, looking up occasionally when she'd recognize a word. Rosa pressed her lips into a harsh line but nodded. No doubt she'd have something to say about it later, though.

With a relieved relaxing of his shoulders, Bobby nodded to Tony. With casual ease, Tony removed his gloves, putting them nearby on the couch and then smiled at the girl next to him. "Ziri?"

She looked up and matched the smile. Tony spoke slowly and carefully, keeping his voice concerned and pleasant. "Do you remember driving here—to the rocks where she found you?" He pointed right at Cara, and Ziri turned to beam a smile at her. She nodded to Tony. "Yes . . . *sí*."

"Those men who brought you . . . did they hurt you?"

Her face changed. It was subtle, but it was obvious she

understood what he was asking. Rosa opened her mouth but Cara raised her hand to stop her. Her sister crossed angry arms over her chest, but kept silent.

Ziri couldn't keep her eyes on Tony. She ignored the question and returned to her braiding, her fingers now moving faster and with more purpose. Her scent revealed her increasing agitation.

Tony paused and watched her for a moment, taking in every aspect of Ziri's actions. His voice turned into a soothing warmth that brimmed with gentle concern. Cara hadn't thought he was capable of such delicate emotions. "You're mad at them. *Waa'lay*? They lied to your *naa*. Lied about why they were bringing you here, didn't they?"

Was he speaking Mayan? Several of the words sounded like those Lucas had used, and they were having an impact on Ziri. Her hands started to stutter, the fluidity gone, and her jaw set tightly. Had he really prepared for this interview to that extent?

Then he changed tactics. He pointed at the work in her lap and smiled again. "That's pretty. May I look?" He reached out his hand, palm up and she shrugged. She reached across the short distance and placed it in his hand. But at the second their hands contacted, he closed his fingers around hers. Everything changed in that moment. She went still, as though frozen—held by magic, except there was no magic in the room. Bobby nodded with a small smile while Rosa looked on with curiosity plain on her face.

Neither Ziri or Tony seemed in any distress. They were just frozen. Cara stepped closer and whispered to Bobby. "Are they all right?"

He nodded as Tony reached his other hand up and pushed forward, as though opening a swinging door. "They'll be like that for awhile. He's started his hindsight. We should probably give them some privacy. Tony tends to get annoyed when people watch. You don't want him annoyed."

"No, you don't." Tony's whispered words came out of a motionless mouth, as close to a ventriloquist as Cara had ever seen. "I can hear just fine, and you're distracting me. This is going to take a few minutes, so go away now."

"Oops." Cara shrunk back a little at the admonishment. She certainly didn't want to do anything to interrupt the process. Ziri's face had taken on a dreamy quality, her eyes locked on Tony's, as though she was quietly contemplating happy things.

Bobby stood up and motioned for Rosa to do the same. "We'll wait in the kitchen. Yell if you need anything." While it appeared Rosa wanted to stay and watch, she grudgingly followed when it didn't appear Ziri was in any distress.

They left the room, with Bobby holding open the slatted door to let her and Rosa enter first. They sat down at the table while the slender dark man walked across the room to open the refrigerator. "No beer. Pity. It was a long drive."

Rosa got a startled look on her face while Cara adjusted her holster so it didn't dig into her waist so much. "There isn't? Here, let me get some out of the shop." She got up and exited the back door, leaving the screen standing partly open.

Leaning her elbows against the table, Cara motioned toward the living room—and the people beyond—with her chin as a light breeze tugged at her hair. "How long's it going to take? What all does he do?"

Bobby shrugged and grabbed the chair. "Tough to say how long. He told me once it's like looking through old newspapers on microfiche. Sometimes you find the information right away, and other times it takes all day. But *we* have other things to discuss, as you know, so let's not avoid the subject. How much have you told your pack?"

"Told us about what?" Rosa stepped through door, carrying a six-pack of sweating Coronas in one hand, and a small bag of limes in the other.

The blush that heated Cara's face probably told Bobby everything he needed to know. Rosa looked at them both in turn and then raised her brows. "Let me get some limes cut up for the beer."

Bobby reached out his hand expectantly. "I'm good without the lime."

Her sister snorted and pulled the cardboard carton out of reach. "You most certainly are *not*. Nobody drinks beer in this house without salt and lime. Now, you two just forget I'm here." She walked to the counter and removed a knife from a spinning rack attached to the bottom of the upper cabinets.

Yeah, right. She was the worst gossip in the pack. Cara shook her head and Bobby smiled before motioning to the back door. "We'll be back in a minute, Mrs. Ruiz. Keep the beer cold."

Her sister's scent turned to the burnt metal of frustration, but she didn't comment, instead turning on the water to wash the limes before cutting them. Cara followed Bobby out the back door a short distance away, where the python agent leaned against the pecan tree nearest to the carports. The rain had stopped, but there was a fine, cool mist in the air that would make the humidity miserable tomorrow. "I take it you haven't told them yet."

"I was planning to wait for the next hunt. That's just a couple days away. People would be on edge if I called a special meeting. The only times I've had to do that is when there's bad news. They get like dogs going to the vet—it's not pretty."

Bobby shook his head. "It's your pack, of course, and if you're sure they're going to handle hunting with complete strangers without any warning . . . but if it was me, I'd want to talk to them in private first."

"*What*?" Her voice came out louder than she'd expected, so she hurriedly lowered it and stepped to the other side of the tree, closer to Bobby. "Since when are there going to be people hunting with us on *this* moon? ¡*Madre de Dios!* When did this happen?"

"Hell . . . day before yesterday, I think. Hasn't Adam talked to you about the council meeting yet? I mean, I know Lucas is swamped, but since Adam is going to be your Alpha Male down here come next week—"

Emotions simmered inside her, blending and splitting. Anger, happiness, frustration. Finally anger won. "*Chingada!* Not a word. And I've talked to him twice since he got up there." They'd talked about a lot of things, but her getting no say in the choice and having the new people arrive in just a few days—no, that should have rated a mention. Oh, they were *definitely* going to have words next time they talked. "*Damn it!* When were they planning on telling me?"

"Well, Adam was supposed to be here already, but the storm cancelled his flight. Maybe he was waiting to talk to you in person. I probably just screwed this all up by bringing it up. And hey, didn't Lucas give you any of his cologne? He said he did, but I can smell you."

Cara shook her head in frustration. "It doesn't seem to work on me. Don't know why. Could it be because of my . . . condition?"

Bobby pursed his lips and crossed his arms over his chest again. "Y'know, that's a possibility. You might be one in ten thousand it doesn't work on. When I get back to the lab, I'll try to whip up something for you, and you might really consider letting Adam lead the hunt for a month or two until I can."

The tone of his voice set her nerves jangling. "Why?"

"Afraid they're sending down mostly Alphas. I haven't a clue how your body is going to respond to a rush of testosterone from multiple unattached alpha males. In fact, I think I'll talk to Lucas about that tonight when I call."

Multiple unattached alpha males. ¡Madre de Dios!

She couldn't even think past that thought for a moment, as he continued. "But, for the other, I thought if things were going badly down here, I could be your . . . I don't know—"

She said the words through gritted teeth, her anger riding over her fear for a brief moment. "My *muscle*?" He laughed in response and she shook her head. "Nah. I can handle the pack . . . at least, the *current* pack. Can you give me any hint about who's being sent down?"

Bobby shook his head, now smelling concerned at her annoyance and embarrassed at his faux pas. "Sorry. I'm not that much in the know. I just know Lucas wants the Alphas out of Minnesota."

She looked down at the shaggy lawn and squished a nearby pecan into the moist sod while muttering an angry curse. "I should be the *first* one to find out this shit. Oh, he's gonna *pay* for this." Bobby flicked out his tongue several times. It was a vivid reminder of the snake in the canyon but she was too pissed right now for it to bother her like it used to at the academy.

The screen door slammed at that moment and they both turned their head. Tony was walking their way, his face set in serious lines and his leather-tipped fingers tapping a staccato on his jeans.

Bobby raised his chin. "So, did you find out anything interesting?"

He stopped and snorted. "Sure, if you consider finding out that we're all completely *screwed* to be interesting. We need to pack up our shit and move this discussion down the road 'cause it's way too hot for the ladies inside to hear."

Anger to worry was a pretty short step, so when Cara went back inside to tell Rosa they were going up to her house to continue the discussion, her sister gave her an odd look. The Coronas had already been placed at the table, a salted lime stuck in each bottleneck. Cara tried to ignore the fact that leaving without sharing a drink that had been prepared was the height of rudeness in her family. But Cara's expression made Rosa's brow furrow nervously and she sat down, fingering one of the bottles. "What did he see, hun bun? Is Ziri in trouble?"

"I don't know yet." Noticing Rosa's curiosity was winning out over worry, she realized she would have to give a gentle reminder. She reached out and touched her sister's shoulder and brushed back a hair that had strayed from the braid at her neck. "You do know that even when I find out, I won't be able to tell you, right? This is like the files at the office. Wolven stuff is just like my regular job—confidential."

Rosa got an incredulous look that matched her scent and she pushed away Cara's hand. "No, this is about our pack, Carita . . . those birds and Ziri. This isn't office stuff. You can't keep secrets that involve *us*. That's against the rules the pack voted on."

God, if she only knew how much the pack rules were about to change. She pasted on a smile that her sister would see right through. "Look, I'll call you tomorrow, 'kay? Just make sure you keep Ziri here and out of sight. No town runs for y'all unless I'm with you." She walked out hurriedly, before Rosa had a chance to respond.

"T-1, DISPATCH."

"Go ahead, Sheriff." Maggie's voice bordered on laughter. She wondered what might be going on in the office.

"Show me on a courtesy stop out on CR sixty-one. Some folks following an uncovered load hit a mesquite branch and got a flat. The shoulder's a little narrow, so I'm gonna run my lights 'til they're done." It was a lie, but a plausible one . . . so long as nobody happened to notice she wasn't actually on County Road 61, which was unlikely since it wasn't on a regular patrol route. She was going to have to hurry with the discussion at her house and get back. There was so damned much to do at the office, even if Yolanda was covering for her. She was starting to wonder when she'd have time to fit in Wolven investigations if this is how much time it took. She'd have to ask Will how he managed it.

"Copy that, T-1. Let me know if you need backup or a tow truck."

"10-4. T-1 out." She released the radio button and eased back out of the cab, then checked the radio on her hip to make sure it was on, but the volume was low. Bobby and Tony were waiting on her front porch. Their cars would be hidden from the main road, and she'd made certain to lock the gate to the ranch so nobody could follow.

In a few minutes they were seated at the kitchen table and Bobby was taking his second draw from an ice-cold beer, while Cara waited for water to boil. If Adam was coming back this soon, along with a bunch of other alphas . . . well, she'd better keep drinking tea. She might be mad at him, but she wasn't stupid. With the way her emotions were swimming today, it was a good thing both Tony and Bobby were mated.

Tony leaned back in his chair and took off the gloves with a frustrated sound. At a glance from Cara, he shrugged. "I *hate* gloves. They're damned hot. Just stay on that side of the table and we'll be fine." He pointed at Bobby with an exasperated look. "You, too. I've had my fill of visions from you this trip."

Bobby snorted. "Oh, and you becoming a seer is somehow *my* fault?"

"No, you grabbing the salt this morning at the diner is your fault. Just fucking wait until I'm done with it and pass it to you next time. I'm not going to spend every goddamned meal fumbling with my fork through gloves because you can't remember not to touch me. I'm getting tired of living out the kinky shit you do with your wife."

Cara felt her brows raise and she hid a smile with a cough. Tony shifted his glare to her. "That's how hindsight works . . . at least for me. I'm *living* the memories with the subject. Whatever powerful events they see and feel, as they remember it." He motioned to Bobby with his chin and continued with sarcasm thick in his voice and his scent full of annoyance. "And when my *partner* spends an hour on the phone with his wife before breakfast, then what's on top of the pile is the last time he had sex with her. You don't want to know what a snake and a dragon consider *fun*."

He reached out and grabbed his beer and took a long swallow while Bobby offered Cara a sheepish smile and a small chuckle. It made Tony shake his head angrily. His voice lowered a few notes and took on a decidedly Italian accent while he stared at the slender black man with deadly calm. "Laugh it up, slither boy. But I swear to God—one more time and I'm gonna shoot something off that'll take a damned long while to grow back. *Capisce*?"

Bobby sighed and the dry, sandy scent of embarrassment rose from him enough for Tony to nod. "Okay, okay. I'll be more careful. Now, how about you tell us about Ziri."

The tea kettle whistled in the background and Cara stood up. A brief stutter of static made her listen for a second. The Garcias were at it again—he *really* needed to start eating lunch at a restaurant. She shook her head and then looked back over her shoulder as she turned off the stove and reached into the cabinet for a mug. "Go ahead. I'm listening."

"Okay. Well, first, she's really good at lying through her teeth." That stopped Cara cold. She turned, the kettle poised over the mug.

"What's she lied about? I don't know that anyone's been able to question her with the language barrier."

Now Tony smiled. "See, *that's* what she's lying about. She speaks fluent Spanish, but she doesn't want to let on. Don't ever play poker with her, because she takes everything in and never shows any sign. Not even a scent. But I wish all of my sessions were as vivid as her memories. I didn't have to use rewind but once or twice. She takes it *all* in."

Cara opened her mouth to ask what he meant, but Tony must have realized he said something unusual because he added, "Memories are like a video. You have to rewind the tape to get to the right spot. Sometimes you overshoot and have to fast forward. That's why I started to ask Ziri questions about the men and her family before I touched her. It helps get the memories back *close* to the right spot. I was just guessing when I asked if the men lied to her mother about where she was going, but apparently nailed it. I figured scattering in a few Yucatan words Lucas taught me would help, too. Her memories rewound straight back to her village and telling her mother good-bye. Handy, because I'll recognize the place when we go down there."

Bobby nodded. "John-Boy would be proud of you. You're really starting to pick up on this interviewing stuff."

This time Tony laughed and the sunny, penetrating scent of oranges rose into the air. "You say that like I had to step *up* to his level or something. I was *always* better at couch sessions." He noticed Cara's curious expression while she scooped tea into the small metal infuser and lowered the chain into the hot water in the mug to steep. "John Corbin is a psychiatrist buddy. He decided to do it for a living, but I got better grades in all our psych classes together. I might add that he's pretty damned envious of me for the hindsight. Think about how many shrinks would kill for the chance to get the real scoop on their patients' problems." He snapped his fingers. "Just like that—diagnosis and start to fix it. Ten minutes, tops."

Cara walked back to the table with her cup, the small silver chain clinking lightly against the glazed ceramic. "Wow. I've never heard much about hindsight. So does that mean you get everything that happened to the person . . . emotions, sensations, sights, sounds . . . the works?"

"Depends on the person. Most people don't consciously focus on sounds and scents, so I have to dig around to get the whole picture. But in Ziri's case, you betcha. That girl's a goldmine of information. I'd lay odds she's a musician and artist, because she thinks of voices in keys and even categorizes different shades of yellow. Want to make her day? Give her a print of Van Gogh's *Sunflowers*. She'll be entertained for a week, but you might have to remind her to blink."

Tony leaned forward, resting his forearms on the table and met each of their eyes in turn. "Okay, just so you know—I probably shouldn't be telling you guys this before I talk to Lucas, but I figure we're leaving here and he's busy up there." He pointed at Cara with purpose. "You need to get a forecast of the storm that's coming, Salinas, because the horizon's an ugly color right now."

The tale he related made Cara forget to even take the tea ball from the mug. She just continued to dip it into the water, over and over, while Tony told a vivid account of Ziri's terrifying journey to Texas.

"So five girls started out in the van with her?" Bobby was taking notes in that same strange shorthand he'd used at the academy. It never mattered whether he left his exam notes sitting out in plain sight. Nobody could read them anyway. "Were they all from her village?"

Tony shook his head. "No. Only two others—names Oomay and Torgi. That's phonetic, by the way. You'll have to ask Lucas for spellings in that language. She doesn't know what happened to them after they were taken from the shack on the border where they were kept prisoner for about a week, but she has opinions. Ziri figured out pretty quickly that some of the girls were bound for a brothel somewhere, instead of the restaurant jobs they were promised. One of the goons beat one of the girls, a young Mexican girl named Inez, pretty badly for refusing to strip for them after dinner one night. Then they raped her while the others listened."

"*¡Madre de Dios!* The poor thing . . . no wonder she's been trying to forget." Cara hissed in a breath and finally realized the tea was almost black when Bobby touched her hand and pointed down. She pulled the infuser out of the now lukewarm water and placed it on the folded paper towel next to the cup. The first sip made her grimace enough that she was forced to add some sugar. She couldn't afford to pour it out. There wasn't enough left to waste. Bobby flicked his tongue multiple times and furrowed his brow. Then he picked up the infuser and let some of the remaining liquid drop into his palm. But he motioned with his chin for Tony to continue, just before he licked up the small amount of tea. Cara couldn't decide who was more interesting to watch.

It was Tony tapping his fingers on the table that caught her attention. "Don't count her out so fast. Mentally, she's fine. She's a tough one. No, Ziri's keeping quiet because she discovered they wanted *her* and the other two girls from her village for something different and she doesn't want them to know *she* knows. Even though we're being nice to her, she's not entirely convinced that all of us aren't involved. After all, she's already seen several of the locals—you included—change forms just like her captors did. No, she's just biding her time."

That made Cara's brow furrow. "Biding her time for *what*? What did they want her for?"

Tony moved his tapping fingers to the side of the silver

can and let out a small snarl. "Biding her time to *escape*. We need to get Adam's butt back here because things are going to start to get dicey pretty quick. Someone's apparently started a Sazi raptor factory down here. Ziri and her friends were being saved to become attack victims." He let them process that information for a moment, nodding his head at their shocked expressions. "See what I mean about *hot*? According to what Ziri overheard, after the girls were turned, they were either going to wind up murderous feral birds that would hunt meat for the flock, or—and this is my worry—they were going to be turned over to some sort of . . . *creature* the men wouldn't even mention without crossing themselves and muttering prayers—*as food*."

Chapter 24

"OFFICER MUELLER?" ADAM turned his head while struggling to pull his briefcase from the overhead compartment in the now-empty plane. He saw the slender, dark-haired flight attendant who'd waited on his section. "Don't forget these."

She held out a paper-wrapped bouquet, the stems dripping water on the carpeted aisle. He tugged and the compartment finally released his case, so he held out his hand for the flowers. "Thanks. I appreciate you putting them in water for me."

Her smile and raised brows had a knowing hint that seemed right at home with the soft Southern accent. "Well, wilted flowers aren't much of an apology and believe me when I say y'all might want to consider adding chocolates."

"Yeah? Why's that?" He lifted the case over the backs of the seats and edged sideways down the row.

"You said your lady friend is a sheriff down here?"

He nodded as she stepped back between the seats so he could get by. "Yeah."

Another smile, this one with real amusement that showed in her scent briefly before disappearing into the vents overhead. "Well, there's a very pretty, and *very* annoyed-looking lady with a badge pacing the concourse in front of this gate. Oh, and she's armed."

Adam grimaced and clutched the flowers a little tighter. "A hazard of cops dating each other. It's occasionally surprising we survive to breed." It had been a convenient excuse to get the flight attendant to find a vase during the flight, but he was starting to wonder if it wasn't the truth. He certainly had the same butterflies as if he was dating her.

She chuckled and waved her hand toward the exit, obviously wanting to stay carefully behind him as he left the plane. He took a deep breath and walked down the corridor, his weight making the walkway bounce with each step. The phone call last night hadn't gone so well. He really believed that Lucas was going to tell Cara about everything, so he hadn't mentioned it. But when the elder wolf had told him that *as of now* he was the Texas alpha—he'd been expected to take the lead on getting information to Cara. So, now he was in hot water from both sides. Thankfully, though, he didn't have a planeload of pack mates with him. The phone conference with Bobby and Tony last night had changed things. Only Tommy, Jill, and Jenny would be arriving tomorrow because Jill was very close to a breakdown. She needed a change of scenery. The rest of the people would follow in a week, after the moon—when wolves on both sides were a little . . . calmer and Bobby could make some formula for Cara to replace her tea that would solve her scent problem. So, he and Cara only had a week to integrate two packs *and* find a murderous flock of birds with some larger, more sinister motive than just abducting girls. *Terrific*.

He looked inside the paper tube in his hand again, still not sure about this bouquet. His first choice would have been roses, but Reggie had assured him that would only make things worse. He hadn't told his ex-partner what he'd done, just that she was mad. "No, amigo, you need poinsettias if you've screwed up. A chica will throw roses right back in your face." It'd taken hours to find a florist in the cities who had a poinsettia plant this time of year. He'd finally found one in the middle of St. Paul, with just barely enough time left to cut off the blooms and catch his flight. *I hope Reggie was right*.

Cool air filled with scents and sounds hit him in the face when he entered the main airport, the bouquet carefully hidden behind his back. Chief among the smells was fur and anger. It wasn't hard to spot Cara in the crowd. With a frown under mirrored sunglasses, hands on hips, and a stance wide and solid, she could have posed for a statute of the goddess of vengeance in nearly any culture. She was bleeding enough Sazi magic that everyone on the concourse was giving her a wide berth. Probably the reason for the sunglasses. And yep, she was armed.

And even still, the sight of her—dangerous and nearly feral, sent his pulse racing and magic flaring, reaching out to her . . . and not in a *what a great pack leader she is* sort of way. Maybe Lucas had been right. Shit.

He took a deep breath and walked toward her, skirting the bank of plastic chairs secured to the floor. It wasn't until he was standing just a few feet from her that he realized anger was only one of the emotions going on inside her. He might just have a chance to make this better, after all. He tipped his chin and crinkled the plastic behind his back. "Sheriff Salinas. Good to see you again."

"Officer Mueller. Wish I could say the same." The words came out sneering and sarcastic, but they didn't match her scent at all. She looked around furtively and lowered her voice. "Who in the *hell* do you think you are, keeping vital information like tha—"

He pulled the bouquet from behind his back and held it out. "I'm sorry, Cara. I screwed up."

She ignored it for a moment, her jaw clenching, but when he tipped the white paper tube so she could see inside, she faltered. He softened his voice and pushed the bouquet a little closer. "I'm *really* sorry."

Her hands clenched into fists over and over until she finally reached up and snatched the bouquet out of his hand. The next words were harsh and rushed and the fiery pepper scent was taking on a thick wet quality that made him want to pull her against him and bear the pounding of her fists on his arms and back. But this wasn't the time or the place. "The truck is parked out front. Get your baggage and meet me there."

It took nearly a half hour for the carousel to cough up the two suitcases he'd had time to pack. He'd loaded everything he could think of, because this might be it. He might never make it back north. David and Mom had promised to pack up his house if that's what winded up happening. While his mother had been very upset by the circumstances, she'd also apparently been briefed by David about Texas . . . and Cara. She'd sat him down when he stopped by. Patted the couch next to her like she always did when he was a child and she wanted to give needed advice. "Give it a chance, son," she'd said. "Now, you're just like your father don'tcha know . . . both you boys are. He was a great pack leader, but he could never let himself show anything.

Typical for a Minnesotan, I suppose, but your new pack is going to be different. Remember I lived in Texas until I was ten. People are more open down there. They're going to expect you to speak your mind, and the pack members from up here are going to look to you . . . are going to take their clues on how to respond by how *you* present yourself." She'd smiled then, with both motherly concern and womanly amusement. "And that includes how you interact with the Alpha Female." She'd patted his hand when he frowned. "Just give it a chance."

Give it a chance. It sounded simple, but when he arrived at the truck to see Cara's frowning face, it might not be so easy in practice. She opened the driver's door as he approached. "Put 'em in back." Then she got in and closed the door with a sharp pull.

He swung the first case over the bed wall and took a moment to glance into the cab through the back window, his eyes searching for the bouquet. Reggie had told him that how a Latina dealt with the flowers was a good indication how the apology was going. At first, he didn't see them at all, which might mean they wound up in a trash can on the way out of the airport. But then he spotted them propped in the corner of the extended cab. As he arranged his two bags to protect the briefcase, and the laptop inside, he was pleased to see the stems were now safely in water again, in a tall glass vase that still bore the price tag from an airport shop.

As he got into the passenger side, he was very careful to keep his scent neutral and a smile off his face.

"I STILL DON'T think this is a good idea." Cara stared at the card key Adam held out toward her. "We should head back tonight. I'm really worried about Ziri."

"Just to turn around and come back before dawn?" The

burnt metal of his frustration tainted the lush scent of the poinsettias curled in the crook of her arm as he reached forward and picked up her hand to press the credit-card-sized piece of plastic into it. "You said it yourself—there are at least four good reasons to stay over. Look, I'm sorry things haven't been going your way today, but that's the way it happens sometimes."

She looked down at the richly colored carpet lining the hallway of the exclusive Riverwalk hotel and fought off a shudder. "But *two hundred dollars* a night? We could have stayed at the Motel 6 by the airport for about forty."

Adam sighed for probably the tenth time since they'd checked in. "Yes, but the airport is the *last* place we need to hit in the morning. It doesn't make much sense to fight our way back to this exact spot during rush hour in the morning, does it? At least the jeweler was embarrassed enough at not finishing the engraving on the necklace you ordered that he's going to come in specially in the morning and bring it to you in the coffee shop next door."

He touched her hand again for a second and a full blown shudder ran through her. No fighting this one off. His magic was teasing her arms again, and she doubted he even realized he was doing it. But it was getting more disconcerting how much it was affecting her—especially since Bobby had thrown a fit back at her house and had poured the rest of her tea down the garbage disposal. A *stash*, he'd called it. Well, how was she supposed to know some of the herbs Ten Bears used were *narcotics*? But she understood the python agent's concern. If she ever had to do a random drug test—belladonna, peyote, and even, *¡Madre de Dios, poppy tar . . . opium*! No wonder the old seer had taken off in such a rush, especially if he'd had a vision Bobby was coming. And he'd been a career *cop*? At least Bobby had let her explain and said he would see what he could come up with to replace it, using legal substances.

But here she was . . . at a hotel with a man who made her condition a dozen times worse with no way to stave it off. Even with separate rooms, it was going to be a long night.

"Cara . . . *hello*? Did you hear me?" She started sharply and realized she'd been staring down at the carpet again, not even listening.

"Oh. Uh . . . no. Sorry."

He shook his head with a small smile, smelling slightly amused. "I asked what order you wanted to do things in the morning. I was thinking we'd have a quick breakfast downstairs and then go to the coffee shop. Meet the jeweler, then head over to the police station for the paperwork on that prisoner you transported down here yesterday."

The snort that erupted was inevitable. "That still pisses me off. They had me drop everything to rush him here and then didn't even bother to get a copy of the signed order from the court so I could release him. Any other day, I would have turned right around and taken him back until they could get their shit together. But they swore it would be ready at nine and at least the court clerk said the order existed. So yeah, that would probably work . . . and I can probably call the party company about finalizing delivery of the balloon arch on my cell at the coffee shop. We might not have to actually stop there. I shouldn't have even promised to do that, but Rosa was really ticked off that I wouldn't tell her what happened during Ziri's hindsight session, and it was a way to keep the peace. But I didn't realize your flight would be late and I'd miss them."

Adam nodded. "And speaking of flights, we'll finish up at the airport and pick up the Taylors. Are you *sure* you don't mind? It's going to be a pretty full truck all the way back to Santa Helena."

"It's silly to make them rent a car when we're already here. Besides, there'd be no place to leave it when they got there. We don't have a rental agency in town." Annoyance tugged at her insides again, but there was no point in arguing any further. It was going to happen, whether now or later. She couldn't help but blush as she glanced at his face. There was still a bit of red remaining along his jaw from where she'd hit him. But she had to give him credit. He'd seen it coming and hadn't dodged out of the way after their screaming match in a secluded corner of the Riverwalk. But there was no way she was going to let her pack be bound. She couldn't even *imagine* that the people up north would allow an Alpha to control their actions like some sort of puppetmaster!

That he backed down showed he respected her authority as Alpha . . . a lot more than her own pack did—not that either of them expected it would knock him back so hard he'd smack his skull against the bridge. She'd never had that kind of power before. It was a little unnerving and she was starting to wonder if the tea had been tamping down more than just her pheromones. But it had been a release she needed and he seemed to realize it. The trip back to the hotel along the meandering pathway next to the light festooned river had resulted in a much calmer talk, where she could relax and actually enjoy the sounds of laughter and water lapping against the sidewalk as boats of tourists passed. He hadn't brought up the incident since.

"So, we should probably turn in then, huh?" His voice seemed unsure as he lifted his chin toward the adjoining doors and reached down to pick up the largest suitcase. "Tomorrow's going to be a long day, Carita."

Nodding while hiding a small smile at the name, she picked up the handles of the elegant bag from the gift shop downstairs. The change of clothes and toiletries she'd purchased—for an ungodly price—would at least make her presentable to her new pack members tomorrow. "Yeah. Okay, then." She lifted the vase lightly. "Thanks again for the flowers . . . and the dinner—especially the *sopapillas* for dessert. I don't think anyone's ever gone to this much trouble just to apologize to me before."

He paused and then his voice softened as he slid the card key into the door slot and turned the knob when the green light blinked. "Nobody's ever been *worth* the trouble before . . . my Alpha." Magic tingled her again, but this time it was intentional. With a small gasp, she looked at his face, and immediately got lost in his drowning deep blue eyes— flickering with the same ethereal power that danced over her skin like a thousand tiny fingers. Panic spread through her in a wave and she backed up a pace, bumping her back against the wall next to her door. He didn't follow, didn't press his advantage, even though a small part of her wanted him to. Instead, he offered a small smile, pulled back his magic, and walked through the door with his bags while she stood, frozen in place, trying to get her heart to start beating again.

Chapter 25

ADAM PRESSED THE button on the remote to change the channel again and watched ambulance doors fly open on the screen. It didn't have as much impact with no sound, but he'd really hoped to hear a knock on the connecting doors between their rooms and didn't want to miss it. He added another pillow to the pile behind his back, and crossed his jean-clad legs on the bed while reaching for the bottle of water on the night stand.

His tongue pressed his molar again and was glad it was starting to firm up in the gum. Maybe this sip wouldn't hurt as much as the last one. A quick touch of his fingers against his jaw confirmed that the swelling was nearly gone. Man, could that woman punch! He hadn't taken a shot like that since Josef pounded on him for the newspaper article about wolves last fall. Another quick glance at the door didn't make it any more open than a second ago, but he couldn't help himself. Was she still mad?

I would have sworn Reggie had been right on the money about how to make up to her. She'd responded like clockwork to the flowers, the dinner, and the fight. It wasn't in his nature to argue about pack politics, but he had to admit it was sort of cathartic—especially this close to the moon. Even though taking the punch full on and hitting his head had really rung his chimes, it *had* shocked Cara out of yelling enough that she raced to pick him back up and spent the next few minutes apologizing until he convinced her to stop.

And oh, baby—the sensation of healing magic after she'd helped him to a bench to shake it off—that definitely made it worthwhile. It had boiled his blood enough that he nearly threw her to the ground, right there on the cobbled path. The glittering strands of lights under the star-filled sky hadn't had anything on those glowing golden eyes as power flared between them. But he'd been so damned dizzy for those first few minutes that he hadn't dared any quick movements. Still, the way she reacted just now to the light touch of magic, he'd been sure—

"Damn." He shook his head in frustration and turned off the television, and then swung his feet to the floor while muttering. "Face it, Mueller, you had your chance and screwed it up. Let it go."

It really was going to be a busy day tomorrow, so maybe it was best to just take a shower and go to bed.

Still . . . just to be safe. He silently unlocked the deadbolt on his way to the bathroom.

* * *

CARA TOOK ANOTHER sip of way too expensive bottled water and tugged at the bodice of the pale yellow night-gown she'd purchased downstairs. It pushed and pulled in all the wrong directions and was going to be miserable to sleep in. *Why in the world didn't I try this thing on before I plunked down my card?*

The answer in her head came in the form of Yolanda's voice. That was the problem with having an opinionated, smart-aleck best friend—she'd even managed to infect Cara's own logic center. *Because you didn't expect to wear it all night, stupida!*

She looked from the spray of pink poinsettia blossoms in the cylindrical glass vase on the dresser to the door that con-nected her room to Adam's. How long had it taken to track down the flowers at this time of year—and when was the last time she'd gotten flowers from a man *at all*? Another glance at the door didn't change anything, although she could have sworn she heard a noise a few minutes ago. But nothing had happened since and now her nerves were starting to get to her. Was he mad that she hit him? She supposed he had every right to be—especially if they were really supposed to be corulers of the pack. He hadn't really said anything that she didn't already know. But she hated this whole situation . . . hated the complete lack of control over the lives of so many people, and she'd taken it out on him.

She stood up and slipped on the matching silken knee-length robe and crossed her arms over her chest—which threatened to pop her breasts right out the top of the nearly translucent fabric. Again she flipped back her hair and tugged it up, even as a part of her was wishing she had the nerve to just take it off and knock on the door, stark naked, and ask him for what she wanted. She just couldn't deny it anymore. She wanted him to toss her on the bed and make her body *feel*. The tiny bits of magic he'd been throwing at her all evening were a nearly constant torment that quickened her breath every time she moved. Did he feel it, too? Was he waiting for her to make the first move? The way he'd looked at her out on the path . . . and there was no denying the increasing musk in his scent as their arguments moved from terse, nearly whispered words to yells that probably reached the street above the river.

Just do it. Stand up on your hind legs and do it! Again, Yo's voice in her mind taunted her, even ending with the same frustrated harsh breath. *What's the worst he's going to do?*

Laugh.

Wasn't that what she was really afraid of? That a powerful Alpha, years older than her, would laugh at her for throwing herself at him like a crushing teenager?

"But I'm not a teenager. I'm the Alpha Female of a werewolf pack, and I get to be attracted to an Alpha Male." Her own voice sounded strange to her ears, and she paused, as though she was waiting for someone in the empty room to contradict her.

Taking a deep breath, she reached for the door, turned open the deadbolt, and opened it to reveal . . . another door. She stared stupidly at it for a space of a few seconds then let out a sharp bark of laughter. Of *course* there'd be a second door in a hotel. Not that many guests arrived in groups large enough to need two rooms and who would want someone to be able to just waltz into their room? She heard water running in the background, but she couldn't tell if it was in Adam's room or the one overhead.

Here was the real test now. Was *his* door unlocked? She reached for the knob, feeling nearly apart from herself, but then stopped. *Maybe it would be better to knock.*

Even the little Yolanda in her head couldn't argue with that logic and she raised up her hand. The tentative knock still sounded far too loud, but the water turned off instantly, and her stomach fluttered as distinct footsteps created fine tremors in the carpet under her bare feet. Her fingers clenched on the handle of her own door, her every muscle screaming to slam it shut . . . ignore this for another day.

But then it was too late, because his door opened, and she froze anew, her eyes wide with both panic and sudden, irresistible desire. The running water had apparently been the shower, because he was naked from the waist up, his lower body covered only by a fluffy white towel that reached his knees. The dark hair she'd wanted to run her fingers through all evening was damp and smelled of herbal shampoo and fur and his face was clean shaven again. Would his jaw glide against her chest, or her thighs? Would she like it better than the stubble?

He didn't move or speak. He just stood there, barely breathing, his hand mirroring hers on the edge of his door.

Droplets of water covered his neck and broad, muscled chest—with only one remaining scar across those rock solid abs to mar the perfection. Steam rose from his skin when the air conditioner suddenly clicked on. She couldn't seem to take her eyes off one drop, larger than all the others, that quivered in the hollow of his throat.

The voice that reached her ears was a harsh whisper that pulled at things low in her body. "Go ahead. I know you want to." Adrenaline musk filled her nose and suddenly there was nothing but the sound of her own heart and the trembling bit of water on smooth skin that she had to taste or fear going mad.

Cara was suddenly powerless to stop herself and stepped forward, across the threshold, and flicked out her tongue to catch the water as it escaped. He didn't move, but the tiny growl that escaped him vibrated his skin beneath her frantically moving lips and tongue. God, he tasted so good! She lapped up drop after drop of clean, cool water, like melted snow that smelled of pines and fur. It wasn't until the last drop was gone that she came partially back to her senses. She moved back her head . . . only to discover his fingers threaded through her hair, holding her tight against him.

"Don't stop. Jesus, don't stop now." His voice was rough; needy, and she finally looked up to see his eyes burning with dark intensity and his nostrils flared. "Not now." He lowered those velvety lips to hers and an ache of pleasure ripped through her as he claimed her mouth with a hunger her own body matched, movement for movement. Ten times more intense than the stolen kiss in the dark alley or even in her kitchen—he raked her body with magic, no longer trying to hide what he was . . . or what he wanted.

His erection pushed at her stomach, and when he wrapped his arms tightly around her and stepped backward, pulling her into his room, the towel dropped away and his pulsing cock brushed against her naked leg. With a movement so quick it drew a gasp from her that exited into his searching mouth, he had her legs wrapped around his waist. Cara suddenly remembered she wasn't wearing panties, and couldn't remember if it had been intentional. But the feeling of him rubbing between her legs was nearly enough to make her pass out.

He apparently realized it, too, because he didn't even try to pretend. He reached down and took hold of himself while at the same time pressing her up against the wall. She didn't even have time to breathe before he slid himself inside her.

She could feel it happening again . . . felt the roar of the wolf race through her veins and then suddenly she didn't care anymore that there was no condom, no protection. She didn't care about anything but the aching need and the scent and sound of a growling wolf as powerful as the one inside her. She answered his growl as his tongue began to thrust against hers, matching the movements of his hips.

Her muscles clenched around his swollen organ, pulling him ever deeper inside. Magic made her skin burn and her nipples ache as he drove into her, again and again—taking her higher than she ever dreamed possible.

His fingers dug into her lower back, then moved to cup her thighs as he began to raise and lower her whole body, sliding her up and down the wall, while he drove into her. It was too much sensation and she tried to push him back, tried to lower her rising panic as a massive orgasm grew inside her belly. She could feel it building with every movement but she couldn't break free of his desperate mouth against hers—his lips, teeth and tongue pulling as much pleasure from her as the frantic movements of his hips. The scents that filled her nose, musk and cinnamon and her own maddening pheromones, caused a series of spasms that was pure, delicious torture.

Then he started to toy with her, taking her right to the brink before easing back, slowing his thrusts, but never taking his mouth away, or relieving the pressure keeping her against the wall. Her own body betrayed her head as she dug her fingers into his muscles, desperate for him to continue.

The pressure of the impending climax made her legs tighten on his hips, pulling him closer. And then it was too late, too late to do anything but scream into his mouth as a wave of pleasure claimed her. White lights erupted behind her eyelids as she came and her muscles clenched around him hard enough that his movements became more labored. She was suddenly, abruptly tight and hot enough to burn—every nerve was awakened and she could feel his power, his magic, slice deep within her. It intensified the sensation enough that a second orgasm ripped through her before the first was done.

Energy burst from her in a shock wave that slammed shut the door to her room and threatened to drop them both to the floor. That was too much for him. With a deep moan she felt him swell inside her, scorching already sensitized nerves as his own orgasm took him. It was a half dozen more thrusts before he finally slowed, but his kisses became less desperate and more passionate. By the time he pulled himself free of her, he was butterfly kissing her nose, her cheeks, her eyelids.

It wasn't until he'd lowered her to the ground that she realized he had been wearing a condom after all—though when he'd found time to put it on was beyond her. She motioned downward at his crotch as she tugged and shifted cloth to fit her chest back inside the teddy. "Um, thanks for that." Even though she wasn't positive she was thankful. It was something she still struggled to fit in the confines of her beliefs.

He smiled and it was both thick with satisfaction and lecherous. "Hopefully I'll remember next time, too. Now, how about we get you out of that sweat-soaked robe and nightie and into a hot shower? 'Cause it's going to be a long, long night . . . *my Alpha*."

Chapter 26

SHE'S IN THE shower and she's nervous. Adam tucked his hands behind his head and closed his eyes, luxuriating in the thick sheets and pillowy mattress while breathing in the scent of her body and their shared pleasure. Was he just imagining he could see her in the shower in his mind—looking wet and soapy and utterly delicious? *Reaching for the shampoo. Oops. She dropped the bottle.* The barely discernable thunk that reached his ears over the running water confirmed it and he nodded once.

I'm mated. He tried it out loud next, just to see what it sounded like, but in a whisper too low to be heard. "I'm mated."

It didn't sound *too* horrible . . . and it wasn't like he was the first Sazi male to have it happen. Hell, even Lucas was mated. He opened his eyes and stared at the ceiling, tracing the shadowy shape of pink poinsettia leaves in the light from the twin lamps next to the bed. They made a much more interesting pattern of intertwined images in the pre-dawn darkness than if they'd stayed in his room all night. But after Cara had complained that her bed was more comfortable than his, well . . . they had to test the theory. And she'd actually been right.

The shower shut off and the sudden silence pressed against his ears. Part of him wanted to get out of bed, go into the bathroom and wrap himself around her—hear her moans as his magic inevitably sought hers out and teased her. But the larger part of him was utterly exhausted . . . happily so, but still, he could barely move.

A small smile curled his lips as the blow-dryer came to life behind the closed door. If he'd had this same night when he was younger, he'd probably have wanted to crow about his prowess. How many times had he taken her—and in how many ways? The scent that shut off his brain, that maddening smell of her readiness, had pushed them both far beyond human limits and each successive time inside her had increased the struggle to hold on to his humanity—and tightened the mating ties to her.

The door to the bathroom opened, the light from inside chasing away the shadows overhead. He turned his eyes and watched her walk back into the main room. She was wearing that flimsy little robe that revealed all her curves again, and it made her skin look all the more golden in comparison. Her thick, auburn mane of hair flowed around a face he couldn't tear his eyes from. Adam felt his body start to stir again. Yeah, he was a goner all right. "Hey."

"Morning." Her voice sounded almost painfully shy— probably getting the morning after guilts. He couldn't really blame her, since he wasn't in much better shape.

He held out his hand. It was probably time to tell her. She was going to find out soon enough anyway. "C'mere for a second."

She shook her head and turned her back to open the shopping bag on the chair. "We probably need to get dressed and get started."

His eyes flicked to the alarm clock on the night stand and he picked up his watch to confirm it. "It's only five. Nothing's open yet."

She didn't stop, her agitated movements matching the scent of rising panic. With one smooth movement he pulled the covers away and stood up. He was across the room with his arms around her shoulders before she could take a single step. Her whole body was shaking and the distress tore at him. "Shhh," he whispered, and kissed her hair softly before resting his cheek against the back of her head. "What's wrong?"

She tried to pull away, but only half-heartedly, so he didn't let her go. Eventually she leaned into him and tightened her own arms around his. "I couldn't stop." The words were a harsh, desperate admission that had deeper meaning than they first appeared. The scents of sorrow and fear were nearly equal.

"Did you *want* to stop at some point?" What was she saying? That some of what happened . . . had she felt *forced*?

"I . . . I don't know. Some of the things—I've never done them—never even *considered* them before. But I couldn't stop . . . even when it . . . *hurt*."

He felt his breath still and a rising horror clench his

stomach. "I hurt you?" He stepped back and spun her around, raising her chin so he could see her eyes. But, that wasn't *possible*! He couldn't harm his mate. "Talk to me, Cara. *Did I hurt you?*"

She shook her head, but there were tears in her eyes. "They were things *I* suggested, things I started and . . . it felt really, really *good* at the time. I wanted them or, at least, my wolf did. But this morning—I'll heal, but . . . why couldn't I stop, Adam? And what in the hell are we going to do if it happens again—when there are other alphas down here? Bobby threw away all my tea."

He pulled her against him, wrapped his arms around her, and held her tight. It was a good question, especially because of . . . him. He kissed her hair again and took a deep breath. "I'm mated to you, Cara. I won't be *able* to let anyone else touch you. I'll protect you, or die trying."

MATED. IS THAT what he just said? Cara pushed against his chest and raised her eyes to his incredulously. He nodded seriously as she felt her jaw drop. "How do you—I mean, how can you know that?"

He sighed, lifted her hand, and led her to the bed where he plopped down on the edge. He patted the mattress next to him and she sat, just before her suddenly rubbery legs gave out. "You remember telling me about the truck hitting you?" She nodded and he let out a small chuckle. "I was walking up from the basement of our pack headquarters when that happened . . . remember I asked what time it happened? Well, at that instant, a wave of exhaustion hit me, like all the energy had been sucked out of my body. I blacked out and fell down the stairs. I nearly broke my neck." He paused. "Lucas is the one who suggested being mated. The guys were trying to figure out why I looked like . . . well, like a truck hit me."

Her head was swimming and she started to shake her head, tiny little movements that didn't clear her mind at all. "But that could be anything. Coinciden—"

Adam raised his hand and put his fingers against her lips. The mixture of emotions that rose from him was just too confusing for her nose to sort. "How about that punch in the jaw that sent me flying ten feet? Ever been able to do that before? You're drawing on *my* power, my abilities. Strength is my biggest ability. And just now, while you were in the shower, I could *see* you. See you inside my head. I *watched* you drop the shampoo bottle, like I was standing next to you. And I knew you were worried in there, before your scent ever could have reached me." He let out a nervous chuckle. "Trust me, if I could delude myself into believing it was *anything* else, I would. No, I'm mated to you."

She put her hand on his and pulled it away, wrapping her fingers around his while he gave her a sad smile. "But that means you won't ever be able to—" She couldn't even finish. Mated was *forever* for a Sazi male. He would never be interested in another woman, Sazi or human. He'd never be able to have sex with anyone else, ever again. And it was just a few days ago she'd wondered what it would feel like to have a powerful Alpha mated to her. It felt . . . odd.

"I know." He chuckled again, and this time it was amused. "I guess you were just too much woman for me." He gave a great, heaving sigh that was filled with mock resignation. "*Qué mujer fatal.*"

She couldn't help herself. A giggle escaped her. "*What* did you say?"

Dry, sandy embarrassment rose from him in a flash and he blushed. "Did I say that wrong? What did I say?"

Another fit of giggles overcame her. "You said, 'What a femme fatale.' I've just never heard Spanish spoken with a Minnesota accent. *Dios Mio!* That's *too* funny—say it again." Wetness began to fill her eyes, but not from sadness this time.

He wiggled his eyebrows this time and did a bad Sam Spade impression. *"Qué mujer fatal . . . sweetheart."* The twitching, curling lip started her laughing again and now she was really wiping tears away.

"You have *got* to say that to *Abuela* Carlotta—my grand-mother. You'd make her whole day!"

He raised his brows with a hint of mild insult. "Why? So she can laugh at me? You're asking a lot there."

Cara nodded. "She'll laugh, but in a good way. She doesn't speak any English and if you take the time to say *anything* to her in Spanish, she'll think you're terrific— even with that accent. All of my pack can speak English, but a lot of the older, fringe relatives don't. And Gloria's Quinceanera will have a *lot* of fringe relatives. You can't imagine the size of my *familia*—my family. There will probably be twenty-five or thirty cousins who'll be walking under that balloon arch . . . oh, you'll just love my *Prima* Carmen, and José! Oh, he's—"

She was babbling but couldn't seem to stop herself. Sweet Jesus, she was starting to think of him as *part* of the *familia* . . . and she wanted him to fit in. She wasn't at all upset when he put light fingers over her mouth again and then caught her gaze. "I'll be honored to meet your family, and your grandmother. If she's anything like you, she prob-ably *is* a femme fatale." Then he moved his fingers, easing them down the line of her jaw and behind her neck to rub gently. "And you don't have to worry—I won't let anyone bother you on the moon, *mi amor.*"

My love. If he was mated, he really meant that. Did she love him back? She just didn't know. It was still so damned early, and she barely knew anything about him. But she didn't stop him when he pulled her closer and her hands reached for him just the same. The kiss was slow and soft, and his magic eased around her, lulling her into languid bonelessness. But when he started to roll her over onto the bed, she stopped him. "My turn."

His scent spoke his amusement. "I didn't know we were taking turns." With fluid grace that took her breath away, he stretched out on the bed. His arousal was becoming evident as she let her eyes roam over his muscled chest and firm abdomen. "But please, don't let me stop you."

She rose to her knees and leaned over him, letting her hair dangle in his face for a moment. His stomach muscles twitched when she ran a light finger across his skin. He breathed in her scent with flared nostrils and rubbed his cheek against the strands as she whispered. "No wolves. Is that possible?"

He met her eyes seriously and nodded before reaching for her waist. "No wolves. Just a man and an utterly, devastatingly beautiful woman."

Now, how could a girl not smile at that? So she did, right before lowering her mouth to his for a long, slow taste. It was hard to hold the wolf at bay, especially when his fingers snaked down between her legs to rub her. When his mouth moved to her breasts and started to lick and suck, she nearly lost the battle, so he slowed, bringing her back from the brink.

"We *can* keep your wolf out of it," he said and then pulled her over to straddle his waist and flipped her onto her back. "But you need to let me lead." He slid down until she could only see the top of his head between her legs, past the rise of her breasts. The first slow flick of his tongue inside her put her heart in her throat. Her back arched and her wolf reached out for his magic, but didn't find it. He'd pulled as much of what made him Sazi as he could inside and so the man who was licking and sucking at her was just a man—who happened to be *really* good at what he was doing!

It wasn't very long at all before she was clawing at the bedsheets and screaming his name as another orgasm turned her mind to putty. But when he crawled back up and kissed her cheek the wolf was already satisfied and didn't growl for more. "See? We just need to get you off first. I thought that might work. Nothing to it."

He reached for another square package from the night stand but she stopped him before he could rip it open. "What happens, happens. There's always families who can't ever have kids." She'd never gotten involved in the breeding program, but there really were so many families where both partners were Sazi . . . but couldn't bear children. Only Alpha females or humans could successfully have children with a male werewolf. Her guilt at the packet in his hand was probably increased by the fact that her golden Virgen de Guadalupe medallion had wrapped in her hair and was cutting into her neck. Maybe that was a sign that it was time to look, as so many had told her lately, to the future of *all* of their kind.

Adam didn't argue. Possibly he couldn't argue, if he was truly mated. He just began to rain slow kisses on her face and neck, and when he entered her, his groan collapsed him onto her chest. He didn't last long enough after that for her to do much more than moan softly and taste the salty sweat that rolled down his neck as he took his pleasure. She wrapped her legs around his hips and held him to her as he climaxed with a shuddering moan and a whisper of her name. She kept holding him close until he naturally slipped out of her. His breathing was soft against her ear when he spoke. "You're so beautiful . . . so incredible, Carita. Do you know that? Do you have any idea how good you feel under me?"

She smiled as he threaded his arms under her, and just held her. His scent, like warm bread and cookies baking, told her what she needed to know. It might not be love yet,

but there was definitely contentment. It felt good—his
warm weight on her, and the thick cool sheets underneath,
as the sun began to creep over the horizon and fill the room
with soft light.

Chapter 27

"So? HAVE ANY bright ideas how I'm going to pull this
off?" Cara leaned back into the comfortable wicker chair,
grabbed the bottle of Dos Equis beer from the glass-topped
end table and used it to salute the incredulous look that
greeted her rambling account.

Eduardo Ruiz shook his head and closed his eyes for a
moment as she took a deep draw of the amber liquid. "*Jesus bambino,* Cara! This has all happened in a *week*?"
When she nodded at his strange but somehow fitting curse,
he blew out a slow breath and stood up, frustration and
anger overshadowing his normal scent, similar to boiled
raisins with oatmeal.

Immaculate and handsome as ever, in polished cowboy
boots, a starched western-style shirt and dark jeans that
had been pressed until there was a sharp crease, Paco's
twin oozed the same Latino style and masculinity as her
brother-in-law—despite his sexual preference. Eddie reminded Cara of how Paco looked on the day he married
Rosa . . . young, strong, virile. But then, Eddie actively
worked to keep his physique, and Paco's desk job had softened him over the last sixteen years.

He took two steps from the living room and was suddenly
in the kitchen of the tiny efficiency apartment. Opening a

refrigerator that barely reached his chin, he pulled out his third bottle since she arrived. One more and she'd have to suggest switching to coffee. She knew he was trying to cut back since almost getting hauled in for a DWI. *Dying for a drink* had nearly become literal last fall when Will pulled him over after a pack hunt. Sazi who got locked up never reached their trial. Cara felt a small shudder pass through her at what nearly happened. She learned after that incident not to leave a hunt until after she'd seen everyone safely on their way, no matter how big the emergency. Thankfully, they'd still been on the ranch property and Luis had been with him. Will just made Eddie move to the passenger seat before they hit the highway.

"So, let me get this straight," he said as he sat down opposite her with a squeaking of varnished fibers and put the bottle on the other table. "The Sazi council told you that we have to share our territory with a bunch of timber wolves, and the guy you've been hanging out with is going to be our new Alpha?" She nodded and he continued. "And, there's some sort of big plot going on where raptors are stealing livestock around the valley and kidnapping young girls, including the girl—who I might mention is the same age as Gloria—that's staying with my brother . . . *and* that it's all somehow tied to the pack that's joining us." He held up a finger in a good enough imitation of a trite infomercial that she chuckled. "But *wait*! There's more! Just to screw things up further, the Wolven snake who was here took away the only thing that keeps you from going into heat, and the Alpha Male is *mated* to you, so he causes you to go into heat even faster because you can't keep your hands off each other . . . and he'll proceed to *kill* any of the pack that accidentally touches you." He raised both his arms, like some enraptured televangelist. "*Sí, sí!* It can all be yours, for the low, low price of just—" Now he turned deadly serious and dropped his arms, and all the humor disappeared from his face. "The love and respect of your entire *familia*."

Cara let out a harsh breath and banged her fist down on the armrest. It bent downward sharply as she felt extra power flood her from the sudden anger. Would Adam be able to see this conversation now? Would he be mad at her for telling Eddie about him? "I *knew* you were going to say that! Damn it, Eddie!" She crossed her arms over her chest and shook her head. "I don't know why I even bothered to tell you."

His voice softened, but was no less serious. "Because you knew that I'd be the *most* receptive to the situation . . . unfortunately. Paco is going to go ballistic, Cara. You know that, and Rosa is going to be stuck square in the middle. You've known about this shit for a whole week—you've introduced people to us and *lied,* saying they were just visiting . . . and it's just *now* you're telling anyone? On the first night of the moon, when there are already new wolves here that will need to hunt with us?"

She shook her head. "I didn't lie. Not exactly—you guys would have smelled that. They *are* visiting right now. They'll just be visiting for . . . a really long time. And they won't need to hunt tonight. They're alphic."

"Oh! Even better! *Rationalize* lying and then rub the Second's nose in the fact that the newcomers are better than him. *Jesus bambino!*" She felt her face redden, because she knew he was right.

"It's not fair, Eddie. I didn't have any say in this, but I'm going to take the heat for everything. We don't have any *choice*! Doesn't that count for anything?"

He ran his fingers through his short, wavy black hair and stared at the table in the corner, filled to overflowing with candles in glass jars bearing the image of the Virgin and her baby. He had more to pray about than most anyone she knew . . . until recently, anyway. She was pretty sure her candle count was higher this week. He started to tap one finger on his leg and she felt herself perk up a little. He was thinking his hardest when that happened and he was unusually brilliant when he started to really work on a problem. Paco couldn't believe the day when Eddie had gotten the invitation to join that club, Mensa, in the mail—only to have Eddie laugh and throw it away. *Why would I join a snooty bunch of librarians who don't even know how to fiesta?* he'd asked. *I just took the test for fun.*

After a few moments where she didn't dare even breathe for fear of breaking his concentration, he finally started to nod and a slow smile spread across his face. "Refugees."

Cara felt her brows raise. "Excuse me?"

He flicked his gaze to her, his eyes filled with fiery intensity. "The Minnesota people. They're *refugees*—running from an insane Alpha dictator. A wolf version of Castro, and we have to take them in. We're Sazi . . . family. We can't turn them away. I saw the scars on Tómas . . . and so did Paco. If you're right and Jill is as traumatized as you say, then it could really work. You saw how Rosa was around her when they stopped by with Adam yesterday. Even your sister saw there was something haunting her. And the girls are already *hermanas*—just like sisters." He shrugged mildly. "Jenny's hair and clothes are a little Goth, but she's nice enough and offering to photograph the Quince made Paco happy—I mean, *damn*! She's had her own *gallery* showing up north! It would save him a bunch of money. It might just work."

She brightened for a moment but then felt her heart sink. "But the Alpha is dead up there now. Why still run?"

"A pack without an Alpha is a pack headed for extinction, Cara. What sane person wouldn't run from a civil war where everyone is trying to fill the top slot?"

Refugees. Eddie was right. That might just work. "Wow. That angle would *never* have occurred to me!" She stood in a rush of movement and bent down over him to hug his shoulders. "Thank you so much! You're the best!" A weight lifted from her and she smiled. The room seemed brighter and the air cleaner. She shook her head in amazement. Once again, he'd come through for her.

"But," he added, with worry tinging his scent, "that first hunt with *all* of them . . . you'll need to lay down some ground rules."

She nodded and stepped back to take her seat again. "Already covered. Lucas said the council approved everyone in this pack remaining in their current rankings. They'll all be coming in at the bottom until things settle down."

Eddie took a sip of beer and fingered the bottle. "That's good, but it's not what I'm worried about. Rosa was pretty ticked off when she found out how the Minnesota pack treats non-shifters."

She reared back a little in surprise. "Which is *how*?"

"They're not considered *pack* at all. They're not even *invited* to the hunt fiesta. They're like glorified babysitters who handle all the menial details, like cooking and caring for the children, while the high and mighty shifters hunt. Not only do the wolves not offer them the first deer of the hunt like we do, they don't get *any* meat. I guess Jenny was complaining to Gloria about it and Rosa caught wind of the conversation last night when the girls had a slumber party. Jenny's getting ready to change, and she hates the thought of joining . . . what did Rosa say again? Oh yeah, she didn't want to become like those *bourgeois elitists*."

That was what had been bothering her—ever since the first conversation at the restaurant! He'd called the non-shifters *family members,* not pack. Yeah, that was definitely something that was going to need to be discussed. No way would people be joining her pack and not be included in everything that bound them together as Sazi! She looked at him seriously. "I'll take care of it. I promise." She happened to notice the time on her new watch—she never did find the old one, damn it!—when she reached for her beer again.

"*Chingado!* I've been here for two hours already! I'm so sorry, Eddie. I've been totally monopolizing the conversation, and you were the one who called me here to talk!" She looked again at his handsome face, noticing again the puffy dark bags under his eyes, and the wet scents of sorrow and fear that seemed to hang around him like a funeral shroud. "I've been really worried about you lately. Something's been on your mind. I'm guessing it's pretty serious, or you would have already talked to Paco about it."

He shifted his eyes away but then took a deep breath and smiled a bit. "Actually, I think I figured out a solution while we've been talking. I have a feeling it's not going to be a problem much longer." He raised his bottle in toast. "So here's to solving two *problemas* in one day!"

She laughed and took a drink. "Well, if that changes, you let me know. I'll do anything I can to help."

His eyes filled with comradery and warmth. She really couldn't ask for a better brother-in-law, or friend. "I know you will. So, how's work? Any better? Have you checked in on Carl lately?"

She sighed and tucked both ankles under her and fought off a wave of frustration. "Let's not talk about work. Carl had another episode while I was in San Antonio. One side of his face is paralyzed now and it's really hard for him to talk—and even harder for the rest of us not to stare at him when he tries. I stopped by last evening. The doctor didn't put him in the hospital, and *thinks* he'll get the use of those muscles back eventually, but—"

Eddie grimaced. "*Ay chi!* So that means he probably won't be back before elections, huh? You gonna put your name on the ticket?"

"Hell, yes! I'm not even sure I want the job anymore, but I'm going on the ballot." At his questioning look, she continued. "I just found out from Yo that two of my deputies are having an affair . . . or *were*. Right now they can hardly stand to be in the same room together, so I'll have to figure out how to make their shifts opposite. I can't afford to lose either one right now. We're already down a person." Eddie opened his mouth but she held up a hand. "And no . . . don't suggest that Adam could apply. *¡Madre de Dios!* Can you *imagine* what that would sound like in the donut shop, now that people have seen us around town together?"

He raised his chin in sudden understanding. "Ah! Yeah, you're right about that. I wasn't thinking. So, who are the two unlucky lovebirds?"

"You didn't hear it from me, and if I hear it spread around, I'll swear to God I'll beat you bloody—but Stephanie Dion and . . . *Billy,* if you can believe it!"

Eddie nearly dropped his bottle. "That racist, woman-hating son of a bitch—with *Stephanie? Jesus bambino!* She deserves better than him! What in the world is she thinking?"

Cara nodded, still incredulous at the revelation. But Stephanie had finally confirmed it when cornered. No wonder Elliot had been avoiding looking at them. He was friends with them both and probably stuck in the middle—hearing both sides and trying to avoid *taking* sides. She still couldn't believe she hadn't noticed, hadn't smelled any attraction. Then again, maybe it wasn't a matter of attraction.

"I don't know how it started, and I don't want to. I'm just hoping if I can keep them apart for awhile, maybe it'll settle down." They shook their heads at nearly the same speed, and it let her take a deep breath. "Oh hey, I nearly forgot. I got lucky on one front, so the day's not a total loss. I had a long chat with Rick Seguin. Remember I told you I thought he was sneaking around my back to make me look

bad?" Eddie nodded. "Well, turns out he was actually trying to cut me a break. He's been telling everybody that *I've*
been doing the stuff he's been doing, like setting meetings
and shit, in hopes people will think I'm on top of things . . .
and maybe accept me as the permanent sheriff." She
paused and then stood up. "Well, I should probably be going. I need to get the barn ready for the hunt tonight and
then stop by Rosa's. You sure you don't need to talk about
anything?"

He shook his head and stood up, picking up his tall-
crowned straw cowboy hat in the process. "Nah. I've got to
get moving, too—I have a few things to do before the
hunt."

She pointed at him seriously. "Not a word to Paco. Okay?"

He held up one hand while putting on his hat with the
other. "I won't even be seeing him before the hunt. I'll be
going in the other direction."

"WELL, I THINK you're being too hard on yourself, Alpha." Jill took another sip of canned ice tea and leaned
closer to Tommy. She'd been needing to touch him almost
constantly since the battle—maybe to prove to herself that
he wouldn't push her away. She let out a small sigh when
her husband put his arm around her and kissed her hair
lightly. "Cara seems like a perfectly reasonable woman and
she's obviously crazy about you. I don't think she'll react
nearly as badly as you think."

Adam leaned back into the motel's chair and sighed. He
understood now why Lucas had selected this motel. The
thick, adobe walls allowed them to speak freely without
anyone outside the room being able to hear—unless they
were standing right at the door. He'd discovered it just this
morning, when Tommy told him Jill had been up crying all
night again. He hadn't heard a thing, even though he hadn't

been sleeping either. "I should have just told her. It was the perfect time. But I chickened out."

Tommy shrugged. "It's not like you had any choice in the matter either. And it's not the *whole* group that'll be here tomorrow. Just Mike and Sheila. They were the only alphas who could travel on the full moon."

"And Cherise," Adam corrected. "Even if she's only going to stay a few days, long enough to talk to the people at the economic development board, she still needs to hunt. But that's still *six* people, which just about doubles Cara's current pack. I can't *believe* Lucas would decide to do that!"

Jill's expression was worried, but the scent wasn't much different from the profound sadness that masked her normal flowery aroma. "Is there maybe somewhere else we could hunt this month . . . just *our* pack, that is?"

"This *is* our pack now, sweetie. We're not part of the Minnesota pack anymore." Tommy's voice was gentle, but it still had a startling effect. She jerked as though struck and started to shake. Tommy closed his eyes and pulled her head closer to his chest. "It's going to be okay, Jill. You'll see."

She broke into sobs that nearly tore out Adam's heart. "But I can't *feel* them anymore, Tom. They're all gone, and I'm . . . alone!" She touched his face with trembling hands. "I mean, you're here. I can see you, but I can't *feel* you anymore. I can't tell if you *really* forgive me, like I always could before. I didn't mean to hurt you. I have to feel you again."

Tommy sighed and looked up at Adam with desperation plain in his face, and his scent. "We need to be bound again, Adam. You know it—you have to be feeling it, too. We're all pining, but Jill and Sheila are the worst. We can't exist like this forever, no matter what this new pack does."

Adam stood up, walked to the small refrigerator, and

pulled out a 7-Up. He silently offered one to Tommy, but he shook his head. "I know, Tom. I really do. But I've talked to Cara about this twice now. It's just that she's never been attached to a pack before. She doesn't understand how hard it is for us. She really thinks of it as a horrible thing, and unless I can find some way to convince—"

A knock on the door made Adam put his fingers to his lips and Jill wiped away her tears with the back of her hand. He stepped the few paces to the door and opened it. The tall, slender Latino on the other side was one he recognized, but he was certainly surprised to see him. "Eddie? What can I do for you?"

Eddie swept off his cowboy hat and held it nervously in front of his ornate belt buckle, his gaze firmly fixed on the turquoise and green shag carpeting under Adam's feet. "May I speak with you, Alpha?"

Adam exchanged a surprised look with Tommy and Jill before responding. "Oh. Uh, sure."

Tommy pulled away from Jill and started to stand up. "We were just leaving. Adam, we can finish this another time—"

Eddie's head raised and he nearly shouted. "*No*! That is . . . um, this concerns you both, too. I'd like you to stay, if, um, the Alpha is willing to allow me to speak."

He sounded very timid, much more shy suddenly than the charming, engaging man Adam had spoken to twice now. His scent was thick with worry and bordered on ammonia panic. Sadly, they matched what was already in the room. Adam stepped back and motioned him forward with a sweeping gesture. "Fer sure. We might as well make it a party, that is . . . a *fiesta*, right?"

That managed to even pull a small smile from Jill and caused Eddie to laugh and step inside the room far enough for Adam to shut the door behind him. "*Sí*! Except not so happy of a fiesta as we would like, Alpha."

Adam snorted and then let out a sad sigh. "No. You've got that right." He sat down on the edge of the bed, offering Eddie the last chair. He sat down on the very tip of the cushion, tense and nervous, and started to spin the brim of his hat as it hung down between his slightly open legs. "So, Cara finally told the pack about us, huh?"

Eddie shook his head. "Not the pack, Alpha. Just me. She asked my advice, because I know how Paco thinks." He tapped his temple with one hand while continuing to rock the hat forward and back with the other. "Sometimes it works that way with twins, you know. She told me about *everything* and, well . . . maybe she shouldn't have told me as much as she did, but I was grateful because I need your help. I haven't got anywhere else to turn."

Adam started slightly. What could he possibly do that Cara couldn't? "What's the problem, Eddie?"

He took a deep breath and glanced at Tommy and Jill again, then spoke directly to Jill. "You're sad, *sí*? You feel something missing . . . here—" he tapped fingers over his heart. "Inside you?"

Jill nodded, tears just below the surface again, but couldn't speak. She didn't need to, though, because Eddie kept on, his words tumbling over each other now as though he was afraid to stop for fear of never starting again. "See . . . I feel that same thing and I need to make it stop." Another deep breath and then he looked Adam straight in the face. "I did something bad, Alpha. I didn't know it was bad at the time, but now it's done and I can't fix it. I only hope, God willing, that *you* can make me not do it again."

Drugs? Alcohol? Adam could think of a few things that would qualify in what Eddie just admitted. He raised his chin in understanding. "You fighting an addiction, Eddie? Something you don't want Cara to know about? Is it drugs or something?"

The other man let out a slow breath. "*Sí* . . . an addiction. But not to *something*. It's a some*one*." Embarrassment rose from him in a dry, dusty cloud that chased away the cloying, wet scent of tears. He clutched his hat a little harder, causing the starched straw to crackle under the pressure. Another deep breath and he continued. "I think you've already figured out I'm gay." Adam nodded but the fact raised brows on both Tommy and Jill, who looked at each other in surprise. "I don't know if there are any other gay Sazi. I've asked around, but, cautiously, if you understand. There's one or two women who are bi, but I haven't heard about any other men."

"I'm sure there probably are." Adam knew there weren't any in his own pack, but there were rumors that had drifted in from other packs. He leaned forward, toward the man, and put a light hand on his shoulder, just a touch, before releasing. "But it can't be easy for you."

Eddie let out a small smile and smelled of gratitude. "It's not. At least in Texas. But I thought you might have a more liberal attitude coming from a big city. Anyway, I've been spending a lot of time in bars in Dallas, with . . . *mayates*." He froze for a long second with rising panic, obviously waiting for a rebuke or worse, but Adam didn't understand the situation well enough to do either. He held up his hands and shrugged.

"Is that bad?"

With a sharp bark of laughter, Eddie suddenly sat up straighter. "*Jesus bambino*! That's right! How could you know what's good or bad down here?" He paused again, but this time it appeared to be to put his thoughts in order. "Okay. *Mayates* are newcomers from south of the border. There's no distinction to the word in whether they arrived . . . *legally,* if you know what I mean."

Sudden understanding flooded through Adam. Eddie was

flirting with danger—the sort that could get him killed. He closed his eyes and took a deep breath. "And you got involved with one."

Worry and fear flooded the air around the slender Latino again. "*Sí*. He has a green card, though." He stopped and got an odd look on his face and then sighed heavily. "Or maybe he doesn't. He's lied about everything else. Anyway, Juan Carlos and I have been dating for months now. I go up to Dallas most weekends lately—I'm the ranch manager for Cara, so I have a more flexible schedule than he does. It's easier for me to go there."

Adam put up a hand. "Cara runs a ranch?" That was news to him. "I mean, I know she has some land, but—"

Eddie nodded. "Oh sure. We raise whitetails and javelenas—wild boars—and do guided hunts every year. We charge five grand a gun for a trophy hunt." At the incredulous look from Tommy and Jill, and probably himself, the other man continued. "You have to understand—there's hardly any public land in Texas. Most of the larger ranches that don't want to run cattle or goats had to do something so they didn't get taxed out of existence. Property taxes pay for *everything* down here. There's no income tax. With as much land as the pack owns, we would have lost everything unless we converted the use to wildlife conservation. The guided hunts are just a by-product, but they pay for the upkeep and my salary. I earn it, too. There's growth management and tagging the herds, testing for disease and lots of other stuff. Of course, the whole ranch is fenced to keep the deer inside, so we have to cull periodically—the moon hunts take care of that, and add breeding stock. It's a real job to keep up with all the paperwork I have to send the state and feds."

Ah! Now the ear tags made sense. They weren't experimental animals—they were *livestock*. Wow. Apparently there was still a lot he needed to find out about life down

here. But that was for another time. "Okay. Good to know.
But let's move on. You go up to Dallas—"

Another deep breath said Eddie would have preferred to
continue talking about the ranch. "*Sí.* I've been spending
more time there, because . . . well, I fell in love. The real
kind, where I've been seriously thinking of asking him to
move down here—tell him about *us.*"

Meaning the Sazi. This was pretty serious, because none
of them did that lightly. To bring in a human to become
family—it was a big step.

"That's nice for you." Jill's voice made Eddie look at her
and flash a smile filled with straight, white teeth.

"But something went wrong, didn't it?" Adam's voice
sounded flat, because he knew full well there was another
boot yet to drop. Might as well get it over with.

Eddie tensed again and readjusted his feet on the floor.
"*Sí.* The last time I was up there, I was helping him clean his
apartment, and he asked me to throw away the junk mail. I
set aside the bills, but underneath the last envelope there
was a letter from his family down in Mexico, dated just a
few days before. Maybe I shouldn't have looked, or maybe
he *wanted* me to see it. I just don't know. But, I read it. His
mother wanted him to come home. They appreciated the
money, but—" He looked up at Adam with the same plead-
ing desperation in his brown eyes that had been in Tommy's
just a few minutes before. "He's only . . . *sixteen*, Alpha."

Adam winced just as Tommy let out a harsh swear. He
put a hand to his forehead to ease the sudden headache that
was pounding his skull like a triphammer. How many laws
had Eddie just broken? Of all the things he might have encountered as his first official act, this hadn't occurred to
him. "Shit, Eddie. How in the hell—"

The other man looked truly stricken and fairly green.
The shame that rose from him was thick enough to choke.
"I swear I didn't know. He has an adult driver's license

from Mexico and it looks *real*. Nobody at the bars has ever questioned it. He has a green card, he has a good job that he's held over a year now. *Jesus bambino*—he shaves every morning!" He looked nearly ready to cry and his voice started to crack. "I feel like *shit*, Alpha. Lower than dirt. I *swear* to you I have no interest in children. I'm not a predator." He sighed and hung his head. "I can't see him anymore. I know that. But . . . I *love* him. If he calls, I know I'll go to him. I'll find some way to rationalize it and if we're ever caught together—so, I need your help."

Jill spoke up quietly, her voice soft and sad. "But what if you're wrong, Eddie? What if you misunderstood?"

He turned his head and now a single tear traced down his cheek before he wiped it away with a flick of his thumb. "I hoped I had, so I asked him. He denied it, but he doesn't know I'm a wolf and can smell emotions. He lied so hard I sneezed from the cloud of black pepper. Lied about everything . . . that is, everything except that he loves me, too."

Adam ran fingers through his hair and raised one knee onto the bed so he could face the other man better. "What can I do to help?"

Eddie turned to him and squared his shoulders. "I want you to bind me."

Adam frowned and opened his mouth to reply, but Eddie raised his hand. "Please just hear me out. I can't ask Cara to do this, any more than I could ask her to change who she votes for at the polls. She believes what she believes, but I think she's wrong. I told you I talked to other people, other Sazis. I know all about binding and it would be a wonderful thing for our pack. I think it's just because people here don't understand what it is . . . so they don't know what they're missing. But Señora Taylor needs it—I can see it in her eyes. She looks like I *feel*. We could help each other get through this." He moved his gaze to look at Jill. "*Sí?* You want to be bound again?"

Jill nodded, her face moving from panic to sure, defiant belief. "Yes. Yes, I want to feel my pack mates again. And I'd be honored to help you through this."

Adam let out a frustrated sound. "There are more things to consider than—"

"What things?" Eddie's voice was growing more sure, more confident. "Really. What things are more important than helping people who need help? You're the Alpha. You have power and strength. You would know when I was getting weak and could stop me from falling." He moved his head from side to side briefly. "Maybe it wouldn't have to be forever. But at least until Juan Carlos is twenty-one. If it's real, he'll wait for me. And if you bind me now, before the pack meeting tonight . . . then people here can see that I'm just the same as before. If they don't notice anything, and I'm happy, then maybe they'll reconsider. Maybe *Cara* would reconsider. It's not the same as mating, but—"

"He's right, Adam." Tommy spoke up again. "It's not the same as mating, but I *do* miss feeling Jill in my head, even a little bit. It's like I'm missing part of a sense, like being deaf in one ear."

That described it just about right. Adam only noticed it *not* being there, and only at odd moments. "And really, Cara hadn't noticed it before she knew, so why would it matter if some members were bound and others not?"

"*Sí,*" Eddie said with a sharp movement of his head that was too strong for a nod. "It doesn't affect my brother and the others any more than my being gay. They can like it, or not like it, but what is . . . is."

Maybe he was rationalizing it because he really missed being bound, too, but Adam found himself looking down at his faded jeans and Pig Eye beer T-shirt, and then scoping out the room. "Well, this ritual is normally a more *formal affair,* in the deep forest where there aren't any people around, but I can't see any reason why we can't do it right here. The walls are boundary enough and with the thick adobe, nobody outside the binding circle should notice. And I suppose I don't have to break skin with my teeth to mix our blood for a mild binding." He looked at the three people, who were staring at him with enraptured attention, then sighed. "If you're all sure—"

The bright, penetrating tang of citrus chased away the tears, accompanying the shouts of "Yes!" "Thank God!" and "¡Sí, sí—por favor!"

Adam stood, centered himself between the three chairs and took a deep breath. He looked at Eddie. "You don't have to do a thing, except not leave the room. It might feel a little strange at first, since you've never been bound, but it'll pass. Just try not to fight the power when it starts to pull."

"We trust you, Adam." Jill's voice was soft and nearly reverent. When he looked that way, her eyes were filled with tears, but there was a smile on her face. Tommy winked and gave him a thumbs-up sign. Eddie had already closed his eyes and leaned back into the chair, his breathing slow and deep.

Closing his eyes, Adam turned his attention inward and began to focus on his own heartbeat. In moments, the traffic outside disappeared and he felt a cool wind caress his skin. It was the first night of the moon, and the weight of it pressed against him, filled him and boiled his blood. He let it burn through him, and called on the power deep inside him to raise up until it danced over his skin like invisible fire. He pointed his face toward the source of the magic— the ceiling being nothing against the pull of the moon, and let out a low, quiet howl.

Three howls joined his own, answered the call that pushed aside their humanity. His nostrils flared, drawing in the scent of the others. They were strong, healthy—worthy of becoming pack. He let loose the crackling fire, threw it out like three solar flares and felt the first resistance of their own magic. But they weren't strong enough to resist and he easily slipped through their unconscious defenses. Then he began to pull them toward him in his mind, pulled a tiny thread of their own magic inward, like twine attached to a post.

Now came tricky part. He had to bind them into a single unit, braid the threads into something that was stronger. He raised more magic and fed it back out, hearing the gasps of pain as Tommy, Jill, and Eddie suddenly became aware of one another. Adam could see their minds now . . . and their hearts. Yes, Eddie was wounded, his heart was scarred and bleeding from deep, searing grief and fear. But he could be healed and the pack would make him whole.

Adam opened his eyes and dizziness wrenched his stomach and threatened to drop him to his knees. He managed not to vomit, but only just . . . a nice change from the last time. The world appeared in multiple focus, layered with shades of color that hadn't existed a moment before. But now he was no longer just seeing through his eyes. The eyes of the pack were his to command as well. He looked at them and he could see himself through their eyes. But it still wasn't done. He flooded them all with power a second time and this time, their whimpers were of near pleasure, rather than pain. They were beginning to taste unity.

This last step would finalize the binding, so he yanked hard on the threads of magic, pulled them into cords, and then into ropes as the others gasped. Close, so very close—

And then the world dropped out from under him.

He heard a scream in his mind that tore at his heart, and ammonia panic, fear and . . . *peaches* filled his nose as he stumbled and crashed into the table—scattering the contents of the coffee tray against the wall.

The scenery shifted and he was in Rosa and Paco's house, staring down at their bloodied bodies. Then he heard Cara's voice, calling out for the children in panic—feeling her feet stumble down the hallway to the bedrooms.

Relief flooded through Adam as though it were his own as she picked up little Felix from his crib, whole and safe, and hugged him to her with enough desperation to make him squirm and cry.

Raul, wide-eyed with fear, came racing out of his room and clutched at her leg, crying hysterically, screaming about birds that came and took away Gloria and the other girls, and how Mama and Papi fought them. Now Tommy and Jill's fear added to Cara's, but there was nothing he could do to break away.

He watched as Cara put Raul back in his room with the baby, told them to stay put and blocked the door to be sure they did. Then he felt her returning to the slashed and broken bodies on the blood-soaked carpet. Sobbing freely now that the children couldn't see, enough to nearly break his heart, she knelt beside Rosa first and began to fill her with healing magic. But her sister was human and it took every bit of Cara's limited ability just to bring her sister back from the brink—close the worst of the gaping wounds. Near collapse, she moved to Paco's side. But even a Sazi can only take so much damage . . . there was no pulse. His heart had stopped.

She didn't let that stop her. His skin was still warm, and her magic could feel a delicate, fragile thread of life still inside. She leaned back his head and centered his body and started CPR. Breathe twice and press three times—then slam his heart with magic like some sort of metaphysical cardiac defibrillator. Adam felt her heart start to slow even as the spark of life grew in Paco. But it wasn't enough. He was too far gone.

Jesus! She was going to kill herself if she didn't stop. But in those few seconds in her mind, he knew she wasn't planning to stop. Pack was pack—*familia* was everything, and if she died so they could live, so be it. That was the duty of the Alpha.

Adam felt his heart race. He had to help. He couldn't let his mate die. More important, he didn't *want* her to die, not now . . . not when they'd just—

He rose to his knees and opened himself, tried to offer up his power to her through his mating tie. But the binding ritual was preventing his magic from reaching her . . . unless—

There was no permission necessary. He felt the three wolves in the room offer themselves to the struggle. He called again on the moon, summoning every ounce of magic in his body, until he was a pillar of pure fire. He pushed out another flare of magic, a fourth thread, pulling on the unity of the nearly bound pack to increase the strength. It passed beyond the circle of the group like a spear, cutting the air with fine precision. Beyond the parking lot and past the highway, magic pushed through the alien environment of asphalt and brick until it reached the forest of pecans and a little adobe house. Near the end of his own strength, he finally felt her, now collapsed over Paco's body. There was no time to ask, and her reserves were at their end so she wouldn't be able to resist.

"Cara?" He breathed the word into her mind and felt a spark of recognition just before he felt the binding magic slice through her body. A ragged scream erupted from her that caused Raul to begin shouting her name and banging on the bedroom door.

Far from the careful, slow transition to awareness the others had, Cara was immersed in the tiny pack in his room. Her heart started to beat painfully fast and she held her hands to her eyes to stop the stinging as fire burned across her mind. He felt the pain along with her and wished it didn't have to be this way.

What's happening? She screamed the words into his mind. *What in the hell is happening to me?*

We're here for you, Cara. Adam kept his voice low and

soft and let himself wrap around her, let her feel his presence and concern. *Draw on our strength. Finish healing Paco while you still can.*

Adam? He heard the surprise in her voice, felt her head spin from side to side, trying to find the source of the voice.

Yes.

The others joined in. *And Eddie,* mija. *We're familia now, Cara. Do as the alpha says. Take my strength to save my brother.*

And mine, said Jill, softly into their minds.

Me, too, Tommy added. *Pack sticks together.*

Tears were running down her face and Adam could feel them as though they were his own. She shook her head, both in confusion and pain. *I don't understand.*

Like you did with Lucas, Carita—to save me. *Now it's my turn to repay that. Take from us to heal your family.*

And with a breath of hope that made his new pack smile, she began.

Chapter 28

CARA POURED THE last bucket of water, brown tinged and smelling of blood and vomit, down the toilet—then flushed. She paused at the sink long enough to stare at the dark circles under her eyes in the mirror and slosh and spit some mouthwash from a tiny paper cup covered with seashells. It took two tries before she could get the foul taste out. Only Raul had seen her throw up, but the scents from the battle, combined with the disorientation when Adam cut off the flow of magic had just been too much.

After stowing the bucket in the hall closet, she stood at Rosa and Paco's bedroom door, watching them breathe slowly on the double bed while Raul snuggled between their pale, injured bodies, twitching fitfully in an exhausted sleep. She'd nearly lost them and even now it would be touch and go.

Then she looked around the living room. It would have to do—she'd done as much as she could. Company was going to be here any second. The big area rug from the bedroom covered the stains on the carpet. The scent lingered, throwing images into her mind every time she caught a whiff. But the bare spot next to the wall was the hardest to look at and her eyes immediately moved away from the blank white paint. The whole room felt . . . wrong. She'd hated to throw Paco's favorite recliner into the fire pit behind the shed, but there was no salvaging it. She'd have to buy another for the day he walked down the short hallway from the bedroom again.

If he ever does.

She could heal broken bones and torn muscles, but she just didn't know what to do when the parts were *missing*. Could he grow back most of his right foot? Would he ever be able to run with the pack again if he couldn't? Would he lose his job? How would she explain the scars on both of them to the town without involving the hospital or filing a report with her own office? Rosa almost lost an eye and without plastic surgery . . . well, people would *notice* a four-inch long jagged scar running from her temple to her jaw.

So many questions—not the least of which were the ones that haunted her, reminded her of her failings. *Why didn't I stop by before I opened up the barn? Why was I stupid enough to make all the calls to the pack to cancel the fiesta, except for the hunt? Where the hell have they taken the girls? Are they even still alive?* A buzzer from the tiny room off the kitchen made her start. The clothes were ready for the dryer—another reminder. She looked down at the simple sundress she'd grabbed from Rosa's closet after ruining her outfit when her stomach heaved. It all came back to one thing. *I should have been here.*

A car door slamming outside and footsteps running toward the house made her stomach roil again. She couldn't face them, not right now. She was out the back door before they made it in the front. Not even hearing Eddie and Adam calling her name stopped her as she bolted into the thick stand of trees.

It was close to an hour later when she felt the crackling of Adam's magic approach. The difference from just a day ago was amazing. He'd been powerful before, but now there was a sense of *majesty* to his aura—one she'd never felt before, except in Lucas and some of the council members. He stayed out of sight for a long moment, but he didn't try to hide his scent. It was filled with worry and concern and just a trace of horror . . . apparently he'd stayed in the house long enough to see the carpet and the wounds. Cara didn't greet him. She continued to sit cross-legged under her favorite old live oak, picking cactus spines from the soles of her shoes with ragged fingernails and squishing fire ants, which managed to sting her bare legs. Would he approach? She knew she should call out to him, just as she should move away from the ant hill, but she just couldn't seem to care.

It had seemed such a good idea earlier to ask the pack members who didn't shift not to come tonight. *Rosa and the kids aren't feeling well,* she'd told them with appropriate sympathy—all so she didn't have to introduce Adam to more than those he would hunt with. Rosa had agreed, and wasn't terribly surprised that he would be joining the pack. After all, it had been the first man Cara had ever brought to her home. How could he *not* wind up pack? So, Rosa had offered the excuse, suggesting the flu so the human pack members would be happy to stay away.

Every lie has a price, her mother had always taught. *And those made for prideful reasons are doubly expensive.* How many choices lately had she made for prideful reasons?

She spoke without planning to. It was just supposed to be musing. "Would I have known?" Looking up, she could just make out the line of his body past the thick bower of twisted ivy that draped down from the branches. Now that the words had reached air, she had to know. "If the pack was bound, would I have known they were in trouble? Would Sharon, Luis, and Eddie have known; have come to help?" He paused for long enough that she stopped plucking spines. "Please don't lie to me. I need to know."

He pushed apart the tangle of green and stepped inside her haven, where she'd always hide when bad things happened or she needed to think. God, he was so handsome, even when he looked sad. But even over the sorrow, he smelled brave and proud and she felt tears come to her eyes, because she knew the answer. But she couldn't pull her gaze from his face as he sighed, tipped up his head to stare at the mass of waxy leaves, and ran his fingers through his hair, smelling of sorrow and burnt metal frustration.

"Yes. You would have known."

She nodded and lowered her gaze to her task again, not caring that tears were running down her cheeks to wet the thin cotton dress as she plucked out another needle-sharp spine and tossed it into the distance. "I looked for tracks before I started cleaning. There's not so much as a feather, or even a scent to follow. The girls could be anywhere by now."

"We'll find them."

She nodded even though she didn't believe him for a minute. Taking a deep breath she gathered her courage to

speak. The words were harder than she'd thought they'd
be. It took more than one try and her hands startled to
tremble. But she had to do right by her family. "The pa . . .
the pack is yours now, Adam. You were right, I was *wrong*."
The next deep breath was marred by a thick, wet gasp. "So
very wrong. I failed my people. I don't deserve to be
their—" She couldn't finish. All she could do was bury her
face in her hands and cry, great heaving sobs of grief and
fear that shook her shoulders. She couldn't even take a full
breath without it cracking, breaking into a thousand bits of
sound.

Cara heard him, felt Adam come to her, sit down and
wrap himself around her. She didn't want him to, and yet
she did. Pushing at his chest only served to make him pull
her closer and press the side of her face against his warm
neck. He held her until she stopped struggling and clutched
at his back, and then until her tears slowed. Long minutes
passed where all she could hear was the steady beating of
his heart and the rustle of the leaves in the wind.

Finally, when the pulsing of his power against hers had
lulled her into resting quietly against his body, he spoke.
"You weren't *wrong,* Cara. You did what you thought was
right for your people." He pulled back slightly and raised
her chin to look into her eyes. His scent turned to determination, with a healthy dose of pride. "*Your* people. You
can't second guess the past. You can't know you could have
gotten here in time, and you did something I never could
have. You *healed* them. If I'd been the pack leader instead
of you, Rosa and Paco would be *dead* now."

She snuffled as he released her chin, then she rubbed at
her swollen nose with the back of one hand. "Fine. I'll be
the pack's healer then. But I've never really been an
Alpha—not like you have. I . . . *saw* things . . . while we
were connected. I never knew what real Alphas have to go
through. I've just been fucking *playacting,* pretending I'm

adult enough to run a pack. And my family has suffered because of it."

Adam snorted and pulled away from her, leaning back against the trunk of the tree and crossing his arms over his chest. "Oh yeah. I've been a *great* Alpha, a *terrific* one." He held up a finger and his scent turned fiery hot with anger. "I run the pack for one night—just *one*, and I manage to screw up all our lives forever. Those skiers saw our pack hunting because of *me,* Cara. I picked the route. I ignored everyone's advice to stay to the deep woods, because I was *tired*. I'd just come off-shift and didn't want to drive for an hour each way." He shook his head, eyes now glowing a bright blue. "I should have just let Tyr take my position when he challenged me. I deserved to move out of second position for breaking the First Rule and letting the humans live to report what they saw. But instead, I killed him."

He must have noticed her surprise, because he nodded. "Yah, you heard right. Tyr Isaacson was the pack leader's son. He confronted me when he read the newspaper account of the massive pack of wolves the two hikers saw. I saw them in the trees, just like Tyr did. They would have been easy targets and nobody would ever know . . . but they were just kids. I couldn't bring myself to order the pack to hunt them down. And when he challenged me, in private—instead of blowing it off, I accepted."

A profound sadness swept across his face and he closed his eyes. "Tyr's dead, Josef's dead, and so are Mark and Vivian's sister, Tabitha. Who knows how many girls have been enslaved and tortured on my watch. Christ, Cara! I'm a *cop*. Following the rules is all I *have*—it makes me . . . me." He looked at her with eyes blazing and self-loathing bleeding from every pore. "You have nothing to apologize for, and are a far better Alpha than I'll ever be. You offered your *life* for your pack."

"So did you." She ignored his startled look and confused

scent to continue. "Just now. You didn't have a clue what
would happen when you broke that ritual—but y'all did it
to save *me,* and *my* family. And like you said, you can't second guess the past. Not a whole lot of other people would
do what you did today." She took a deep breath, letting it
out slow, her thoughts flashing back to her conversation
with Ten Bears. It was time for her to let go, for the good of
all of them. "Maybe you *don't* deserve to lead the Minnesota pack—I don't know. I can't judge who did what for
how many cookies. But you've earned your place in *this*
pack. I don't think there's any question anymore that my
people will accept you as their leader, especially after Eddie talks to them tonight. I didn't offer you my place for
laughs, y'know. I *wouldn't* offer it unless I was willing to
step down and follow you, my Alpha."

Cara bowed her head and waited for him to respond. But
instead, he rose to his feet, pausing to stare down at her
briefly. She couldn't sort one scent from the next and
looked up to see his face. He'd already turned, though, and
she watched him walk out of the grassy, acorn strewn
hideaway—leaving her to wonder what would happen to
her family if he refused.

Chapter 29

WE FOUND THE birds, Alpha.

Adam's eyelids snapped open, the tiny bedroom filled
with a young boy's toys suddenly superimposed with the
image his pack was seeing miles away. Adrenaline started
his heart beating faster. He shifted Cara's arm, wrapped

tightly around his chest, so he could grab his watch. It was already after seven. Night was nearly here. He ruffled his fingers along the edge of Cara's aura and was relieved to find that Jill's advice had been on the money—staying in close contact, skin on skin, had allowed her to heal faster than if she'd just tried to tough it out. He just hoped she wouldn't be mad when she woke up and found him here with her.

He shifted his body on the narrow twin bed and let his vision slip inward until he could see the steep cliff face clearly. The long crack in the rock must open into a cave. He could only pray the girls were with them. Five birds, or were there six? Was that a sentry in the nearby tree? *Don't approach them,* he whispered into the minds of his wolves. *Stay low, keep upwind and get back here.*

Eddie and Tommy turned and slunk back into the trees, moving with flawless precision, born of the mind-link. Eddie knew the territory well and Tommy stayed glued to his left quarter, letting the smaller red wolf guide him safely home.

Then he focused on Jill and slipped into her mind to see the long expanse of highway and the familiar sound of a man and a woman talking animatedly. The flight from Austin had arrived right on time. They were on their way here. It hadn't been cheap for Mike and Sheila to coax that young family out of their place on the plane, switching them for their own tickets a day later, along with a fistful of cash—but it had been worth every cent. They needed every possible wolf here if they had any hope of getting the girls back. Luckily, Lucas had agreed an offensive strike was their best chance. Admittedly, he was more concerned about Ziri than the other girls, but then he apparently had gotten a report from Bobby and Tony that worried him. It was frustrating to Adam that the Wolven chief wouldn't reveal what the situation was—only that it was serious enough that every wolf in this pack was suddenly expendable.

Adam didn't plan to lose anyone tonight, though. *Nobody* else was going to die on his watch, except a flock of murderous birds. For that to happen, they were going to need split-second timing, and a fully bound pack. He wished he could trust the information that had been leaked to them by an anonymous caller. Unfortunately, every cop knew that information was only as good as the source. He wasn't sure. It made him nervous. The whole thing seemed almost *too* convenient.

Adam looked down at the woman in his arms again, marveling at the play of hard muscles under smooth honeyed brown skin. He let out a sigh that rumbled with a small chuckle. Yah, he was falling for her, hard and fast, and was pretty sure it wasn't just the mating talking. The scent of her turned his mind to putty, and fer sure he had to struggle nearly every minute not to rip off her clothes and take her . . . but there was more to it. He *respected* her— her fierce loyalty and intelligence. And she was good in a crisis. She kept her head and could analyze as well as any cop he'd ever met. But she was beaten down right now, questioning her own decisions. He understood that well— had seen it in plenty of other guys on the squad after an operation went bad.

No. He wasn't going to let her give in to it. She was a good Alpha and he'd be damned if she was going to slink off with her tail between her legs. He'd be proud to share the pack with her. Together, they could rise above this setback.

A sudden heat swept through him as the moon crept over the horizon and froze his breath in his throat. He caught a glimpse of the glowing orb through the little window half-covered by a white bookcase crammed to overflowing with Dr. Seuss books. The moon magic was unusually strong tonight . . . or maybe it was just because Cara was nearly naked beside him. He leaned down and kissed her hair gently, and felt her respond with a sigh and a tightening of her arm around him. She was more powerful than she knew and with the right prompting, he might be able to help her reach her potential.

If what Mom told me on the phone earlier is right, there's a chance this tiny little group could wind up one of the strongest packs in the country. Myrna Mueller was the pack's historian—knew every bit of Sazi folklore that stretched back to when the world was new. If she said it was possible, then it was. It was just a matter of handling the meeting tonight properly. And if it worked, well, those birds weren't going to know what hit them.

But as much as he was enjoying the warmth of her body that made his skin tingle, it was time to get moving. There was a lot to do. He shook her shoulder lightly.

"Carita, *mi amor,* wake up. It's time to get going."

SHE FELT THE power of the moon first—a burning tingle that both pushed and pulled at her. Then scents began to penetrate her brain. Pine and cool soil, swollen with melted snow, along with rich, downy fur and clean soap made her suddenly amorous. She blinked her eyes and Adam's pale chest filled her vision. She fought off the urge to flick out her tongue and taste the dark nipple only inches away. What would she find if she glided her hand down? Would he be hard and ready under the thin sheets? Did he want her again, like she wanted him?

But beyond the broad expanse of his chest that she ached to fondle was a poster of a glacier, with a Spiderman action figure glued on so it appeared he was climbing the ice. Shit! She was in Raul's room . . . not the comfortable Riverwalk hotel. And the memories of the past few hours

swept back through her again like a foul dark wave that
churned her stomach and brought tears to her eyes.

She had hoped, for a brief, shining moment, that it had
all been a horrible nightmare.

Adam raised to a sitting position under her, loosening
her grip and forcing her to move. She couldn't remember
how he came to be in bed with her, but she was definitely
nude from the waist up. The murmur of voices from the
next room opened her eyes wider. The pack was just on the
other side of the door and here she was—half-naked with a
man in her nephew's bed! *¡Dios Mío!*

She rose up so suddenly she hit her head on the planet
mobile that hung over the bed. Adam reached out to shift
the papier-mâché Jupiter out of the way and separated a
section of hair that attached to the chain holding the sun in
place.

"Whoa, there! We're not in *that* much of a hurry. It's still
going to be a few minutes before Jill gets back from the airport, don'tcha know. Take it easy." He let his fingers drift
slowly down through her hair and the warm glow in his
eyes made her breath stutter. She half-expected him to pull
her closer into a long, slow kiss. She realized abruptly it
was what she wanted him to do, even checking to see if
he'd shaved. She liked him freshly shaved, liked the
smooth, nearly rubbery texture of his skin against hers.

But instead, he just eased his fingers away from her hair,
then touched the tip of her nose lightly with his index finger and winked. "Feeling a little better?"

She blinked several times, trying to process the question
and realized . . . she did. A tentative stretching of her arms
and back didn't match with the reality that *should* be. She'd
nearly died healing Rosa and Paco, did a frenzy of cleaning
and then curled up for multiple hours on a lumpy mattress
that wasn't nearly big enough for two. "You know . . . I do.
But it feels completely *wrong*—it's not logical."

He chuckled and sat up straighter, then wadded the pillow against the flat headboard and leaned back while smelling of light citrus amusement. "Not such a bad thing to have a mate, huh? Jill suggested it after you fell asleep earlier. She's a registered nurse and worked at the clinic with our healers. You pulled power from me to heal yourself while we slept. Now, how about you go in and take a shower and Eddie and I will take the pack over to your barn to start introductions. Don't take too long. We'll start the binding ritual as soon as the others get here." He paused and locked his eyes with hers. "Are you sure about this? You want *me* to bind the pack, rather than doing it yourself?"

She nodded, not trusting herself to speak past the lump in her throat—both for her decision and because he was willing to share his energy to heal her. He opened his mouth to say something, but then changed his mind and returned the nod. Then he swung his legs off the bed and stood up. "Your brother Jorge brought along a good set of walkie-talkies with a ten-mile range and a couple of shotguns with silver shot. He's going to stay here to guard the family and let us know if anyone shows up. The pack can be back here in less than a minute once we're bound." He put his hand on the doorknob and turned his head back. "We know where the birds are, Cara. We're going to bring the girls home tonight . . . and then the people who hurt this pack are going to *pay*." The set of his jaw and the fierce intensity in his eyes made her believe him.

For the first few minutes after he walked out of the room, she just stared stupidly at the closed door with the tiny multicolored handprints that crawled all the way up to the ceiling, trying to decide what to do next. They were really going to do this—against everything her papi ever taught her, she was going to allow someone to bind her pack.

But it's not anymore. It's not my pack. I won't be their

Alpha. Was that good . . . or bad? She wanted desperately to trust Adam as much as his own people trusted him. She could see it in their eyes—Tommy's, Jill's, and now Eddie's, too. She touched the worn golden medallion around her neck and raised her eyes toward the ceiling. *Please, please don't let me make a mistake here—not with so many lives at stake.* She blinked rapidly. She'd promised herself she wouldn't cry again, so she just wrapped her arms around her knees and rocked on the bed until the threat of tears passed and the house grew quiet.

"Carlita?" Jorge's voice came through the wooden door a few minutes later, and he knocked lightly as a follow up. "You okay in there?"

She let out a slow breath and tried to put a smile in her voice. "Fine. What's up?"

"Eddie just called on the radio. Jill and the others are at the barn. They're waiting for you, to start."

A burst of adrenaline made her leap to her feet and she looked at the Mickey Mouse clock on the dresser. *¡Madre de Dios!* She'd been curled in a ball, praying for strength, for almost an *hour*! She looked out the window to see the moon halfway up the horizon. Thankfully, speed was one thing she could do well. "Thanks, Jorge. Tell them I'll be right there."

One nice thing about being late is it doesn't give you much time to think. She jumped in the shower, not caring that her hair would be damp when she arrived, then tossed on the first thing she found in the closet in the guest room: a pale lavender top with painted lilacs and a pair of dark purple jeans she'd forgotten she left over here. Fashion didn't really matter at pack meetings because clothing didn't last very long before the moon called the wolves from inside. Still, she wanted to meet the new people looking halfway decent, so she brushed her teeth, added some makeup, and, as an afterthought, fluffed her hair with the blow-dryer. Then she gave a quick kiss to each member of her family. She hoped Rosa would remember it . . . if she didn't make it back.

Cara stepped into the night and the moon called to her, pulling a long, mournful howl from her throat before she could stop it. She turned back to the door, embarrassed at forgetting herself with her brother still in the house. But Jorge was standing in the doorway, Felix bouncing on his hip, a smile on his face. "Go. Bring home our Gloria. We can't have a Quinceanera without our princess, can we?" Then he raised the shotgun in his other hand and rested it on his shoulder with enough fire in his eyes that he should be turning with the moon tonight.

Cara raced into the forest, running would be faster than taking the car. Her eyes filled with filtered moonlight. Suddenly it was as bright as midday. Grabbing a familiar branch as she reached the tall game fence separating Rosa's property from the hunting grounds, she swung her body up and over. Energy flooded her muscles and fur began to tickle under her skin, fighting to get out. She held back, but didn't really want to. Her nose pulled in scents that she shouldn't be able to smell if she were only human . . . traces of deer musk on that tree, a rabbit's frantic tracks away from her through the cactus. Even closed for the night, the wildflowers were incredibly fragrant. She wanted to run and run until the night was over, chase something to ground to calm the burning in her stomach.

And then the barn appeared, surrounded by cars. She slowed as she approached and heard Adam's voice from inside.

"So, we're agreed then? You're all certain you want to give it a try?"

Eddie was the first to speak, and it really surprised her. Usually he was quiet during meetings. "Absolutely! It sounds like the best way to bring Gloria and the others home. Luis will eventually come around. I'm sorry he attacked you and I thank you for sparing him, Alpha. But you'll have to make him pack by force . . . as you saw."

"He made his choice and he failed," replied Adam and then he raised his voice slightly. "What we'll be doing is a little different in a full binding. There'll be some pain, and I'll need you guys to all change form."

Cara started to step forward but then stopped with one foot still in the air, when he continued. "We'll add in Cara last, like we discussed. It has to work that way, in case there are problems."

Oh. Sure, that made sense. What if instinct kicked in and she attacked him without realizing it? It wasn't just the human side of a Sazi that came up with authority challenges. The moon touched a much more primal instinct. She backed up until she was outside the wide circle of light surrounding the tall steel building and started to take off her clothes. She might as well turn into wolf form and be ready for his . . . *attack*. Cara wondered abruptly if he'd explained it to them—that he would have to close his jaws around each of their throats and tear flesh until they submitted to his authority. She did know *how* to bind a pack, even if she had always disapproved.

By the time she let the moon slice through her defenses and pull the wolf from inside her, she could hear Adam doing the formal side of the ritual. "Does anyone object to my rule?" No response. He raised his voice and let a low growl play along the edge of each word, readying himself for the moon to take him. "Does anyone challenge my right to lead this pack?"

She heard a rustling and a growling that she recognized. Luis must have woken up. He couldn't help himself, as she knew he wouldn't be able to. He was the third male, and with Paco not here . . . he let out a deep snarl, apparently already in his animal form.

She could feel the swell of energy as Adam descended on him and the snarls and growls as they fought. Luis was no match for an alpha timber wolf. He probably even knew it, rationally—but logic didn't mean much on the first night of the moon. She winced inwardly as a sharp animal yelp cut the air and she prayed that Adam hadn't gone too far. She forced herself not to race to her pack mate's defense, and lay down on a bed of pine needles in the darkness, closing her eyes so she couldn't see, and digging her claws into the ground to hold on.

One by one, wolf screams split the air and each subsequent whimper cut her heart. She wished there was another method, but there just wasn't. It was the Sazi way. He didn't mean them any harm, and blood had to be spilled for the binding to complete.

Power began to grow around her until even the branches of the trees shuddered and moved upward with a protesting creak. The air was alive with magic. It called to her, pushed aside her human mind until there was little left but the wolf, scenting the air and waiting . . . waiting for him to come for her.

Then she smelled him and her eyes opened. He was in human form, bathed in moonlight that paled to the glowing power from under his skin. "It's time, Cara."

She rose to her feet, front legs splayed and hackles raised while a growl formed deep in her chest. No! She was supposed to be submissive, the human argued. No, replied the wolf. He would have to *prove* his dominance. She was no whelp, to roll over and bare her throat. Only the strongest should lead.

He smiled, laughed at her snarl. Blood painted his mouth—the blood of her pack; now *his*.

The laugh enraged her wolf. With barely a thought, she flung herself at him, aiming for his neck. She expected him to back up, to run, even to shift forms. So she wasn't prepared when he opened his arms and caught her—pulled her against him so tight she couldn't turn her head enough to bite, and whispered, "Right idea, wrong form."

The mass of energy in the air descended on her like an axe and she howled . . . fought to be free of the magic that sliced through her and stripped the fur from her body. She was abruptly human again, but her mind was still mostly the wolf's.

"*No!* I will not submit!" Again she fought to be free, but he'd apparently gained some of their speed already, because his mouth dropped to her throat before she could react, while he adjusted his hold around her to her new form, tight enough to bruise, trapping her arms against her body. She shrieked as his teeth, feeling every bit as sharp as a wolf's, broke skin and wetness began to flow down her naked chest as he fed; swallowed the last bit of her pack necessary to bind them.

The shock of sensation broke through the moon haze in her mind and she gasped. Lightness flowed through her limbs. Dizziness overcame her as he pulled back to meet her eyes. "Adam! I'm sorry. I didn't mean to fight—"

"You may not be done yet. We'll have to see." Then he gripped her hair in his fist and pulled her mouth against his in a fierce kiss. His tongue forced the mingled blood into her mouth and pushed until she swallowed involuntarily. No! This wasn't right. He was going to ruin the ritual. He had to . . . had to—

Again he sent his magic into her, but for a different purpose this time. He growled into her mouth and dug fingers into her back. Her wolf responded, suddenly shifting gears from wanting to kill him to wanting to . . . *mate* him.

¡Madre de Dios! Dear heavens, he couldn't actually be considering . . . the pack was just a few yards away. And the wolf in her wanted them. Wanted them all under the light of the full moon until she was sated. With all her

strength Cara pulled back, fought against the moon that threatened to open her pores; start the frenzy. But he was stronger now, with the power of the pack behind him. She stared into those glowing blue eyes, as haunting and foreign as the stars overhead. "Adam, you have to let go. I don't know if I can control myself much longer."

He smiled again, a baring of teeth stained with red. "Oh, you're not *going* to control yourself—I'm going to make sure of that. You're going to give yourself to me with every last ounce of the fury I know you have inside, and then we're going to rule this pack . . . *together*. The others are already bound but I've frozen them. They'll just have to suffer through my mating you and wait for me to finish turning you into a smoking, satisfied puddle before I release them. They'll have to wait for their *Alpha Pair* to return and lead the hunt."

She felt her heart still and a buzzing filled her ears. *Alpha Pair*? There was no such thing, not in truth. There was an Alpha Male, who ruled the pack, and an Alpha Female, often his wife or mate, or sometimes a female who just wished to rule alongside. "There's no such thing as an Alpha Pair. It's a myth."

"Then I'm about to go all kinds of mythological on you." A loud roaring sound rose up over her head and she looked up to see leaves and bits of debris sailing in a circle around them both. It was a tornado of magic, and they were at the center. He raised his arms into the wind and then closed them together and the magic compressed, pushed inside her as if driven by a battering ram. She screamed, cried out, shrieked—over and over, as fast as she could draw air. But it wasn't a scream of pain.

When she opened her eyes her entire body was one throbbing mass of need and the wolf inside her was not going to allow this to pass. Not again. Her glands opened fully, drinking in the moonlight, pulling on the energy

around her—searching for the pack, but finding only one
wolf—*the wolf*, who was hard and hungry and growling.
She could taste the colors in the air, see the scents as the
world dimmed behind the glowing man in front of her. He
smelled of fur and sex and blood and she wanted him.
Needed him beyond reason. His every muscle was highlighted by moving shadows from the trees and his lightly
twitching erection made her suddenly wet and ready to do
anything he asked.

But he didn't have to ask, because she could suddenly
see it in his mind—she could feel him in her head; she
knew what he wanted. And she finally understood what *she*
needed, what she'd needed all along.

Chapter 30

CARA DROPPED TO her knees in front of him and Adam
could feel her smile pull at his own lips. He reached out
and touched her hair, that silken mass of red and brown.
She let him guide her forward. She took him into her
mouth in one smooth movement and the sensation nearly
dropped him to his knees. Her lips were smooth and slick
and her mouth so cool that it felt like ice water on his su-
perheated skin. The wolf in him wasn't overriding his mind
tonight when he caught her scent. They were of the same
opinion, had the same needs. Her fingers dug into his hips
as she suckled him, teased back and forth with her tongue
and lips, until he was nearly mad. When her hand slid between his legs to rub the muscle just behind his swollen
sac, he nearly lost his mind. "You need to stop," he gasped,

and pulled back on her hair, even though he was desperate to have her finish him this way. "I won't last long enough to finish the ritual."

She growled just a bit and nipped the head of his dick lightly as she moved off, causing him to utter a strangled sound that was half pleasure, half pain. Instead of leaning back onto the springy bed of pine needles, she turned around and dropped to all fours. She wiggled her hips just a bit and fire filled his mind. It was the way it should be. His mate needed him and he had to give her what she wanted.

Adam dropped to his knees between hers and used one hand to slide himself inside her with one smooth movement. He caught some of her juices on his fingers and couldn't resist a taste. The scent nearly shut down his brain, even as he struggled to keep his senses enough to finish the ritual. But oh yah, she was slick and hungry for him. Cara gasped in pleasure as his hips bumped hers, the force and the angle causing contractions that pulled at him. It made him pull her hips tight against him to give her more of the same.

"Oh God, yes!" She dropped to her elbows on suddenly boneless arms while he began to take her, make her his, make her the *pack's* one and only Alpha Female.

A long slow lick of his tongue down her sweat-soaked spine brought a deep groan and lowered her head nearly to the ground. The human in him was moved by the sight and scent of her—it wasn't just the animal in him that needed this. He bent over her, slowed his movements and began to toy with her nipples while she moaned. "Carita," he whispered into her neck, "This isn't just about the pack. I want you to be mine, *mi amor*. Just mine. I'm falling in love with you."

"Adam—" She breathed it into the night air, and the word was filled with almost too much emotion to be real. "Yes, God help me, yes. *Make me yours.*" She adjusted her

balance and grabbed one of his hands, moving it to her lips
to kiss each finger and then his palm. When she reached his
wrist, he knew what she was going to do and braced himself. It didn't hurt when she bit through the delicate skin
and drew blood. In fact, it felt pretty damned good. Then
she flipped her hair over her shoulder and turned her face
back, past her shoulder.

It was time.

He had to raise onto his toes to kiss her and remain inside her, but it was worth the effort. Fire exploded as the
last piece of the puzzle slammed into place. The blood of
the pack mingled in their mouths and their consciousness
suddenly spread out, found the waiting pack in the barn.
Energy flowed through them, feeding the cords between
them all until they were solid as steel. And they ruled at the
top together as one unit; one mind. He saw inside her for a
flash as the pack opened, each baring themselves to the
whole. Pain was washed away in the unity, in the complete
acceptance of the pack. He felt Eddie take comfort, and
knew he would have enough strength to get through his
grief. And Jill's joy as her mate fully touched her mind
again made her tail wag until it was nearly a propeller.
Even Luis . . . poor prejudiced Luis was swallowed in the
magic of the night until he forgot why he even was against
this.

Adam was looking elsewhere, though. He saw Cara's
past, felt the pain of her childhood, knew her faith and discipline, and the strength that was *familia*.

They were still moving together, though they could
probably stop without release. But he wasn't done with her
yet, even though the binding was complete. There was no
reason to end this until she'd had her pleasure and so he began to rub her tiny, swollen clit and move inside her harder.
She gave up any pretense of self-consciousness and began
to push back against him, crying out with each thrust of

him into her—no longer caring if the pack heard, or saw. They did, and it was good and right.

Adam felt a new energy begin to build inside her, pulled from somewhere deep within. The moon rained down pale fire that heated the very air around them and he released his hold, drew the pack from the barn to marvel in the sensation of the magic and the sight of the glowing pair of humans taking their pleasures. She bucked against him, and he could feel the wolf inside her thrill to his touch. But this wasn't all about the wolf. He wanted to watch her face when she went. He pulled out of her and she spun her head, her eyes hungry—oh so close to the edge.

Adam pushed her over and she went. She scooted over so she wasn't lying on bare dirt and then held out her arms to welcome him. He leaned over her and flicked his tongue over each nipple, then used his lips to suckle and nip, until she was arching her back, rubbing herself against his stiffness and holding his head against her chest. "Oh God! Please . . . Adam, *please!*"

The pine needles weren't so soft anymore, but he hardly noticed as several of them dug into his knees. But he did lift up her hips so more . . . sensitive parts would be protected. She understood and kept them there, her feet on tiptoes to match his height.

He began to thrust into her, watching as her chest heaved in mindless bliss, with eyes closed and lips parted. Suddenly he couldn't stand it anymore. He had to claim that mouth, those pouting lips that tasted of *pack*. He bent to taste her mouth, pushed her down into the pine needles while kissing her as if his very life depended on it. Perhaps it did, because he felt a similar power building in him. It was more than an orgasm—much more, but he didn't quite know what it was. It was new and different, frightening and exhilarating, and he raced toward it, desperate to see what was at the end of the fire-filled tunnel.

But he wanted to watch her go over first, and he really
did want to see if what happened in her kitchen had been a
fluke. He eased his thrusting and raised to his elbows, then
reached forward with both hands, placing his thumbs
alongside her nose and began to rub—long, slow strokes
along her whisker glands that matched the movement of
his hips. Cara's eyes shot open wide and she took a deep,
frantic inhale that couldn't seem to fill her lungs, and her
fingers began to convulse in the dirt. Her back arched as
she gave into an abrupt climax, and she wrapped her legs
around his back to pull him inside deeper.

The sudden spasming of her muscles around him set off
a chain reaction he never could have imagined. He felt the
first swelling of his cock inside her, felt the movement of
fluid and then burning, searing fire began to flow through
his veins and erupted to soak into her skin. It was met by an
answering flame that grew as fast as an out of control wildfire. He collapsed onto her and buried his face in her hair as
magic shot out of them both in a wave. It was nothing like
in the hotel room, where a door merely slammed shut. It
spread out in a growing circle while they remained locked
together desperately, unable to so much as breathe against
the storm. A shock wave raced through them both . . . them
all, as the wave of magic blew through the bodies of their
pack, pulling howls from them that filled the night air. But
it didn't stop at the edge of the barn, the limit he'd set for
the ritual. It flowed outward like a dam breaking, sending
water over the land. The magic touched the little adobe
house and found another pack mate . . . Paco. He was
brought into the binding as though skewered with a spike.
Another line reached out and found the woman on the
bed . . . a woman who was soon going to turn on the
moon—but would have *wings*.

An attack victim. By rights she should have died, but
instead was only turned because of Cara's intervention.

Adam felt his mate's sorrow, and her joy, as Rosa took the step she had always wanted to take. She'd spent her whole life wishing to be true Sazi and knew the form wouldn't matter to her. And she would heal now; wouldn't be disfigured for life. But she wouldn't ever be pack.

Or would she?

The magic wouldn't be denied, the blood inside her was wolf-born—*familia*. Adam felt Rosa's back arch and a strange, awful cry tear from her as the power claimed a raptor as *pack*—something that should never be.

But even then it wasn't done. Little Raul, only seven, but so close to turning, was next. He welcomed it with all the trust of a child, throwing open his arms as though waiting for a hug. Adam could suddenly see Jorge's terrified face through the boy's eyes. He knew something was wrong, but it wasn't something he could fight. Instead, he was on his knees, seeking guidance from above in frenzied, heartfelt Spanish.

Cara, still in the throes of pleasure and pain, called out to Jorge through Raul's mouth. "It's okay, little bro." Jorge's head whipped up and stared at his nephew open-mouthed, trying to comprehend his sister's voice coming from the little boy. *"They're pack now. We're all pack now."* She smiled with tiny pearl-like teeth. *"No need to fear."*

Then she left him, was torn from the boy as the magic spread even farther, seeking more people to bind. Adam tried to pull it back—there weren't any more Sazi *to* bind, but the moon disagreed.

Adam suddenly found himself thrust inside the mind of another, in a car hurtling toward them with lights flashing. Another raptor, and the binding ritual tasted of old magic, ancient similarities—close to family. And this one was stronger . . . good pack material. The car veered off the road as the magic began to spear Will Kerchee. But he was strong. He righted the car after a quick dip into the barrow

ditch and withstood the pull of the magic until he changed
his mind. Adam felt a small smile of acceptance and an
amount of amused resignation at his surprise. *Better than
wrecking the car, Mueller. And it might be useful tonight.
We can always sever it later. Oh, and by the way, I've called
in the representative for the birds, Angelique Calibria. She
was in California and is on her way here as backup. She's a
falcon, so it won't take her long to arrive.*

With the added power from Will, the magic surged
again, roared in his head—became a tidal wave that found
a crevice in the towering cliffs outside town . . . a break in
the limestone that opened into a cave. And it found a young
wolf, newly turned by anger and adrenaline-laced fear,
who was bound to the wall with silver shackles.

They'd found Jenny.

Chapter 31

THE YOUNG MINNESOTA girl had turned without pack
guidance—without a healer present. She wasn't thinking
human thoughts at all. Cara could sense the damage in her
mind, and knew they only had one chance to bring her
back. The magical wave was nearly at the end but she could
sense there were many Sazi in the room, bird after bird . . .
some with minds, but many without, along with a pair of
snakes. She struggled to control the magic as it swept
through the high-arched room of stone. There wasn't
enough magic left to bind them all properly, and it would
risk the entire pack to try.

The magic found Gloria and Ziri, still human . . . yet,

with a spark in their blood that would someday make them turn. But there wasn't enough there for the magic to reveal the type of animal or grab it, so the power moved on. A young owl with silver manacles on both burned taloned feet revealed herself as Ume. The magic speared her, the girl recognized Cara and Adam from Ziri's description, apparently after she'd been recaptured. The little Mayan girl didn't fight back against the magic at all. With a breath of trust and a shuddering leap of faith, the bond formed. She was pack.

Cara struggled for all she was worth to control the magic, turn it back to the wolf. She felt a shout of frustration and effort erupt from her mouth, but she couldn't hear it over the roaring in her head. At last, with infinite slowness, the magic turned, halted in mid-motion and she turned it back to Jenny and let it spread into her like a wave, and waited.

But the binding refused her. It flowed in and through her like a doorway, finding nothing human to attach to. They were losing the girl to the wolf. She was going feral. Again Cara forced the magic to change direction, pushed it through Jenny while the wolf howled in agony and fought against its chains.

Still nothing.

She pulled on the strength of the pack and tried again, hoping that the touch of her parents' mind would be enough to reach the screaming wolf.

"You have to stop, Cara." She heard Adam's voice from a distance and felt her shoulders being shaken. The forest came into view again, pulling her out of the torch-lit cave in the bluff. She looked into Adam's stricken face and snarled with frustration. She couldn't leave yet. He had to let her finish. She tried to close her eyes to return to her task, but Adam reached forward to hold open her lids. The wave of magic shuddered as they fought each other for

control of it. Finally, it broke apart and fell away. "*Stop it!*
You're only hurting her and the pack can't afford to lose
any more energy." There were tears in his eyes now and he
didn't fight to hide them. "We've lost Jenny. There's nothing more we can do for her now."

We've lost her? But—"No! I can do this, Adam. There's
still time to bring her back."

He'd pulled out of her and was kneeling next to one leg.
He put a quiet hand on her cheek and she could feel, smell
the sadness rolling off him in waves that broke her heart.
"No. There's not. We're all out of time. They know we're
coming now—they had to have felt the magic. We'll lose
them *all* if you keep going, Carita. We'll lose *Gloria*, too,
and Ziri."

Her niece—*familia,* who would be pack someday. The
image of the pretty, smiling girl, twirling in her pink ball-
gown in the kitchen flowed through Cara's mind. But no
less pretty was the girl that Cara saw through the eyes of
her parents . . . who might have electric blue stripes in her
pale hair and wear a studded dog collar around her neck,
but was good and sweet, filled with purpose, brimming
with artistic talent.

And little Ziri, not as pretty in the narrow image of this
country, but who was equally beautiful in the eyes of their
newest pack mate Ume—and as talented and brave as any
of the rest.

She looked around at the circle of wolves. When had
they come from the barn and surrounded them? She knew
she should be embarrassed, but she wasn't. She raised to a
sitting position, addressing her pack mates. "We'll bring
them home tonight. We'll bring them *all* home." The feroc-
ity in her voice startled her. But it wasn't just her own voice
now. It was the voice of many. It was Jill's voice, and
Tommy's . . . Eddie's and even Mike and Sheila's—who
she'd never seen before, but *knew*. She knew them all with

the intimacy as if they'd grown up in the same house, shared the same experiences.

She suddenly saw the strength in binding and was sad it had taken a crisis like this for her to understand. It was the ultimate democracy—the many speaking as one. Each voice in her mind a counsel, bringing intelligence and experience through thought and emotion. It wasn't dictatorship as her papi had feared and she suddenly knew her mother didn't have to die. She and Papi could have shared this same thing. They could have taken their love to a new level.

Could have taken their . . . love.

Her eyes moved to Adam's, now a solid blue, no longer glowing. He smiled and nodded and she knew he'd been following her thoughts in his mind. "We'll talk about it later. After we've brought them *all* home, *my Alpha.*"

THE KIDNAPPERS HAD time to prepare, but there was no helping it. At least the three lead birds and the snakes didn't realize Ume was one of the pack now, didn't know she was feeding them everything her bright black eyes took in, like a remote camera.

Wolves raced across the dark prairie, the landscape lit only by the moon, now high in the sky. The pack followed in her and Adam's wake, pads and claws silent on the rocky ground. Eddie and Tommy had marked the trail well—they were able to move swiftly through the trees and cactus without stopping to get their bearings. It wasn't long at all before the bluff came into sight. They slowed to a trot and then to a stalk as they tried to get close enough to see.

"I can smell them." Adam breathed the words into her ear and motioned with his muzzle to her left.

She nodded and mentally ordered the pack to spread out to search for the kidnappers. She had to stand still as she

C. T. Adams and Cathy Clamp

watched through the eyes of a dozen wolves, fearing she
was going to fall over from being so dizzy—it was like
standing in the center of a crystal prism and trying to follow each separate image.

It was so hard to watch for danger and since Luis's nose
wasn't his best feature, the shot rang out before anyone
nearby could scream a warning. Cara felt the silver pellets
fracture his front leg as though it was her own, and he went
down in a screaming heap. The big Minnesota female,
Sheila, so black she was invisible in the shadows, crept up
and leaped at the guard, riding him to the ground with his
throat in her mouth until he stopped struggling. The scent
and smell of blood seemed to center the images in her
mind. The focus cleared and she could think again.

Adam was right at her side as she reached Luis. His
front paw was hanging limply, part of the foreleg blown
away by the shotgun blast. She looked to Adam for guidance. Did she dare heal him? Would it weaken them too
much?

He muttered a curse under his breath and nodded, mentally agreeing with her logic. They couldn't leave him here.
The scent would bring the birds right down on top of them
and he would be a sitting duck. Of course, the gunshot
would bring them as well, but it would be better if they
weren't slowed by his injury.

Luis looked up at her with pain-filled eyes and she drew
a deep breath and turned human. It was so much easier to
heal when she could use her hands and fingers. With the
strength of the full pack behind her, she felt her ability
multiply and warmth turned into heat as she held the mangled leg. Skin began to flow and bone rebuild as she
watched. She'd never been able to do this much this fast
before. It seemed only moments before Paco's older
brother was back on his feet, limping—but on his feet all
the same.

He dropped his head before her and tentatively flicked out his tongue to touch her hand. *Submission . . . from Luis?*

"Miss Cara?" A dozen pair of eyes turned to the brush, where a ghostly figure wearing pale blue sweat pants stood, her scent hidden in the strong juniper scent of the trees. Adam snarled and crouched, but held himself and the rest of the pack back.

Cara patted Luis's head and stood up, stared into the trees and let her eyes glow above her naked body. "Yes. It's me. But why are *you* here, Missy? And where is Brittany?"

Will was in the air and nearly to them, but the shock of hearing the woman's name made him slam against an updraft and tumble for a moment.

Missy Foster's voice took on a panicked tone. "No! I would nevuh . . . she's with Mama . . . hidden where they can't find her—I *think*. I didn't tell you before, in the hospital. But I'm so tired of running. They keep finding us, Miss Cara, it's why I found you to tell you. But I couldn't just stay away. Only ways we'll ever be safe is when all dem birds is dead."

The pack was getting restless, circling the trees and growling, and Missy backed away with wide eyes. But Cara had a feeling this would be important. Ten Bears said it would come back around. There wasn't time to explain it to them, even in her head. They'd just have to trust her. She slammed out stinging energy and a word. "*Enough!*"

The wolves flinched as a unit, as though struck, and backed up enough that Missy stared at her wide-eyed. "Are these *yo'* dogs? Booray, they're big 'uns!"

Cara stepped forward until she was right under the woman and looked up with hands open wide and pushed forward a bit of warm magic, trying to use the persuasion Will could do so well. "Yes, they're mine. You shouldn't even be out of the hospital, Missy. How did you know where to find me?"

"I wasn't lookin' for yo, Miss Cara. I came here to kill those blasted birds, once and for all! Yo gave me a second chance, ma'am, and that means I need to follow my heart. I ain't gonna let them torment ma baby no more. Yo showed me not all yo animal people is bad, even though they said—"

Had she been in contact with the birds since the accident? How could Cara have missed the scent in her room, or was she speaking from further back in time? "We're not bad, Missy. Not all of us. But the men in those caves *are* bad. They kidnapped my niece Gloria, even took a little girl away from her mama in Oklahoma. We're here to make sure those girls get home . . . just like I made sure Brittany got home. But we know where they are. You need to go home and let us take care of it." She paused and watched emotions chase each other on the woman's face, streaked with bruises and tears. "You need to go be with your little girl."

"No. I *know* what they planning. They took me from my mama, too—got me with child. The things they did . . . *nobody* else should have to—but Brittany's *mine*. She's *ma* baby . . . not theirs. She won't never know 'bout *them*. Not every girl wants babies, but I did. Eileen didn't and she let them take it. Not me—I ran, with my belly full of my little girl, so they couldn't take her. Couldn't ever do to her what they did to me." She paused and then the cold steel scent of determination chased away the sorrow. Missy's face grew defiant and she pulled a shotgun from among the branches of the juniper and threw it at Cara's feet. "I ain't got nothing to offer you 'cept my own life to help, Miss Cara. But I know all 'bout them birds and every nook and cranny of that 'ole cave. This has been goin' on too long and I wouldn't be able to look ma baby in the eyes again iffen I don' help." Missy's words swam through her brain. Brittany was at least seven. How in the fuck long had this been going on—right under her nose?

Cara smiled, though—a baring of teeth shared by her pack members, and by the woman in a pale blue jogging outfit. How could she turn away help, when the person knew the consequences? Would she do any different in the girl's place?

"*Ecouté*! Let's you and me and your wolves go do us a little bird huntin', so I can hold ma head up to ma baby."

Chapter 32

ANYTIME TWO PREDATOR species meet to battle, things are bound to go badly. Add in supernatural strength, and the stakes are raised. The night erupted into the hellish stench of blood and gunpowder brief moments later, accompanied by anguished howling and unearthly screeches. The kidnappers had released the feral birds and they followed the scent of blood straight to the pack—to Luis.

There was nothing so dangerous as a feral Sazi, in Adam's opinion. With the mindless rage of a rabid animal, and the power to turn flesh and bone to ribbons, they were something even trained Wolven agents feared to face. Coordinated attacks could drive them back, but they had no fear; felt no pain and lived for nothing except to feed and destroy.

One was difficult to handle and usually two or three agents, fully armed, were sent to take it down. But here there were *six*.

Adam heard Cara cry out in pain and panic as Luis was pulled into the air and literally ripped apart before the startled eyes of the pack. There was no running, no time to fight.

He felt the line to his new pack mate shred and fall away from his mind. It happened so fast there was no response possible, other than instinct. He leaped into the air and grabbed one of the birds by the talons—pulled it down to earth with muscle and magic. The entire pack attacked as one. Fangs and teeth flashed in the moonlight as the beautiful snowy owl became nothing more than meat and feathers, as they took revenge to struggle past the pain of Luis's loss.

He was gone . . . just like that—and his new pack felt anguish, remembering the soft-spoken, loving father of three. Despite Luis's wolf forcing him to attack Adam, Luis had actually championed Adam's plan to make Cara his coruler, even shouting down the dissents of some of the others who didn't believe she'd earned the right to rule. But there would be time for tears and remembrances later. Now, Adam had to focus their minds.

Will arrived and their collective eyes took on a new perspective. He attacked the second bird from above, just as Missy's shotgun roared again. She clipped a wing of the great horned owl and sent it spiraling into a tree for the pack to take down, then turned the barrel toward the massive bald eagle, jacking another round into the chamber as she smoothly swiveled her shoulders.

Cara shouted to her. "*No, Missy*! Not Will—the bald eagle! He's with us!"

The woman in blue turned her head in exasperation and shot a different bird full in the beak, then pumped a second round into the chest—as though she knew exactly how to kill their kind. Her voice had taken on a thicker accent during the fight, as though she normally struggled to make her speech fit in better. "Well, hell's bells, Miss Cara. You gots to tell me that stuff! Lessen dey talk, I don't know the difference. The wild birds, dey don't talk."

Adam raced by her on the way to finish off the wounded owl. "You're damned good with that thing."

Another shell loaded and was fired, just missing Will's tail feathers, but hitting his opponent in the leg. She didn't seem at all startled by a talking wolf. But then, he had no idea what sort of strange things she'd seen in her young life. "I've had to be. Daddy taught all us girls how to bring home dinner for when there was no money. Coon, deer, cocodrie . . . you name it, I can hit it." She ducked under a branch and fired off another shot as swooping talons took a handful of hair from her head. "Galee, but I hate these wild ones!" She tapped Adam on the snout and pointed to the other end of the bluff. "Dere's a second entrance back dat way. Look for the hose pipe going inside. You can't see the windmill, but it's dere. It's how I got out tonight after they grabbed me at the Town and Country store. I bet yo girls are inside, but I'll bet with all this ruckus, dey'll be moving dem. Dey've got a Hummer back there—not the sissy ones you find in town—but the real thing, so dey won't need no roads."

Adam suddenly felt his heart race as blinding pain and rage filled his mind. Cara was hurt! He turned and bared his teeth as a massive golden eagle rose back into the air. He raced to his mate's side but she was already on her feet, hopping on three legs toward the shelter of a massive oak, and smelling of pain and anger.

"*¡Madre de Dios,* but that hurts!" She reached back to lick the twin holes in her thigh and pushed healing magic into the wound while Adam stood watch. Their wolves were fighting well, and Will's contribution was invaluable. But they were grinding down and hadn't even reached the cave. Mike was panting heavily and Eddie had collapsed under a thick stand of mesquite, where the birds couldn't reach. And neither he nor Cara had any idea what they still had to face.

Cara nodded her head and he heard frustration play through her voice. "We'll have to go alone—split our attack.

If they keep sending waves of feral birds, they'll eventually pick us off, one by one, while they escape with the girls." She looked at the three dead birds already on the ground and let out a sound close to a sob. "Is it horrible of me to feel proud for making it this far—knowing that they were once human girls who were loved by their families as much as we love ours?"

He walked over to her and rested his forehead against hers for a long moment, letting his magic soak into her to ease her heartache. "We didn't make them this way, Carita—and there's no way to bring back a feral Sazi. You know that. We're upholding the First Rule, and doing our duty as Wolven agents."

She sighed and then they winced in unison as Penny's ear was cut by a slicing beak. She howled and snarled and pulled out a mouthful of tail feathers, and they felt that, too. There were as many disadvantages as benefits to being bound in a full-out fight.

With a mental instruction to the pack to keep fighting until the birds were down and then follow, he and Cara headed toward the cliff. He marveled at her resilience as she pushed past the pain in her leg to easily race ahead of him.

Just as Missy promised, there was a rubber coated canvas hose threading through the brush on the other side of the bluff, and a primer gray Hummer, covered by camo netting, weeds, and mesquite cuttings. It appeared to be a firehose that had been modified down to fit on a windmill irrigation pipe. There was a leak at the connection and Adam took a moment to lap up some water from the deep puddle that had formed. Cara happily joined him and they drank from the cool mineral spring until they could stand no more.

They looked at each other and tried not to think about what was to come next. Like any crisis situation, all they could do was focus on the goal and take things as they came. Adam suddenly realized there wasn't anyone else in his life he would trust more to fight at his side, except maybe David. A ghost of a smile passed through his mind as he remembered his brother's words in the cab of his pickup, and how he would now respond. *It was during that battle to save the girls in Texas last spring for me.*

A slippery slope indeed.

ADAM SMELLED OF amusement, but was keeping his thoughts to himself and just shook his head when she gave him a questioning look. But there was no time to ask, because they heard movement from the mouth of the cave—a dragging, scraping sound, accompanied by muffled yelling.

Cara recognized that particular string of curse words—the ones Gloria used when she knew her mother wasn't around to slap her on the back of the head with a *chancla*. When they finally came into view, she recognized another person. The man dragging Gloria and Ziri by their arms was the snake from the canyon. He was alone. Obviously he didn't feel threatened by the girls, but Cara wasn't a *girl*. She was the Alpha Female of the Texas pack, and this time, that snake was going *down*.

She didn't wait for Adam. He'd follow along . . . or not. But she couldn't pass up the element of surprise. She raced forward at top speed, faster than she ever had before and hit the snake full in the chest with teeth and claws, mere fractions of a second after she bolted from the brush.

His hands were torn from the girls, taking along part of one sleeve as they hit the rock cliff together and bounced apart. The snake had expected resistance, though, and was as fast as Cara *used* to be. He turned in an instant, rising up to his full height and sizzling his rattles with fangs bared. It pulled a scream of terror from both girls and the overpowering scent of ammonia terror flooded the air. She could sense Adam in her head, moving the girls to safety and then turning back human to remove their gags and the ropes securing their hands and feet.

She didn't have time to concentrate on them, though. The snake struck, but she easily avoided it and took a bite from where his neck should be. He hissed with virulence as she spit out the vile, bitter-tasting meat that burned her tongue.

"So, you've improved since our last meeting, *muchacha.*" He struck again, just barely missing her leg and then tripped her with his tail. She tumbled and heard Adam call out to her in panic.

"Stay with the girls unless there's no other option! They have no protection!" It was an order; a command and she feared he might ignore it. The mating tie might be too strong to resist. She rolled over the back of the snake and dug in claws, ripping long bloody strips through his thick hide.

"You'll pay for that, *puta!* I'll make your death so slow you'll beg."

"I'll never beg to the likes of you! But you will be telling me every single secret about this place, and why you're kidnapping humans." She spun and dived under another strike, but the wounded leg gave out for a moment. It was enough. One fang scraped along the leg, adding burning venom to the talon holes and she screamed.

She heard a howl of rage and then Adam was on the snake, tearing at its body while it thrashed and tried to spin to strike. The scent of rattlesnake venom was enough to choke on and even its blood was pungent and bitter.

Cara knew Adam wasn't fast enough for this battle, but the distraction was enough. She launched herself at the snake and tried the same trick that had worked before Yolanda arrived in the truck. She gathered her strength and pushed moon magic through him. He was expecting it this time, and fought back, but the strength of one lone snake, however alphic, couldn't overcome the power of her pack. With Adam still riding him, she pulled on his power—added it to her own, and the snake turned to man with a scream that sliced the night air. The human neck snapped under the grinding pressure of the predator's teeth and when the head severed from the body, there was silence—save for the frightened weeping of the girls under the tree.

A moment later, the sobs turned to screaming. She and Adam turned as one. A new man with olive skin was standing behind the girls, a machete held to their throats with one hand while the other held a fistful of hair. Their eyes were wide with panic, contrasting sharply with the slightly amused expression of the man. But they weren't so much as breathing. He was holding them magically so they would remain still and not struggle.

That expression . . . the way he holds himself—

Cara took a step toward him, over the body of the other man. She searched the new man's slender bare arms for a tattoo similar to the one on the arm of the man under her, but they were clean of ink. She deliberately flared her nose, then huffed out air from her side nose slits to gather the purest scent possible, pushing away the warm copper that filled the air. Definitely Sazi, and another snake. A viper, too, but she couldn't figure out the species. "Do I know you? You seem familiar."

He smiled now, patient and slightly pleased. His voice had a slight Middle Eastern flair that she couldn't place. "You know someone I *used* to be. But I'm not that man anymore."

Adam came to stand by her side. "Who are you, and what do you want? You know we're not going to give up the girls. I can have the rest of my pack here before you could get away."

The man shrugged fluidly. "Things aren't going so well

for your pack right now. You know it as well as I do." And
he was right. Several of the pack—Tommy, Sheila, and
Carmen, were struggling desperately against horrifying injuries. Fortunately, they had released more birds . . . one of
which was Ume, who was now battling on their side. Between she and Will, two more birds had gone down.
"Frankly, I think you should get back there to help them."

Adam spoke up. "You'd like that, wouldn't you? But
you're going to have to go through *all* of us if you expect to
get out of here alive—because there's no *way* we're leaving
without our family. You will not take our girls."

Now the man's face went pleasantly blank. Only his eyes
held a small amount of amusement. "I think we need to
make one thing perfectly clear." A wave of magic began to
flow from him. It roiled around them like hot steam, burning them enough to drop them both to the ground
howling—screaming in pain that was everywhere at once.
The pain began to flow through the pack connections and
Cara desperately fought to close down the binding, separate themselves from the whole. They could all die if the
pack leaders did.

The man left his spot behind the girls and was crouched
down in front of Adam so quickly that even Cara's eyes
couldn't follow it. He spoke quietly, with all the politeness
of discussing politics at dinner while they thrashed on the
ground in such intense pain that Cara felt as though her
eyes were going to explode. "*I can do whatever I want to.* If
I wanted you dead, you already would be." He lifted
Adam's muzzle so their eyes met, and she couldn't do a
thing to stop him. "But I don't *want* you dead, Alpha
Mueller." He flicked out his tongue to taste the scent of
their surprise. "Oh yes, I know who you are. You just did
me a favor by eliminating Manuel here. His taste for young
American girls was becoming a nuisance. And your pack is

destroying those abominations made by another traitor to the cause, saving me the trouble."

With a breath of a thought, he released his magic and was standing by the girls again, twirling the sharp blade, before either of them could catch their breath. "You've probably already noticed that the three raptors who attacked you the other day haven't joined the frey. That's *my* contribution to the operation."

Adam finally managed to struggle to a sitting position and shook his furred head. "Again . . . who in the hell *are* you and what do you want?"

He shrugged again, still spinning the blade, flashing moonlight into their eyes like a strobe. "Call me Roberto. That will do for now. As for what I want, I've already got it. You eliminated Manuel and the abominations and there's no hint I was involved. It's unfortunate that I need to shield my cards, but I can't afford for my partners to think me untrustworthy."

"So you think we're just going to let you walk away with the girls, because you happened to have killed three birds?" Cara snorted and stepped to the side, while Adam moved one step in the opposite direction.

"Again, I don't *want* the girls. In fact, I want you to take them far away so nobody can ever find them again." He tapped Ziri on the head absently with the flat of the blade and another wave of panic rose in her scent, even though she couldn't move. "Especially *this* one. The council needs to hide the Mayan girl somewhere, put her and her family in the care of someone who can protect them."

"*Why?* Why are you helping us, Roberto?" She might as well try to get as much information as possible. She adjusted her feet again, as though restless and stepped another pace from Adam. Maybe if they flanked him—

He chuckled. She and Adam were both just suddenly

frozen . . . caught in a wave of magic that exploded with the same speed as the snake could move. "What is it about wolves that you feel the need to martyr yourselves to the greater good?" With an abrupt movement, he threw the machete toward her face, then stopped it, mere inches from her nose. The moon, half covered by clouds, was reflected in the polished blade. "Would you *prefer* to die, Alpha? That's all attacking me would accomplish." He released them a split second before he released the blade. She barely had time to move before it cut through the air where her head used to be. "Now, I'm helping you because you're helping *me*. This operation was started—without my input, I might add—in a time when it might have done some good. But that time is gone. Those in power here couldn't see the futility of continuing a course that had no goal."

"And what *is* the goal?" Adam came to stand by her side and she could feel his frustration and rage at their inability to act.

Now Roberto went deadly serious. He crossed his arms over his chest and looked at each one in turn. "A new age is coming and this pack will be on the front lines of the battle as it surges north. You need to prepare yourselves. I'd suggest learning to master sword fighting. You'll stand a better chance."

"What is this new age? *What* is coming? Can't we stop this before it starts?" Cara felt as confused as if she were talking with Ten Bears, hearing prophecies that said everything and nothing.

He shook his head, to her immense frustration. "There's no stopping this, any more than you can stop the movement of the stars or the shifting of the poles. She—the greatest snake of all eternity—will be born again, and the predators will become prey once more. But it's her *allies* that will be in the first wave and those are what you'll need to prepare for." He paused and then smiled. "Think of the *Two Towers* for potential scope—with no annoying Elvish poetry." He turned his back on them and started for the Hummer, releasing the girls so they dropped to the ground, coughing. The girls limped to them, and Cara could smell that her niece's leg was probably broken. Gloria wrapped her arms around her and wept into her fur. "Remember, Alphas—protect the Mayan girl and her progeny . . . or the snake that is to come could wind up a *goddess*." He blew away the covering on the Hummer with a flare of magic that moved like a wind and put his hand on the handle. "Sane people don't bring something into the world that is beyond control. And I am most definitely *sane*."

He picked up a duffel bag that smelled of bird, got into the Hummer, and started it, while Adam and Cara tried to figure out what to do. They couldn't just let him *leave*, could they? They could still stop him. The pack had eliminated the birds and were headed this way, slowly rebuilding their strength from the whole. Roberto rolled down the window as they started toward the vehicle, apparently noticing that Adam was looking into the distance, watching for them to arrive. "Oh, and before you decide to order your pack to attack me, you should know that I've already bitten the wolf inside the cavern—the pretty blue-haired girl. She'll die if you chase me. But you might be able to bring her back . . . *completely*, if you hurry. Venom can be a powerful stimulant, with the right magic to bend it. *Healing* magic, for example."

They looked at each other frantically and Gloria nodded, her eyes filled with hot tears. "He did! That's why we were screaming when the other snake was dragging us out. We have to go back for Jenny! *¡Por favor* . . . please, Tia Cara! She's my amiga."

Roberto turned on the headlights while they were distracted and locked both doors before rolling up the window, leaving just a crack for his voice to escape. "I'd suggest you hurry. She doesn't have much time left."

Chapter 33

THE LOVELY BLACK and silver timber wolf inside the cavern was barely breathing. As they heard the Hummer roar into the distance, Adam raced over to her still form and mentally ordered Will and Ume to follow Roberto—keeping a safe distance so he couldn't hurt them. Adam knew Will could easily see for nearly a mile and he presumed Ume had excellent night vision. The girls didn't need to see this. They'd have nightmares enough for weeks to come. "Tommy, watch the girls."

"Call us back if you need us." Will's voice sounded tired, and he hated to push his old partner this hard. But they didn't have many options. The big sable wolf, his best friend, nodded and guided Gloria and Ziri to a small room near the entrance.

Adam looked at Cara, who had turned and was running her hands over the young wolf. "What do you think? Is there any hope?"

She smiled quietly. "There's *always* hope, Adam. It's the one thing that truly separates us from the animals."

The rest of the pack arrived and the lesser wolves fanned out to guard the entrances and search the rest of the cavern for anyone still hiding, picking their way past the headless bodies of three massive birds. That bag Roberto had put in the Hummer . . . did he take—

Jill turned human and hurried to Cara's side, then looked down at her daughter and let out a little sob at the horribly swollen, bluish tongue and seeping fang holes in her shoulder. She picked up the girl's muzzle to unstick the dry tongue from the dusty rock floor, gently closed the mouth and checked her eyes. "There's faith, too." She looked at Cara with tears welling and touched the other woman's hand. "I have faith in you, my Alpha." Then she turned her eyes up to meet his. "I have faith in you *both*. Bring back my little girl."

Cara patted Jill's hand and then turned her lightly glowing eyes to look into his. There was something deep inside that golden power that he couldn't place, but it make him feel warm and safe. She held out her hand to him. "I've always been the strong one—always been the one who people could count on. But this time . . . I need you, Adam. Please help me bring her back."

He went to her. How could he *not*? Jill backed away with head bowed. She knelt at Jenny's feet, and put a light hand on the fevered paw—still needing to touch that small bit that was her daughter.

Adam snuggled in next to Cara's nude body, wrapped warm fur around her shivering body. Even as hot as it was outside, the cave was cool and damp and smelled strongly of bird feces and something fainter, in the background— perhaps bats had used this cave before the others moved in.

The instant they touched, he felt a roar of power race through them both, born of both mating and binding. Cara called on the web of them all, turned the magic in on itself, until they *were* the power—all of them. They were a single unit of energy and she was the focus. He felt her power touch the girl, the wolf, the *Sazi* at their feet. She placed her hands over the sticky, oozing bite marks and pushed warm energy into them. Jenny's body lurched, as though an electric shock ran through her. Jill began to weep when the girl's legs started to convulse as the poison raced through her body, sped up by the magic. Her lips drew back to bare fangs and Adam had to press his forehead to her temple with brute force to keep it from slamming against the stone during the spasms. There was no other way to heal her except to let the venom run its course through the rest of Jenny's body and protect her heart and head. Cara attached her power to the heart, and Adam pushed pure energy into her mind to make a magical barrier, shielding her brain from the toxins.

The venom was the most virulent Adam had ever encountered. It chewed at his magic like acid, burning through his mind and pulling whimpers from the lesser wolves by the cave entrances.

But they were already so beaten down . . . so very tired. Despite Adam's better judgment, Cara began to pull from farther away. Will's and Ume's wings began to slow and it became a struggle to stay in flight. Soon even Paco and Rosa and little Raul were called on in the desperate attempt to help Jenny pull through. The shield was shrinking and it was all he could do to keep the venom from reaching her mind.

"Wait!" Cara's voice startled him out of his concentration. "We're doing this wrong!"

"What?" His voice sounded thick, like he'd had too much to drink. "Wrong, how?"

"He said we have to *use* the venom. We're forcing it out of her system."

He struggled to sit up on his haunches, but was growing more alert as he caught the scent of excitement. He looked down at Jenny. Her tongue was back to a normal color and the wounds were nearly sealed. But she was still a wild animal. He couldn't feel any spark of human inside. "Why should we believe him? What if he wants to kill us all by making us think there's a chance to save her?"

Her eyes were bright and she shook her head. "It feels like acid, doesn't it? Some acids are good things—can be bent to our will to benefit us. What if we can use the acid to cut through the scar tissue from the turning? What if we can use it to—"

"Bring her back?" Jill caught the excitement and nodded her head. "Maybe it's like Alzheimer's. Maybe there's some sort of magical build-up that turns some shifters feral, while others not." She reached forward and grasped his paw. "It's at least worth a try, Adam."

He let out a frustrated sound, between a growl and a bark and slapped his tail on the ground. "And if you fail, and the magic in the venom gets in the binding . . . then what?"

Cara looked at him with calm assurance. "It won't. I swear I won't risk the pack." She smiled gently and leaned down to kiss the tip of his ear before whispering, "I won't risk losing *you,* my Alpha. Not when I've just barely fallen in love with you."

He let out a small growl that was mostly filled with defeat, but he knew his scent was pride and happiness and the warm scent of cookies baking that even made Jill smile. "Do what you need to do."

With a nod, she used her fingers to reopen the fang wounds and then closed her eyes. He didn't try to do anything, but let her draw on him as she closed her mouth over the hole and pulled some of the venom onto her tongue.

This is madness. We can't have any idea what this will d—

FIRE ERUPTED INTO Cara's mind as the magical venom touched the binding and began to burn through their links. More howls joined her own and soon they were all thrashing on the stone, with blood leaking from around their eyes and frothing on their tongues. Will and Ume let out terrible screeches and dropped from the air like twin stones, landing in the treetops and crashing to the ground.

¡Madre de Dios! Adam was right. She was going to kill them all! Her heart started pounding so hard she could feel it in her eardrums. Again she drew on her healing ability, felt it recoil against the powerful venom. But she surrounded it, coaxed it, and finally felt it halt in its path. But it was still in their binding and she had to move it out of their system and into Jenny's mind. The only way to do that was to *become* the venom. She pulled on the bitter acid, pulled it out of bodies of the others and into herself. She heard Adam shout a warning and suddenly turn human, as he reached for her inside her mind. But she slammed the connection shut once the stinging power was inside her and then she threw herself on top of Jenny's body and locked her arms around the warm wolf, now beginning to wake.

I can't risk the pack, and if I fail, Adam might still survive.

She reached outward and found the wolf's mind. There was nothing human here, but her own wolf understood the mental processes. This time, her wolf didn't fight her because the young one was sick; needed healing. She felt her body lurch as Jenny woke and tried to rise and Cara finally managed to find her voice. "Keep her still. Hold Jenny down!"

Adam raced to comply and then she felt the touch of Jill's slender fingers and Tommy's thicker ones. The wolf snapped and snarled and dug claws into her legs as she opened herself to the wolf, let healing magic, laden with burning venom, flow into the girl's mind. The wolf screamed under her, then started slavering and throwing venom-laced froth to land on bare skin.

Cara ignored the pain, and the screams and swearing as she was doused with cold water to ease the searing flesh.

She just kept her eyes shut and sent flooding magic into the scarred brain. She wished there was time for delicacy, but there was none. She couldn't let the others know she was pulling from her own reserves, rather than from the pack. Little by little, her body started to shut down—her fingers and toes growing numb and cold and then her limbs, as the venom cleaned mental passages.

Finally, all that was left was her own heartbeat and even that was slowing, but she felt a spark in the wolf's mind—a spark that was most definitely human. More power, that last little bit, even though there was no more to spare. Then a stray thought reached her and it made her smile. *I wonder what froth would look like in black and white?*

Just before the last stuttering thump closed her eyes, she felt Adam's strong arms wrap around and pull upward frantically. And she heard a hoarse, muffled voice from underneath her that made it all worthwhile.

"Mom?"

Chapter 34

"I SWEAR TO God! If you ever do anything like that again, *stupida*—" Yolanda's frustrated voice drowned out even the bright mariachi music from the band at the front of the room.

"It wasn't stupid." Cara looked at her friend, whose face moved from anger to worry. She clutched her hand and Cara winced. The acid burns were still a little sensitive. Jill said her healing would have to rebuild over time, so they'd had to concoct a story about her car battery exploding to explain the scars on her face and hands. She motioned to the dance floor with her head. "Does that look stupid to you?"

Gloria was entering the room on Paco's arm, resplendent in her Quinceanera dress. The cast on her leg had been custom-dyed to match, but it still wasn't quite the effect her niece had hoped for.

The band moved into a slow waltz. She couldn't believe that Paco was going to try this, considering he'd had to fill one shoe with tissue paper to get it to even stay on. But it was his little girl's day and how could she reach adulthood without her Papi?

Her three new amigas—Jenny, Ziri, and Ume—watched her in only slightly less elegant, matching dresses with pride in their scent and tears rolling down their faces. They held hands fiercely as their adopted papi, Paco, took a deep breath and handed his cane to Eddie. Ziri's fingers still had a little yellow oil paint on them that even the scrubber sponge couldn't remove. She had been trying to re-create Van Gogh's style for the better part of a week now.

For Ume, Paco really was the only father she had left. Tony and Bobby had arrived to find their village destroyed and many of the people killed, probably by the same men who had taken the girls. Ziri's family had been moved and Ziri would soon join them in some hidden location, but Ume would remain here so Will could train her in her new abilities. After all, she was *familia* now—part of the pack.

Paco held out his hand to take Gloria's and she looked up at her father warmly. In her golden necklace, strapless gown that showed her very adult curves, and a beautiful smile under a cascade of fresh and waxed flowers, she truly did look like a princess today. The lights in the room dimmed and the slowly spinning disco ball threw dancing lights of all colors around the room.

Cara smelled pine trees and lemongrass enter the hall and smiled. Adam had made it after all. But she didn't search for him with her eyes. She could feel him walk across the room to talk to Will. Instead, she watched Paco and Gloria stumble through a few steps before the girl's date stepped in to whisk her away—as much as one can be *whisked* in a cast. Rosa looked so proud as he limped back to his chair. It had only been a week since nearly dying, and here he was, dancing! Rosa felt her smile and met her eyes happily before helping her husband into his chair. Then she sat down next to Papi who watched his granddaughter with the same pride and warmth. She knew she'd be able to convince him eventually to join in the binding. He, too, was noticing the closeness of the pack and she sensed the longing of the wolf in him for a pack to call his own.

"No, not so *stupida*, I suppose." Yolanda's voice was soft and close to her ear, so only Cara could hear, but she could make out the slight cracking in the words that matched the emotions that rolled off her.

"I'm very proud of you, Cara." She looked up at the table's other occupant with mixed emotions. Ten Bears had returned early from the powwow, brought back by Will from near Albuquerque. So much had changed between them in these few days. He'd moved from her most trusted confidante to . . . something else. But she didn't know what. He still looked the same, yet so very different now that she knew the truth. Will was the true shaman, had always been the shaman—while Ten Bears only repeated what he was told to keep up the appearance to her pack; to protect his great-great-grandfather's secret identity. He couldn't offer more information because he didn't have any to give. But did that negate all the long talks over quiet dinners where he'd given good advice? Did it take away the honest emotion that she'd smelled over the years, or the tea—however illegal—that had gotten her safely this far?

"Thank you, Ten Bears. I'm glad you could be here for this."

He dipped his head in acknowledgment. "I'm glad so many of us could be here for this. When Will told me of the future he'd seen—"

It was a good point. "Why did we only lose Luis? Didn't you say that *several* of my pack would die?" She still couldn't quite get over the fact that her Tio Luis was gone. He'd meant so much to them all. They were dealing with it in the only way they knew how, with tears and prayers. Penny had the pack to help her through it; helping her to be strong for her children. Luis, Jr.—Louie—the oldest, would take over the store, and had helped set up the supposed *accident* that had claimed his father's life. The police bought it. Luis had been known for working too long, and drinking too much, and taking risks at the store without helpers. The tendency had put more than one cast on his body, because he wasn't a strong enough shifter to heal without help. So finding him crushed by a massive antique oak wardrobe hadn't seemed out of line to the officers or ambulance attendants. Of course, it helped that Will happened to be shopping for furniture that day, and helped *convince* them.

Ten Bears smiled, that quiet, patient smile she'd known for so long. Was it really Will's smile she was seeing, faked for so long that it had become his own? "You changed the future, Cara. It was *Paco and Rosa* who were meant to die . . . not Luis, but I couldn't bear to tell you. When you accepted the help of another, the timeline altered. Five years ago, or even one, you wouldn't have allowed yourself to get close to Adam. You would have fought the binding and your sister and her family would have paid the price."

"I know." He was right. But her family *had* paid a price, one she wasn't sure could ever change. One of the pack was gone, would never return. And as she looked out over the crowd, she saw how the pack members gathered together at tables—including the new members who nobody except the wolves ever met before today. She could see the suspicion in the eyes of her *other* pack, the dozens of human *familia* who now felt a difference. They saw a closeness among the shifter members that hadn't been there a month before and jealousy had been born out of the noticing. She didn't have to walk up to each person to smell it . . . the fans in the room corners carried it to her nose. However slight, there was a rift now—and she vowed she wouldn't let it grow to the level of fear and hate that she'd experienced through the minds of Jenny, Jill, and, yes, Adam. The Minnesota pack had allowed it to go too far. No, she would find some way to include the others in the circle. Maybe they could all help with Luis's float. It was now going to be a tribute to him and their family's contribution to past Tequila Days events. And just for this year, it would *be* Tequila Days. The city council had agreed to honor Luis with that small gesture . . . after the impassioned pleas of many older citizens at a special meeting. Definitely, the whole pack would participate. They were all Sazi, would be Sazi for as long as she ruled. She would keep her pack *whole*.

"I know you will." She looked up to see Adam smiling down at her and touching the chair next to her. "We'll keep it whole together."

Cara believed him, because she could feel the determination inside him. She felt other things, too, and they made her smile. "I was afraid you weren't going to make it."

"I should have made *you* work with Councilwoman Calibria. She's a total pain in the ass."

She chuckled, remembering the tall, demanding Belgian woman who'd arrived and treated them all like the lowest of peasants who were expected to do her bidding and then *thank her* for the privilege. She threaded her fingers through his and raw power flowed through her, giving her a little boost of strength as he nodded a greeting to Yolanda and Ten Bears. Yo touched Ten Bears's hand and they both stood up and offered excuses to give them a little privacy. Cara

368 C. T. Adams and Cathy Clamp

watched Yo walk across the small room to chat with Stephanie, who was looking a little lonely in the corner. Billy had put in his notice yesterday and the deputy couldn't quite decide how she felt about it. Ten Bears wandered over and clapped Will on the shoulder.

"Thankfully, she doesn't like me. I couldn't stand to be around the woman even back in academy, especially since her voice is high-pitched enough to shatter glass. It hurts my ears to be in the same room as her. I can't imagine how you stand it. But has she had any luck with the investigation?"

Adam rolled his eyes and snorted. "Her *voice* doesn't bother me too much. It's the rest of her I can't stand. But she is remarkably good with cleanup and thinks she might know who our *Roberto* really is. She just needs to bring in another council member to be sure before she says anything. Of course, that doesn't mean they can find him, since Will and Ume lost his trail." He looked down at her hand, which had started to tremble again. She just couldn't seem to hang onto energy since healing Jenny. It came and it went again. Jill said it would probably take months to get back to normal. "You doing okay? Do you want to leave and go lie down and rest for a bit? I'd be happy to drive you home."

She reached her head up to whisper in his ear. "If *you* take me home to lie down, I won't get any rest." The proprietary chuckle that slipped out of his mouth made her happy. He cupped her chin and gave her a slow, light kiss that was filled with his tongue and his scent. But the wolf was too tired to play and ignored the invitation. Probably time to change the subject. "Has anyone heard from Missy Foster?"

Adam nodded. "She apparently left a note in Will's car. The pack didn't notice her leaving when they followed us to the cave. She's leaving town and is going to go back to the bayou to stay with her father for now. Will used a little persuasion on the hospital staff to make them believe they authorized her release. He said he's going to wander that way as soon as he can get a few days off. She's ready to talk, I think, and we need to find out more about the history of this group. Bobby and Tony can only do so much. They're on their way to Columbia based on information they found at the village, but it sure would help to find out what they're going to walk into before they arrive."

Thinking of Will made her smile, and she could feel his irritation in the back of her mind. "Is he still pissed that the whole pack knows his secret?"

"Oh, probably. He was doing okay until your papi asked for his autograph after hearing about it from Paco—not teasing like I did. But for real."

She shrugged and then whispered, "Well, sure! Papi's always been big on all things American, and *¡Madre de Dios!* how often does a person meet a real living national icon?"

I'm not an icon! came a terse male voice in her head that sounded very much like an eagle's screech and she smiled.

Adam laughed and lowered his voice, too. "And yet his picture is on every piece of currency in every wallet here."

Who'd have thought there was a real, physical *model* for the eagle on the dollar bill . . . and the quarter?

Again Will Kerchee's voice filtered into her mind through the warm pack connection. *Hey, can I help it if his first engraving looked like crap? I offered to sit around for a few hours so he could get it right. Who knew the design would stick around this long?*

Her alpha's laugh, rich and rolling, shivered her skin. *You're a classic, dude. Just accept that you're gorgeous.*

Will made a rude noise and shut down the mental connection as they both laughed. Then Adam looked at her. "So, have you decided? Should we tell them today?"

Cara looked out over the happy crowd. Everybody was

dancing, including Jenny, who had bleached her hair back to blonde so she didn't take away from Gloria's thunder today. Even Eddie was taking a turn with Yolanda now, putting a happy face on his sadness. She was sorry he hadn't felt he could come to her earlier about his lover, but really—what could she have done? She didn't know what the future held for him, but she was going to actively search around to see if there were any potential suitors for him among the other Sazi in the world. It wasn't fair that he couldn't share his life as the rest of them did, with a partner. With someone to love and have forever, like she had now.

Should they announce their engagement? She smiled at the man who had proposed to her just this morning. "No, not today. Let Gloria have her day without everyone fawning over us. The pack knows *already*. They'll wait until we're ready to announce it."

An elderly woman walked in the room and she brightened. "Oh, look! There's *Abuela* Carlotta!" She stood up and pulled on his hand. "I want you to meet her. She's *amazing!*"

Cara literally dragged him across the floor to where her grandmother had settled herself, holding both hands on a sturdy black cane in front of her legs and looking stern. She slowly introduced Adam to her, trying to use words that she had already taught him so he could follow along.

Abuela Carlotta looked him up and down slowly while he smiled at her graciously. "*So this is the new Alpha of your pack.*" She nodded once. "*I suppose he'll do.*"

Cara nudged Adam. She'd taught him an easy, respectful speech of greeting and prayed he remembered it. She pushed the instruction into his mind again. *Simple. Very simple. Just say hello and it's a pleasure to meet you.* But he'd shut down the connection and she couldn't see his thoughts.

He cleared his throat and bowed slightly. "*Buenos tardes, Abuela. Es un gusto conocerle.*"

She let out a breath she didn't realize she was holding as the older woman raised her brows in surprise, and a small smile twitched the corner of her mouth at his accent.

But then Cara's heart rose to her throat as he elbowed her slightly and continued. "And you were right, *mi amor! Que mujer fatal!*"

Cara froze with wide eyes and talking stopped at three surrounding tables. The scents were too many to sort—everything from embarrassment to amusement to indignation. Everyone turned to see what was going to happen.

The older woman had shock plain on her face as she stared up at Adam. But then he picked up Cara's limp hand and kissed it lightly and *winked* at her grandmother with a sly smile.

The lights and music in the room were nothing compared to the music in her heart when her grandmother laughed, patted his hand and welcomed him into the *familia*.